8/30/18
$26.95

9/18

Withdra

D0394857

SOLEMN GRAVES

SOLEMN GRAVES

A Billy Boyle World War II Mystery

James R. Benn

Published by Soho Press, Inc.
853 Broadway
New York, NY 10003

Library of Congress Cataloging-in-Publication Data

Benn, James R.
Series: A Billy Boyle WWII mystery ; 13

ISBN 978-1-61695-849-7
eISBN 978-1-61695-850-3

1. Boyle, Billy (Fictitious character)—Fiction.
2. World War, 1939–1945—Fiction. 3. Murder—Investigation—Fiction. I. Title
PS3602.E6644 S65 2018 813'.6—dc23 2018016741

Printed in the United States of America

10 9 8 7 6 5 4 3 2 1

For Debbie, as always.

Are we not like two volumes of one book?
—Marceline Desbordes-Valmore, 19th century French poet

To the solemn graves, near a lonely cemetery,
my heart like a muffled drum is beating funeral marches.
—CHARLES BAUDELAIRE

SOLEMN GRAVES

JULY 1944

NORMANDY, FRANCE

CHAPTER ONE

THE FIRST DEAD body I saw in Normandy was a cow, tangled in the branches of a shattered tree at a crossroads by the edge of a field, a good thirty feet off the ground. More of them lay scattered across the pasture, the thick green grass dotted with gaping holes of black, smoking earth.

A few cows were still upright. One wandered into the ditch alongside the road, trailing intestines and bellowing, her big brown eyes crazed with fear and pain.

"Stop," Sergeant Allan Fair said from the front seat, placing a hand on the driver's arm. "Easy like." The driver, a skinny kid who looked like he might shave soon, if he lived that long, let the jeep roll to a halt. Fair got out, planted his feet, raised his M-1 to his shoulder, and squeezed off a round that found a home between those two brown eyes. The cow collapsed into the ditch, and silence filled the air.

"Damn," Fair said to no one in particular, and got back in the jeep. The driver eased into first gear and took off slowly, carefully navigating around a shell hole on one side of the hard-packed dirt road. We passed a sign at the crossroads, tilted lazily to one side and peppered with shrapnel.

Dust means death.

As we drove on, the roadside was decorated with the burned-out hulks of vehicles whose drivers had not heeded the warning. The bovine casualties had likely been the result of a nervous driver who barreled down the road, kicking up a dust storm and making it through before the German shells rained down on the intersection.

"I didn't think we were close to the front yet," I said from the back seat, as we proceeded at a dust-free twenty miles an hour under the hot morning sun. "I mean, for Kraut artillery spotters."

"It's close enough. They're up in those hills," Fair said, sweeping a hand toward the distant rise to the south. "With a good pair of binoculars, they can pick out a swirl of dust five, ten miles away. Plus, they left spotters behind, hiding out in barns or in the woods."

"Scuttlebutt is, they pay the French for any dope they bring them about targets," the driver said.

"Hard to imagine any Frenchman would sell information to the Germans," Big Mike said.

"How long you been in Normandy?" Fair asked.

"We got here yesterday," Big Mike said.

"Figures," was all Fair said.

"We seen pictures," Big Mike said. "People throwing flowers at GIs, stuff like that."

"Anyone throw flowers at you, kid?" Fair asked the driver.

"A Kraut threw his helmet at me when his rifle jammed," he said. "But no flowers."

"See? So don't believe everything you read in *Stars and Stripes*," Fair said. He spat into the road, ending the conversation.

Big Mike looked at me, eyebrows raised. Or looked down at me, I should say. Big Mike—Staff Sergeant Mike Miecznikowski—was tall and broad and took up most of the cramped back seat.

"I was looking forward to the flowers, Billy," he said. "In Sicily, all they threw were stones."

The jeep moved slowly, past open fields and into more hedgerows. Here, the roadway became a narrow, sunken lane with a deep ditch on either side. For centuries, farmers had been mounding earth to mark the boundaries of their fields and to keep livestock in. Topping it all off was a tangle of trees and bushes, their roots intertwined with the gritty gravel, dirt, and stone base.

Hedgerows made every pasture a fortress, every lane a death trap.

"How long have you been here, Sergeant Fair?" I asked. Fair had been ordered to take Big Mike and me from First Army headquarters to the outskirts of Bricqueville, where a dead body was waiting for us. Not the sort that ended up in a tree or torn apart by explosives, but the kind that found itself wearing a slit throat in the sitting room of a French villa, safe behind the lines, and wearing the uniform of a US Army captain. Simply said, it was murder, an almost quaint and old-fashioned custom these days. Killed In Action was the usual phrase, and here in hedgerow country—the French call it the *bocage*—there was a lot of it going around.

"I been on the line since D+3," Fair said, his voice a low mutter as he turned to study me. He did his best to look unimpressed. My ODs were clean, and from the SHAEF patch on my shoulder, I was obviously nothing but a headquarters feather merchant out for a joyride. Fair was headed back to the front, where he'd been since three days after D-Day. His olive drabs were worn and muddy, bleached by the summer sun to a shade not found in any Quarter-master's stores. The bags under his eyes were as dark as midnight sin, and crow's-feet arced from the corner of his eye, an occupational hazard from squinting over the sights of an M1.

His mouth was a thin slit of insolence. His eyes were narrowed, wary, and suspicious. He didn't bother saying "sir," but I didn't care about that. At the front, there was an unspoken rank, and it wasn't based on an officer's bars or a non-com's stripes. It had to do with how long a man faced death and kept going despite it. All Fair knew was that Big Mike and I still had the smell of London about us, and that made us nothing but nuisance cargo in his book.

I didn't blame him one damn bit.

"Anything else, Captain?" Fair said, his eyes scanning the road as it curved ahead. Which was obviously of greater interest to him than any stupid questions a desk jockey from Supreme Headquarters, Allied Expeditionary Force had. Probably why he was still alive.

He clamped a hand on the driver's arm, signaling him to roll to a dustless halt.

"Look, he's making a run for it," Fair said, pointing to a flurry of road dust off to our right, where the land sloped away.

"Who?" Big Mike asked.

"The jerk who got all those cows killed," the driver said.

"They're dead meat," Fair said, leaning back and shaking a Lucky Strike loose from a crumpled pack. He lit one, ignoring the sound of distant booms and the screaming crescendo of shells coming in from the German lines. "The Krauts got a crossroads over there zeroed in."

Explosions *crumped* a mile or so away, just ahead of the dust cloud, belching smoke and fire as they ripped through trees and shrubs.

Then it was over. Fair drew in his smoke as if it were oxygen, cupping the cigarette even in broad daylight.

"Shouldn't we see if they need help?" I asked.

"Naw," Fair said, shaking his head at what to him was obviously a silly question. "Lemme finish my smoke." He did, tossing the butt into the road as two more shells landed out where smoke from a burning vehicle was already curling into the sky.

"Krauts always send a few in after the fact," Fair said, signaling the driver to move on. "To pick off guys who don't know any better."

Meaning us.

The driver eased his way around the curve, keeping the speed down. Down so much we could have walked and kept pace. But I didn't complain, since I liked not being blown up.

"They ain't going to like keeping a stiff around this long," Big Mike said, meaning our murder victim, who had apparently bled out in the sitting room of a farmhouse.

"There's stiffs all over the place," Fair said. "Ours, Krauts, and plenty of French who can't get out of the way fast enough."

"Out of the way of what?" Big Mike asked.

"Pissed-off Krauts, our planes bombing and strafing the hell out of everything, artillery, land mines, drunk GIs, you name it," Fair said. "If I was them, I'd have gone south."

"I think they like the idea of being liberated," Big Mike said.

"Yeah, it's working out just swell for them, isn't it?" Fair said.

He had a point. Along our section of the line, the bridgehead from the beaches to the front lines was no more than eighteen miles deep, after a month of hard fighting and heavy casualties. It was a killing slog for the GIs, but French civilians were often worse off, caught in a cross fire of bullets, shells, bombs, and brutality.

Things weren't going all that well, truth be told. By now we should have broken out of the bridgehead, our tanks rolling toward Paris. But the Allied armies were still cooped up in Normandy, fighting for every hill and hedgerow and paying a heavy price.

"Look," our driver said, pointing to the source of the smoke. A supply truck was on its side, burning, the rubber tires sending up thick, acrid smoke. Two bodies were in the road, thrown from the cab when it had been hit.

A couple of Frenchmen knelt by the bodies. They glanced up as we quietly rolled to a halt twenty yards away. One, caught in the act of rifling through the pockets of a dead GI, hastily stuffed a pack of smokes in his jacket. His pal let the arm of the other corpse flop to the ground as he filched a wristwatch.

Both soldiers were shoeless, their boots laced and draped around the necks of the Frenchmen. Farmers, by the rough cut of their worn clothes, although most residents of Normandy looked ill fed and poorly clothed these days.

"Goddammit," Fair said, stepping out of the jeep and advancing upon the men. I followed, noticing bits of paper scattered in the dirt around the bodies. Photographs and letters, tossed aside as the bodies were looted.

The men muttered in rapid-fire French, sounding apologetic, shrugging and smiling as they gestured over the two corpses. I couldn't make out what they were saying, but I could guess. *Sorry, we found them like this. It is a shame for good boots to go to waste when we have so little.*

Fair shot them. Two sharp cracks, a bullet each to the chest. They were both dead before the second shell casing hit the ground, bounced, and rolled to a stop.

"Fucking looters," Fair said. He slung his rifle and moved the GIs off the road, taking a dog tag from each of them. They wore the same shoulder patch as Fair, the red-and-blue 30th Infantry Division insignia. He gathered up papers and stuffed them inside each man's jacket. Then he took the boots and watches from the Frenchmen, left a pair of boots next to each GI, and shoved the wristwatches into their shirt pockets. He stood for a moment, shaking his head slowly.

"It's not right," our driver said, his hands resting on the steering wheel. "Stealing from the dead. Especially when them boys are from our own outfit." He sounded angry and apologetic at the same time.

"They were idiots, driving like that," Fair said, stuffing the dog tags into his jacket as he returned to the jeep. "But no one has a right to take from our dead. Right, Captain?"

"You could have turned them over to the military police, Sergeant," I said.

"What, and make you and your pal walk? Sorry, Captain, but I got my orders. No one loots our dead, and I take you to Bricqueville. So mount up."

We drove on at a snail's pace, past the dead, both the young and foolish Americans who had come to liberate France, and the old and foolish French who stole their boots. None of them expected to die today on this dusty stretch of road, but there they were, shattered bodies in a ditch.

"I don't know if I would've shot them," Big Mike said in a low voice, leaning in close. "But I wanted to."

"Yeah, I didn't like seeing them paw over our boys," I said. Which was true enough. But I also didn't like Sergeant Fair much either. Maybe because he did what I, like Big Mike, wanted to do myself. It's not pleasant to see the worst of yourself in another man, so I tried to think about something else. Like the dead body waiting for us down the road.

Dust means death. Like that line from Genesis that scared me back in Sunday school: *For dust thou art, and unto dust shalt thou return.*

"Keep it slow," I told the driver. "The dead can wait."

CHAPTER TWO

A WEATHERED SIGNPOST pointed the way to *Pressoir* Janvier, off the main road to Bricqueville. This was our destination, a farm of some sort, run by Madame Regine Janvier. That was about all we'd been told back at First Army HQ, other than to get a move on.

"What does *pressoir* mean?" Big Mike asked. I knew some French, picked up mostly from French Canadians I'd thrown in the slammer back in Boston, where I was a cop—until the war came along and ruined things seven ways to Sunday. My French was better suited to the drunk tank, so I had no answer but a shrug.

"It's an apple press," Fair said from the front seat, as we drove down a narrow lane between hedgerows so tall the branches grew across the road, forming a dark green canopy. "They make apple brandy, what they call calvados. Back home we called it applejack, but this French stuff is a damn sight better."

"Sounds good," I said. "Any left?"

"Sure. Officers took the place over soon as they smelled the booze. Our outfit had a signals company stationed in a barn for a while, while the rest of us dug in on a hill to the south. Then battalion HQ set up in the farmhouse, and Madame Janvier started making money selling the stuff to the brass. You know how it goes."

"I hear the booze wasn't the only attraction," the driver said.

"Shut up," Fair said. We emerged from the hedgerows and passed open fields filled with rows of apple trees, maturing fruit weighing down their branches. The orderly columns were marred by mounds of blackened earth and charred trees, marking the progress of recent combat. Burned-out vehicles and the scorched hulk of a German Tiger tank marked the site of an impromptu cemetery off the road, rough wooden planks with scrawled letters in unreadable German script topped off with Kraut helmets.

Ripening apples and decaying corpses—the scent of Normandy.

We followed a lane winding through the orchards, scarred here and there by lines of tank treads and crushed trees, their limbs twisted and broken like the bones of men. Soon the apple trees gave way to planted fields of flourishing green—potatoes, turnips, beans—whatever was easy to grow and plentiful enough for the Germans not to confiscate.

Another sign announced we'd arrived at *Pressoir* Janvier, the farmhouse visible through low-hanging leafy branches. A three-story stout granite building, it anchored a line of several outbuildings done up in the half-timbered and thatched style typical of the region. MPs from the 30th Division stood guard at the front door, near a collection of jeeps and half-tracks. GIs milled around, smoking, talking, and generally doing nothing.

"Captain William Boyle?" It was an MP second lieutenant, calling out from the front door of the farmhouse. A wiry guy, he had a carbine slung over his shoulder, a military police brassard on his arm, and an impatient look on his face.

"That's me," I said, stepping out of the jeep with Big Mike. I told Fair to hang around in case we needed him. Maybe the killer had confessed, and he could take us back to headquarters. Or maybe it had all been a misunderstanding, nothing more than a fistfight and a bloody nose after too much calvados.

"Glad you're here, sir," the MP said. "Madame Janvier has been none too happy with the mess in her sitting room."

"I got here as soon as I heard some French lady was upset, Lieutenant," I said, disappointed that my theory about a misunderstanding hadn't held water. "Tell me about the corpse, why don't you?"

"Hey, Captain," Fair shouted from the jeep. "Can I go now?"

"No, you can't," the MP answered for me. "You've been detailed to look after Captain Boyle and his party."

"Some guys have all the luck, Sarge," our driver said, laughing as he drove off. Fair sat himself down on the stone steps and lit up a smoke, flicking his Zippo shut with a bored finality.

"Your dead man is Major David Jerome," the MP said, checking a small notebook he'd pulled from his pocket as we stood on the front steps.

"Wait a minute," I said, holding up a hand. "Who are all these guys hanging around? Have they been inside?"

"Most of them are from the battalion's headquarters company," he said. "And none of them have been inside."

"You're certain?" I asked.

"Absolutely. We're bivouacked in those trees, just past the pressing house. The housekeeper came running over right after dawn, screaming her head off. We were on the scene in minutes and kept a cordon around the house, waiting for you."

"So this crowd just gathered to watch the fun?" Big Mike said. "Sir?"

"Well, yeah. The colonel and most of the other officers are up at division for a briefing, and after chow guys started asking questions and waiting for something to happen. Nothing wrong with that, Captain."

I thought I heard Fair choke up a hollow laugh. "Who are those clowns, Lieutenant Sewell?" he asked, pointing to a clutch of GIs leaning against a half-track.

"They're from Second Armored," Sewell said. "No idea what they're doing here."

"You weren't in police work before the war, were you, Lieutenant?" I asked.

"Nope. Ran a hardware store," he said.

"Well, pay attention, and you'll learn how to run an investigation. Big Mike, find out what those Second Armored guys are doing here. Find out if any of these other goldbricks saw anything, then clear them out."

"Will do, Billy," Big Mike said. "Come on, Fair, you can help me with your pals."

"I don't have any pals in this bunch," Fair said, standing up as slowly as possible.

"That comes as a great surprise," Big Mike said, grabbing hold of Fair's sleeve and pulling him along.

"You know Sergeant Fair?" I asked Sewell.

"Sure. He's been around awhile. Good soldier, from what I hear."

"A little tightly wound?"

"Who isn't? Now, about the stiff," Sewell said as we entered the house, stepping into a poorly lit hallway decorated with paintings in heavy, dark frames and a chest of drawers which might have been new back when they chopped off King Louis's head. "Major David Jerome, commanding officer of the Signals Company, Second Armored Division."

"Hold on," I said. I wanted to see the body, but this curveball from Sewell stopped me cold. "Same division as the guys who showed up outside after you found the body?"

"Well, yeah. Sir."

"Okay, Lieutenant. Go outside and order those guys not to leave. Then get back in here, pronto." Sewell took off, and I glanced into the first room on my right. It held a desk and shelves of books, bright light flowing in from a south-facing window, beneath which an easy chair offered a soothing spot to curl up with a book. It was tempting, but I had a dead officer and a ticked-off Frenchwoman to deal with.

The sitting room was down the hall and to the left, across from a staircase.

It wasn't a pretty sight.

Major David Jerome, late of the Second Armored, lay sprawled on his back in front of a fireplace with a smoke-smudged stone lintel. A chair and side table were knocked over, shards of glass littering the floor. The windows were closed, and the room gave off odors of brandy and blood.

Calvados, I corrected myself, mixed in with the coppery stink of dried blood.

A lot of blood. A lot of booze, too, judging by the shattered, thin-necked bottle on the hearth. I stood back, studying the scene, trying not to draw conclusions and let the room talk to me. It was one of the things my dad had taught me, or tried to, back in Boston. He was a homicide detective, and as soon as I got my badge as a rookie cop, he dragged me along to watch and study him at work. Whether it was a prostitute knifed in a Scollay Square alleyway or a Beacon Hill snob dead in his bed, he went through the same routine.

So here I was, carrying on the family business in Normandy, wearing khaki, instead of home in Boston, wearing blue.

"Captain Boyle," Sewell said from behind me. I held up my hand, blocking him from entering the room. I needed to see it as Jerome had. As his killer had, after the deed was done.

The carpet was bunched up at Jerome's feet. He'd taken awhile to die and thrashed around while he waited. His right hand was at his throat, where he'd tried to stanch the flow of blood, which was impossible as far as the carotid artery was concerned.

A chair stood next to Jerome's body, undisturbed. A small couch opposite was untouched as well, a glass and ashtray on the table nearby. A vase filled with flowers was on a table by the leaded glass window, a rocking chair next to it. Paintings hung on either side of the fireplace, country scenes of fields and forest.

A comfortable room, marred only by a dead man and the spray of arterial blood on the wall. Some of it had decorated one of the paintings. And the killer as well, unless he'd been behind Jerome. That would require a closer examination.

"Is there a doctor close by?" I asked Sewell. "A field hospital, maybe?"

"Captain Boyle, they left," Sewell said. It took me a second to realize he wasn't talking about doctors.

"Those Second Armored guys," Big Mike said, stepping into the room. "They said they were scouting out locations for a headquarters, since they're taking over part of the line here. Their lieutenant said they wanted to get out of our way and took off damn quick. Right before Lieutenant Sewell came out."

"Just in time to wave goodbye," I said. "Never mind, we'll follow up on that later. Now tell me, Sewell, can we get a doctor in here?"

"That would be tough," he said. "Nearest aid station is a half mile down the road, but there's only one doctor, and he won't leave to look at a dead man. We got a good medic right here, though."

"Okay, get him, willya?"

"Sure, Captain," Sewell said. "Sorry about letting those guys take off. This is the first murder I've ever seen. Think it could have been German commandos?"

"Don't sweat it, Sewell," I said. "We'll find those guys, and you can help interrogate them."

"And don't worry about Kraut commandos, Lieutenant," Big Mike said, ushering him out of the room. "They wouldn't have smashed up the booze."

"What do you think, Big Mike?" I asked. He walked around the body, keeping clear of the blood. Big Mike had been a Detroit cop before the war, and he still carried his policeman's shield with him as a good-luck charm. Sometimes I half expected to see a blue tunic under his field jacket.

"There was a struggle, but not much of one," Big Mike said. "That table's knocked over. So's this chair, which could have been where he was sitting. But nothing else."

"You're right," I said, kneeling to study the shards of broken glass. "This could have all happened when he fell."

"The killer could have walked behind him," Big Mike agreed, mimicking the movement. "Casual like, chatting, and out comes the knife."

"He was standing when the blood sprayed," I said as I pointed out the arc of red on the wall, five feet up.

"Okay, so he catches a glimpse of the blade, or maybe he was already suspicious," Big Mike offered. "He starts to stand, but the killer grabs him and slits his throat. Not perfectly, since the major kicks up a storm before he checks out from blood loss."

"Yeah. Maybe our man hesitated. He might have known Jerome, or he was not used to killing up close."

"That would let a lot of suspects off the hook, this close to the line," I said. "We need to find out more about who had access to the house and why Jerome was here."

A knock sounded at the door. "Captain Boyle? You needed a medic?"

"Not for my health," I said. "Or his. But I want you to take a look and give me your medical opinion."

"He's dead, Captain," the medic said, his brow wrinkled in confusion. He carried a musette bag and wore a helmet with a big red cross on a white background, the same symbol on an armband, and Private First Class stripes on his sleeves. He was thin and pale, shifting nervously from one leg to the other. It was obvious he wanted to be anywhere else.

"That's why we're here," I said, trying to avoid the sarcasm ready to roll off my tongue. "You heard about this, right?"

"Sure, Captain. Everyone's talking about it," he said.

"What are they saying?"

"That some officer got stabbed," he said. "And all sorts of crazy scuttlebutt. German spies, commandos, French criminals, that sort of thing." Nothing very helpful, since the rumors avoided mention of anyone who was actually within spitting distance of the dead major.

"Have you ever seen this officer before?" I asked.

"No, never laid eyes on him, honest."

"Any other officers or GIs from the Second Armored come by recently?"

"No, I heard there were a few here this morning, but I guess they took off." He looked shaky, like he was worried we were going to finger him for the knife work.

"What's your name, kid?" Big Mike asked, clapping the medic on the shoulder like they were old pals.

"Aaron Kaplan," he said.

"Well, Kaplan, we need your help. You been a medic long?" Big Mike said.

"I was premed back in Chicago. They made me a medic during basic, and I've been on the line a month now," Kaplan said, sounding more sure of himself.

"Damn, you mean the army actually gave you a job in your field?" Big Mike asked.

"Yeah, must have been a mistake," Kaplan said, warming to the subject. "So you want me to confirm the cause of death?"

"Just take a look," I said. "Cause of death is pretty certain, but I want to be sure we're not missing anything. Another pair of eyes always comes in handy."

"Okay," Kaplan said, laying his bag on the couch and removing his helmet. He knelt by the body and moved Jerome's hand away from his neck. "The arm's stiff. Rigor mortis is advanced." He checked the jaw and neck, which I remembered was where rigor began.

"Any estimate of time of death?" I said. This kid was no coroner, but it didn't hurt to ask.

"Jeez, Captain, it's hard to say. Probably before midnight, but don't hold me to it. The nights are cold here, even after a warm day, so that could have some effect." He began to study the wound at Jerome's throat. Now that the hand was moved aside, it was more visible, beginning at the center of the neck and moving up to the jawbone.

"Not very professional," Big Mike said, leaning over to gaze at the wound, which Kaplan was spreading open between two fingers. "I'm not even sure this was made from the back. Look at the angle."

He was right. The knife had gone in midway up the throat, and the cut went up from there, not as deep and ending below the ear, where it was little more than a bad shaving nick.

"He might have made it if there was a doctor close by," Kaplan said. He widened the cut and stuck his fingers inside the mess that once was a human being. "See the jugular? It was cut but not severed. This was serious, don't get me wrong, but maybe he could've been saved."

"Could he have walked? Called for help?" I asked.

"Called out, no. Walked, maybe. At least out into the hallway," Kaplan said, standing as he wiped his hands on his ODs.

"But he just stayed there," Big Mike said, frowning.

"Shock, maybe," I said. "Physical or emotional, depending on who knifed him. Hard to say. Anything else, Kaplan?"

"Well, the eyes," he said.

"What about them?"

"They're dilated. It naturally occurs to some extent after death, but his are really wide. See for yourself. I'd say the major was on something when he was killed."

I leaned in and stared at two dead eyes. The pupils were like saucers.

"Kaplan," I said, "if I ever need a doctor in Chicago after the war, you're the man I'll call."

CHAPTER THREE

WE SPENT THE next half hour sorting pieces of shattered glass. There was a dribble of calvados left in the bottle, and I took a careful taste, watching for slivers. I'd never drunk it before, but it tasted like booze. No surprise there.

The surprise was finding two broken glasses on the floor. With the intact goblet on the table by the couch, that made three. That one still had half an inch of liquor in it, so I knew one person had been sitting on the couch.

The calvados glasses had thin stems above a wide bulb and a narrow rim. I picked up the remnants of one, the stem shattered and the rim cracked. A drop of amber-colored drink still rolled around in the bulb, and Big Mike and I both dipped a finger in for a taste.

"Nothin' but hooch," Big Mike said.

The third glass was cracked, with most of the rim missing. Tiny shards of glass lay at the bottom, and I shook them out onto a newspaper. There was no liquid left inside, just a pale, whitish residue.

Big Mike wet a finger, pressed it to the dried dregs, and tasted. He made a face. I went through the same routine, right down to the grimace. It was bitter.

"Could be a lot of things," Big Mike said. "But there's one bitter substance close by."

"Morphine," I whispered, glancing at the doorway. Kaplan had gone, and I wanted to be sure no one overheard. "Keep it under your hat for now."

"Got it," Big Mike said, wrapping the broken glassware in a handkerchief. This was beginning to look a lot more serious than I first thought. I'd expected a beef that had gotten out of hand, or a drunken brawl. But a spiked drink was premeditated. Someone had wanted Major David Jerome dead, and they wanted him doped up enough so the odds were in their favor.

But why?

We needed more information, like why Jerome was at this 30th Division battalion headquarters, and who had easy access to enough morphine. Right now, we had nothing to go on.

"Tell Sewell he can take the body away," I said to Big Mike. "We're done here."

I settled down on the couch and kept Jerome company, leafing through the letters we'd found in his pockets. One was from his girlfriend, the other from his mother. The first was breathless and cheerful, the way people were when they were trying too hard on paper. The second was oddly formal, which I thought was strange coming from a woman writing to her son in a war zone. Then I felt ashamed for judging Jerome's mother, given the next communication she'd be receiving from the army. I wondered if their letters were a clue to how the two women would react—hysterical and stoic, perhaps. But you never knew, it might be the other way around.

I leaned back on the couch and stared at Jerome, feeling an odd affinity with the man. After all, we shared a secret. No one else who cared about him knew he was dead.

Except for whoever murdered him, that is. They cared a great deal.

I began to get that feeling, the one where the hair on the back of your neck stands up, and you want to turn around but you don't because you're afraid of looking silly. Soon I couldn't stand it any longer and glanced to my rear.

A girl stood in the doorway. Bloodstains covered the front of her dress. Her gaze was calm, her face pale, almost ashen. Her eyes glimmered with tears that seemed ready to spill over, but somehow stayed balanced on the edges of her eyelids. A haunted, fragile, ethereal beauty.

"Hello," I said, getting up slowly, afraid of spooking her. Why, I couldn't say. She obviously wasn't spooked by the quantity of dried blood decorating her bosom. *"Bonjour, mademoiselle."*

No response. She wasn't looking at me or at Jerome. Or at anything I could see in the room, for that matter. I edged closer.

She looked to be twenty or so. Her hair was strawberry blonde, her eyes azure blue, and her cheekbones were set high above full lips that looked like they hadn't cracked a smile in months. A faint scattering of freckles fell across her nose and cheeks like a distant memory of childhood.

She was thin, like most French boys and girls who'd grown up without enough to eat during the Occupation. A light blue dress hung limp on her frame, an embroidered vine of flowers barely visible beneath the blood. It buttoned down the front, with a belt cinched tight around the waist. It didn't look like the dress of a farm girl, more like what a young lady would wear with white gloves and a nice hat for an afternoon of shopping. One hand held a white handkerchief, which she pressed to her lips.

"Yvonne," a soft voice said from behind her. A hand appeared at her shoulder, turning her gently away from the sight of Jerome's body, not that it seemed to upset her.

"You will excuse us," the woman said, guiding Yvonne into the hallway, as if blood-soaked young women and dead officers were an everyday experience. She said it in such a firm tone that I didn't question where she was going or ask who the hell Yvonne was. The blood, unless there was another stabbing victim close by, spoke for itself. The girl was clearly in shock, so it made sense to leave her be. For now.

I watched them go upstairs, Yvonne being led by the older woman. Madame Janvier, perhaps? She looked every inch the proprietress of *Pressoir* Janvier, dressed in old corduroys, a worn sweater, and a leather vest. Her dark hair, decorated with streaks of gray, was pulled up on top of her head in that casual fashion French women seemed to wear so well. She was slim but strong. Her posture was ramrod straight, even as she climbed the steps.

"Who's that?" Big Mike asked.

"Jesus! Don't sneak up on me like that, okay?" I'd nearly jumped when he spoke.

"Hey, Billy, I didn't sneak, I walked. And I'm not exactly light on my feet," he said.

"Sorry. This was a tad strange, that's all." I told him about Yvonne, as much as I could.

He looked at me, his eyebrows furrowed. "You okay? It sounds like she got to you."

"Hell no, Big Mike. There's just something strange about her. And she's a beauty." I tried to deny it, but there was something haunting about her. I'd have to make sure she didn't get under my skin.

"Oh yeah? Like Betty Grable beautiful?" he asked.

"Nothing like that," I said. "It's just hard to describe. We'll talk to her later. Right now, she's pretty shook up."

"Maybe you got a thing for blood, Billy. But if you want strange, I've got stranger. Lieutenant Sewell is gone. I've got Fair out searching, but he's nowhere to be found."

"What a goddamn mess," I said. "You keep looking, and I'll find out what's the story with Yvonne."

"Okay. Some guys from the Quartermaster company are right behind me. They'll take care of the body, so you can give Madame Janvier the news. A little bit of scrubbing, and her sitting room will be as good as new."

"Yeah, it's time to get him out of here. Make sure Kaplan has a chance to check the body for any other wounds," I said, as GIs carrying a stretcher made their way inside. I stepped back and watched them hoist Major David Jerome onto it like a sack of potatoes.

Big Mike was right. Some elbow grease on the floor and walls would do the trick; good as new. I wasn't so sure about Yvonne. Her ten-thousand-yard stare said otherwise. Maybe she'd knifed Jerome, and all that blood pushed her over the edge. Or perhaps she was standing too close when he was cut and was nothing more than a traumatized bystander. She also could have found him and tried to help. Did they know each other? Did she embrace him as he lay dying, or did she twist the knife?

Where was the damn knife anyway? And if this had happened last night, why was Yvonne still wandering around covered in Jerome's blood?

"I am sure you have many questions, Captain Boyle," said the Frenchwoman from the hallway, as if reading my mind. She seemed not to want to enter the room. "I am Regine Janvier. Come, we will have coffee."

"I should speak with the young woman, Yvonne," I said, as she walked down the hall to the rear of the house.

"You may speak with her all you wish," Madame Janvier said. "But it will do no good."

I had a lot of questions. But Madame Janvier had the coffee, so I followed her to the kitchen. It was a long, enormous room with a well-worn brick floor and high windows facing a large walled garden. Shade trees stood beyond the waist-high wall, the tiled roof of a barn visible beyond it. The pressing house, someone had said.

I sat at the table, the dark walnut wood polished to a shiny gloss by decades, maybe centuries, of use, while Madame Janvier busied herself with making coffee. She got water boiling and dished out coffee from a can of Uncle Sam's finest into a French press.

"Real coffee," she said, finally looking me straight in the eye. "After years of ersatz coffee made from roasted chicory and acorns, it is heaven."

"Yes, ma'am," I said, deciding to keep the conversation easy and make my way carefully to Yvonne and Major Jerome. "You barter for the coffee and food, I imagine."

"Oh yes," she said, pouring in steaming water. "It has been hard to bring in the crops these past few years, but we have enough calvados put away to trade for food. Your officers are most generous."

"It's easy to be generous when you're trading the army's goods and not your own."

"*Exactement!*" she said, with a light, lilting laugh. "It is amazing to see truckloads of food and clothing delivered every day. Such wealth you Americans have! The Germans took riches from us, while you bring them to our door. Liberation is delightful, *n'est-ce pas?* We must enjoy it while it lasts."

"What do you mean, Madame Janvier?"

"Oh, the Germans may return. You must admit it is possible. Your armies have not gotten very far in the past month. Why, when I was a young girl, we would ride our bicycles to the beach in a morning. The one you call Omaha. So we can take nothing for granted. Your men are very brave, but so many have died for such small progress. Forgive me, but I remember when the *Boche* came in 1940. It was all over so quickly, they defeated our army as well as the English and seemed to be everywhere, racing through the country with their tanks." She pressed down on the *cafetière's* plunger, filling the room with the aroma of hot coffee and haunting dread.

"Was it very hard for you? The Occupation?" I asked.

"My husband died in 1941," she said. "Natural causes, but he was really a casualty of the first war. He was gassed, and his lungs never fully recovered. It was a slow death, painful for both of us. After that, our son Paul fled the roundup of young men for slave labor in the Reich. He joined the *Maquis* in the south, where no one could connect him to me and the family business. That was eighteen months ago, and since then I have heard nothing. Perhaps that is good news, who knows?"

She set out coffee cups and offered sugar, which I declined, knowing how precious the stuff was even with *beaucoup* calvados to trade. Her movements were slow, her appearance weary, as if telling that brief story had wrung all the energy and emotion from her. Life with the *Maquis* was dangerous, and any mother would worry about a son living as a guerrilla fighter on the run.

"I'm sorry," I said, as she filled our cups.

"It could be much worse," she said, her hands wrapped around the delicate cup, drawing in the warmth. "The Germans killed many. Took the Jews and Communists off to God knows where. So many of the old people died last winter, with not enough to eat or fuel to stay warm.

Forgive me if I make light of your American chocolate and coffee. Otherwise, I should only weep."

She sipped her coffee and sighed. I tasted mine. It was bitter. Chicory. She was still mixing it into the real thing. Maybe she'd gotten used to the taste. Or she wanted her coffee to last in case the Germans came back. A sad, smart woman.

A Kraut comeback wasn't impossible. Out on our eastern flank, British General Bernard Montgomery was fighting to get into the city of Caen, where he faced serious opposition. He'd planned on taking it on D-Day, a long, hard month ago. Here, the front was narrow, offering the Germans a chance to split the Allied forces in two. I drank more, savoring the bitterness as best I could.

"Your English is very good," I said, to move the conversation away from defeat and dead husbands.

"I studied it at school, as many did," she said. "But during the last war I worked at a British army hospital in Arromanches. My English improved speaking with the patients and boarding with English nurses. I still write to some of them, or did until the Germans came. I must send them a note to let them know I am alive. As I hope they are." She gazed out the window, a brief smile playing across her face.

"Tell me about Yvonne," I said, after a silence had settled between us.

"There is not much to tell," she said.

"Start with the blood," I said.

"She was like that this morning. I found her sitting by the window in her room, as she always does. I went to check on her as soon as I heard the cook's screams."

"That was the first thing you did?" I asked.

"Yes."

"Why?"

"I expected it might have been her. When I saw her, I thought she had hurt herself." Madame Janvier made a cutting motion across her wrist. "But then I saw it was not her blood."

"Did she say anything?"

"Yvonne never says anything," Madame Janvier said.

"Is she mute?"

"Who can say? We know her as Yvonne Virot, but that is not her real name. Nothing is known about her. She eats, sleeps, and stares out the window. Little more. But men find her very attractive. Did you, Captain Boyle?"

"Well, yes," I said, seeing no reason to lie. "In some inexplicable way. Bewitching, as if she came from some other place."

"That she did, Captain. Too bad we do not know where."

"Billy?" Big Mike shouted from the hallway.

I heard his heavy steps heading our way and called to him. "In here."

"You ain't going to believe this, Billy," he said, stopping to nod in our host's direction. "Ma'am, sorry to interrupt."

"So?" I asked, impatient to hear his news.

"Sewell's gone because he was transferred out. Him and his MP commanding officer, First Lieutenant Moretti."

"When?" I asked, struggling to understand what the hell this meant.

"About an hour ago, according to the other MPs," Big Mike said. "No one knows why, just that a flash message came in from Corps HQ ordering them out immediately."

"You have a very strange army, Captain Boyle," Madame Janvier said.

Ain't that the truth.

CHAPTER FOUR

I HAD A lot more questions about Yvonne, but from the little Madame Janvier had told me, her houseguest wouldn't be going anywhere soon. As I left, she continued to stare out her window, her thoughts unknowable. Big Mike and I marched to the MP platoon area to see what we could learn about these mysterious transfers, part and parcel of our own unknowable present. The MPs were set up in one of the barns, sharing it with a swayback horse and an assortment of smells ranging from worn leather to fresh manure. Slit trenches were dug outside, some covered in logs and netting to camouflage the defensive positions. They'd made themselves at home inside, where a small table stacked with papers and a lantern marked their headquarters in one well-swept corner of the barn.

"I got no idea what happened," a sergeant told us. "Sewell and Moretti got an order from Signals and packed up their gear without a word. It was the damnedest thing."

"Where's the order?" I asked.

"You got me," he said. "They didn't leave nothin' around."

"Did they say where they were headed?" Big Mike asked.

"You don't get it. It was like they was spooked. I saw Sewell packing and asked what was happening. I thought we was all moving out. He told me to not ask any questions and to bring the jeep around. Moretti said they were being transferred, then they got in the jeep and left. End of story."

"Where's the radio room?" I asked.

"Over in the annex, at the back of the main house," he said. "Good luck, Captain." He whispered this last bit. Up front, you don't call an officer by his rank or say "sir" out in the open. It was a healthy habit; there were plenty of Kraut snipers and forward artillery observers around. For the same reason, officers didn't wear their rank insignia or walk around with binoculars draped over their necks. There were plenty of ways to get yourself killed without hanging a target on your chest.

While we were at the front, as far as the battalion MPs were concerned, this wasn't the sharp edge. A GI in a foxhole along the MLR—main line of resistance—would probably laugh at the precaution this far to the rear. Basically, the closer to the front line you were, the more disdainful you become of anyone thirty yards or more behind you. Still, we were within artillery range, so I welcomed the MP's restraint.

As we left the barn, I saw why this was such a good spot for a headquarters unit. The hill to the south shielded us from German observers, and the orchards gave ample cover for tents and vehicles under camouflage netting strung between leafy apple trees arrayed in orderly rows. I wondered if Madame Janvier had played host to any Germans who also appreciated the layout.

The annex was a single-story extension off the back of the house. It held six rooms, each facing the garden, with double doors wide open to the warm air. GIs wearing headsets were busy fiddling with radio dials, while the slow clack of typewriter keys echoed from the rooms. Communications wire was strung from the roof and went off in every direction. Aerials sprouted from trees beyond the annex, well hidden from prying eyes.

"Who's in charge?" I bellowed, my frustration with this case getting the better of me.

"That'd be me," said a lieutenant, standing from behind a desk and stepping outside. "Friedman, in charge of the Signals section. You're investigating this murder, I hear." Friedman looked a little old for a lieutenant, maybe early thirties or so. Long face, pencil mustache, and dark hair.

"We are. Right now I want to know about the order received earlier concerning those two MP officers. What can you tell me?" I said.

"Moretti and Sewell? I was sorry to see them go. We played poker, and they were both lousy at it."

"I mean, who sent the order? Do you have a copy?" I said.

"It came direct from the Provost Marshal's office at Corps head-quarters," Friedman said. "We should have a copy here somewhere."

"Why do you say direct?" Big Mike asked. "That sounds like it was unusual."

"Yeah, it is. Standard procedure is for transfers to come from Division. But this order had priority stamped all over it, so I didn't ask questions," Friedman said. "You want to see it?"

We did. Friedman began sorting through a box filled with carbon copies and handwritten notes. He came up empty.

"Hey, Sullivan," he shouted to the radio operator. "What'd you do with the order for Sewell's and Moretti's transfer? I can't find it."

"I didn't file it, sir," the operator said. "When it came in, it said no copies, so I just typed one up for them and didn't file anything."

"You wanted unusual?" Friedman asked us. "That's unusual."

"Wait a minute," I said, walking into the garden along a path set between beets and green beans. Big Mike trailed me as I tried to figure out who was behind the transfers. Was it just another example of the army not making any sense at all, or was someone pulling strings from higher up the chain of command? What advantage would it bring? And to whom?

The killer?

Who would have enough juice to get Corps HQ to issue two transfers? The 30th Division reported to XIX Corps, along with the Second Armored and a couple of other infantry divisions. A Corps headquarters meant plenty of big brass.

"Billy?" Big Mike asked. I realized I was standing there, arms folded, tapping my finger against my lips. Same way I'd seen my dad do it back in Boston when he was working a case. Except with him, it was usually followed by a snap of the fingers and the announcement of a revelation. Me, I had nothing.

"Yeah," I said. "Get Fair over here, willya? I need to ask him something."

"Okay," he said, then cocked his thumb in the direction of the MP's bivouac. "Looks like Sewell's and Moretti's replacements are here." Two officers were unloading duffels from a jeep as a couple of MPs came out to greet them. Occasionally the army moved quickly. But not often enough for me to think this wasn't part of the setup.

"We'll talk to them later," I said. "Maybe they have a clue." I sure didn't. I strolled back to Friedman's office, where he sat at his desk, lighting up a Chesterfield. He offered me one and I waved him off.

"Anything else I can do?" he asked.

"Are these your quarters?" I asked, noticing a cot set up in the corner of the room.

"Yeah," he said. "All the comforts of home, if your home is a shack on a bombing range. Why?"

"Did you hear anything last night? See anyone who didn't belong here?"

"Captain," he said, leaning forward and blowing smoke, "we may be a headquarters unit, but we're close enough to the front that anyone who doesn't belong here would get shot up pretty badly. As for hearing things, it was quiet except for a dozen guys snoring within easy earshot, plus the artillery fire. There's a 105mm battery about a quarter mile to the rear, and they send a predawn wake-up call to the Krauts most days. That's when their kitchens haul up coffee and bread, so our guys do what they can to ruin breakfast in bed for Fritz. So if you think being on duty for twelve hours and then trying to sleep through all that left me any time to watch for a murderer tiptoeing around, you're not much of a detective."

As if on cue, the thunder of artillery sounded, fire from multiple cannons echoing against the hills.

"Is that the battery you mentioned?" I asked.

"No, that's coming from a different direction. There must be a new field artillery unit set up down the road, on our right flank," Friedman said, his head tilted to one side to listen to the booming fire. "Big stuff, maybe 155 millimeters from the racket they're making."

"The Krauts are bound to fire back," I said. "Let's hope they don't drop any rounds our way." Not that I wanted them to hit our own artillery, but being so close to those big guns made me nervous. Then I heard it—a shrill whistling that pierced the sky like a scream.

"Incoming!" shouted the radio operator as he dashed out of the room, Friedman right behind him. Being a better detective than he gave me credit for, I was hard on his heels. A slit trench had been dug on the other side of the garden, and we tumbled into it, along with a dozen other guys trying to make themselves as small as possible.

Rounds landed around us, some crashing into the woods and others sending geysers of earth sky-high as they exploded in the cultivated fields, dirt pelting my back like hail. Explosions sounded off to our right, closer to where our guns had fired from. There was no return fire; hopefully they'd gotten off their shots and skedaddled before the Germans zeroed in on them. All it took was some Kraut up a tree with a pair of binoculars to spot the smoke, and the artillery duel would get underway.

We waited. I peeked out over the mounded earth, ready to duck down again if need be. But instead of incoming, there was the *bang* and *swoosh* of outgoing mail, as the 105mm battery to our rear joined in, probably having spotted the German battery. They kept it up for a while as we cheered, happy to be alive, knowing they must be doing some heavy damage. Hoping and praying, in my case, since that meant fewer artillery shells coming my way.

I hated artillery. Not that I enjoyed enemy machine gun fire, but at least there you had a chance to fight back. But all an infantryman can do under shelling is hunker down in the ground and beg the good Lord to let him live one more day. So I cheered along with the rest of the boys, whooping and hollering like a kid, urging our steel on to render German steel and flesh torn, shattered, and useless against us.

Our fire tapered off, finally ending as silence gathered around us, men still crouched below ground with hands clamped over their helmets. The absence of explosions and shrieking shells ushered in a shocking stillness, unnerving after the back-and-forth volleys and falling rounds.

"It's over," Friedman said, standing and dusting himself off. "I think we got the better of them, don't you?"

"Let's hope," I said as we trudged back to his office, men joking and laughing in high voices as only those who have cheated death can manage. The shelling hadn't caused us any damage, leaving nothing but a few craters in the fields, marked by blackened earth and trails of wispy smoke. "Just a couple more questions, and then I'll let you get back to work."

"Fire away," Friedman said, smiling at his own joke as he sat and lit another smoke.

"Who was on duty when the body was found?" I asked.

"My sergeant, but he got me out of the chow line, and I composed the message that went up to Corps," he said. "A smart non-com knows when to hand off the hot stuff to his superior officer."

"Corps HQ?" I said. "Not First Army?"

"First Army? I'm not crazy, Captain Boyle. Why would I do that? We report up the chain of command. First I reported to Division, then I notified the Provost Marshal's office at XIX Corps that we had what looked like a murder here and requested assistance. Lieutenant Moretti concurred; he definitely wanted it kicked upstairs."

"What did you hear back?"

"Well, the message was for Moretti. He was ordered to secure the area, touch nothing, and await an investigator. That'd be you," Friedman said, crushing out his Chesterfield.

"Far as you know, he kept the area secure?"

"I don't check up on other people's work, Captain. I have enough of my own. And if you have nothing else, I'd like to get back to it."

"All I need is the name on the message from the Provost Marshal's office," I said.

Friedman sighed and called out to the corporal manning the radio set, asking him to dig out their copy of the message. "Have it in a second," he said.

"Thanks. You haven't had any signals about the Second Armored Division, have you?" I thought I might squeeze in one more question while we waited. I'd hoped Friedman might have received a radio message about Jerome's visit.

"Nope. That's the dead man's outfit, right? We didn't get any notice."

"I saw him," the radioman said, handing me a piece of flimsy paper.

"Who?" Friedman and I said at the same time.

"That major," he said. "It was during my shift last night. Sarge took over at the radio while I went to the latrine. On my way back, I saw this major walking around the farmhouse, and he asked me if I'd seen any other Second Armored guys. Said he was supposed to meet them here. I told him he was the first I'd seen, then we chatted a bit, since he was a Signals officer. About our gear and stuff, you know. Shop talk. He was real friendly. Then he went inside, looking for Madame Janvier."

"You didn't tell anyone?" Friedman said, his voice raised.

"I did, sir. But I went off duty at 0500, before anyone found the body. I got some sack time and came back on duty this morning. That's when I heard he'd been killed. I told Lieutenant Sewell what happened, but all he did was tell me to keep my mouth shut."

"When was that?" I asked. "And you're sure he mentioned Madame Janvier?"

"Yeah, I'm sure. I saw Sewell an hour ago. When I brought him his transfer papers."

"I'm keeping this," I said to Friedman, holding the orders in my hand.

"Fine. We do everything in triplicate," he said. "Except when we're told not to. Now get out of our hair, okay?"

"Not yet. I need you to send a priority message to First Army HQ. This thing is getting out of hand."

"Okay," Friedman said, his hands up in mock surrender. "Sullivan will take care of it."

"Who to, sir?" the radioman asked.

"Colonel Samuel Harding, SHAEF Office of Special Investigations, First Army HQ. Tell him I need Lieutenant Piotr Kazimierz here immediately. Got that?"

"Got it, Captain," he said, taking down the spelling of Kaz's name as I went through it. "Polish guy, huh? I know the radioman on duty at First Army, name of Nowak. He'll get a kick out of this."

"Polish Army-in-Exile," I said. "And a baron to boot."

"Wow," he said. "Nowak will get this to him right away, believe me."

Kaz had that effect on people. He was part of our little group, dedicated to the rooting out of common crimes in uncommon times. When this trip didn't seem like it would amount to much, Kaz volunteered to stay behind at First Army with Colonel Harding, interrogating German prisoners, especially those Russian and other nationalities who'd volunteered to fight for Hitler rather than die in POW camps. Kaz knew a bunch of languages, which made him a valued interrogator. He could impress people all right, but he also had a steely resolve that put the fear of God into anyone who got on the wrong side of him. Being Polish, that meant anyone in a German uniform, whatever their mother tongue.

Kaz also understood the language of murder, and I needed his help translating what I'd found here before another body cropped up. I couldn't put my finger on why, but a chill along my back told me it was going to happen soon.

CHAPTER FIVE

"HERE HE IS, Billy," Big Mike said, escorting Sergeant Fair as if he'd just collared him. "I caught him snooping in the house outside that girl's room."

"I wasn't snooping, dammit," Fair said, giving Big Mike a hard glare. "I was checking on Yvonne to see if she was okay."

"Yvonne, huh? Well, you can explain that to me along with a few other things while we get some chow," I said. "I'm hungry." And if I was hungry, I knew Big Mike was about to fall over from lack of grub. Fair led us along a path through the orchard to a tent set up under camouflage netting. The cooks were offering beef stew with vegetables, served into mess kits. Our gear was still packed away, so Fair scrounged up a couple of tin plates for us. At the end of the line, slices of fresh-baked bread were tossed on top. I had to hand it to the army; one thing it did well was feed us. Guys griped all the time about chow, but with a mobile bakery turning out fresh bread within shelling distance of the enemy, I found it hard to complain. About the bread, that is. The explosions I could do without.

"Okay," I said, as we sat on crates of C-Rations under the dappled camouflage, plates balanced on our knees. "Tell me about Yvonne. Why were you hanging around her?"

"Jeez, Captain. You saw her, right?" Fair said.

"I spoke to Madame Janvier, remember," Big Mike said, his eyes fixed on Fair. He didn't say anything else, just shoveled stew and stared.

"Okay, okay," Fair said. "I'm supposed to stay away from the house."

"From Yvonne, specifically," Big Mike said, rubbing his sleeve across his lips.

"Well, yeah. I sort of took it on myself to watch out for her," Fair said. "Some of the officers were paying way too much attention to her. No disrespect meant, Captain, but some of them think they can get away with anything."

"Like murder?" I said.

"No, that's not what I said. Come on, you know the type."

I did, but kept that to myself. "You're talking about the battalion staff?"

"Yeah. Not Colonel Brewster. He's the CO. Decent guy. But some of his officers, they were following her around like wolves," Fair said.

"Who specifically?" I asked.

"Mainly it was Major Johnson. He's the Battalion G-2."

"You'd think an intelligence officer on the front lines would be too busy for funny stuff," Big Mike said.

"Yeah, well, he made the time, believe you me. He claimed she might be withholding information, since she just sorta turned up one day, according to Madame Janvier, anyway," he said.

"Who else?" I asked.

"Lieutenant Friedman was a close second. He was in and out of the house all the time, bringing Colonel Brewster messages, when he could have had a clerk bring them," Fair said. "He always stopped to bother Yvonne."

"But he wasn't the one who got kicked out of the house," I said. "Was that the colonel's doing?"

"Naw, that was Madame Janvier. She can kick up a fuss when she wants to. She has the officers to dinner a lot, plays up to them. They like the attention, I guess. And she's doing pretty well in the bargain," Fair said.

"Can't blame her for that," I said. "Tell me why Johnson thinks Yvonne is hiding something."

"Well, Johnson is big on working with the Resistance, since they know the area. He's got some contacts with them, and there are rumors Yvonne might have been a German spy. There's some crazy story about her and a Kraut officer. I can't believe it, though. Some of these Resistance types are just out for revenge. A lot of scores are being settled, I hear."

"The FFI, they call themselves now," I said. *Forces Françaises de l'Intérieur*, as General Charles de Gaulle had named them.

"Yeah, I see trucks with FFI painted on the side everywhere," Fair said. "They come here now and then. Johnson has a guy he works with, Claude Legrand, a liaison with the Resistance. He's got one of those German jeeps, a *Kübelwagen*, with FFI splattered all over it."

"Anyone else other than Major Johnson and Lieutenant Friedman bothering Yvonne?" I asked.

"I think Legrand didn't like Johnson visiting her," Fair said. "Maybe because he's French or maybe because he's got a thing for her too. I don't know, I just try to make sure she's okay whenever I can."

"So you're her protector," Big Mike said, mopping up stew with his bread.

"Listen, I know it sounds corny, but yeah, I fell for her. Johnson complained, probably because Yvonne doesn't mind me being around. She turns away whenever Johnson gets close. She doesn't communicate much, but that tells you something. But Madame Janvier took Johnson's side, and she read me the riot act. Said she'd go to Brewster if I set foot back in the house, especially in Yvonne's room."

"But you did anyway," I said.

"I wanted to make sure she was okay after finding that body. I had to, that's all," Fair said. He looked out into the orchard, his eyes hidden from ours. The guy was an on-the-edge battle-hardened veteran, but he was also totally enthralled by Yvonne. So I ate my stew, giving him a few minutes to pull himself together.

"What exactly were you doing up at First Army?" I asked.

"My squad," he said, and turned away again. He cleared his throat and spat, as if the truth was caught in there somewhere. "My squad was shot up. Out on patrol in the hedgerows. We lost contact with the rest of the platoon. We dug in for the night, and I figured we'd find the way back at first light. Those damned hedgerows and sunken lanes all look the same after a while, you know?"

"What happened?" Big Mike asked.

"We moved out as soon as I could see my hand in front of my face," Fair said, holding up his right hand as if it held a map of the *bocage*. "But we ran right into a Kraut attack. Or they ran into us. Probably a full company, looking to take back ground we'd gained the day before. They chewed us up real bad, killed five men right off. A grenade got another guy right next to me, and the explosion left me stunned, my ears ringing. Then another GI got wounded, and I had to leave him behind. No way to carry him without getting both of us hit. Kraut mortars took out my corporal, and then there was only Brady and me."

"Just two of you made it back?" I asked.

"Sort of. Soon as we got close to our lines, Brady took a bullet in the throat," Fair said. "Maybe they called for a password, but I was having a hard time hearing, so I mighta missed it. The funny thing is, it was one of my replacements who shot him. Can you beat that? That sonuvabitch kid would have gone out on patrol with us if he showed up a few hours before. Probably woulda got himself killed. Instead, he misses the patrol and shoots Brady. Goddamn."

"That's what got you to First Army?" Big Mike asked.

"I told you Brewster's a decent CO," Fair said. "He needed a courier to take some documents up to First Army. Told me to get a shower, new ODs, and a hot meal. Said I should take my time. Which meant he didn't want me going off the deep end, at least not around the replacements. Spooks 'em."

"You didn't get new olive drabs," I said, eyeing his mud-stained trousers. He had a two-day growth of beard and a lingering smell that said he hadn't taken a shower either.

"Didn't feel like it," Fair said, resting his arms on his knees. I'd seen this before. Guys who'd lost their pals couldn't bring themselves to enjoy even the smallest pleasure. For a non-com who'd lost men in his charge, it had to be even worse. "I did get something to eat. Then an MP came and found me. Said they needed an escort back to

Bricqueville, so I said sure. Didn't really want to hang around all that brass anyway."

"Did the MP say who gave the order?" I asked.

"No. Not that I asked. He mentioned the Provost Marshal's office, but I wasn't paying much attention," Fair said. "I'm going to get some coffee, okay?"

I nodded, finishing up my food and waiting for him to get out of earshot.

"So Friedman contacts 30th Division and Corps HQ about Major Jerome," I said, working out the timeline of events as I spoke.

"Must've been around 0630," Big Mike said. "Dawn, from what everyone says."

"Yeah. Then *tout suite*, Corps gets onto the horn to First Army, kicking it upstairs even further. Then before we finish our first cup of coffee, we're on the road with Sergeant Fair, who can't wait to get back to his unit. Not to mention Yvonne."

"All of which means there had to be some heavy brass behind this," Big Mike said. "Things don't happen that quickly unless there's a general throwing a fit somewhere. And Sam had to know something was up."

"But he acted as if this was nothing but routine," I said. Colonel Sam Harding was our boss, and he reported directly to General Eisenhower. Harding was a no-nonsense West Pointer, an intelligence officer and combat veteran of the last war. Nothing got by him. But apparently, a lot got by me.

"There's something we don't know," Big Mike said. "When did Fair leave here, and when did he arrive at First Army HQ?"

"Jesus," I said, seeing Fair head back with a cup of steaming joe. He sat, shook out a smoke from a crumpled pack of Lucky Strikes, and lit up, sighing with satisfaction. It was a small comfort, and I hated to spoil it. But that was my job. "Sarge, just to get everyone's movements straight, when did you drive up to First Army?"

"Last night," he said, blowing on his coffee. Then he looked at me over the cup, steam drifting up before his eyes. "Hey, you're not going to finger me for this, are you?"

"Don't worry," I said. "We just need to know where everybody was. It doesn't mean you're a suspect. But it does help, so we can spot someone spinning a yarn."

"Yeah," Big Mike broke in. "Say you left around sunset. Then another guy says he saw you in the house at midnight. Then we know he's lying, see?"

"Sure, sure," Fair said. "I get it. Okay, I left around eight. It was getting dark, but I had to wait for Brewster to get some reports together."

"Who'd you deliver them to?" I asked.

"First Army G-3," Fair said, sucking in a lungful of smoke. G-3 was Operations, responsible for combat planning. "It was a report on working with the local French Resistance. Using them as scouts, that sort of thing. Leastways, that's what Brewster said. He made it sound important."

"Got a name?" Big Mike asked.

"No, I tossed a thick, sealed envelope on some duty clerk's desk," Fair said, irritation creeping into his voice. "It was a big tent with a wooden floor and a woodstove keeping those guys warm, with plenty of coffee close at hand. I didn't hang around and make friends."

"What time was this?" I asked.

"I dunno. Late," Fair said, field-stripping his butt and scattering the remaining tobacco. "I had to go slow driving up there, with the blackout. You can't see much with the headlights taped over except for those tiny slits. Then I had to wait for a convoy to pass at a crossroads, which took forever. It was after midnight, but I wasn't really paying attention to the time."

"See?" Big Mike asked, clapping Fair on the shoulder as we stood. "That wasn't so bad, was it? Now we have a time frame."

"I guess," Fair said, finishing off his coffee. "What's next, Captain?"

"Well, where's our gear, and where are we bunking tonight?"

"Madame Janvier had a room free. I brought your duffel bags up there. Second floor, last room on the left. Nothing fancy, but there's beds and sleeping bags I scrounged," Fair said.

"Is that what you were doing when Big Mike found you at Yvonne's door?" I asked.

"Yeah. I couldn't resist," Fair said.

"Okay. But make room for one more. We have another man on the way," I said. "And stay away from Yvonne this time."

"Sure, Captain," he said.

"What about you, Fair?" Big Mike asked as we walked back to the house. "Where do you hang your hat?"

"Me and the boys were dug in real good on the line," he said. "Had a dugout with pine logs for a roof. Deep, too. But some other squad's got it now."

"So where do you sleep?" I asked, stopping to face Fair.

"Sleep?" Fair said, as if it was the dumbest question he'd ever heard. "I don't know, Captain. I really don't. I got my gear in the press house. I'll be there if you need me, okay?"

"Sure," I said. Fair trudged off in the direction of the *pressoir*, following a couple of local workmen in their blue coveralls and berets. Fair with his M1, the workers with pitchforks. Even in the midst of war, there was work to do. But I bet the Frenchmen got more sleep than Fair.

"You know what this means, Billy," Big Mike said.

"I do. Fair could have doubled back here and still had time to get to First Army, if he didn't have traffic problems." HQ was outside of Grandchamps, on the coast, not far from Omaha beach. A morning's bicycle ride, as Madame Janvier described it.

"Maybe he snuck in to visit Yvonne, found her with Major Jerome, and went nuts. He's close to the edge as it is," Big Mike said.

"But that doesn't explain the morphine," I said. "Which was put in the glass on purpose. Premeditated. What you're describing is spur of the moment. I could see Fair pulling a knife on some stranger going after Yvonne, but not planning out some elaborate poisoning."

"Yeah, besides, Jerome would have been too woozy to be much of a threat," Big Mike said.

"Assuming he drank from the glass containing the drug," I said. I stuck my hands in my pockets, a chill in the evening air.

"But Kaplan said he could've made it out of the room if he wasn't drugged," Big Mike said.

"Maybe the glass was for someone else, and he interrupted a carefully planned killing. There's some sort of struggle, and his neck gets sliced. The killer holds him down, then dumps the drink down his throat."

"Billy," Big Mike said, shaking his head, "that's crazy. Who was the killer? Little Yvonne? Where'd she get the morphine? And who was the intended victim?"

"Okay, I admit it," I said. "I'm not making sense. But let's talk with Kaplan about any missing morphine."

We headed back to the farmhouse and the pair of medic's tents behind one of the barns. In front of the house we found an ancient truck with FFI on the side. Next to it was a German *Kübelwagen* with a similar paint job. Heavily armed *résistants* milled about, but one fellow stood out. He was tall and wore a black beret with even blacker hair curling out from beneath it. He carried a German *Schmeisser* submachine gun slung over his shoulder, one hand resting on it, his finger inches from the trigger.

But it wasn't his height, his darkness, or the weapon that made him stand out.

It was the hole where an eye should have been.

CHAPTER SIX

"WHO ARE YOU? And where is Major Johnson?" demanded the one-eyed man. Skin was puckered and scarred around his eye where it had healed, if that was even the right word for the knots and swirls of flesh. A chunk of his cheekbone was gone, replaced by a gnarl of scar tissue. Shrapnel, or maybe a bullet, had grazed his face and took half his sight with it.

"Who are you, buddy?" Big Mike asked, stepping between me and the gathering Frenchmen. He didn't like our new friend's attitude one damn bit.

"I am Commandant Legrand. Everyone knows of me," he said, turning to his men with a quick aside that brought laughs, probably at our expense. "I have news for Johnson. Where is he?"

"Up at Division headquarters," I said. "I hear they'll be back in the morning."

"This cannot wait," he said, puffed up with his own self-importance. "Take me to Colonel Brewster." He spoke English slowly, with a heavy accent, but he knew the lingo pretty well, so I figured he was the Resistance liaison Fair had described.

"Sorry, but Johnson and the rest of the battalion staff are with the colonel," I said. "What's so important?"

"Who are you?" Legrand asked again, ignoring my question.

"Captain William Boyle. I'm here to investigate a murder." I watched Legrand to see if he betrayed any knowledge of the killing. Nothing.

"The *Boche* have murdered many," Legrand said. "Which of their victims has brought you here?"

"It wasn't the Krauts," Big Mike said, still going toe to toe with Legrand. "An officer from Second Armored was killed last night. His throat was slit inside Madame Janvier's house."

"What?" Legrand dropped his imperious tone as his remaining eye went wide in surprise. "Yvonne, is she safe?" With that, he brushed by us and stomped into the house, calling out for Yvonne.

"Fair was right," Big Mike said. "He definitely has a thing for her."

"I'm going to talk with him," I said. "You go check with Kaplan about the morphine, and ask him if he found anything when he checked Jerome's body." The medic wasn't a coroner, but he seemed sharp enough to spot needle marks.

"Okay. I'll be glad when Kaz gets here," Big Mike said. "We sure can use another guy."

"You got that right," I said, taking the steps into the house. Maybe half a dozen guys, all as smart as Kaz, would help. I followed the sound of footsteps up to Yvonne's room. She had a spot at the end of the long hallway, a room with a big dormer window overlooking the gardens and barns. She sat in a rocking chair, her eyes fixed on the scene outdoors, with the sunlight filtering through the treetops in the distance. Legrand knelt at her side, whispering to her, stroking her hair as if she were the one upset.

Yvonne flinched at his touch, but it did not deter him.

She was finally out of the bloodstained dress, wearing a yellow skirt and white blouse, her skin looking even paler against the fabric. In her right hand, she still clutched a white handkerchief.

"*Sortez!*" Madame Janvier said, entering the room in rubber boots, still clinging to pruning shears from her work in the orchards. She was out of breath, her mouth set in a grimace of anger.

Legrand stood, drawing himself up to his full height, nearly hitting the low rafters with his forehead. All the gentleness he'd summoned up for Yvonne—no matter how unwanted—vanished into a sneer of disapproval. He said nothing, then stalked from the room, brushing by Madame Janvier, almost toppling her.

"Captain Boyle, will you please leave as well?" Madame Janvier said, one hand on the wall to steady herself, her gaze settling on Yvonne.

"Sure," I said. "I only wanted to make sure everything was okay. Legrand was upset when he heard about last night." I looked at Yvonne, hoping for some response, but she kept her gaze focused on the gardens outside.

"He is always that way," Madame Janvier said. "Now please leave. It is not good for Yvonne."

I wasn't sure exactly what was not good, but I got the message. I shot one last glance at Yvonne as she let her hand fall to her lap, her fingers relaxing their grip on the handkerchief.

There was blood, a line of scarlet where she'd pressed it to her palm. I started to say something but stopped myself. There would be no answer from Yvonne. So I asked Madame Janvier about the cut.

"It happens often, what can I say? Now please leave her in peace."

I followed Legrand out, wondering what secrets Yvonne held and why Madame Janvier was protecting her.

As for her and Legrand, it was obvious they knew each other well, the way people do when they hate each other. But why? Was it about Yvonne, or was there personal history between them? Yvonne's wound, and how she'd come by it, could wait.

"Legrand," I said, catching up to him at his vehicle.

"Commandant Legrand," he corrected me as he opened the door, snapping his fingers for his driver.

"Very well, Commandant. Tell me what your relationship is with Yvonne."

"Why does she concern you? She is not a murderer. She barely moves and does not speak."

"She was found this morning covered in blood, so she managed to move downstairs on her own," I said. "She was involved somehow." I kept the news of that slice on her palm to myself.

"If that is so, she must have tried to help the poor man. How was he killed?"

"I never said it was a man, Commandant Legrand," I said.

"There are many men in the house, it is obvious," he said. "An

American, of course. Which officer? And yes, I know it is an officer because your army would not send you to stick your nose in over the death of a common soldier."

"Major Jerome from the Second Armored Division," I said, not liking his attitude, but knowing he was close to the mark. "Any idea why he was here?"

"We need tanks," Legrand said, shaking his head. "I told them that last night."

"Who?"

"The soldiers from that armored division. They were here last night," Legrand said, lighting up a smoke, then passing the pack of German Juno cigarettes around to his pals. He didn't bother to offer me one.

"Are you sure?"

"Yes! I was here to talk to Johnson, but Lieutenant Friedman told me he was gone. I hoped he would be back by now. As to the soldiers, yes, they all had that patch. A triangle, with the number two and *Hell on Wheels* written below. We could use some of that Hell, let me tell you."

"How can you be sure Major Jerome wasn't with them?" I asked.

"Because there were no officers! Are you an idiot? Or do you think I am? It was a half-track full of men, right where you are standing. A sergeant, but no officers," Legrand said.

"Friedman saw them as well?"

"*Oui.* Now I must go. When you see Major Johnson, tell him to watch his battalion's right flank. There is no one there. We patrol the roads and see no one. Except for a *Boche* patrol, and we kill them. So you are safe for the moment."

"We heard artillery firing from the right flank today," I said, thinking Legrand was overreacting and too damn full of himself.

"Then they ran away," he said, shutting the door on the *Kübelwagen* and tapping his driver on the arm. "You should hope the Germans are as unaware as you."

"A horrible man," Madame Janvier said from the doorway as he drove away, her arms folded across her chest.

"Capable of murder?" I asked, wondering how much of what he told me was true.

"He has blood on his hands, that much is certain," she said. "But do not believe everything he says. Legrand means 'the great' in French, but it is only his *nom de guerre*, which he chose for himself. This tells you much about his character. As does the fact he goes without a patch to cover his missing eye."

"Why does he?"

"To frighten people and show he has been in combat. He wears that horrible wound like a badge," she said.

"How did it happen?" I asked.

"I do not know. He returned bandaged after our armies were defeated. The Germans thought him too badly wounded to take prisoner, so they let him go home to Bricqueville. He never told anyone what happened. It adds to the mystery."

"How long has he been with the Resistance?"

"From the beginning, according to him. Again, who can say? His men are loyal and do not speak against him. They have fought the *Boche*, to be sure, but they also have taken property of the *collabos* who fled as the enemy retreated," she said, using the term for pro-German collaborationists.

"There's money to be made in a war," I said.

"Yes, and old scores to be settled. People were first denounced to the *Boche*, and now to Legrand and his gang," she said.

"You make it sound like everyone is on the take," I said. She raised an eyebrow, unfamiliar with the term. "Corrupt. Out for only themselves."

"Ah, yes, I understand. Perhaps, Captain Boyle, it sounds that way because all those who fought honorably for France are now dead, leaving only the evil and the frightened behind."

Following her into the kitchen, I returned to more recent events. "Madame Janvier, Legrand said he was here last night, looking for Major Johnson, and that he saw soldiers from the Second Armored at your door."

"I saw nothing," she said, turning to busy herself at the sink. "There are always soldiers coming and going. First our own men, but they were all fleeing. Then the Germans. Now you Americans. I look forward to the day when I no longer see uniforms everywhere. *Bonsoir*, Captain Boyle."

I wished her a pleasant evening as well and strolled back to the Signals area, finding Lieutenant Friedman seated by the garden, smoking and drinking a glass of calvados.

"Join me, Captain?" he asked. "There's a bottle and glasses on my desk."

"No, thanks," I said. "Just one quick question. Why didn't you tell me you ran into Legrand last night?"

"That puffed-up Frenchman? Why's that important?"

"Everything's important in a murder investigation," I said. "So tell me about it."

"Nothing to tell, really. I went around to the house and saw him chatting with a bunch of GIs. He asked me where Johnson was, and I told him Brewster and his staff were up at Division. He went on about our flank being threatened, and I told him I'd pass the message on. That's it."

"Nothing else?"

"Not that I recall. Legrand thinks he's de Gaulle. Don't pay him much mind. Johnson can't stand the man, but he speaks good English, so he's the best choice for liaison work."

"Did you recognize the GIs he was talking with?" I asked, giving Friedman a chance to come clean.

"Nope. We're just off a main road here, so we get plenty of traffic from other units. Didn't really pay much attention."

"They were Second Armored, same as the victim," I said.

"Really? Wonder why they left, then," Friedman said. "Were they the same crew that was here when you arrived? I heard they vamoosed pretty quick."

"Good question," I said. "Now, one more for you. What were you doing in the house?"

"Hey, I'm in and out all the time, delivering signals to Colonel Brewster, that sort of thing," Friedman said, taking a last drag on his cigarette.

"Brewster was gone. You said so yourself."

"Yeah, well, I did drop in to visit Yvonne. Just for a minute."

"You and she have a nice chat?" I asked.

"Come on, Captain, you know she doesn't speak. I like to say hello. Maybe she's awake inside and understands everything, you ever think of that? A little human contact might go a long way, that's my theory."

"That's great, Friedman. Anything else you didn't think was worth telling me?"

"Can't say there is, Captain," Friedman said, draining his glass of calvados and giving a satisfied smack of the lips.

"You weren't worried about Legrand's warning about our flank?" I asked.

"You heard that artillery on our right flank today," he said. "That's evidence he was wrong. Besides, I've been picking up their radio signals since yesterday, so they've got to be close by. Legrand wants to prove he's vital so we'll keep supplying his men. There's quite a bit of competition among the Resistance types for food and fuel, and right now Legrand and his bunch are on top. How much actual fighting they do is up for debate. But I included his message in some reports I sent up to Division. Never hurts to put a warning down on paper. In triplicate."

With that, he ambled off to his quarters, pleased he'd done his duty, or at least the bare minimum. Me, I sure felt a whole lot safer knowing a report had been filed and sent up the chain of command. If the Germans attacked, I could show it to them.

I headed back to the house, the late summer sunset finally settling down behind the tree line. Distant *crumps* of artillery and the occasional volley of rifle fire were all that set this starlit twilight apart from a peaceful country evening anywhere else in the world. It was quiet enough now, but soon patrols would be heading out, men from each side probing and testing defenses in the dense hedgerows. Then things would get loud, dark, and deadly.

As I mounted the staircase, I resisted the temptation to peek in on Yvonne. I understood the attraction. Men far from home, hungry for female company, each of them thinking they could play Prince Charming to her Sleeping Beauty. But even the mention of her name was beginning to wear me down, so I happily turned the other way and found our room.

There was one bed and two army cots, with a small table set under a dormer window. A couple of rickety chairs and peeling wallpaper completed the décor. I flopped down on a cot, unlacing my boots. I left the bed for Big Mike, since he'd likely break the cot or keep me up all night complaining about hanging over it.

I lit a lamp and pulled the curtains tight as Big Mike entered the room with a bottle of calvados in one hand and three glasses clasped in the other. "From Madame Janvier," he said. "I traded for Hershey bars."

"Good man," I said. "What'd you find out from Kaplan?"

"He draws his stuff from the Quartermaster who's headquartered in Bricqueville in a local warehouse," Big Mike explained as he poured. "Kaplan said it was pretty secure, but that a supply truck headed here got caught in a barrage last week, and they lost a lot of stuff including morphine. And what was left was brought back in bits and pieces. There were open cases of morphine syrettes stacked up outside. Anyone could have helped themselves."

"Okay, that doesn't do much to narrow our field of suspects," I said. "Legrand told me he saw some men from Second Armored here last night. No officers, just a sergeant and men in a half-track."

"That's strange," Big Mike said. "The Second Armored guys here this morning didn't mention anything about that. Funny that the only ones we've seen were near the crime scene. If they're moving into the area, where the hell are they?"

"That's a good question, but right now I'd prefer answers. Like why Friedman didn't mention he was in the house last night. Legrand saw him go in and gave him a message for Johnson about our right flank hanging loose."

"When was this?" Big Mike asked.

"Sometime after Brewster and his officers left. Late evening, I'd say."

"So we have more suspects," he said. "Legrand and Friedman. Both sweet on Yvonne. That dame's trouble."

"We need to find Second Armored headquarters," I said. "First thing in the morning."

"Hope Kaz gets himself here by then," Big Mike said. He and Kaz were great pals, and as different as two guys could be, except for their common Polish heritage.

"I hear my name being bandied about. I do hope you are paying me compliments," a voice said from the hallway. Kaz himself, right on cue.

"Naw, we were just debating whether to save any calvados for you," Big Mike said. "Come on in and take a load off."

"Cheery accommodations," Kaz said, tossing his cap onto the table and dropping his duffel. As usual, Kaz looked dapper, even this close to the front. His British army battle dress was tailored for his slim figure. And I mean tailored, as in Savile Row bespoke uniforms for gentlemen and royalty. Kaz was both, being filthy rich and also a baron of the Augustus clan. He was probably among the few Polish barons left alive, after both the Nazis and then the Russians exterminated any Poles who might resist their rule. Kaz had been lucky enough to have been studying in England when the war broke out. His family's luck, back in Poland, had been nonexistent.

But the war had damaged Kaz in a very real sense. Besides losing his family, an explosion during our first investigation left him with a scar that ran from the edge of one eye all the way to his jawbone. That same explosion had also killed the woman he loved. For a long time, Kaz didn't care if he lived or died. Then he decided that staying alive allowed him to exact retribution from the Nazis for all they had done to his homeland, his family, and his one true love. He'd recently received news that his youngest sister might still be alive, fighting with the Polish Underground. I had never seen Kaz hopeful before that news. Hope looked good on him.

"How did the interrogations go?" I asked, pouring him a healthy measure, thinking what a blow it would be to him if that news turned out to be false.

"Mostly Russians and Ukrainians frightened at the prospect of being returned to the Soviets," he said. "They'd been forced into German service or volunteered simply to avoid starvation as POWs. Some may have been genuinely anti-Communist, but most of them surrendered as soon as they could. All of them begged not to be sent back to suffer Stalin's tender mercies."

"Is that the plan?" I asked.

"So goes the rumor, but I have no idea. Since they have served in both armies that dismembered Poland, I must admit to little sympathy for them. Although I did talk with two Koreans who were quite interesting. I wish I knew Korean, but we got by with a mixture of German and Russian."

"Koreans? They're a long way from home," Big Mike said, raising his glass. *"Na zdrowie."*

"Na zdrowie," Kaz said, taking a gulp and working not to show any effect. "Yes, very far. They were impressed into the Japanese army and fought the Russians in a border skirmish. They were taken prisoner and forced to join the Soviet army at the time of Stalingrad. They then escaped and were captured by the Germans, who conscripted them for one of their static defense units along the Atlantic Wall. They couldn't wait to surrender."

"Jeez," Big Mike said. "One army is enough for me."

"My sentiments exactly," Kaz said, raising his glass in my direction. "Now tell me about this murder of yours."

Which is what I did, in between glasses of calvados. After a few rounds, things began to make sense. After a few more, nothing did.

CHAPTER SEVEN

THE MORNING DAWNED sunny and warm, which only made my head hurt. Madame Janvier fawned over us, pouring steaming coffee without a trace of chicory and setting out plates of bread and plum jam made from her own orchards. It was only when she called Kaz "baron" and Big Mike sent a wink in my direction that I tumbled as to why. This wasn't the first time Big Mike had laid the groundwork for a good meal by letting Kaz's baronial status slip.

The French, like most Europeans, loved aristocrats. Madame Janvier was no exception. She smiled and chatted in French with Kaz, who thanked her on our behalf for her hospitality, gracing her with a brush of lips over her hand as we departed.

A convoy of jeeps pulled in as we left the house. Some of them sported mounted machine guns, and they all carried GIs with weapons at the ready. Officers sat in passenger seats, recognizable by their clean shaves and tanker jackets.

Tanker jackets were hard to come by, and every GI wanted one. Snug and comfortable, the knitted cuff and waistband made for a better fit than the drafty M41 field jackets most of us were stuck with. Supposedly only issued to tank units, they could turn up anywhere, especially in rear-echelon units where men had easy access to supplies meant for the front.

One of the jeeps braked to a halt as the others continued to the back of the house. My shoulders tensed as tires sent up puffs of dust, tiny swirls that disappeared into the overhanging branches of a beech tree. A colonel, by the rank insignia on his helmet, got out and dusted himself off. This had to be Brewster.

"Boyle? You the fellow looking into this killing?" he barked.

"Yes, sir, Colonel Brewster," I said. "This is Lieutenant Kazimierz and Sergeant Miecznikowski."

"Are you not in the habit of saluting superior officers at SHAEF?" Brewster said, his hands clasped behind his back.

"At SHAEF, yes, sir. Up here, I thought you might appreciate not being pointed out." With that, I gave him a fast salute. Kaz and Big Mike followed suit, and Brewster returned the favor.

"Captain, if we have snipers this close to battalion headquarters, then we're in big trouble. We wear our rank and perform the proper military courtesies. In my headquarters, at any rate. Man would be a damn fool to do it up on the line, but here we need to set an example. Now report."

"Nothing much of substance yet, Colonel," I said. "Major David Jerome of the Second Armored Division was killed inside the house two nights ago, shortly after you and your party left. We're following up leads now."

"You think any of my men were responsible?" Brewster asked.

"Too soon to tell, sir," I said. "We're heading out to the Second Armored HQ to find out what Jerome was doing here. Seems like no one was expecting him."

"I wasn't, I can tell you that much."

"Might you have any idea where Second Armored is headquartered?" I asked.

"No. Haven't seen a single tanker. Heard them moving up in the woods outside of Bricqueville, though," Brewster said. "The sound of a Sherman is music to my ears." His eyes moved past me, and his face tightened. "Jesus, Sergeant Fair, don't you know how to follow orders?"

"Sorry, Colonel," Fair said as he shuffled toward us, offering the faintest of salutes. Front-line habits died hard. "They grabbed me at First Army to guide Captain Boyle down here."

"That's no excuse for your appearance, Sergeant," Brewster said. "Get yourself cleaned up." Fair was still unshaven and filthy.

"Will do, Colonel, soon as I get Captain Boyle and his men back here. They're bound to get lost on their own," Fair said. "Probably drive themselves right into Kraut lines."

"All right, you do that, Sergeant," Brewster said. "Report to me tonight. Cleaned up, got that?"

"Sir," Fair said with a nod, and took the driver's seat in our jeep.

"Boyle," Brewster said, leaning in and whispering, "find that killer. And take care of Fair. Bring him back in one piece or you'll answer to me." As he went into the house, I wondered if his first stop would be Yvonne's room.

"Ready, Captain?" Fair said, starting the jeep.

"Let's go," I said, eager to leave Yvonne and the silent magic she worked on men behind. I took the passenger's seat while Kaz and Big Mike squeezed in the back.

"Where to?" Fair asked, easing the jeep slowly down the drive.

"Head west," I said. "We need to make contact with a Second Division unit on our flank and find somebody in charge."

"Funny we ain't seen any more of them guys," Fair said, getting the jeep up to speed. "Since yesterday morning, I mean. I swear I heard tanks last night, not too far away."

"I didn't hear a thing," I said.

"It was the calvados," Kaz said. "Or perhaps Big Mike's snoring drowned out the noise."

"Well, I heard it," Fair said, turning onto the main road. "Other guys did too. We'll swing through Bricqueville and see what we can find out. The town anchors our right flank, so beyond it we oughta find Second Armored. Or somebody."

"Long as it ain't Krauts," Big Mike said. "You heard the story Legrand was selling? That there's no one covering that flank?"

"He's crazy. I know tanks when I hear them. If I thought he was for real, I'd hotfoot up to the line and tell my company commander," Fair said. "We're stationed on the far right. I'd hate for the Krauts to sneak around them."

"You going back on the line?" I asked.

"Yeah, I think Brewster'll cut me loose pretty soon. There's a new batch of replacements headed our way, and he'll need an experienced squad leader. Damn few of us left in one piece," Fair said. After a month of constant fighting, any front-line noncom left standing was a walking good-luck charm.

We passed more of Madame Janvier's orchards, and I realized we'd only seen a small portion of her property on the way in. One field that abutted a forested hilltop looked like it had taken a beating from the air. Huge craters gouged the earth, and apple trees were upended, their charred roots on display. Elsewhere, trees hung heavy with young apples in shades of yellow and red.

"Is this all part of Janvier *Pressoir*?" I asked.

"Yep," Fair said. "Madame Janvier worries about the harvest a lot. As if the shooting war will have passed by come fall."

"It better," I said. The good Madame seemed to be a wealthy lady, at least in terms of land. Funny that so many men were fawning over poor, penniless Yvonne, while the widow Janvier, her business, and her lands were right there as well. Sure, there was gray in her upswept hair, but she was a good-looking, trim woman on the sunny side of fifty. I wondered what she thought of Yvonne. Did she resent her?

"Bricqueville," Fair announced, pointing to a signpost ahead. We left the narrow dirt lane and drove on a paved road into town, low stone buildings on either side of us. Several were in ruins, rubble strewn out into the street. As Fair navigated around the debris, a roar of voices rose from ahead. We drove around a curve and the road emptied out into the town center, filled with a cheering crowd of a hundred or so. They were gathered around a statue in the center of the cobblestoned square, one of the monuments to a bygone war and the local dead to be found in every French town.

On the steps of the monument, Legrand stood tall above all others, haranguing the crowd, waving his arms madly, pointing at two men before him, their hands tied and arms held roughly by his men. The crowd surged forward, kicking and striking out at the prisoners. Legrand laughed, and his followers did nothing to stop the abuse.

It was a festive atmosphere. Not for the captives, of course, but everyone else was enjoying themselves. Smiling, laughing, clapping one another on the back and congratulating those who struck the hardest blows. These were common folk, hardworking country people. Women in their aprons and worn wool stockings, kids in short pants, men in dirty corduroys and slouched berets. Nice people, most likely.

Except today they were a mob.

"Ah, Captain Boyle!" Legrand called out, holding up his hand to still the crowd. "Come. You will see how true Frenchmen deal with *collabos.*"

"If they collaborated with the Nazis, put them on trial," I said, stepping out of the jeep.

"Why, that is what we have done," Legrand said, his one eye lit with fervor. "Now for the sentence." He launched into a tirade, pointing at the two men as he addressed the crowd.

"He says they are *profiteurs de guerre,* war profiteers," Kaz translated. "They ran the black market in this area and paid off the Germans to let them operate. The sentence is death."

One of the bound men shouted back at Legrand. The other hung his head, blood dripping from a cut on his cheek.

"He says Legrand wants his pig farm and knows he has no heirs. He denies working with the Germans and says everyone bought from him on the black market," Kaz continued. "Including many of those who yell the loudest against him."

"It won't make any difference," Fair said, holding his M1 in his arms.

The shouts and screams of the townspeople proved him right, as did the two Resistance men who took up positions behind us, fingers on the triggers of their Sten guns, leaving no question as to who was running the show. Legrand yelled a command, and the crowd backed away and quickly quieted, as the two prisoners were forced to their knees. Legrand's men stepped behind them, pistols at the ready. He nodded.

Two shots cracked in the still air, echoing off the stone buildings surrounding us. The men slumped forward, hands bound behind them. Dark red blood pooled on the paving stones under lifeless eyes.

Another cheer went up from the assembled villagers, not as

enthusiastic as the previous shouts had been. This one was to reassure themselves that they were in the right and on the side of justice, no matter how roughly delivered. And to let their neighbors know they were on Legrand's side. Because once a mob commits to killing, there's no telling who may be next.

"Jesus, they ain't gonna kill those girls, are they?" Big Mike said, pointing to a clutch of young women being pushed through the crowd. Four of them, holding onto one another as people spat at them and began tearing at their clothes. By the time they stood before Legrand at the steps of the monument, they were left with nothing but shreds of their dresses covering their undergarments, hands crossed over their breasts.

"Now, Captain Boyle, you shall see how we punish the *collaboration horizontale*," Legrand said, laughing as his men forced the four women to sit on the steps. But not to receive a bullet. Theirs was to be a less lethal, but still cruel, punishment. Men with scissors and hair clippers grabbed them roughly, pulling up their hair. They held them that way for a long minute as the townspeople heaped abuse upon them. At a sharp command from Legrand, they began hacking away.

"We call this the *coiffure* '44," Legrand said. "You see, we can show mercy, Captain Boyle. Do not judge us too harshly. If we did not do this now, they might be killed later. Hair will grow back. Necks do not."

"This is mercy?" I asked, watching the girls. One wept, while another held her head high, maintaining what dignity she could. Another was noticeably with child, while a younger girl twisted and turned as the clippers were put to work on her auburn hair. But it was the faces of the townspeople, people who knew these young women well, who had likely watched them grow up, knew their parents, and went to church with them that stunned me.

They were gleeful. They jeered at the girls, taunted them, reaching forward with wagging fingers of righteous disapproval. Deep groans of satisfaction arose as the old clippers drew blood. Wild, shrill laughter rang out from hearts and throats unrestrained by pity.

The villagers pressed in close for their chance to spew humiliation, shame, and degradation. The crowd became a tight knot of flesh closing in around four girls who were perhaps foolish, or stupid, or at worst uncaring and unthinking. But not deserving of this. How could they ever live again with these people?

How could their tormentors live with themselves?

Legrand stepped back, admiring his work. Big Mike and Kaz were staring in frank horror at the scene before us. Only Fair had turned away. Behind us, he watched the streets and exits, scanning rooftops, his rifle at the ready. Of all of us, only Fair remembered there was another enemy out there, an enemy who could strike while other men catered to their worst instincts.

He turned in my direction and I caught a look of strained anguish on his face, and in that moment it seemed as if he was searching hopefully, desperately, for his old, well-known foe. Men like him who fought, killed, suffered, and died in the tangled hedgerows and open fields. Not those who turned on their own young with leering, superior grins.

He kept looking, seeking out what soldiers finally come to know when they've been fighting long enough. That they may have arrived at the point where they have more in common with their enemy than anyone else. Including those they have come to liberate. Or conquer. The intensity, horror, and death of the battlefield has a way of burning away all that is base, tawdry, and disappointing in humanity. Like the shorn locks of hair left on the cobblestones in the small village of Bricqueville.

CHAPTER EIGHT

WE DIDN'T SPEAK much as we drove out of the town center. What was there to say? That the dead men and the shamed girls had deserved it? Or that it was all a part of war, and what the hell did we expect, flowers and parades at every turn? Liberation wasn't always about the liberators. Today, it had been about power. The kind of power that wormed its way in between the conqueror's retreat and the return of the old order, leaving plenty of room for the settling of scores.

Maybe we needed to explore that gap between the old and the new, and see if Major Jerome had somehow gotten caught in the cross fire. Nothing else made sense, so why not? Did he have any contacts with the French Resistance? He was in Signals, so there might have been radio communications of some sort going on. A long shot, but at least a shot.

"That's the Quartermaster building," Fair said, pointing out a two-story brick warehouse set close to the road. Double doors were rolled open, revealing crates of supplies stacked floor to ceiling. GIs worked at unloading a truck, carrying cases of grenades and Spam, each deadly enough in their own way. "You wanted to stop there?"

"No," I said. "We were going to ask about thefts of morphine, but Kaplan told us a truck with medical supplies was shelled near headquarters, and some might have gone missing. You know anything about that?"

"I didn't take any, if that's what you're asking," Fair said, giving me a quick glance, anger flashing in his eyes. "Swiping officers' booze is one thing, but stealing morphine this close to the front? That's a god-damn crime."

"Hey," Big Mike said, slapping Fair on the shoulder from his perch in the back seat. "If you heisted some scotch from the Quartermaster's stocks, my hat's off to you. Billy didn't mean you stole the morphine, pal, so just answer the man."

"Okay, okay," Fair said, holding up one hand. "Yeah, I was close by when it happened. Coupla supply trucks got clobbered by Kraut artil-lery, about halfway between Bricqueville and HQ. I was in a jeep with my lieutenant and a fresh replacement—both dead now—and we went to help. Krauts must've spotted 'em somehow, since it was a half dozen rounds and done. Both trucks wrecked and the drivers dead. There were uniforms, boots, and K-Rations scattered everywhere. When we saw the medical supplies, we figured it wasn't smart to leave a dozen crates of morphine syrettes by the side of the road."

"Where'd you take them?" I asked as we left the warehouse behind.

"Back to HQ," Fair said. "We left them with Colonel Brewster."

"All of them?" I asked.

"Well, some of them crates was smashed open. I grabbed some loose syrettes for our medic, and I know Kaplan took some too. But the rest Colonel Brewster took charge of. Did an inventory right on Madame Janvier's kitchen table."

"That's it?" Big Mike said as Fair slowed the vehicle. We'd left the paved road and the town behind, emerging into the now-familiar countryside. Fields, hedgerows, and dusty, narrow lanes.

"That's it. Brewster sent out a party to recover the bodies and the rest of the supplies, and we went back on the line. I gave our medic the syrettes, about ten or twelve, I think. Lucky thing I did, he was almost out. Needed them the next day."

"What happened then?"

"Nothing good," Fair said. Good was in damn short supply around here.

We emerged from the narrow lane, hedgerows giving way to a small valley with a stream flowing through it, a stone bridge to our front. A thick forest of fir trees shaded the roadway on our right, while on our left the rocky ground sloped away toward the fast-running water.

"There," Fair said, braking and pointing to the firs dead ahead. The muzzle of an anti-tank gun protruded from the branches, camouflage netting strung over it. Beyond the gun GIs were dug in, their helmets dark against the thick and gloomy pines.

"Hey, fellas," Fair said, tilting his helmet back on his head.

"Jesus, Sarge, where you been?" one of the men asked, a corporal, by the stripes on his sleeve.

"Brewster's got me ferrying these VIPs around," Fair said. "What gives out here?"

"Quiet," the corporal said, his red-and-blue shoulder patch showing him to be part of Fair's 30th Division. "Patrols, nothing too heavy. Where you headed?"

"We're looking for Second Armored," I said. "Seen any tanks?"

"Nope," the corporal said. No salute, no calling me "captain" or "sir," which I liked. And worried about, since it meant we were at the shooting edge of this war. "We keep hearing them move around the other side of that hill, but they ain't come out in the open. Can't blame them, you know?"

"Yeah," I said, looking out past the stone bridge to a wooded hilltop opposite. I strained to listen for the sound of tank engines and clanking treads, but the trees gave up no secrets other than a flight of crows. "The road ahead safe?"

"Should be," the corporal said. "Stay away from the mines along the gully, and you'll be fine. We're the end of the line as far as it goes for 30th Division. Next guys you run into oughta be tankers. Ours, if you're lucky."

"You get much artillery fire here?" I said, eyeing the stone bridge and thinking the Germans must have it zeroed in.

"No, the Krauts ain't shelled us much lately. Think they got the shit end of a few duels with those Second Armored boys, from what we could hear."

"Yeah, I saw how quick them tankers pulled out the other day," Fair said. "Now get back undercover and keep your head down." The corporal and his men disappeared into the woods, and we drove off, crossing the stone bridge and following the road as it curved around the hilltop.

"What'd you mean," Big Mike asked, "when you said you saw how quick the Second Armored artillery withdrew? We heard a lot of firing, but it didn't sound close."

"I took a ride to check things out," Fair said. "I found the spot where the Krauts shelled them. A few tire tracks and a lot of shell holes. But no trace of Second Armored artillery. They gotta be fast on their feet."

Big Mike explained to Kaz what had happened, how the artillery fire had caused the Germans to strike back, only to have their own positions revealed and pounded by the bigger 155mm guns to our rear.

"Remarkable," Kaz said. "And you saw no evidence of casualties or wreckage?"

"Nope," Fair said, glancing back at Kaz. "Just a few odd-looking shell casings. Must be some new kinda round." Fair slowed around a curve, downshifting as he navigated deep ruts in the road as it wound around the forested hillside.

I wasn't all that curious about artillery rounds, especially if they weren't being aimed at me. What did get my attention was a half-track pulling out onto the road about twenty yards ahead and swerving across it, blocking our path.

Not to mention the GI manning a .50 caliber machine gun mounted on top.

Pointed directly at us.

Fair braked, spinning the wheel and bringing the jeep to rest a few feet from the half-track. A couple of GIs appeared behind us, Thompson submachine guns at the ready. The driver's door on the half-track opened and another soldier got out, this one resting his right hand on the butt of his .45 automatic pistol.

They all wore the shoulder patch of the Second Armored Division. Hell on Wheels.

"We seem to have found them," Kaz said.

"Okay, fellas, turn her around," said the half-track driver. He didn't wear any rank insignia—none of them did—but he had an officer's swagger to him. I could swagger too, but it was tough to get one started seated in a jeep with the muzzle of a machine gun staring you down.

"Captain Boyle, from SHAEF," I said. "Who are you?"

"Doesn't really matter, Captain," he said. "This is a restricted area. And too damned close to the front lines for sightseeing. So turn around and head back down the road."

"We're looking for your division headquarters," I said. "How about you tell us where it is, and we'll head out thataway?"

"What do you want at HQ?" he asked while crooking a finger in the direction of the woods. Three more men stepped out, weapons at the ready. "You boys really ought to get out of here before the lead starts flying." Whose lead might fill the air, he failed to specify.

"Hey, Captain, why don't we just head back?" Fair said, eyeing the hardware pointed our way.

"I think I'd like to know this man's rank before we decide anything," I said, swinging my legs out of the jeep. Big Mike vaulted out of the rear seat and landed neatly on his feet, no mean trick for a guy his size. Fair sat still, hands gripping the steering wheel. Kaz sighed, as if this was all a great inconvenience, and languidly unfolded himself from his perch.

The GI on the .50 caliber swiveled it in its mount, keeping all of us covered. He looked nervous. Hell, *I* was nervous and began to wonder if these might be Germans dressed as Yanks. Something was off about them. They sounded tough but looked scared.

"And I think I'd like to know what business you have with headquarters," he said, drumming his fingers on the butt of his holstered pistol. Nervous in the service, as the saying goes.

"It has to do with a murder investigation authorized by First Army," I said. "You know, the brass who are the boss of your general's boss."

"You got orders?" he asked, his jaw raised in defiance. "Written orders?"

"I don't need—"

"Billy, please calm down," Kaz said, sauntering by me with his hands clasped behind his back. "And you, sir, may we have your name at least?"

He smiled, the grin lighting up his face behind his steel-rimmed spectacles. Well, one side of his face that is.

"Burnham," the GI said, relaxing a bit. Kaz had that effect on people. The posh accent and the Continental style worked every time.

"Well, Mr. Burnham, you of the uncertain rank, why don't you tell the young man with the machine gun to stand down? If he pulls that trigger, he'll cut your men down as well. Look, see how he's sweating?" Kaz said, pointing to the gunner as he came to Burnham's side.

It's a natural thing to look where someone's pointing, especially when it's to a Browning .50 caliber M2 machine gun, capable of firing five hundred rounds a minute. So everyone did.

By the time eyes were back on Burnham, Kaz had the barrel of his Webley revolver snug up under Burnham's jawbone. Now, Kaz had done a lot of risky things armed with nothing more than his Webley and strong sense of outrage, but this was the first time one of our own had been on the wrong side of his gun barrel. Burnham looked scared. So was I, for that matter. A little too much pressure on that trigger, and there'd be no going back.

"I'm afraid I must insist," Kaz said. "And tell your men to drop their weapons."

"Sure, sure," Burnham said, his hands raised high, his eyes pleaded with me for mercy. Apparently, he was smart enough to pick me out as the soft touch.

"Do as he says," I told him. Burnham nodded, wincing as his chin dug into the sight at end of the barrel, then told the gunner to step down. Big Mike relieved the others of their rifles, stacking them in the back of the jeep.

"Jeez, Captain," Fair said, not budging from his seat. "You're gonna get us in a world of trouble."

"*Au contraire,*" Kaz said, taking the automatic from Burnham's holster. "You are in a world of trouble when a man aims a heavy machine gun at you. Now that threat has vanished. Don't you feel better?"

"Not a whole lot, no," Fair said.

"Here, a souvenir," Kaz said, handing the Colt automatic to Fair as he stepped back from Burnham, who looked more confused than angry.

"Okay, thanks, I guess," Fair said, pocketing the piece.

"Listen, give us back our weapons, turn around, and head out," Burnham said. "We'll forget all about this, okay?" Sweat dripped down his temples. He had no idea who we were or what we might do. Good. This was a table I liked turned, now that Kaz was less likely to blow his brains out.

"Maybe we ought to take you back with us," I said. "For all we know, you're Kraut infiltrators."

"No, we have to stay here. You don't understand," Burnham said, looking even more worried.

"Make me understand," I said, going face-to-face with Burnham. "Now."

"We wouldn't have shot you," Burnham said, avoiding the question. Still, it was nice to know.

"Listen, pal, all we want to do is talk to someone at Second Armored HQ," I said. "We aren't spies, and we won't say anything about your restricted area. But if you don't cooperate, I will turn this jeep around, get back to a radio, and stay on the horn with First Army until I find out what I want to know. So you might as well save everyone a lot of aggravation and tell me now."

"Sorry, I can't do that," Burnham said. I looked at his men, herded against the half-track by Big Mike. Not a peep from them. These guys were hiding something, and I decided that if we turned around to radio First Army, we might never find out what.

"Back this half-track up," I said to Burnham. "We're going down that road, restricted area or not."

"No," he said, folding his arms across his chest. "We're not helping you."

"Then step aside," Kaz said, nudging Burnham in the ribs with his pistol. I nodded to Big Mike, who stepped into the cab and started the half-track, slamming it into reverse and plowing several yards into the woods.

"We'll leave your weapons a couple of hundred yards down the road," I said. "As long as you don't follow us."

"Our orders are to stay here and man the roadblock," Burnham said. "And that's what we'll do."

"What will we find down the road?" I asked. "Another roadblock?"

"That's for you to find out, Captain. Remind me of your name?"

"Nice try," I said. "Tell me, does everyone go back down that road after you train that .50 caliber on them?"

"No one wants trouble," Burnham said.

"You were no trouble at all," Big Mike said, emerging from the woods. We piled back into the jeep and took off, leaving Burnham fuming. Around the bend, we stopped and left the M1s and Thompsons stacked by the side of the road.

"Here," Fair said, reaching into his jacket for the Colt automatic. "I don't want it. It'll just get that guy in trouble for losing it. And maybe me too."

"You're a fine chap, Sergeant Fair," Kaz said, placing the pistol next to the rifles. "I myself do not respond so kindly to the threat of violence."

"Aw, those guys weren't going to shoot us," Big Mike said. "They were too damn nervous, you could tell."

"Exactly the sort to pull the trigger at the wrong moment," Kaz said as we drove away. "They were strangely ill suited for their role, don't you think?"

"How so?" Big Mike asked.

"They weren't ready to back up their tough talk," I said. "They were used to getting their way, and Kaz shocked the hell out of them."

"Outta me too," Fair said, downshifting as we left the thick woods, the road winding through open country. Tall grasses blanketed the ground, where before the war, cows and sheep grazed. Many were confiscated by the Germans or killed in the battles that flowed through these small Normandy villages. The empty fields looked deceptively peaceful.

"Hey, pull over," Big Mike said, tapping Fair on his shoulder. "Look down there."

The pasture on our left sloped down to a grove of trees. I could make out another field beyond as the contours of the land folded out toward the German lines. But that's all I saw.

"What?" I asked.

"Down in the trees. See them? Tanks," he said.

I did, after scanning the woods below. Hidden in the shadows were three Sherman tanks, facing the open land beyond. I could make out camouflage netting draped between the trees, which is why I had a hard time spotting them.

"That's odd," Fair said, shielding his eyes with his hand. "They got the netting up to their rear, not the front."

"Backwards," Kaz said. "Unless we are on the wrong side of the line."

"Nope," Big Mike said. "Their turrets are facing the other way. Guess they like their privacy."

"Let's pay them a visit," I said. "Maybe they can put us in touch with their HQ."

"If they don't shoot us on sight," Fair said, shaking his head at the stupidity of officers looking for trouble. "You see a way down there?"

The road curved off into the woods in the opposite direction. The field itself was rocky and uneven, not an inviting prospect even in the jeep. Fair got out to study the terrain for a better approach.

"Jesus H. Christ!" he said, pointing to the tanks. "Lookit that."

Two GIs, oblivious to our presence, had gone under the netting and walked to either side of one tank. They lifted the vehicle, moving crablike about ten yards before setting it down.

"I don't believe it," Big Mike said. "It ain't possible."

"Cripes, do we have Superman on our side?" Fair asked.

"What the hell?" I said, blinking to make sure I wasn't seeing things.

"Quite strange," Kaz said, with less astonishment than the rest of us. "Perhaps we should consider the principle of Occam's Razor."

"How does a razor explain a tank so light two guys can pick it up?" Fair asked, rubbing the stubble on his chin.

"It is a philosophic principle," Kaz said. "Simply put, it says that when presented with competing hypotheses, the one with the fewest assumptions is usually right. So we are not looking at real tanks, or supermen, for that matter."

"We're looking at phony tanks," Big Mike said.

"Does that mean we're looking for a phony Second Armored too?" Fair asked, looking to Kaz.

"Excellent deduction, Sergeant," Kaz said. "The evidence to date is easier to explain by their absence than their presence. It is all fakery."

The sound of engines revving rose from the woods ahead of us. Treads clanked and gears ground, harsh and threatening, seemingly nearby but invisible through the cover of the forest.

"That ain't fake," Fair said, climbing back into the jeep and shooting a glance down the hill. "Well, I'll be damned."

The phony tanks were disappearing, vanishing before our eyes, melting into the ground. GIs began to pull down the camouflage netting, revealing more vehicles. Real ones, maybe, but I wasn't about to start trusting my eyes.

There wasn't time to discern the fake from the real. They'd seen us, if the waving arms, shouts, and running about were any indication.

"Let's get out of here," I said, craning my neck to watch the men at the base of the hill. A few pointed at us, but most had returned to pulling down netting and loading vehicles. They didn't look threatening, but I didn't want to take a chance on meeting another half-track with a .50 caliber aimed square at us.

We drove on, the road leading through a grove of trees. The groaning, grinding sounds of heavy iron on the move increased in volume as we craned our necks, looking for the column of tanks that had to be just around the next corner.

Trees crashed into the road about fifty yards ahead, followed by a Sherman tank. A real tank, crushing branches beneath its treads.

"That's one helluva roadblock," Fair said, braking as we came closer. "Pretty damn convincing too."

"I don't think a revolver will get us out of this one," Big Mike said from the back.

I was about to agree when the hatch opened and a tanker popped up from the turret, his Second Armored shoulder patch easy to spot.

"What the hell are you guys doing here?" he shouted. "Get a move on." He waved us through, the tank pivoting to make room. I waved back and we did just that.

"He must figure anyone who got past the checkpoint is okay," I said.

"Yes, but where are the other tanks?" Kaz said, speaking up to be heard over the din of treads and engines. "And why did he want us to leave so precipitously?"

"This doesn't add up," I said. "Phony tanks, one real tank, and it sounds like an entire column is right on top of us."

Behind us, the tank lumbered forward. Ahead, a jeep rounded a bend and drove toward us. A GI manned a mounted .30 caliber machine gun from the rear. In the passenger seat, even with his helmet tilted low and behind his aviator sunglasses, I recognized the man who might be able to explain everything.

Colonel Samuel Harding. My boss. I was surprised to see him, but I shouldn't have been. Not one damn bit.

CHAPTER NINE

"GODDAMMIT, BOYLE, CAN'T you investigate a murder without sticking your nose where it doesn't belong?"

Colonel Harding tilted his helmet back and removed his sunglasses, pointing them at me just like the nuns used to do with their rulers back in parochial school. The only difference was, the colonel wasn't about to rap my knuckles with his fancy sun cheaters.

"Sorry, Colonel, but we're looking for Second Armored HQ," I said.

"Hey, Sam, what are you doing here, anyway?" Big Mike asked. Now, Big Mike was a sergeant, and Sam Harding a colonel, but Big Mike never had a firm grip of military courtesies, on the battlefield or in a London office. Many officers liked him for it and enjoyed his casual banter. After all, who wouldn't want the biggest and most broad-shouldered non-com in the US Army to be their pal? Especially when he was such an excellent scrounger.

"Don't you 'Sam' me, Sergeant," Harding said, clearly steamed. "Not after the stunt you pulled at the checkpoint."

"That was me, Colonel Harding," Kaz said, waving a nonchalant hand. "Purely my idea."

"Why does that not come as a surprise?" Harding said, then shot a thumb in Fair's direction. "Who the hell is this?"

"Sergeant Fair is our guide," I said. "He knows the area, and he was the one detailed to drive us here from First Army. Where you ordered us to investigate the murder of an officer from the Second Armored Division." I thought it might be smart to remind him of that.

"I didn't tell you to enter a restricted area by force," he said, even louder. Well, maybe it wasn't such a great idea.

The tank pulled up behind us, stuck in our little traffic jam. Not a good situation if there was a Kraut spotter with binoculars anywhere nearby.

"Big Mike and you," he said, pointing to Fair, "turn this jeep around and go back the way you came. Do not mention anything you saw out here, or you'll finish out this war and the next one at Leavenworth. Understood?"

"I won't tell anyone what I saw," Fair said. "They'd throw me in the loony bin."

"That's the right attitude," Harding said. "Boyle and Kazimierz, you come with me." He ordered his driver and rear seat gunner to go with Big Mike, with orders to escort them out of the restricted area and to make sure they didn't return.

"Shoot them if they turn back," he said.

"See ya later, Billy," Big Mike said as Fair backed up the jeep. "I hope." This with a grin and an insolent wink.

"Hubba, hubba," the tankman yelled, slapping his hand on the steel turret, wanting to get a move on and oblivious to Harding's rank. Even without visible insignia, he was every inch the senior officer. Tall, ramrod straight, professional army all the way.

"Hold your horses," Harding yelled, taking the driver's seat as Kaz and I climbed aboard. He backed up, slammed it into first, and took off as fast as the rutted road would allow.

"I'd ask what's going on, but I don't even know where to begin," I said.

"I would start with why you are here, Colonel," Kaz said from the back seat. "The answer to that will explain much, I think."

"It's easier to show you," Harding said, taking a side road that turned into a narrow lane, overgrown with trees and weeds. The tank kept going on the main road, but the sounds of many roaring engines still filled the air. Like magic. "This is *top secret* information. I wasn't kidding about Leavenworth, so keep it zipped."

"Does all this relate to Major Jerome, late of the Second Armored Division?" Kaz asked.

"I hope not," Harding said. "Just hang on."

"Colonel, are we headed into the middle of an attack? It sounds like a company of tanks forming up not too far away. The Krauts are bound to notice and call in their heavy stuff," I said. An artillery barrage was not high on my list of enjoyable ways to spend the afternoon.

"That's the general idea," he said. Then it dawned on me why the tanker was in a hurry to get out of Dodge.

Harding steered the jeep into an apple orchard, halting about a hundred yards in.

The sound was deafening. But there were no tanks. Only four half-tracks, spread out under the apple trees, with the biggest loudspeakers I'd ever seen mounted in their rear compartments. Men wearing the shoulder patch of the Second Armored were all around, but I was beginning to think that insignia was just for show, as phony as the distant sounds of armor we'd been hearing just over every hill.

An officer waving his arms signaled to the GIs manning the speakers. Within seconds the clanking of treads slowed and engines cut off, as if twenty Shermans were all getting into position. Commands shouted by the angriest non-coms imaginable reverberated from the speakers, along with fading mechanical noises.

"Astounding," Kaz said as we got out of the jeep. "It sounds perfectly real."

"State of the art," the officer said, introducing himself as Lieutenant Ray Williams. "We're the 3132nd Signal Service Company, and sonic deception is our game." He was grinning like a maniac, which might have come from having his eardrums rattled by all that noise.

"I didn't know you could get that kind of sound out of loud-speakers," I said. "There's no static or distortion at all."

"That's because they're not loudspeakers," Williams said, as the men on the half-tracks disassembled and stowed their gear, covering it with tarpaulins. "Loudspeakers can project noise, all right, but they lack the timbre and range of frequency of actual sound. These acoustical devices project real presence with no background interference. They have a range of fifteen miles, believe it or not."

"Amazing," Kaz said. "You can project other sounds as well?"

"Sure. We use magnetic wire recorders. Stainless steel wire spools with hours and hours of sounds we recorded back in the States. We can mimic engineers building a Bailey bridge, tanks, marching troops, trucks, you name it. Love to tell you more, but you'll have to excuse me; we're closing down the show. Time to exit stage right." Williams waited until the last half-track passed us, then got in, tossing off a jaunty wave.

"Let's go," Harding said. "There's not much time."

"For what?" I asked, as he sped between the rows of trees, dodging fallen limbs and bomb craters.

"To see the finale," Harding said as the jeep crested a hill. Below us, more half-tracks. GIs were busying with some sort of tubes set into the ground, long rows of them dug in between the apple trees.

"These your guests, Colonel Harding?" asked a lieutenant, as several of the half-tracks started up and left by a narrow lane. Exiting stage right, I guessed.

"That's one way to put it, Lieutenant Rosen," Harding said. "I'm giving them a crash course on what goes on here. Can you give a quick briefing?"

"There's not much time, Colonel. I need to radio headquarters and report. I'll have one of the men explain things," Rosen said, waving his hand to one of the GIs. "Hey, Blass, get over here. Give these guys a tour, but make it snappy."

"Okay, Saul," the GI said. "Private Bill Blass. Come on." We didn't bother with salutes or more introductions. Everyone seemed nervous and in a hurry. Which made me nervous too.

"What unit are you with?" I asked, as he led us to the line of tubes, maybe twenty or so. "That sonic company?"

"Nope. We're *camoufleurs*. The 603rd Camouflage Engineers. We hide, we disguise, we confuse. Today's going to be a special show," Blass said. He was a good-looking guy with sandy hair and gleaming white teeth. His clean uniform stood out. Everyone else's was dirty and stained, while his looked like it had just been pressed.

"Are you guys from the USO?" I asked, half seriously.

"No, but a lot of guys are from the theater. We've got plenty of artists, designers, you name it. But today we're more into pyrotechnics. We're pretending to be a 155mm artillery company."

"With these?" Kaz asked, pointing to the steel tubes dug into the earth. "They seem awfully small."

"It's all about the illusion," Blass said. "These are made from 90mm antiaircraft shell casings. We've tried different things, but a half pint of black powder set off in each tube gives a tremendous flash-bang effect. Looks like heavy artillery fire."

"So you already know the Krauts are watching this area. That's what the sonic bit was about. To draw their attention," I said.

"Exactly," Blass said. "We have observers in the hills to both sides, and a Piper Cub in the air. When the Germans fire on this position, they'll spot their flashes, or even calculate their position by the trajectory of the falling shells. Then presto, our big stuff opens up and closes the curtain on the Germans."

"There is one small problem," Kaz said. "We are here. Where the German shells will hit before the end of the play."

"That's why everyone else is pulling out before the curtain comes down. We'll do the same once we get the order to light these up," Blass said, pointing to wires that led from each tube to some sort of electronic gadget hooked up to a battery. "Damned fast, I might add."

Blass grinned, the same sort of crazy smile the sonic guy gave us. I began to get the feeling these deception types lived in a world of their own. A very theatrical world. Blass certainly looked like he was enjoying himself, probably more than was normal for a guy about to call down tons of Krupp steel on his head.

"Let's go!" Rosen shouted and ran to the battery setup where he and Blass fiddled with copper wires. "I'd suggest stepping back, gentlemen."

We did. All the way back to the jeep.

The explosions went off one after the other, earsplittingly loud and accompanied by intensely white flashes. Smoke curled into the sky as Rosen and Blass whooped and hollered.

"Hell, I wasn't sure it was going to work," Rosen said, as he ran back to the remaining half-track. "Get a move on!"

We exited. Stage left. Harding put his boot down hard on the pedal, not giving a damn about dust clouds. We raced through the trees, dodging thick roots and making for the dirt track to the main road as branches snapped against the sides of the jeep. The half-track sped ahead of us, Blass and two other GIs in the rear compartment, hanging on and staring up at the sky as patches of blue and bright sunlight blazed through the green canopy. Waiting for the Krauts to take the bait.

They didn't have to wait long. Screeching artillery shells tore through the sky, landing off to our right, slamming into the rows of apple trees, shattering trunks and scorching the landscape. The Germans had overshot the mark. We drove on, waiting for them to find their range. Another round of incoming mail ripped the sky and bracketed the narrow lane with explosions. Harding steered through a rain of debris as dirt, stones, and shattered branches peppered the air. He jerked the wheel and a tire caught an exposed root, the jolting swerve nearly sending me flying.

"Colonel!" Kaz shouted, grabbing Harding by the shoulder from his perch in the back seat. Harding kept one hand on the wheel as the other fell limp in his lap. He looked faintly surprised at the sight of a thick wood splinter about six inches long sticking out of his upper arm, blood soaking his jacket.

"Stop," I said, grabbing the steering wheel. Harding braked and clutched his wounded arm. I got out to take the driver's seat as Kaz helped Harding slide over.

"I'm okay, I'm okay," he said, sounding like he was working hard to convince himself. Shrieks of falling shells descended from the sky, but this time the explosions were to our rear. The Kraut artillery spotters had found their range and were busy obliterating a good part of the Norman apple harvest.

I gunned the jeep, still not trusting that a stray round or two wouldn't come our way. I caught up to the half-track as we made it to the main road. Blass was standing in the back, pointing to the sky. Far above us, an L-4 Grasshopper—the military's name for the Piper Cub light aircraft—droned slowly by.

"Won't be long now," Blass yelled from the half-track.

He was right. We heard the thunderous rumble of artillery fire in the distance, sounding as sweet as it always did when you knew it was headed for people intent upon killing you and your pals. The heavy shells arcing overhead sounded like freight trains coursing through the heavens.

"We should find a medic to get you treated, Colonel," I said, raising my voice to be heard over the barrage.

"No, wait a minute," Harding said, wincing as the pain began to hit him. "This is too good to miss."

He had a point. In the distance, we could hear the shells detonate as they struck, then the firing of our heavy stuff again, and the screaming passage of outgoing mail. When the firing finally stopped, the woods went silent as a cathedral, nothing but the distant *crumps* of explosives obliterating metal and flesh in some faraway field.

Then, total silence. Except for a bird, chirping away high up in an apple tree. Life went on. For some.

We followed the half-track for a mile or so, turning off into an apple orchard draped with so much camouflage netting it looked like the circus had come to town and put up the big top. Which was pretty close, considering what these guys were up to.

"Medic!" Blass shouted from his perch on the half-track as we pulled up to a row of tents. GIs swarmed our vehicles, most of them celebrating the big con they'd just pulled, passing around bottles of wine.

Two medics helped Harding out of the jeep, but he shook them off. Tough guy.

"Blass, give these two the lowdown while I get patched up. And don't let them leave," Harding said.

"Get some chow, Bill," Lieutenant Rosen said as he joined Harding, whistling at the chunk of wood in his arm. "Make sure our friends here understand how important this work is."

"Will do, Saul," Blass said, as Rosen and Harding followed the medics to a tent with a red cross on top. Expertly camouflaged, since that was the name of the game around here.

"You all wear the Second Armored shoulder patch," Kaz said, as we followed Blass through the maze of tents and vehicles.

"All part of the show," he said. "We can be any unit on demand. All we need is a little time to create the proper illusion."

"To fool the Germans into thinking they are facing a certain division, when it is miles away," Kaz said, as we stepped over cables and wires leading to a large tent with the flaps rolled up. Inside, operators sat in front of dozens of radios and electronics.

"Yes, but it's more than that. We draw fire, as you saw today. We create the illusion of a threat, which the enemy then feels obliged to respond to," Blass said. "We've been practicing for weeks, and today was the big test. It worked."

"So if you do your job right, the Krauts think you're an entire division," I said. "Kind of dangerous if they decide to mount a direct attack, instead of only firing artillery."

"You make it sound downright suicidal," Blass said. "I assure you, no one here has a death wish."

Famous last words.

"What unit are you really?" Kaz asked.

"The 23rd Headquarters Special Troops," Blass said. "A meaningless enough name. Hides a multitude of sins. These guys are our Signals Company. They can mimic any unit's radio net, sending out enough spoof messages to impersonate a division. They set the stage for the deception, fooling the Germans into thinking there's a big radio operation. By the time the sonic company gets to work, the enemy is primed to hear the performance we've planned for them."

"Then you come in with the phony tanks and pyrotechnics," I said.

"Right. We camouflage them as if they're the real thing, but leave just enough showing so the Germans can spot them now and again. We use half-tracks, bulldozers, and the occasional real tank to make tread marks all over the place. We provide the illusion of what the Germans expect to see and hear."

"We saw a couple of guys lift a tank up like it was cardboard," I said.

"Close," Blass said. "We use generators to pump up a skeleton of inflatable tubes and cover it with a skin of neoprene, painted with the markings of an M4 Sherman."

"That's what we saw collapsing, then, before we met up with you," I said.

"Right. We were waiting for those guys to pull out before we set off the fireworks."

"But why is everyone wearing the Second Armored shoulder patch this far beyond the lines?" Kaz asked.

"That's thanks to the combat engineers," Blass said, leading us into a mess tent. We grabbed hot coffee and chow, pulling up empty crates under the shade of the canvas. "The 406th is a combat engineer company assigned for perimeter guard duty, construction, that sort of thing. They weren't trained in deception, but they got into the spirit right away. They came up with the idea of everyone wearing the false patches, and painting unit identification on all the vehicles."

"Smart," Kaz said, blowing on his coffee. "There are reports of the Germans leaving agents behind the lines. Pro-fascist French, for the most part. Greed plays a role as well."

"That's what we figured," Blass said. "Even if there aren't actual spies, gossip travels fast. Our guys from the 406th make a point of stopping in every village café and bragging about how the Second Armored is going all the way to Berlin, that sort of thing."

"Quite the unique outfit," I said.

"Nothing like it in the history of warfare," Blass said. "It's like Broadway invades Europe. We have stagehands and spear carriers from the combat engineers. The Signals Company provides dialog, scripts, and impressions. We *camoufleurs* provide the props and illusions. Inflatable tanks and every other kind of vehicle. The sonic engineers are the orchestra. They play the score we want the Germans to buy. And everyone contributes to atmosphere."

"What do you mean by that?" Kaz asked.

"All the little things that make a con successful. Like everyone wearing the shoulder patches. Trucks driving around in looping convoys through a village so it looks like thousands of GIs are in the area. Impersonating senior officers in cafés and spouting off about a big push coming up, that sort of thing."

"So who's the star?" I asked.

"That would be Captain Fox," Blass said without hesitation. "Fred Fox. He keeps saying we're trying to be too military and not show business enough. He's right. After all, we're a bunch of artists, designers, magicians, sound engineers, and con men. We're here to put on a show. But it's a show that will save lives, I'm sure of it."

"Wait a minute," I said. "You called the Signals Company impressionists, right?" Blass nodded. "And everyone wears the Second Armored shoulder patch?"

"Right. It's easier just to have everyone in on the scam."

"Does the name Major David Jerome mean anything to you?" Kaz asked, picking up on where I was going.

"No. But Captain Fox has authorized us to impersonate officers whenever we need to. A lot of guys carry different rank insignia with them in case they have to chase off an officer. So anyone could have used that name."

"I think Colonel Harding would have told us if the victim was from this unit," Kaz said. "Especially after he came upon us here."

"Victim? What victim?" Blass said. I filled him in on the death we were investigating and explained that was what led us on this wild goose chase for the Second Armored.

"An impressionist must know something about who he is imitating, does he not?" Kaz asked.

"Right. So Jerome was a Signals officer from the real Second Armored. I saw a bunch of Second Armored guys hanging around the morning his body was found. That was at a 30th Division headquarters in Bricqueville," I said, eyeing Blass. "And as we know, the Second Armored is nowhere near that part of the front."

"Hey, don't look at me," Blass said. "I'm a fashion designer, not a murderer."

CHAPTER TEN

"YOU! AND YOU!" I pointed at radiomen as I stalked the rows of GIs under the tent, hunched over their Morse keypads or wearing headphones. "You too!"

"What the hell is going on here?" a second lieutenant barked as he came running toward me. "Step outside, Captain. You can't interrupt our work like that."

"I'm investigating a murder, Lieutenant. I'll interrupt whatever I want." I was plenty steamed. These guys might be great at fooling the Krauts, but I was damned if I'd let them fool me. Some of these signalmen were outside the house where Jerome was killed. They must have been there to meet him and get the inside dope on how Second Armored ran their radio net. Code names, frequencies, everything they'd need to mimic that unit could have been provided by a Major Jerome from Second Armored Signals.

Trouble was, I couldn't think of a reason why any of these jokers would slit his throat.

"What's the problem here?" a lanky, bespectacled captain asked, as he got out of the jeep that had just braked to a halt by the Signals tent.

"Fred," Blass said, introducing us to Captain Fox, master of ceremonies, "these fellows think we killed someone."

"I should hope so. That's what we're here for. Al, take this stuff to the mess tent, willya?" This last bit was directed to Fox's passenger, still seated in the jeep. The fact that Al wore a bird colonel's silver eagle on his collar didn't seem to mean very much. He got right to work hefting cases of wine out of the back seat.

"I'm investigating a murder, Captain Fox," I said, stepping aside as Al strode by with a load of vino. "It seems some of your boys may be witnesses, at the very least."

"This is a murderous business we're in," Fox said, and then told the second looey to get his men back to work.

"I thought you were in show business," I said, once I got his attention again. He looked ready to be anywhere but here, answering my questions.

"Clearly, you've never worked with a producer," Fox said. "Come on, let's straighten this out." He dismissed Blass and led us to his tent. He sat on the edge of a cot and motioned for me and Kaz to sit on two rickety wooden chairs around a small table. It was strewn with maps and schematics for dummy vehicles, along with a sewing kit and a box of shoulder patches from a whole slew of units. Tools of the deception trade.

"Captain, your unit is most impressive," Kaz began, smoothing the way with his usual diplomacy. "Very efficient and quite original."

"Thank you, Lieutenant Kazimierz," Fox said. "I can see you fellows have a good routine. One of you rants and raves while the other lays on the charm. And I mean that as a compliment, being in the business of putting on an act myself."

"It looks like you've pulled one over on the Krauts today," I said.

"Yeah, but I was referring to before the war. I was trying to catch a break in Hollywood when the Japs attacked Pearl Harbor. Now here I am, playing a classified role no one will ever see. An actor's worst nightmare—after getting no work at all, that is."

"Since you see through our act, perhaps we should simply be honest with one another," Kaz said. "We have a duty to find a killer. An odd thing during wartime, I admit. I find it quite disagreeable that Major Jerome was murdered. Such a waste, don't you agree?"

"I don't know that I do," Fox said. "Death is death. Your Major Jerome can never tell us what he thinks, so who am I to judge?" His voice faded to a whisper and his gaze dropped to the ground.

Something was bothering him, and he wasn't entirely comfortable with his own words.

"You've heard about what happened?" I asked.

"A little. Why? Do you think our signalmen were involved?"

"Captain Fox, what have you heard?" Kaz asked. "And who told you? Being in a restricted area must limit your contact with other units."

"Oh, it's only scuttlebutt," Fox said. "GIs are always spreading rumors."

"The only people who could have told you anything are the ones I saw wearing Second Armored shoulder patches outside the house where Jerome was killed," I said. "And there are several of them in your Signals unit. Maybe one of them is our killer. Maybe we need to bring in a crew of First Army MPs and interrogate the whole bunch."

"Or, Captain Fox, you could tell us the truth right now," Kaz said, leaning forward, his voice almost a whisper. I realized we'd gone into our act, although it wasn't really an act. It was just the way we did things, and it was usually effective.

"Jerome was already dead," Fox said. "There wasn't anything anyone could do."

"Who?" I asked. "Were you there?"

"No. And there's no need to question my men. Our work is too important here. I'll tell you exactly what they told me," he said.

"I can't promise anything," I said. "But I'll listen."

"Okay," Fox said, rising from the cot and pacing the length of the tent. "Second Armored was originally holding this part of the line. They were moved out and we were brought in to deceive the Germans into thinking they were still in place."

"We saw the dummy tanks and pyrotechnics today, along with the sonic unit in action," I said. "Private Blass laid things out for us."

"Okay, so you know the Signals Company works at sending messages out that represent normal radio traffic for whatever unit we're imitating. If you've ever seen an impressionist, you know they achieve the illusion by exaggerating known traits."

"Yeah, I saw a guy in a USO show once," I said. "He did Sinatra, Cagney, guys like that."

"An impressionist has to be a good observer," Fox said. "You study the character you're imitating until you know him inside out. We have to do the same. That's why Major Jerome was in Bricqueville. He was meeting with some of our signalmen in the morning to deliver this."

Fox knelt and took a thin leather briefcase from under his cot. He began to hand it to me, then sat down instead, clutching it in his lap.

"What's in it?" I asked.

"Frequencies, code words, daily radio logs, all the details necessary to impersonate the radio net of Second Armored. Without this, our little charade would be a lot less convincing."

"The Germans are expert at listening in to radio traffic," Kaz said. "Even if much is encoded, they can draw conclusions from the number of messages sent, or piece together information from communications sent in the clear."

"Everything we do is based on giving the Germans a complete picture of what we want them to believe. Visual, sonic, and through the airwaves. If any one element doesn't hold up under scrutiny, everything falls apart. We needed a seamless transition from the real unit to our deception," Fox said.

"Okay," I said. "I get why the briefcase is important. But tell me about Jerome."

"Bricqueville was chosen as the rendezvous because it was in another division's area, but close by. That way no one would pay us much mind. The battalion HQ staff was called away to Division so we'd have the place to ourselves."

"That was part of the ruse?" Kaz asked.

"It was. Our guys were to meet Jerome at 0600. I'd spoken to him by telephone the day before. He planned to head out that evening. He said he didn't like driving in the blackout and wanted to get there before dark."

"No one else came with him? He didn't have a driver?" I asked.

"Nope. That way only he'd know about the deception. Need to know, as they say."

"Okay, so what happened?"

"I sent a sergeant and a few other of our best signalmen. They got there early, about 0530. The sergeant saw a light on inside the house, so he went in. He told me he found Jerome. Stone cold dead."

"He didn't alert anyone?" Kaz asked. "Most peculiar, don't you think?"

"You have to look at it from our viewpoint. This was all top secret. The whole point was for no one to know about the meeting. So he took the briefcase and got out of there," Fox said, running his hand over the worn leather. "It had most of what we needed. Enough to get the job done, anyway. It would have been better if we could have talked with Major Jerome, but we worked it the best we could."

"Yeah, I think the major would have liked that too," I said. "Tell me why your men stuck around. They could have hightailed it out of there."

"They did leave, but my sergeant decided to go back. He figured the brass who knew about the meeting might finger him as a suspect if he took off. They returned an hour later, acting like they were just passing through."

"He was right to be concerned," Kaz said. "Did you speak with these men after they returned?"

"Sure," Fox said. "They were ordered to report to me immediately. They all told the same story, and I believed them. I also said they'd made the right choice. Then I ordered them to forget about it."

"Are you certain you saw them immediately? As soon as they arrived?" Kaz asked.

"That's what *immediately* means," Fox said. "You might not see a lot of spit and polish in this outfit, but my men follow their orders."

"Captain," I said, "Kaz isn't criticizing your guys. He's establishing the fact that no one showed up covered in blood. Is that correct?"

"Oh," Fox said, finally getting it. "Yes, that's right. I saw the half-track pull in and went to meet the men. No blood to be seen. So they're in the clear?"

"As far as murder goes, they are," I said. "There was a lot of blood. Whoever killed Jerome couldn't have gotten away without some of it on their clothes or boots. As for leaving the scene of the crime, that's pretty serious."

"It might have been a German raid on a headquarters unit," Kaz said. "Other lives may have been in danger."

"My sergeant thought about that. A Kraut wouldn't have left a major's briefcase behind, would he?" Fox patted the briefcase in his lap.

"Point taken," I said. As much as I didn't want to admit it, I could see this from his viewpoint. If word got out about what this unit was up to, the Germans would find out damn quick. A captured GI or a pro-fascist Frenchmen crossing the lines—it didn't really matter how the enemy found out. One way or the other, news travels fast, and this news was hot stuff.

And I had to hand it to Fox's non-com. He thought on his feet and did what he thought best for the war effort. Hard to fault a guy for doing his job. His was deception, mine was investigation, and all I knew at that moment was he'd done his work a damn sight better than I'd done mine.

"Does that answer all your questions?" Fox asked.

"Allow me to search the briefcase," Kaz said, holding out his hand. Fox gave it to him, somewhat reluctantly.

"Anything else your sergeant mentioned to you?" I asked, as Kaz searched the case and thumbed through the papers. "Did he see anyone else coming or going?"

"Well, the girl."

"What girl?" I asked, although I knew the answer. Yvonne.

"There was a girl in the house, standing at the top of the stairs. She was the only person he saw. Alive, that is. Her dress was covered in blood, but he said she didn't look upset at all. Just stood there and stared at him. He said it was spooky."

"Anything else?"

"Nothing. Except he did say she was beautiful. Funny, how a girl drenched in blood can look beautiful to a guy. Maybe he's been out here too long, huh?"

"Yeah, real funny. Yvonne's a barrel of laughs," I said. Except the laughs were all inside her head.

"There is nothing unusual amongst these papers," Kaz said, handing the briefcase back to Fox. "It would be a treasure trove for the

Germans, so I concur that it would be highly unlikely a German would go to the trouble of killing Jerome and leave this behind."

"Okay," I said. "One last thing I'm curious about, Captain. What's the story with the colonel in your jeep, carrying off those cases of wine?"

"He's actually a private," Fox said. "Been in a few Broadway shows and can play a colonel or a general perfectly. We visited a tavern over in Saint-Jean. Guy who owns the joint was a Pétainist who informed on his neighbors to the Vichy fascist militia." General Pétain was a French hero from the last war who ran what was left of the French government these days. Which meant doing whatever the Nazis wanted him to do. He still had a lot of followers among the older generation, but for most French people his name had become a curse.

"I'm surprised he's still in one piece. We saw some pretty rough justice today," I said.

"The Resistance hasn't gotten around to him yet," Fox said. "So until they pounce, we're using him as best we can. We stormed into his place today and told him the American Second Armored Division was liberating six cases of wine. He was fuming. I'm hoping he'll cross the lines and tell the Germans all about us just out of spite. And if he doesn't, we still have his wine."

"Quite clever," Kaz said. "If the Resistance justice we saw meted out today is any indication, stolen wine will be the least of his worries."

"Thanks, Captain," I said as we rose to leave. "We'll be in touch if we have other questions for you."

"Don't wait too long," Fox said with a grin. "This road show is strictly a limited engagement. We're opening in Paris soon, or so the scuttlebutt goes."

I didn't know what to say. Fox was a smart guy, and he was using his brains to get an important job done. He'd pulled off a successful con, and he was rightly basking in the afterglow. There was only one problem. He was having too much fun. He was playing a game, a damned important and tricky game, but a game nevertheless. He was making up all the rules and pulling one over on Fritz. But death, suffering, and chaos didn't care how smart you were, or careful, or fast, or how deep you dug in. War will rip you apart, bury you in a stinking shell hole, sever a vein so you can watch yourself bleed to death, and not give a damn.

Fox didn't understand that yet. He couldn't. He was playing cat and mouse with the Krauts, not slugging it out every day and every night at point-blank range and coming to doubt the odds of his own survival. There was no way to tell him, and who was I to ruin his sleep anyway?

So we shook hands and said farewell to Fox, leaving him to his wishful thinking about Paris, saying nothing about how many hedge-rows there were between us and the *Folies Bergère*.

CHAPTER ELEVEN

WE FOUND HARDING seated outside Lieutenant Rosen's tent, his bandaged arm in a sling. His other arm was busy hoisting a bottle of liquor to down a good slug. As soon as he saw us, he took another.

"You okay, Colonel?" I asked.

"Sulfa, stitches, and scotch. What more do I need? Other than answers from you two. Did you find out anything useful?" Harding winced as he shifted his arm.

I glanced at Rosen. "Do you mind leaving us alone, Lieutenant?" I asked.

"Not at all. Just keeping the colonel company until you showed up," he said. "I'll go check on Blass. He's scrounging you a jeep." I waited until Rosen was out of earshot and sat on the empty ammo crate he'd vacated. Kaz sat on another. The sun was low in the sky, a light breeze blowing gently against green leaves. A nice afternoon for a drink, but Harding wasn't passing the bottle around.

"We talked to Captain Fox. He admitted his radiomen went to Bricqueville to get the lowdown from Jerome on their frequencies and call signs. A non-com found the body just before dawn. They grabbed the briefcase Jerome had brought and got out quick."

"These people are very security conscious, with good reason," Harding said, suddenly finding his manners and passing the bottle to Kaz, who declined and gave it to me. I inclined it.

"It made sense to me," I said. "Jerome was dead, and no one else was around except for Yvonne."

"Who's Yvonne?" Harding asked, taking the bottle and capping it.

"A girl who lives with Madame Janvier, the lady who owns the place where the battalion HQ is set up. A *pressoir*, where they make calvados," I said.

"Is this Yvonne a suspect?" Harding asked.

"I don't think so," I said. "My guess is she went to help Jerome after he was slashed and got blood on her dress."

"You didn't ask her?"

"She lives in her own world, Colonel. No one knows where she came from. She never speaks and looks straight through you. Real spooky. Madame Janvier takes care of Yvonne as best she can."

"It sounds like you should be digging into her background," Harding said.

"Yes, sir," I said. I wanted to say we would have been if he'd filled us in on the phony armored division routine. But I learned a while ago that a nice, crisp *yessir* now and then kept most senior brass happy. And off my back. "But we should ask around at the real Second Armored about Jerome, just to be thorough."

"He could have angered someone there who followed him to Bricqueville," Kaz said.

"Maybe," Harding offered with a grunt. "But it seems to me it would have been easier to kill him on the road or even before he left. But go ahead. You'll find them just north of Sainteny, a small town about twenty miles west. I know the division G2. As head of intelligence, he can answer your questions or get you to someone who will."

Harding gave us his name. We decided to send Big Mike on that mission tomorrow while Kaz and I dug into Yvonne's background. Harding was staying with the deception crew tonight, then reporting back to First Army later in the day. Apparently General Omar Bradley, commander of all US forces in Normandy, liked the 23rd Special Headquarters Troops and wanted a personal briefing on their operations.

Blass pulled up in a jeep with 30th Infantry Division markings.

"Careful, the paint's still wet," he said. "I figured you wouldn't want to drive around in a Second Armored jeep. Some MP might think you swiped it."

"Thanks," I said. "Must be hard to keep track of who you're supposed to be some days."

"Not at all," Blass said, getting out of the jeep. "The trick is to remind yourself what role you're playing every morning. And then vanish when the show's over. That's why they call us the Ghost Army." He grinned, flashing those pearly whites of his. Like Fox—maybe even more so because he was a private and had fewer responsibilities—Blass was having the time of his life.

"Are you really a fashion designer?" Kaz asked as he climbed aboard. "You seem quite young to have achieved that status prior to the war."

"Well, I will be, that I can promise you," Blass said. "I've sold some sketches already. I send them off to design houses, and they pay me two bucks apiece if they buy." He pulled a worn notebook from his pocket and showed us. It was filled with drawings of women's fashions, everything from fancy gowns to sleeveless dresses, done in quick, clean lines that left little doubt as to Blass's talent.

"Remarkable," Kaz said. "Especially since you have to work under difficult conditions."

"That's nothing special," Blass said. "Just about everybody sketches in their free time. If you hung around much longer, you'd have a dozen portraits done. Come back and I'll set it up."

"You're too hard to find," I said. He grinned, taking that as a grand compliment.

ON THE RIDE back to *Pressoir* Janvier in Bricqueville, we managed to avoid roadblocks, artillery barrages, and angry colonels. We pulled in as the summer sun was setting, hungry and dusty, and headed to the outside pump to wash away the grit from the road. I filled my helmet with water and dumped it over my head, shivering in the warm air as the cold water hit me. Kaz was a bit more fastidious, cupping his hands and splashing water on his face, then brushing dust from his wool uniform. Such a dandy.

"Baron," Madame Janvier called from her kitchen door. She waved to him, her hand vaguely moving in my direction.

"*Bonsoir*, Madame Janvier," Kaz said, smiling graciously and executing a slight bow. Madame Janvier blushed at the attention.

"Your sergeant was looking for you," she said. "Large Mike, I think you called him."

"Big Mike," I said. "Do you know where he is?"

"He went off to arrange for some supplies, so I could cook for all of you. Come into the kitchen and wait. I just brought up *cidre* from the cellar."

That was all the invitation I needed. We sat at the wooden table while Madame Janvier poured glasses of cider from a jug. It was chilled, crisp, and packed a punch.

"Be careful, *capitaine*, this is not your American sweet cider," Madame Janvier said with a smile.

"We call it hard cider back home, ma'am. And after what we saw today, I prefer this to the kid stuff," I said, taking another gulp.

"Why, what happened?" she asked, pouring herself a glass and sitting next to Kaz.

"In town, we saw several girls have their heads shaved, and otherwise shamed by their neighbors," Kaz said. "And Legrand shot two men. *Profiteurs de guerre*, he called them."

"Legrand is a coward," Madame Janvier said, his name sounding like a curse spat from her mouth. "Old Gautier was forced to sell his pigs to the *Boche*, and for that, Legrand declared him a traitor. I had to sell my calvados, and others were forced to sell their produce, and at prices that hardly left enough to feed ourselves."

"Then why kill Gautier?" I asked.

"Because his pig farm is next to Legrand's property, and Gautier has no family left to inherit his lands. Legrand will get it for far less than it is worth, believe me," she said.

"How will he manage that?" Kaz asked as he finished off his cider.

"The *maire* and local *magistrat* are both pro-Vichy. They urged people to obey Marshal Pétain and not resist the Nazis. Now they live in fear that Legrand will denounce them, so this is a small favor to grant in exchange for their lives." Madame Janvier gave one of those Gallic shrugs that said so much. *What do you expect? This is the way of the world.*

"The gentleman said as much before he was killed," Kaz said. "Why did no one protest?"

"Gautier's son went off to fight with the LVF," Madame Janvier said. "This did not make him popular with the townspeople, even those who favored Pétain. It was one thing to obey Marshal Pétain, who was at least a Frenchman and a war hero. It was quite another to go off and fight alongside the Nazis."

"LVF?" I asked.

"*Légion des Volontaires Français contre le Bolchévisme,*" Kaz said. "French volunteers to fight on the Russian Front. Most of them are dead by now."

"Including Gautier's son and only heir," Madame Janvier said, rising to refill our glasses. "Which granted him a degree of sympathy. He was a rightist, but not a *collabo*, no more than any of us forced to do business with the Germans. If not for Legrand, no one would have raised a hand against him. It is only because of that man's greed that Gautier died."

"One can hope justice will catch up with Legrand," Kaz said, with a glance in my direction. We'd had to navigate the path of elusive justice in the midst of war before. "One way or the other."

"I doubt it," Madame Janvier said, shaking her head wearily. "Legrand fought the Germans, that much is true. But he only went into action after the invasion, when chances of survival improved. He played his cards well, *non?* Now no one can speak out against him in the village, since they are all complicit, those who cheered him on and even those who stood by silently. I don't know how we will live with ourselves when the war is over. I truly do not."

"What about the girls getting their heads shaved? One was pregnant," I said. "I can't see the justice in that."

"I hear such things go on everywhere," Madame Janvier said. "Men who did nothing during the Occupation now wield their shears like swords. Such bravery. Hah!" She finished her drink and slammed the glass on the table. "Last week I saw a girl on the road, her head covered in a bloodstained scarf and her *bébé* in her arms. Thrown out by her family, and no one in her village would help her. I gave her a ride to Saint-Jean, where I made a delivery. She cried the whole way."

"People must be held accountable," Kaz said. "Perhaps those girls denounced *résistants* to the Germans."

"I am sure that has happened. But if all the girls being paraded through the streets and given the *coiffure* '44 had done so, the *Maquis* would have been destroyed long ago. No, this is the work of men who were shamed by the defeat in 1940 and did nothing but live meekly and quietly since then. There will be some like Gautier who are killed for their possessions, but mark my words, once Paris is liberated, there will be a great forgetting. All those men who grew rich running factories and businesses that profited from the war, they are the real *profiteurs*. Do you think they will be marched at gunpoint through the streets, beaten, put up against a wall, and shot? Don't be foolish."

"I am sorry, Madame," Kaz said. "You are of course correct. The weakest among us are often the ones punished for the least of crimes, while the powerful evade responsibility for their corruption."

"Yes, well, the Occupation made everything worse. The corrupt became even more corrupt. Ah, I am so tired of talking about *collaborateurs* and *résistants*," said Madame Janvier, leaning back in her chair and releasing a great sigh. "We all did what we felt we had to do, one way or the other. Such things were decided long ago, before we ever heard the *Boche* in their jackboots marching in our streets."

"What was life like for you?" I asked. The lady was right. By the time it came to make a decision about whether to fight the Nazis, work with them, or stick your head in the sand, a person's character was already pretty well set. We become who we already are.

"After my husband died, all I wanted was for the *pressoir* to stay in business and keep my employees working. The only thing that saved us from ruin was that the *Wehrmacht* bought our calvados for their troops in Normandy. At a ridiculous price that left us little or no profit. But it saved our copper still and presses. Otherwise, they would have carted off the metal to Germany and we would have nothing at all."

"The Germans wanted to keep you in business to ensure a cheap supply?" I said.

She nodded. "And to provide alcohol for the French, I was told. The Nazis were smart enough to know their troops would want strong drink and that our people would need it."

"It must have been hard," Kaz said.

"Not as difficult as some," she said.

"Like Yvonne?" I asked. We needed to look at the young lady more closely, and this was as good a time as any to find out more about her.

"Billy, Kaz!" Big Mike's voice boomed from the doorway. "I thought Sam might have put you two in the stockade. Glad you made it back." Fair followed him into the kitchen, a box of supplies in his arms. Canned vegetables, evaporated milk, cheese, flour, jam, canned meat, and cigarettes. He set them down on the kitchen counter, then backed away from Madame Janvier, who gave him a glare that reminded me of my drill sergeant back in basic. Big Mike had two large cans of coffee and placed them next to the other food, which brightened her outlook considerably.

"Such riches!" Madame Janvier exclaimed, clapping her hands together. "What can I cook for you?" Her eyes gleamed as she asked Big Mike what was probably his favorite question.

"I'm fine, ma'am," he said. "I ate at the mess tent. But I need to speak to these two for a while. Could Sergeant Fair stay? If you don't mind, that is?" Big Mike gave her a grin, one hand resting on a can of coffee, a gentle reminder of the riches he was willing to bring her way.

"Certainly," she said, with a quick nod. "But only in this kitchen. Nowhere else."

"We haven't eaten yet," I said. I wanted to hear more about Yvonne, and I was interested in how Madame Janvier had fared during the Occupation. But my empty stomach was beginning to protest, and I stood up to leave. "Let's grab something at the mess tent, and we'll catch up there."

"Nonsense," Madame Janvier said. "I will prepare omelets for you." She went to work at the stove, cracking eggs and setting out bread and cheeses. And so we sat, obedient soldiers, letting the talk of betrayals, collaboration, resistance, and shame fade away as the sweet aroma of butter in the skillet wafted through the kitchen.

Her omelet was delicious. I felt a momentary pang of guilt thinking about the poor dogfaces breaking open a can of ham and eggs from their K-Rations right now, huddled in a trench and listening for Kraut patrols to come their way. But denying myself wouldn't help them, and besides, cozying up to Madame Janvier was all part of this investigation, so I complimented her on her cooking and sat back, satisfied.

She smiled, set out a bottle of calvados and four small glasses, then left us alone.

"Gee, she ain't never been so nice to me," Fair said, staring at the glass before him.

"Must be you're associating with a better class of people these days," Big Mike said, pouring calvados all around. "Drink up."

Fair downed his in one gulp, grimaced, and smacked his lips. I caught a strange look passing between him and Big Mike. Something was up.

"Do you have something to tell us, Sergeant Fair?" Kaz asked. He'd seen it too.

"Yeah. I guess so," Fair said, inching his glass toward Big Mike. Whatever he had to say, it was going to take Dutch courage to get it out.

"I went looking for Fair to see if he'd cleaned up yet. Colonel Brewster had come around looking for him. I found him still in his dirty ODs and fingering this." Big Mike tossed a lace handkerchief onto the table. Fair grabbed it and buried it between his palms. It was a match to the one I'd seen Yvonne holding in her cut hand. Fair's uniform was filthy, his hair greasy, and his unshaven face needed a scrubbing. But his hands were as clean as a baby's. "We had a serious discussion, and now he's going to tell you all about it. Aren't you, Fair?"

"Okay, okay," Fair said, clutching the fabric to his chest, his head bowed, as if he were protecting it with his body. "It wasn't like I said, the night I drove to First Army."

"You told us you left here around eight and got there after midnight," I said. "Said you got held up by a convoy on the way."

"Well, I did leave at eight, after Colonel Brewster gave me the reports. They were getting ready to drive up to Division for that meeting," Fair said, drumming his fingers on the table. Big Mike poured him another drink and nodded encouragement. "I drove up the road and pulled over. I waited for them to leave and came back."

"To see Yvonne?" I asked.

"Yeah. I had to. I love her. I know she feels the same, I really do," Fair said.

"She told you that?" I asked, keeping my voice soft. Fair was a combat-hardened veteran. I'd seen him kill. But right now, he looked like a kid about to burst into tears.

"Not out loud, no," he said. "You know she can't speak, right? But she likes it when I visit her, no matter what Madame Janvier says. She seems calmer. I think she smiles sometimes too."

"She's very beautiful," I said. "I can see why you want to be with her. But why didn't you tell us this before? Why lie?"

"Because I was here when that officer was killed," Fair said, leaning forward, his hands flat on the table.

"What did you see?" Kaz asked.

"Nothing. I was up in Yvonne's room. We were looking out the window. The stars were real clear that night. I heard a noise downstairs. I was worried it was Lieutenant Friedman, since he hangs around Yvonne every chance he gets, and he'd rat me out to Madame Janvier in no time."

"What else did you hear?" I asked.

"There were people talking, but it was kinda garbled. Remember I told you my ears was ringing pretty bad from that grenade? I couldn't make out what the voices were saying, but they stayed downstairs, so I didn't worry. Yvonne got upset, though. Real upset."

"She reacted to the voices?" I asked. "Wasn't that unusual?"

"Yeah," Fair said. "She's always calm with me, you know? But she cried out and her face got all twisted up. She tried to go downstairs, but I shut the door and didn't let her out."

"What happened next?" Kaz asked.

"I couldn't make out the words at all, and at first it sounded like a normal conversation. After a few minutes, the voices sounded louder and angry."

"Then what?" I said.

"I had to let Yvonne go," Fair said, his voice low, heavy with the truth he was finally admitting. "She kept hitting me trying to get to the door. She was going crazy, and I was afraid she'd hurt herself."

"So you let her out," Kaz said. "And remained in her room while she went downstairs."

"Yeah, I did. I hated to let her go alone, but I couldn't chance anyone seeing me. I don't know how long she was gone. Five minutes? Maybe more. Then she came back up, all calm and collected. She went to her chair and sat down like nothing happened."

"Covered in blood," I said.

"Yeah."

"Then?"

"I waited until it was quiet. I went to leave and saw that officer. He was dead. There was nothing I could do but get in trouble. So I got out."

"You weren't worried about Yvonne? Alone in a house with a killer on the loose?" I asked.

"There wasn't anyone around. I figured it was just someone who had a beef with the guy and took off. Besides, Madame Janvier's room is at the far end of the hallway," he said. Which made me wonder if she'd heard the commotion. Or if it really happened.

"Did you see anyone outside? Anybody sneaking around?" I asked.

"Hell no," Fair said. "If I saw anybody doing that, I woulda sounded the alarm. But everything was normal. The light was on in the comm shack, but they're always on duty. I got in the jeep and headed up to First Army. The only traffic I saw on the road was that Frenchman, Legrand, headed this way."

"With his men?" I asked, since I'd never seen Legrand without his henchmen close by.

"No, he was all by himself."

Interesting. *Pressoir* Janvier was a pretty busy place in the middle of the night, all sorts of people milling about and forgetting to mention the dead body in the living room. The Ghost Army guys, Legrand, Fair, Friedman, Sullivan the radioman, Yvonne, and whoever the hell else traipsed through here.

Someone had blood on their hands.

CHAPTER TWELVE

"REPORT, CAPTAIN BOYLE," Colonel Brewster demanded. He'd caught me coming down the stairs first thing in the morning, Big Mike on my heels. I'd tried to turn around before he spotted me, but Big Mike took up too much of the stairway for a smooth getaway.

"Still investigating, Colonel," I said, following him into the sitting room where this whole thing had started. "We've eliminated some suspects and are following up on leads." Standard cop talk meaning we had zero clues.

"What's next?" he snapped.

"Questioning Second Armored staff to see if anyone there had problems with Major Jerome. Looking into Yvonne's story to see if anyone connected with her could have showed up that night. Sir," I added, trying to sound military and respectful to get him off my back as quickly as possible.

"I thought you went to Second Armored yesterday," he said, his voice a growl. "What the hell were you doing out there?"

"We ran into a restricted area, Colonel."

"Yes. And?"

"That's all I can say, sir."

"Dammit, that's all I could get out of Fair. I don't like having secrets on my flank. Makes me nervous, Boyle, and you don't want me nervous," Brewster said, taking a step closer and giving me a hard glare. I could smell the coffee on his breath.

"Sorry, sir. You know what they say."

"Need to know. And I don't need to know," he said. "Heard it before, but it sounds better coming from a senior officer, rather than one of my own non-coms. Whatever happened out there, it did Fair a world of good. He seems better this morning. Wants to get back out on the line."

"He's a good man, sir," I said, thinking fast. I didn't want Fair up front while we still might have questions for him. I didn't quite buy his whole story, and I wanted him close by if I needed to interrogate him again. "So his hearing is better?"

"What's wrong with his hearing?" Colonel Brewster demanded. "Seemed fine to me."

"He told me he had ringing in his ears from a grenade blast. It was still bothering him yesterday," I said, stretching the truth a bit. I was glad Fair's spirits had picked up and wondered if it had something to do with unburdening himself. Maybe his story was the straight dope after all.

"I'll have him checked out before I cut him loose," Brewster said.

"Good idea, Colonel. Then if we need to talk to him, we'll have another day or so."

"Fine, fine. Now get to work and wrap this up, Boyle. People are getting worried. Let me know what you find out at Second Armored. Toot sweet, okay?"

"Yes, sir. We'll have something for you at the end of the day."

Brewster stalked off, heading to the kitchen where his officers were grouped around the table, papers and maps strewn about. The good news was that I'd convinced Brewster to keep Fair on ice for now, and he thought it was his idea. The bad news was that Madame Janvier wouldn't be cooking us breakfast.

"Let's head to the mess tent," Big Mike said. "Too much brass around here."

I agreed, and we headed out. Kaz was waiting for one of the girls who worked for Madame Janvier to iron a shirt, brush his uniform, and polish his shoes. I'd left him in our room, drinking tea while dressed in his silk bathrobe and cleaning his Webley revolver. Kaz had an elegant way of going to war.

"Captain, you going to need me today?" The question came from a GI leaving the mess tent, but it took me a moment to recognize him.

"Jesus, Fair, you clean up pretty well," I said. He wore fresh ODs, was clean-shaven, and his hair was combed. If he hadn't spoken, I would have walked right by him. "No, I don't think so. But stay close, okay?"

"Well, it's like this, sir. Colonel Brewster said I could go back on the line. He's got a new squad for me. So you'll need a new driver," Fair said. He did seem in better shape today. Focused.

"Brewster wants you to take a day and rest up," Big Mike said. "Because of that ringing in your ears."

"Dammit, I told Kaplan not to mention that," Fair said. "I can hear just fine."

"Don't blame Kaplan," I said, not wanting the medic to take the brunt of Fair's fury. He might have been cleaned up, but he still had a temper. "I was talking to Big Mike, saying how it hadn't seemed to have affected you, and Brewster overheard us, that's all. The colonel likes you, Fair. Could be worse."

"Okay," he said, mollified. "I'll report to him and see what he says. Then maybe I can see Yvonne. Thanks, Captain."

"The guy's got it bad," Big Mike said as Fair ambled off, happy enough to be granted one more day with his almost Sleeping Beauty. "I mean, she's a looker and all, but I do like a girl you can have an actual conversation with."

"Maybe that's the attraction," I said as we entered the tent, mess kits in hand. "Fair's carrying around a heavy load of guilt. When you lead a squad and they all end up dead, it's bound to hit you hard. Maybe she's his escape hatch. With her, he doesn't have to feel responsible."

"Or he's nuts," Big Mike said as a cook ladled scrambled eggs onto his plate, followed by a slab of buttered bread, hot from the bake truck.

"Sure, if you want to get all technical about it," I said. I got my food and filled my steel cup with hot coffee. We sat in the sun, pulling up a couple of empty ammo crates and digging in. I tried the coffee, but as always, the metal cup was burning hot. By the time it cooled down, the coffee would be lukewarm. But I shouldn't complain. I was eating aboveground, and no one was trying to kill me.

I gave Big Mike the lowdown on his job for the day: Drive out to Second Armored in Sainteny and see Harding's pal who headed up division G-2, Intelligence. Get the personal dope on Jerome and find out who might have had it in for him.

"Sainteny?" Big Mike asked, unfolding a map he had stored in his fatigue pants pocket. "That'll take me most of the day, there and back. What are you and Kaz up to?"

"Looking into Yvonne and whatever her story is. That's a blank page as far as we know. Maybe there's a jealous lover nearby," I said. "If you come up with any information, take an extra day. These two leads are about all we have."

We cleaned our mess kits and made our way back to the farmhouse as GIs hustled in every direction, throwing on their gear and mounting up in trucks. Lieutenant Friedman and a radioman piled into a radio-equipped jeep. The wireless took up the back seat.

"Pulling out?" I asked, as the jeep drew up next to us.

"No, but Brewster's got two companies attacking a hill to our front," Friedman said. "He figures with all that armor on our flank, we can take the high ground. You make contact with those tank boys yesterday?"

"Yeah," I said. "We saw tanks, all right." Leaving out the fact that they were rubber blowups and not Shermans made from thirty-four tons of Detroit steel.

"Uh, Billy," Big Mike said as Friedman drove off, falling into the column of trucks headed for the attack.

"Yeah, I know." Brewster was sending his men to attack a hill held by the Germans, thinking his flank was secured by tanks. That would leave him hung out to dry if the Krauts made an end run and counterattacked. "But we can't say anything. Besides, Fox and his boys sure fooled us. I bet the Germans have swallowed the bait too."

"Probably," Big Mike said. "But you're not betting your life. If the Germans punch back, they'll overrun the Ghost Army and chew up

Brewster's battalion from the flank. It's a long shot, but it could be a disaster."

"Okay. Head out now and get to Harding before he leaves for First Army," I said. "Let him figure it out. If you get held up at a roadblock, demand to speak to Colonel Harding or Captain Fox. Radio back here with any news."

Big Mike nodded and ran off, surprisingly swift for a guy his size. Speed was necessary, though, since the lives of eight hundred or so guys might depend on it. I hustled over to the farmhouse, looking for Kaz and praying that the Broadway con artists of the Ghost Army wouldn't be taking their final bows today.

I found Kaz sitting at the empty kitchen table, looking sharp as usual. His wool battle dress jacket was sparkling clean and his Sam Browne leather belt polished perfectly.

"Good morning, Billy," he said, sipping coffee. Bread and jam were set out before him. "Brewster and his men left rather in a hurry. But Madame Janvier provided me with their leftovers. Join me."

Somehow Kaz managed to look at ease no matter what the circumstances. He had a way of seeing the war as a great joke, or at least having you believe he did. I knew different. I'd known Daphne.

I poured coffee and sat opposite my friend.

I'd met Kaz and Daphne on my first day in England. I'd been assigned to General Eisenhower's headquarters, London. In early 1942, the general was head of US forces in Europe, such as they were. I'd barely made it through Officer's Candidate School, graduating last in my class. I was used to how things were done back in the Boston Police Department, like when I passed the detective's exam, helped along by a copy of the test that happened to come my way. Dad was a homicide detective, along with my uncle, who also sat on the promotions board. It was kind of a family business.

When the war broke out, the Boyle clan had pulled some strings to get me assigned to Uncle Ike, then a colonel in the War Plans Department, working in the brand-new Pentagon building in Washington, DC. The Boyle family had both political connections and a strong desire not to sacrifice its oldest boy in a second war to save the

British Empire. Which was how this European war was viewed in my Irish household. Dad and Uncle Dan had lost their older brother in the last war, and they aimed to keep me alive in this new one. I did not object.

Little did we know Uncle Ike was delighted to have a family member and experienced police detective on his staff for his new assignment in England. He was right about two out of three. We were related, and I was on the cops. So instead of a comfy post in the nation's capital, I soon found myself in London, befriended by Kaz and Daphne.

Uncle Ike had expected an experienced investigator. Experience was never an issue back home, where Uncle Dan and Dad were always close by with advice and the occasional cuff to the ear. Over here, I had to make my own way. Kaz was a big part of that. He was also the reason I was still alive. That probably worked both ways. Not that I saved him from the enemy. The greatest danger to Kaz's life was the Webley revolver he wore on his belt and his own trigger finger.

He'd lost the woman he loved, Daphne Seaton, during the course of our first investigation. He lived through it, barely. The scar on one side of his face, from the fiery explosion that had killed her, marked the dividing line of his life. For a long time, he didn't care whether he lived or died, and went about our duties with a recklessness that was often astounding. But somewhere along the way, the pull of guilt, sorrow, and pain had lost its grip on his soul, and Kaz felt life was worth living again.

"Billy, did you hear me?" Kaz asked.

"Sure," I said, blowing on my coffee. "But tell me again."

"Arianne told me some interesting things about Madame Janvier," he said.

"Who's Arianne?"

"The young lady who works here. She cleans house and does odd jobs. Very good with a clothes brush, I might add," Kaz said. "She said Madame Janvier was active in the Resistance."

"Really? She never mentioned it. What did she do?"

"Apparently, there is an old cottage in the woods to the east, on the banks of a river. It was the original home of the Janvier family, generations ago. It's practically a ruin and surrounded by apple orchards. There's no longer a road leading to it," Kaz said.

"Sounds like a perfect hideout," I said. "For downed airmen?"

"Arianne said she doesn't know who was hidden there, but she assumed airmen and others on the run from the Germans. Everyone knew not to speak of it or ask questions," Kaz said. "The people who work here are very loyal. No one ever betrayed her."

"I guess she wants to put the past behind her," I said. "That must have taken guts."

"Indeed. Arianne said she had a code name. Corday," Kaz said.

"Is that supposed to mean something?" I asked.

"Marie-Anne Charlotte de Corday d'Armont is a famous figure from the French Revolution, originally from Normandy," Kaz said. "She killed a violent leader of the Jacobins, Jean-Paul Marat. Stabbed him in his bath. She went to the guillotine for that and earned herself a lasting nickname, *l'ange de l'assassinat*." I knew enough French to figure that one out.

"The Angel of Assassination," I said. "Surprising. I wonder if Madame Janvier did more than hide people."

"Arianne did not know of any other activities, but she told me she made it her business not to know," Kaz said. "It may be nothing more than a convenient label. If she aided a local network, they would have used a *nom de guerre*. It would be too dangerous to bandy about her real name."

"We need to talk to Madame Janvier," I said. "There's a lot of bad blood among these Resistance groups. Maybe someone dropped by to settle an old score."

"And decided instead to kill an unknown American officer?" Kaz said. "It makes no sense. But since nothing else does either, we may as well follow it up. Arianne also told me this house was used by the Germans. A *Feldgendarmerie* detachment was billeted here."

"German military police," I said. "That must have made everyone nervous."

"There were others, including the *Geheime Feldpolizei*, the

Wehrmacht's plainclothes secret police, along with the occasional *miliciens,* which frightened Arianne more than the Germans." The *Milice française* were pro-German fascist militia. Nazis were bad enough. Frenchmen who betrayed their own people and did the occupier's dirty work were worse. We'd run into them before. They wore a blue uniform, a big, floppy beret, and looked their best sprawled on the ground bleeding to death from multiple gunshot wounds.

"Seems there's a whole lot we don't know about *Pressoir* Janvier," I said.

"Including why no one but a simple housemaid thought to mention it," Kaz said. "I would think Legrand might have something to tell us about the *Milice,* if he has time between his hairdressing appointments."

"Maybe he didn't say anything since he was playing both sides," I said. "He could have been an informer for the *Milice* while he was waiting for the Germans to hightail it out of here so he could play the role of the guerrilla chieftain."

"It would not surprise me, given what we know of the man," Kaz said. "It would explain his silence, at least."

"Let's start by asking Madame Janvier. Where is she?" I said, finishing off the lukewarm coffee.

"She left with her pruning shears to work in the orchards," Kaz said. "I have no idea exactly where." He dabbed a napkin at his lips and rose from the table. "Perhaps we should try to communicate with Miss Yvonne in her absence."

"It's worth a shot," I said, following Kaz. I glanced at my watch, wondering if Big Mike had gotten to a roadblock yet. And if reaching Colonel Harding would make any difference to the men assaulting that hill.

"*Bonjour,* Yvonne," Kaz said as he pushed open her door. "*Comment allez-vous?*"

I knew how she was. The same. Today she wore a faded blue dress with white polka dots. It was large on her and frayed at the hem. Something old of Madame Janvier's, perhaps. Other than that, everything was as before. The chair by the window. The vacant look in her dark blue eyes. The chiseled cheekbones and the reddish-blonde hair cascading down her back.

Silence draped across her shoulders like a shawl. In her stillness, she radiated beauty. I saw the attraction to some guys. She was helpless, but she also held the promise of something unknowable, a deep secret that held the answer to her muteness.

"*Parlez-vous anglais?*" Kaz asked. Either she didn't speak English or she didn't want to tell him. Or couldn't. It was the same with a host of other questions Kaz murmured gently to her.

I knelt at her side. Her hands were cupped in her lap.

"Yvonne," I asked, "may I see your hand?" I figured the language made no difference if she wasn't going to respond. I tapped her hand with one finger and tried to make eye contact. "Please?"

When she didn't answer, I lifted her hand as delicately as I could. She didn't protest or pull away. Madame Janvier had told us how she could be led to do the most basic tasks, such as eating and dressing, but little else. I felt a shiver at the realization of how easy it would be to abuse this poor girl.

I turned over her hand so it was palm up, the healing cut on display.

She turned her head away. Progress of a sort.

"Yvonne, what happened that night?" I whispered.

She closed her eyes.

"That's fine," I said, patting her hand and placing it back in her lap. "We'll come back tomorrow. Is that okay?"

Yvonne opened her eyes, watery with tears poised to fall. She blinked once, then again, and the tears vanished, her face again impassive, unknowable. She turned her eyes to the window. I wondered if she saw anything but her reflection in the glass.

CHAPTER THIRTEEN

"WHAT ARE YOU doing, Captain Boyle?" Madame Janvier said from the bottom of the stairs as we came out of Yvonne's room. She didn't sound happy. Of course, if she'd been in a good mood, she would have ignored me in favor of Baron Kazimierz.

"Just paying our respects to Yvonne," I said as we descended the stairs. "The cut on her hand seems to have healed nicely."

"You must leave her alone," she said. "Let the poor girl rest."

"If you have a moment, we have a few questions for you," I said. "About the Germans and *Milice* who were billeted here during the Occupation."

"They were more than billeted. The *Boche* used my property as a headquarters for hunting partisans. It was unpleasant, and I do not wish to dwell upon it," she said, turning away from us. "I have more work to do."

"You did dangerous work yourself, I hear," I said as we followed her outside.

"Do not believe everything you hear, Captain. Everyone lies one way or another about the Occupation. We hide our sins and guilt well these days. Some do it by talking endlessly. I prefer silence when thinking of those years. Please excuse me."

"Madame Janvier," Kaz said, stepping forward and placing a hand on my arm, "I respect your wishes. I can only imagine the choices my own people in Pologne must make every day. But perhaps you can help us to discover more about Yvonne. It is possible that someone seeking her was responsible for the murder of Major Jerome."

"Someone who knew of her, you mean?" Madame Janvier asked. "I very much doubt that. The best I can do is refer you to the *Hôpital* Sarlat. It is not far to the east, in Rubercy."

"Is that where she was born?" I asked.

"It is where she came from," Madame Janvier said with a bitter laugh. "It is *une maison de fous.*"

I glanced at Kaz as she walked away. "A house of what?"

"A house of fools," Kaz said. "I believe she is directing us to a lunatic asylum."

I STOPPED AT the Signals office and grabbed a spare SCR-300 radio. Designed to be carried as a backpack, it had a range of three miles. We were going farther than that, but I wanted to keep tabs on Brewster's attack and any news from Big Mike. Sullivan, the radioman on duty, gave me the frequency and call sign, and confirmed I knew how to work the dials and transmit. We strapped the radio in the rear seat and pulled out, trusting our luck and a good sense of direction to find the town of Rubercy and the local funny farm.

French road maps were worth their price in gold, and just as scarce, so we asked around and got a pretty good idea which direction to take. We took an easterly road, past hulks of burned-out trucks and fallow fields churned up by artillery. We passed GIs guarding German prisoners at work digging temporary graves, mounds of Norman soil piled in neat rows next to bodies covered in tent halves and mattress covers. GI boots stuck out from underneath, and I wondered how many of these Kraut bastards were responsible for the corpses they were putting underground.

Some days I saw German soldiers—the enlisted men, at least—as some other poor schmucks doing a lousy, stinking job. Other days I hated their guts for serving their Nazi masters so fervently. Today was one of those other days. I slowed and stared at them, their ragged uniforms dirty and stained. Dust meant death, and death meant dust if you were knee-deep in a grave.

At the far end of the field, POWs were slapping white paint on crude wooden crosses and the occasional Star of David. Others set them in the ground as GIs with clipboards followed along, recording the names of the dead. I didn't envy the guys from Graves Registration. They had a tough job, and there was no shortage of work here in the *bocage*. And I certainly didn't envy the dead.

Graves Registration had two basic roles. First, to bury the dead with what respect it could on the battlefield, handling their personal effects and recording the location of each grave so they could be disinterred for a permanent burial later. Second, to get the dead underground as quickly as possible for purposes of morale, if not health and sanitation. Personally, I thought the sight of rows of grave markers only margin-ally more morale-boosting than seeing the corpses themselves, but I figured the army knew something about disposing of the dead while delivering fresh troops up to the line.

I drove on, letting the clean, fresh air wash over me, shivering in the warmth as I thought about shovelfuls of dirt strewn over the bodies of young men.

"On occasion, it feels strange to be alive, does it not?" Kaz said, as if reading my mind. "Some of those boys may have been killed their first day at the front. And yet here we are still."

Kaz was the kind of guy who marveled at being alive. Me, I took it for granted. Most days. Today, I kept my silence and drove. Slowly, making no dust.

Rubercy wasn't much of a village. A few farm buildings, a bombed-out church, and dilapidated houses huddled together, all sharing a uniform grayness, as if the war had sucked the life out of them. A smattering of cows and sheep grazed in overgrown fields, indifferent to it all.

I braked to a halt, glancing around at a fork in the road, looking for a helpful sign pointing out the local house of fools. At one of the buildings, a door opened and an elderly woman in a long black dress gave us the once-over. A wooden crucifix hung around her neck, and

I wondered how much comfort it could have given her these past years.

Without a word, she pointed to the left turn and shut the door.

"Is it that obvious?" I asked.

"I am sure she was looking at you, Billy," Kaz said, leaning back and laughing as I drove off. We found a sign for the Sarlat Hospital a half mile down the road and turned onto a long, straight drive lined with sycamore trees, their bushy leaves joining overhead in a canopy of shade, relief from the July sunshine.

The building was three stories high, built of red brick and topped with a gray slate roof. It might have been impressive back before the turn of the century, but today it looked rough around the edges. Missing tiles on the roof and crumbling bricks lent an air of decay, matched by the weedy lawn and overgrown shrubs surrounding it. The windows were barred. Patients in dirty robes sat in wheelchairs, apparently to enjoy the sun, but they were bound to their chairs with strips of cloth. No one seemed happy with the arrangement. Some moaned, others gazed at nothing. Two orderlies patrolled the group, giving us a look as lethargic as their charges.

Entering the front door, a stench of unwashed bodies, urine, and despair hit us. Another orderly sat at a desk, leafing through a newspaper, his chin held up by one hand as the other turned a page. Kaz asked to see *le Docteur*, which seemed to surprise the poor fellow. He took so long to raise an arm and point to a wide staircase that I wondered if he was a patient working off his room and board.

"Cheery place," I said, as our boots clomped up the worn stone steps.

"It must be difficult to run an asylum in the middle of a war," Kaz said.

"Yeah, how can you tell the inmates from the rest of us?" I said, as a wail rose from down the hall. I'd heard pretty much the same on the battlefield.

A fancy brass nameplate on the door announced we'd found the office of Dr. Louis Benoît. Kaz knocked, and we entered. A gray-bearded gentleman sat behind a large desk, shuffling papers and looking startled. I guess his patients didn't often come calling.

"*Puis-je vous aider?*" he asked, in a tone that suggested he really wasn't looking forward to helping us. He pushed his glasses up on his nose as Kaz spoke with him, mentioning Yvonne's name several times. Dr. Benoît grew agitated and shook his head, lifting a telephone and dialing a number. He barked into it and shooed us away with his hand as he slammed the receiver down.

"Are we being kicked out?" I asked Kaz as we left the office.

"No, he called another doctor, one who speaks English," Kaz said. "He was not at all happy to hear the name of Yvonne Virot."

"You must forgive Dr. Benoît," said a man in a white coat as he approached us, the door to a ward slamming shut behind him. "Dr. Mathis Leroy. I will be glad to answer your questions." He spoke slowly but well, with a notable English accent. He was about forty years old, with a gaunt face and tired eyes, his right hand stuffed in a lab coat pocket.

"Captain Boyle," I said, and introduced Kaz. I extended my hand, and Dr. Leroy shook it with his left.

"I apologize, but this arm is fairly useless," he said, lifting his right hand slightly from his pocket. I caught a glimpse of missing fingers and gnarled scar tissue. "Courtesy of a German Stuka outside of Sedan."

"You were in the service, Dr. Leroy?" I asked.

"Yes, I was called up by the army when the Germans invaded. We had barely set up a field hospital before it was overrun. The *Boche* were everywhere. We were bombed, and I ended up being treated by a German doctor. Ironic, yes? But this wound saved me from being sent to a prisoner-of-war camp in Germany, so perhaps I should be glad. Now, what can I do for you?"

"We are here to look into the identity of Yvonne Virot," Kaz said. "One of your patients."

"Ah, I see why Dr. Benoît was upset," he said. "Come, let us walk in the garden." Dr. Leroy unlocked a door, leading us down a corridor. Patients in pajamas and threadbare robes roamed the halls, some jabbering to themselves, some greeting Dr. Leroy in what sounded like normal voices. Others shrank at our approach, furtively backing into their rooms and shutting doors.

"The uniforms scare them," Dr. Leroy said, taking us down a staircase and out the back door. "The Germans searched the hospital many times and were always angry. Very upsetting."

Outside, the grounds had been turned into a large garden, well tended by patients busy weeding between the rows of vegetables.

"What can you tell us about Yvonne?" I asked, eager for answers at long last. I was rewarded with a finger to his lips as Dr. Leroy continued to walk, chatting with his patients. This bunch seemed livelier than the people we'd seen before, smiling as they dug weeds out of the loamy soil.

"This is excellent therapy for them," Dr. Leroy said as he paused to inspect the leafy tops of carrots, running his hand through the delicate greenery. "I think we shall keep up our little farm once the war is over. Dr. Benoît and I are the only physicians in residence, and he does not see many patients. He was about to retire when the Germans came, and decided he would stay on out of duty to our residents."

"It must have been difficult," Kaz said, trying to move the conversation along.

"It was, but Dr. Benoît speaks excellent German and did his best to keep the *Boche* satisfied. He maintained relations with the authorities, and left the running of the hospital to me," Dr. Leroy said as we moved on. At the end of the garden, two rows of apple trees offered a shady glade with benches and a small table. We sat, and Dr. Leroy lit a cigarette.

"We are far enough away from your patients that they will not overhear," Kaz said, giving me a glance.

"*Oui,*" Leroy said. "A long-standing habit. I do not fear they would betray me, but they cannot always control themselves or what they say. And as you saw, the sight of soldiers frightens them. So it was best to keep any irregular activities hidden."

"And Dr. Benoît as well?" I asked.

"Yes, but that was intentional. Better for him not to know, he told me. A frail old man could not stand up to torture, he maintained, and that would have been the ruin of us all."

"That was brave of him," Kaz said. "With no secrets to reveal, his torture would have been terrible if he was arrested."

"He was willing to do what had to be done," Leroy said, drawing on his cigarette and blowing smoke to the winds. "As were many who paid the price. We were simply lucky."

"You were part of the Resistance?" I asked. "You worked with the *Maquis*?"

"No, not the *Maquis*. That would have been too dangerous for our charges. We could not store arms and explosives, or let too many know our secrets. The *Maquis* are brave to fight the Germans, but they can talk too much. Some joined simply to avoid being taken for slave labor to Germany and could not be trusted." He crushed the cigarette beneath his heel. "We worked exclusively with *Réseau Nemo*."

"The Nemo Line," Kaz said. "You were very successful, from the reports I read." I recalled the group too. They were named after Captain Nemo, Jules Verne's character who piloted the *Nautilus* submarine, evading capture while helping the oppressed. *Réseau Nemo* did the same with downed airmen and escaped POWs.

"My part was very small. We took escapees and airmen who were shot down and hid them for a night or two, then passed them on. Only myself and a trusted orderly knew of it. We have a hiding place in the attic behind a false wall. I had made many English friends when I worked at a hospital in Dover after medical school. I felt I had to help."

"Was Yvonne one of the escapees?" I asked.

"Yvonne was a special case," Dr. Leroy said. "She did not come to us in the ordinary way. Why do you ask about her?" His question was the first sign that he felt protective about Yvonne. Like every other guy who'd laid eyes on her.

"To keep her safe," I said, figuring that would appeal to the good doctor. "We're investigating a murder. Yvonne was present in the house when it occurred, and we're worried it might have been someone from her past."

"I hope she is well. She is not injured?" Dr. Leroy asked, glancing between Kaz and me.

"No," Kaz said. "She may have seen the killer, but we cannot be certain. She is not very responsive, as I assume was the case when she was in your care."

"Completely," Dr. Leroy said.

"So help us help her," I said. "We need to know everything."

"Very well," Dr. Leroy said with a heavy sigh. He shook another cigarette from his pack and lit up, settled back, and began to talk. "It began with bombs and carnage on a beautiful summer's day."

It was a low-level bombing attack on a rail line a mile or so south of the hospital, late last summer. Dr. Leroy had seen the twin-engine bombers swoop low over the building and heard the explosions in the distance. He took his medical kit and rode his bicycle to the scene, marked by billowing black smoke.

A train was wrecked, the locomotive gone off the tracks, and several cars burning. As Dr. Leroy neared, fires set off ammunition, shattering the boxcars and killing German soldiers who had been standing nearby, dazed and in shock. Dr. Leroy checked the locomotive first for the French crew. The engineer was dead. Dr. Leroy had known him as a member of *Résistance-Fer*, the Iron Resistance, as the *résistants* of the French railroad were known.

There was no time to look for anyone else or help the injured. A German officer, bleeding profusely from a gash on his head, stumbled toward Dr. Leroy, firing his pistol. The shots went wild, but the message was unmistakable. The *Boche* wanted someone to pay for what had happened, and Dr. Leroy was the only living Frenchman in sight. As the officer called for help, the doctor ran, jumping on his bike and pedaling as fast as he could.

Another massive explosion sounded, spewing debris into the sky. No one followed. As he turned off the main road on his way back to the hospital, Dr. Leroy saw a solitary figure walking across a field. A young girl, her clothes in tatters, her face bruised, and her hair matted. He ran to her, but she took no notice, simply continuing to walk through the grassy field. Figuring she was from the train, Dr. Leroy at first thought her clothing had been singed in the fiery explosions.

Then he looked more closely and saw the bruises were not recent. The torn dress was stained and filthy, as if she'd been wearing it for weeks, not burned in the wreck. He realized the bombs had not injured her. They had freed her.

Dr. Leroy led her to the hospital and installed her as a patient, using the identity papers of a girl who had died a month before. Her family hadn't visited her in years, and her death was unnoticed outside of the hospital. Dr. Leroy had kept her papers in case they were needed for just this purpose.

Her name was Yvonne Virot.

"That is how she came to be my patient," Dr. Leroy said. "I believe she had been a prisoner of the Gestapo. Perhaps the officer who shot at me was in charge of her. Who knows? With all the explosions, the *Boche* may have thought she'd been incinerated in the fires."

"Did she say anything?" I asked.

"Nothing. At first I thought she was in shock from the attack. But as I examined her, it became apparent she had been badly beaten. And raped. She had retreated inside herself, and nothing I could do helped at all. We made sure she was cared for and found she could manage simple tasks, like eating and dressing. Otherwise, it was as if she did not care if she lived or died."

"But why is she still not here?" Kaz asked. "Surely she needs medical care."

"You would have to ask Major Hans Rast of the *Feldgendarmerie*," Dr. Leroy said.

"The German military police?" Kaz said. "I thought you said the Germans never searched for her."

"It was several months after she came here. Rast had taken command of the troops in this area and conducted inspections of all sites that might harbor fugitives. It was more of a warning than anything else, I think, not a search for any single person. He saw Yvonne and simply took her away. He was most solicitous, which is unusual for a security officer. He said she was not under arrest, but rather under his protection. And quite insistent that I should ask no further questions. It was very strange. You are certain she is safe?"

"Yes, safe enough. Any idea where Rast might be now?" I asked.

"*Non.* The military and secret police left shortly after the invasion, along with their *Milice* allies. There is a *Maquis* group operating in the area that captured some of the *Milice* and a plainclothes Gestapo man. The poor fellows were late making their getaway."

"Legrand's men?" Kaz asked.

"No, I mean real *résistants*," Dr. Leroy said. "Legrand built up a cache of weapons and then waited for the Americans to show their faces before he acted. If you can find the *Groupe Rouge*, their leader may be able to tell you more. Ask for Jacques in Les Touvets, about ten kilometers south."

"Isn't that close to the front line?" I asked.

"Of course. That is where you will find Jacques and his men," he said. "Communists, but good fighters. They were hunted by Rast and the *Milice*. If anyone can help you, it is Jacques."

"Thanks. Just two more questions, Doctor. What would it take for Yvonne to act on her own? More than eating or dressing herself. Like walking to another room and responding to what's happening there?"

"I wish she had done so once while she was here," he said. "But if she has, I would think it would be in response to a powerful stimulus. Positive or negative, it would not matter. But something strong enough to trigger a part of her mind that has been shut down for a long time. Sorry, but I cannot be more precise. Your other question?"

"Does every man who meets Yvonne fall a little bit in love with her?" I asked.

"Perhaps," Dr. Leroy said, giving a rueful laugh. "She does have a certain quality. Childlike, yet deeply feminine. Alluring even in her deep silence. That is what struck me as odd about Rast."

"In what way?" Kaz asked.

"He did not respond to her beauty and femininity at all. His attitude was triumphant, I would say. But I never thought he took her for his own enjoyment. At least not in a sexual way."

"Then why did he take her?" I asked, mostly to myself.

"Because he was the conqueror, and she was the spoils," Leroy said, lighting his last cigarette.

CHAPTER FOURTEEN

"WE SHOULD HAVE taken a left back there, Kaz," I said, pulling over to the side of the narrow lane. We were on a dirt road with scrub brush on one side, a pine forest on the other, and a washed-out gully in the middle. Right where the village of Les Touvets should have been.

"No, the farmer told us to go straight. We must be close," Kaz said, standing up and shielding his eyes. As hard as he might look, there wasn't a village in sight.

"Maybe he was pro-Vichy," I said. "And I'm hungry." We'd brought rations along, but given everything to Dr. Leroy for his patients before we'd left on this ten-kilometer jaunt. Which was fifteen kilometers ago, which translated to several miles past lunch.

I got out of the jeep and tried the radio.

"Able Victor One, over. Able Victor One, over." Nothing. I'd hoped we'd gotten so lost that we might have circled around and come back within range, but no such luck. We were just plain lost.

"Perhaps we can find food in the village," Kaz said, slumping back down in his seat.

"Let's turn back," I said. "Maybe that farmer was a fascist, or maybe he has the worst sense of direction this side of Paris." I put the jeep in reverse and started a three-point turn, which was tricky in the rocky and narrow road.

Which was why I didn't see the guy with the rifle. But when I did, it was pointed straight at me.

"Halt!" More men emerged from the bushes. GIs, a good half dozen. A lieutenant with a carbine aimed at my chest stepped closer. "Kill the engine." I obeyed and silence settled over us, marred only by the sound of creaking leather straps and one guy snapping his chewing gum.

"Any idea where we are?" I asked, ignoring the fact that no one had lowered their weapon.

"In Kraut territory," the lieutenant said, lowering his carbine slightly and coming closer to inspect Kaz. "Who are you, pal?"

"Lieutenant Piotr Kazimierz, at your service," Kaz said. "And you?"

"Is that a German accent?" asked the lieutenant, ignoring Kaz's politeness.

"*Skąd jesteś?*" asked a corporal, his Thompson submachine gun at the ready. Kaz answered in a torrent of Polish, and soon they were gabbing like long-lost relatives. "He's okay," the corporal said after shaking hands with Kaz, then assigning men to watch each end of the road.

"What the hell are you doing out here?" the lieutenant asked, scanning the terrain he'd come through.

"Looking for Les Touvets," I said.

"You're way off track and headed deep into Kraut territory," he said. "We're coming back from patrol and still have a half mile to go to get back to our lines."

"See any Germans?" I asked.

"*Beaucoup*, just over that last hill. You keep driving down this track and you'll see them too, a full company. They're conducting a sweep, probably looking for partisans. Things are sort of fluid here; you never know who's going to be waiting around the next bend in the road."

"We are actually looking for a *Maquis* band," Kaz said. "The *Groupe Rouge*, headed by a fellow named Jacques."

"Jacques? He's a tough old bird. We saw those boys this morning when we headed out. In Les Touvets," the lieutenant said. "Can't miss 'em; they all wear red bandannas. Said they were about to hunt down some *Milice* guys who'd shot a local *gendarme* down in Castillon. The cop had left the jailhouse door unlocked for a couple of partisans to escape, so the *Milice* put a bullet in his head and burned out his house. Jacques and his bunch want revenge. They've got a real blood feud going on."

"Castillon is behind the lines?" Kaz asked.

"*This* is behind the lines," the lieutenant said, glancing around one more time. "And Castillon is further behind, with a company of Krauts standing in the way. They might be searching for Jacques, for all I know. Now get a move on. You're in full view out here."

The lieutenant and his squad melted into the firs, vanishing quietly and leaving us feeling naked as jaybirds.

Kaz reached into the back seat and grabbed a carbine. "Well?" he asked.

"It would be smart to turn around," I said. "We're lost behind enemy lines. No one knows where we are. And there's about a hundred Krauts a stone's throw away."

"Who are standing between us and Jacques," Kaz said, reaching back again and handing me my Thompson. "Plus, they are spread out on foot. We have speed and surprise on our side."

"How about we just go slowly for a while," I said. I switched off the safety and laid the Thompson in my lap as I drove slowly through the rutted gulley, watching for any sign of movement through the underbrush. There were certain disadvantages to having a partner with suicidal tendencies, and driving even deeper into German territory was one of them. Still, he had a point. We needed to find Jacques, and it was better if we did before the Krauts got to him.

The dirt track meandered through a copse of trees and ran along a fast-running stream for a few hundred yards. It was quiet and dark beneath the shade of the trees. I stopped the jeep and listened for telltale signs ahead. Nothing. I crept forward in first gear, halting again as the track crossed a paved road which led to a wooden bridge spanning the stream.

Wind rustled the leaves, a *whooshing* sound rising as the branches swirled with the breeze. Water bubbled over rocks, gurgling and splashing beneath the bridge.

A bird sang.

A machine gun ripped through the silence. Then more firing, rifles opening up as other automatic weapons joined the fray.

"Over there," Kaz said, pointing across the stream. I drove across the bridge, heading for the gunfire, hoping that speed and surprise were really all they were cracked up to be.

We drove around a bend and saw two Germans running pell-mell for us, one behind the other, right smack in the middle of the road. Kaz fired as I braked, two bullets into the first Kraut, who dropped his rifle but ran a few more steps before tumbling to the ground. Then the same for the guy behind him, who took two to the chest but kept on until he slammed into the jeep and bounced off in a heap of field gray and blood. I realized they hadn't been so much running toward us as away from the gunfire coming from the tree line ahead.

I jammed the jeep into reverse and pulled back and off the road to get out of the line of fire. From what I'd seen, the Germans were marching across a cultivated field to our right, heading for the bridge we'd just crossed. Several bodies were strewn across the road. They'd been caught as they began to file onto the road, a perfect spot for an ambush. Some Krauts were now making a dash for the bridge, while others retreated across the field. Both groups were taking heavy fire from the woods to our left. I darted the jeep forward again, and this time Kaz and I both opened up, firing on a group of Germans running for the bridge before noticing an officer behind the men, leveling his pistol and shooting them in the back.

A machine gun burst put him down, and I regretted I hadn't had the chance. No matter that these were the enemy. Killing your own men is a special kind of vile.

Two Germans who got close to us threw down their weapons and raised their hands. Kaz jumped from the jeep and made them lie facedown. Men emerged from the cover of the woods, firing on the Germans in the open field. With no cover, it was a turkey shoot.

The attackers wore the red neckerchiefs of the *Groupe Rouge*. Several waved eagerly in our direction as they pressed forward.

"They see us," Kaz said, holding his carbine on the two Germans spread-eagled in the road. He waved back and shouted greetings in French to cement the notion that we were all on the same side.

I was ready to breathe a sigh of relief when more gunfire erupted from behind, clipping branches from the trees and sending us diving behind the jeep. Our two prisoners crawled forward to take advantage of the cover as bullets kicked up clods of dirt around us.

"Watch them!" I said to Kaz as I rammed a fresh clip into the Thompson. I rose up to see an old truck bearing down on us, jammed with blue-uniformed men firing wildly, at us and the partisans advancing against the Germans.

Milice.

I aimed at the driver, barely twenty yards away and closing fast. I saw his face, a snarl beneath a floppy blue beret. I squeezed the trigger. Windshield and face disappeared in shards of glass, blood, and bone. I fired short bursts at the men in the back, taking my time to aim, knowing how hard it was for them to shoot accurately from a bouncing, out-of-control vehicle.

I dropped the empty clip and loaded another, firing as the truck slowed and ran off the road, tipping over lazily in a ditch, tires in the air still spinning from their forward motion.

I glanced back at Kaz, who gave me a thumbs-up, his two charges cowering beneath him. I stepped warily around the truck, hearing cries and groans from the ditch where most of the *Milice* had fallen.

They were a tangle of bloodied bodies and moving limbs. Ten of them, at quick count. One, his face covered in red ooze, tried to draw his revolver. A short burst of .45 slugs convinced him otherwise.

Another crawled out from the ditch, wincing as he dragged his broken leg, white bone protruding from his torn blue trousers. He didn't look troublesome, so I let him be.

"Américain," one of the partisans said, slapping me on the shoulder as he nonchalantly kicked the crawling man square on his broken bone. He signaled for others to drag the screaming man away, while he stepped through the bloody ditch, finishing off two moaning *Milice* and dragging another with a belly wound by his leg.

"Ah, *Polonais!*" he said, inspecting Kaz's shoulder patch. Our two

German prisoners were wide-eyed, one of them weeping. With good cause, by the looks of it. The *Groupe Rouge* herded several prisoners forward, gunshots echoing in the field as others were given the coup de grâce.

"Jacques?" I asked, as his men, about twenty of them, gathered around.

"Oui, oui!" Jacques said, smiling with pride. *"Parlez-vous français?"*

"Only *un peu*," I said, not wanting to trust my jailhouse French to interrogate Jacques about Rast and any connection to the *Réseau Nemo*.

"I speak *anglais*," a boy said as he stood next to Jacques. He was sixteen at most, and didn't even shave yet. But the Sten gun at his side added a few years, along with the red cloth at his neck. Jacques spoke to him, pointing to both of us, Kaz having relinquished his prisoners.

"Mon père thanks you. We did not know the *Milice* were coming," the boy said, slowly and with a thick accent.

"We came to see the famous Jacques and his *Groupe Rouge*," I said. As the kid translated, Jacques puffed up his chest and laughed. Kaz began to speak, but Jacques cut him off.

"We must deal with the *Boche* and *les salauds*," his boy said. "Before others come."

Kaz spoke quickly, gesturing to the Germans. I caught Rast's name a few times, and figured he was telling Jacques we needed to interrogate the prisoners. Jacques strode over to the two wounded *Milice* and barked a question at them. One spitting in defiance, the other shaking his head and holding up one hand in supplication.

Jacques drew his pistol and shot each in the head, then spoke to Kaz.

"They knew nothing of Rast," Kaz translated. "Not that one could trust the *Milice* anyway. He says these are the men who executed the policeman who was an agent for the Resistance, and he is grateful to us for stopping them. Therefore, we may take one prisoner with us."

"The others?" I asked, even though I was sure of the answer.

"Jacques promises justice for them. Meaning a bullet, if they are lucky. Most of them are Russian turncoats, led by German officers."

"Which is why that Kraut was shooting his own men," I said. I remembered Kaz telling us about the Russian prisoners in German uniforms he'd been interrogating before he joined us.

"Yes. Jacques says this unit was known for its cruelty, officers and men alike. Burning villages, shooting innocent civilians. The *Groupe Rouge* had been planning this ambush for some time."

"Okay, let's pick our man," I said. I had no sympathy for Russians who switched sides, but I also didn't want to linger on thoughts of exactly how these men were going to end up this afternoon. "Ask if any of them knows where Major Rast is."

The prisoners were seated on the ground, surrounded by partisans with grim looks and ready trigger fingers. Kaz walked up and down the line, speaking in German and Russian. He ended up shaking his head, one hand resting on his holstered revolver.

"The Russians all say they know where he is, but they are lying to save their lives. None of them agree with the other. The Germans—one lieutenant and a sergeant—refuse to answer," Kaz said.

One of the Russians, a hand clasped over a wound in his arm, began to speak loudly, in French so poor even I could understand much of it. Kaz filled in the rest. He was claiming his innocence. The Germans had captured him and threatened to kill him if he didn't join this detachment. What choice did he have? What choice did his men have? He begged to be turned over to the Americans.

Jacques answered him. If he liked choices, he would give him one. Would he rather be turned over to the Pole or to the French?

The Russian looked at the Frenchmen with the red neckerchiefs gathered around him, their fingers hard on triggers. Then to Kaz, his gaze taking in the *Poland* shoulder patch and the scar on his cheek.

He gave his answer. *"Tue-moi."* Kill me.

"You do not want this one?" Jacques's son asked. I looked to Kaz. He shook his head no. Jacques drew a German Luger from his holster and gave the Russian a 9mm choice to the forehead. His head snapped back in a spray of gray and red, his body collapsing on another prisoner, who pushed the corpse away, scrambling to avoid the gore. Others cowered, pleaded, wept, prayed, and otherwise implored the partisans to spare their lives. Hands on their hearts, fingers pointed out the killers who burned homes and murdered the innocent, denying their own guilt with all the sincerity of a carnival barker.

"I think we should pick our man, Kaz," I said. "Now."

Kaz nodded. He drew his Webley and strolled in front of the two Germans. He spoke to the officer, calmly and slowly, gesturing with his hands as if explaining something complicated. The lieutenant nodded, then spoke eagerly, his *Ja, ja, ja*, almost joyful, while his eyes watched Jacques warily.

As the officer spoke, the Kraut non-com lost his composure for a second, his eyes widening and his mouth turned down in a frown of disgust. The look passed, and his face went impassive as he stared once again at the ground, knowing his lieutenant was leaving him to the *Maquis*. Betrayal is a bitter thing.

Kaz raised his Webley. The sergeant closed his eyes. Kaz swung the pistol around and shot the officer in the head, the *crack* of his revolver loud against the silence.

"This man, I think," Kaz said, smiling grimly at the sergeant who now wore bits of his lieutenant's brain on his sleeve, along with a stunned look on his face.

Jacques snapped out orders, and a partisan produced a length of rope, tying our prisoner's hands behind his back. They tossed him in the back of our jeep, removed his boots, and tied his feet as well. Then Jacques's lad jumped in the back seat, his Sten gun aimed at the Kraut's belly.

"I am Lucien," he said. "We will meet *mon père* in Les Touvets. He will tell you about Major Rast. Please tell this *Boche salaud* I will kill him if he moves."

"Pleased to meet you, Lucien," Kaz said, introducing us as I drove back over the bridge. Then he spoke to the German, who answered in a few quick grunts. "This is *Feldwebel* Krause, and he may well be a bastard, but he is the bastard we want. If you must shoot, do not kill him. He may be quite useful to us."

"I will shoot his legs then," Lucien said and laughed, aiming the Sten at Krause's knees. Thankfully, his finger was off the trigger. It was a bumpy ride, and I didn't want shattered kneecaps littering the jeep.

Rifle shots and cries rippled behind us. Rough justice for Russian and French turncoats.

"What did you say to that Kraut lieutenant?" I asked Kaz.

"I merely inquired if he'd prefer his sergeant to be released into our custody, or himself," Kaz said. "He said as an officer, he insisted on being taken prisoner by uniformed forces. He did not even ask about his sergeant."

"Which you thought might put our *Feldwebel* in the mood to rat out another officer," I said. "Good plan."

"Yes, and it had the added benefit of eliminating another Nazi from the face of the earth. His fate at the hands of the *Maquis* would have been far worse, if you care to look at it from his viewpoint," Kaz said. "Which I do not. From what Jacques said, his security detachment was especially vicious—killing, burning, and raping, often in the company of the *Milice*."

"Men with no home and nothing to lose can do terrible things," I said.

"Are you talking about me, Billy, or the German I shot?"

Kaz laughed and slapped my arm to show he was joking. I hadn't meant him, of course. This was just the way Kaz had of making it through another day of horrors. But at the same time, I knew he existed on a knife's edge, and that his perfectly cultivated outward appearance masked sorrow deeper than I could imagine.

We found the turning where we'd gone wrong, and Lucien directed us to Les Touvets, informing us we were back behind the American lines. We were stretched pretty damn thin along here, and I wished the Ghost Army was at work in this neck of the woods.

We rolled into the village, attracting quite a crowd as Lucien grinned and the locals began cursing and spitting at our prisoner. I parked in front of a café, and people swarmed the jeep, congratulating Lucien, asking for news of partisans killed or wounded, and unleashing pent-up rage against the German sergeant.

"Lucien," I said, gently pushing aside an old man who was shaking his fist in the Kraut's direction. "We need to question this man. I don't want him fearing for his life."

"Oui," Lucien said. "We can take care of him later." He moved the villagers, all the time keeping an eye on our bound captive.

"We can't give him to the partisans," I said. "Not after taking him this far."

"Of course not," Kaz said. His ready agreement led me to wonder if he thought the Kraut might speak English. "Unless he has nothing useful to say."

"Yes," I said, playing along. "Then we'll let the French have him."

For the first time since his lieutenant was shot, he reacted. Looking up, he met my eyes, then Kaz's. He stared at us, then returned his gaze to the rope tied around his ankles.

"Perhaps I chose incorrectly," Kaz said. "We shall see."

I watched the eyes of the villagers lingering over the German. Hatred burned in their glares. Memories of atrocities recent and past, the burden of years of obedience to their occupiers, the shame of defeat and compliance in ways large and small, all simmered in a ferocity that would take only a single word, the movement of a crooked finger, a wink, or a few casual steps away from the jeep to unleash.

Right then I felt like the only sane man in the world, one who didn't particularly like the responsibility of sanity when everyone else seemed pleased with their own madness.

"Do you think we can ever forgive what these bastards have done?" I asked Kaz. "For our own sake, if not theirs?"

"Forgiveness? When those who fell at their hands rise and give their blessing, I will consider it," Kaz said. "Otherwise, I believe forgiveness would be a great injustice to the dead. And to those yet to die."

The *Feldwebel* looked up, not at us, but at the blue sky and green trees at the edge of the village. As if it might be the last bit of beauty he'd ever see.

CHAPTER FIFTEEN

JACQUES AND HIS men showed up an hour later, hanging off a rickety Berliet truck with captured weapons and a few dozen pairs of boots stacked in the back. I still didn't think it was right to strip boots off dead GIs, but when it came to Krauts, I figured it was the one decent thing they could do before marching off to Nazi Valhalla. Shoe leather had been in short supply during the Occupation, and I'd seen plenty of folks wearing wooden clogs. A little looted German footwear was fine by me.

Jacques distributed the boots to the villagers, making sure the elderly got first pick. Everyone treated him with respect and a touch of awe. He was popular, unlike Legrand, who seemed feared in comparison. As the truck rumbled off with most of his men aboard, Jacques spoke with Lucien while eyeing our German.

"*Mon père* asks if you would like him to make the *Boche* talk," Lucien offered, nodding toward our prisoner.

"No, thank you," I said, preferring my own methods. I liked knowing that what a prisoner gave up was reliable, not just what he thought would buy him a few more hours on the right side of the grass. "But we would like some food. The café?"

Jacques led the way to an outside table in the shade of a poplar tree where we could keep an eye on the jeep and Lucien as he guarded our prisoner. With the wariness of a guerrilla leader, Jacques took the seat against the wall, giving himself a good view in every direction. Through

Kaz, I complimented Jacques on what a good lad Lucien was. Jacques said yes, he was brave, but young, and sometimes foolish. He'd raised Lucien alone after his mother died in childbirth, and it was a hard life for them, even before the war. He was glad the fighting was about to pass by and leave his son in peace. Too young to join the French army, he might now have the life of a boy, at least for a while.

The café owner brought a bottle of wine and glasses. A smiling woman carried out a tray of bread and cheese, followed by three bowls of lentil soup. I was overwhelmed by the fragrant smells and the gnawing hunger they'd awoken in my belly. We toasted to peace and drank down the rough country wine, no finer taste to be found this side of a shallow grave.

Which made me wonder about Colonel Brewster's attack, and if Big Mike had gotten to Harding in time to warn him. If not, there'd be rows of shallow graves waiting.

Jacques broke a piece of bread, twisting it apart in his calloused hands. He stopped, the bread falling into his soup. He cupped a hand over his mouth and tears welled in his eyes. I looked to the jeep, ready for a glimpse of some unspeakable agony.

But no. It was Lucien, standing by the jeep, bowl in one hand. With the other he gave *Feldwebel* Krause spoonfuls of lentil soup. Krause nodded his thanks and hungrily took more.

Jacques choked back a sob. *"Mon Dieu,"* he said, then spoke in a choked whisper.

"He says he has taught Lucien how to kill, God help him," Kaz said. "But the boy knows mercy all on his own. He sees his dead wife in Lucien's gentleness, and it causes him great pain, but much joy."

Jacques rubbed his sleeve across his face and drank more wine. We finished our meal in silence, with the father watching his son treat a sworn enemy with a kindness beyond his understanding. Or mine, I had to admit. That might have been me not too long ago, willingly treating an enemy with kindness. But not today. I hadn't given our prisoner a second thought, beyond being happy he was trussed up tight.

"Rast?" I said, once the last of the dishes had been cleared away.

Kaz launched into a brief explanation of our investigation—*le meurtre du major Jérôme*—and how Rast's name had come up.

"*Un homme étrange,*" Jacques said, shaking his head as he spoke to Kaz.

"A strange man, even for a German, claims Jacques," Kaz said. "He came to this area to root out the *Groupe Rouge* and eliminate the *Réseau Nemo.* Although Jacques reluctantly admits the Nemo Line may have been Rast's main priority." Kaz leaned in to speak to Jacques, who nodded his agreement.

"Yes," Kaz said. "Jacques's group had conducted several attacks last year, but there were brutal reprisals, led by Rast himself. Ten men from a village close to where they derailed a troop train were shot and their houses burned. When they assassinated a *Milice* leader, more men were executed and their families sent to camps in Germany. Jacques then received orders from London to cease operations and wait for the invasion."

That fit with what I knew about the *Maquis* in the lead-up to D-Day. They'd been supplied with arms and given targets to hit, but only when the order was given. Any other actions resulted in harsh reprisals and the risk of the *Maquis* being annihilated before the invasion, when they'd really be needed.

"*Les sanglots longs, des violons, de l'automne,*" I said from memory, in what I knew was a terrible accent, more French Canadian than Norman.

"*Blessent mon coeur, d'une langueur, monotone,*" Jacques replied, grinning and speaking rapidly, gesturing grandly with his hands.

The BBC broadcast of the first line of the Paul Verlaine poem— "the long sobs of autumn violins"—meant that the invasion was to begin within two weeks. The second—"wound my heart with a monotonous languor"—signaled the invasion would start within two days, and that the Resistance should initiate major sabotage operations, especially against rail lines. Jacques and many others in touch with the Special Operations Executive had been glued to their hidden radios, waiting for that second stanza.

"The *Groupe Rouge* blew up rail lines and attacked a fuel depot,"

Kaz reported. "Jacques heard that Commandant Legrand, who he says is neither grand nor a commander of anything but a bunch of thieves, claimed some of the attacks were his."

"Tell him we know Legrand is a fraud. Ask if he thinks him a murderer," I said.

"Jacques says he heard we witnessed the executions yesterday and sees that we are not stupid men, so why do we ask such a question?"

"Had he heard of Major Jerome's murder at *Pressoir* Janvier?" I asked, liking Jacques more and more.

"*Oui,*" Jacques said, even before Kaz could translate.

"Legrand is greedy and cruel," Kaz said. "But sly. Jacques doubts he would kill an American. Unless there was much to gain."

"*Beaucoup,*" Jacques said, rubbing two fingers together in the unmistakable sign for money. Legrand was a suspect, although I failed to see how he benefited in any way by Jerome's death. Or how it helped anyone, for that matter.

"Does he know Madame Janvier?" I asked. "Corday?"

"Shh!" Jacques said, raising his finger to his lips and then wagging it at me, spouting off in a lecturing tone.

"He says, with apologies, that the Germans are still powerful and the Americans seem stuck in the *bocage*, while the English are even slower," Kaz said, translating as Jacques spoke. "The Nazis may be back, it is too soon to say otherwise. Therefore, some secrets should be kept until all the *Boche* are dead in their graves or on the far side of the Rhine River."

I nodded, meeting Jacques's eyes. He'd survived four years of Nazi occupation, and he hadn't done it by spouting his mouth off. He was right.

"*Désolé,*" I said, holding up my hand and asking what had happened after the invasion.

"He says that Rast hunted everywhere for their weapons caches," Kaz said, translating as Jacques went on. "He nearly found one, due to a *Groupe Rouge* fellow bragging to a woman, who then betrayed him to Rast."

"Should I ask what became of her?"

Jacques simply drew a finger across his throat.

"But Jacques says the odd thing is that Rast freed the man, Leon Dubois, shortly after the first line of the poem was broadcast. Jacques was certain that Dubois would be executed or sent to a concentration camp," Kaz said.

"Did Jacques think he talked?" I asked, then drew a finger against my own throat, eyebrow raised in a question to the partisan leader.

"No, he does not think so," Kaz said. "There were no further arrests, and the weapons caches were untouched. But Jacques was still suspicious. The Germans are not known for their mercy to suspected terrorists. To be safe, Jacques sent a message to Dubois telling him to stay away from the group, fearing the Germans might be watching him."

"Where is Leon Dubois now?" I asked.

"Saint-Jean," Kaz said. "Just west of Bricqueville. Dubois is a schoolteacher there and lives with his mother, who has a small apple orchard. Apparently, he did not complain about being cut off from the *Groupe Rouge*. Jacques thinks the arrest frightened him badly."

"Time in a German jailhouse will do that to a man," I said. "Or a Vichy French slammer, for that matter."

"Dubois was held in the same jail in Castillon where the *gendarme* released prisoners and was killed for it by the *Milice*. An unpleasant place, by all accounts," Kaz said. "Jacques fears a civil war if the *Milice* are not defeated quickly. There is much hatred on both sides."

"Will there be more reprisals after today?" I asked.

"Likely, if there are *Milice* left in the area, he says. But most of them are running to Paris, where they plan to defend the city. Jacques wishes to know what is taking us so long to get there ourselves," Kaz said with a weary smile.

"Tell him because there are not enough fighting men like the *Groupe Rouge*. And ask what else he can tell us about Rast."

"First, he says you flatter like a Frenchman. Then he says Rast changed after he released Dubois. There were no more raids to search for weapons, or escapees. The Germans still patrolled and manned roadblocks, but it was as if Rast knew the war was going badly for him.

For Germany, that is. Or perhaps Rast lost an informer who had supplied him with information, he does not know."

"Too bad more Krauts didn't take his attitude. Look at the troops we ran into today. Diehard officers shooting their own men," I said. "How bad was Rast before the release of Dubois?"

"Bad," Kaz said, after some back-and-forth. "Very bad. People disappeared under the *Nacht und Nebel* decree, a Nazi policy that resulted in prisoners vanishing into the camps, with no record kept of their fate. No way for family members to know what became of them. It is meant to terrorize those left behind as well as those sent away."

"Nuit et brouillard," Jacques said.

"Night and fog," Kaz said.

"Is Rast alive?" I asked. Jacques shrugged as he spoke.

"He was seen the day the Germans withdrew from Bricqueville," Kaz said. "But never again. Jacques captured some of Rast's men as they left, and they claimed not to know where he was. But they were under quite a bit of stress." This time it was Kaz who did the finger across the throat move.

"The *Milice* and Gestapo men Dr. Leroy mentioned?" I asked.

"Leroy?" Jacques repeated, his lips turned up in a sneer as he whispered to Kaz.

"He knows Dr. Leroy was part of the Nemo Line," Kaz said, keeping his voice low. "He suspects Leroy may have betrayed the last downed airmen to be brought to the hospital several months ago. Since then, Jacques has avoided using the hospital. He says Leroy used to provide medical care when any of his men were hurt, but he no longer trusts him."

"Is he sure?" I asked.

"No," Kaz said. "Which is why Dr. Leroy is still alive. Not that living with all those crazy people is much of a life, as Jacques says."

"Back to the men Jacques captured," I said. "Did he actually interrogate them about Rast's whereabouts?"

"Yes," Kaz said. "He wants Rast to answer for his crimes and still has not given up looking for him. He had hoped Rast would be with the Germans he attacked today, since that unit was under his command. As for the men he captured after the invasion, the *Milice* did nothing but beg for their lives. But the Gestapo man called Rast a traitor and said he'd lead Jacques to him if he knew where he was."

"What did Jacques think of that?" I asked.

Another shrug, another finger across the throat, another drink of wine.

It seemed as if Rast had disappeared into the night and fog of war.

CHAPTER SIXTEEN

IT WAS A lot to chew on. Was Dr. Leroy an informer? If so, had his betrayals led an unknown avenger back to *Pressoir* Janvier and Corday, finding Major Jerome in the wrong place at the wrong time? And what was behind Rast's freeing of Dubois and the easing up of his war on the *Maquis*? Was Dr. Leroy a double-agent for Rast? Did Dr. Leroy get cold feet and refuse to give Rast the inside scoop on the Nemo Line?

No, that last notion didn't wash. Rast would have put the screws to anyone who held out on him. The man was not shy about the application of power and pain. Screws which might have caused Dr. Leroy to betray escapees entrusted to his care and save his own skin to boot. But how did Rast uncover his involvement? Or was Jacques simply wrong in his suspicions? After all, Dr. Leroy was still alive, and if Jacques had any real evidence against him, he'd be nothing more than an anatomy lesson. I made a mental note to question Madame Janvier about Dr. Leroy and see if she shared any doubts about his loyalties.

Jacques and Lucien had already departed, the father telling us to leave word at the café if we needed to talk to him again, and promising to get word to Madame Janvier if he learned anything more about Rast. With his hand around his son's shoulder, they strolled around the corner of the café, Jacques glancing back, still suspicious of who was watching. A wise man.

"We need to question Dr. Leroy again," I said to Kaz as we returned to the jeep.

"Yes, I have been thinking about the good doctor since Jacques told us of his suspicions," Kaz said as we stood outside the café. "There is one thing about our talk with Leroy that strikes me as odd now that I recall it. We told him we were investigating a murder."

"He never asked who the victim was, did he?" I said. I'd been focused on his story of finding Yvonne and hadn't thought back over the entire conversation. It would have been a natural question if he didn't know, and if he did, why hadn't he mentioned it and how he'd come by the information?

"Not that I remember," Kaz said. "I would like to know why and if there is any truth to airmen being taken from the hospital. And why there apparently were no reprisals."

"Agreed. But right now, let's focus on Krause and see if we get anything useful before we put him in a POW cage."

"And we should question Leon Dubois as well," Kaz said. "He may know more about Rast than he lets on. Jacques can be quite intimidating, I think."

"Right. So let's play hardball with Krause. Our well-fed German friend may be in a mood to talk, especially if he thinks we may still turn him over to the *Maquis*," I said.

"Or to a vengeful Pole," Kaz said, his smile creased by that dreadful scar.

Krause avoided our eyes as we approached him. If I were in his place, I wouldn't want to chance catching a glimmer of hatred from Kaz or to be confronted with the self-assured swagger of an American. A few years ago—long years for the conquered people of Europe—Germans like Krause chewed up Poland and then Russia, leaving corpses and fear in their wake. If you had told him in 1940 that one day he'd be at the mercy of Polish and American officers in a liberated French village, it would have been beyond his Germanic comprehension.

Today, he wasn't much of a superman. He had dried blood and gray matter on his sleeve and soup stains on his tunic. I stood next to him, arms crossed, waiting for him to look up. When he did, the fight was gone out of him. His face sagged with defeat and disorientation. The rush and thrill of battle had long worn off. Fear was always present, but the flow of adrenaline had a way of sustaining you amidst a rage of bullets, bodies, and blood. When it was over, the fear returned in company with exhaustion, a weariness of body and soul that grabbed you by the throat. It took time, booze, or both to let it go. Krause was right there.

I took the combat knife from my belt and walked behind him. He stiffened as I drew the blade against the ropes binding his wrists. I could hear his exhale, and it sounded like a prayer, or thanks for one answered. Then I sliced through the rope around his ankles and gestured for him to take the front seat. He rose slowly and stiffly, grabbing hold of his boots, which lay on the floor beside him.

"*Keine Schuhe,*" Kaz snapped, and Krause dropped the boots, nodding his soldier's understanding. It was harder to run cross-country in stocking feet. He flashed a brief smile as he got into the passenger seat. After all, his prospects were looking better. He was alive, he still had his boots, he hadn't been handed over to the partisans, and he'd been fed lunch. Plus, he'd seen the lieutenant who sold him downriver get his brains blown out. I knew plenty of guys who'd be happy with less.

I started the jeep and Kaz got in the back, tapping Krause on the shoulder with his Webley revolver, counseling him on how to behave.

"Let's see if we can find a POW compound," I said. "Maybe near where we saw those Krauts digging graves this morning."

"Or perhaps a quiet spot in the woods," Kaz said, the barrel of his pistol resting against Krause's neck. He gave me a wink, so I'd think he was kidding. But I knew Kaz, and the burden of grief he bore for his family and his country. Not to mention the loathing for his nation's conquerors, Nazi and Soviet alike. If he was joking, it was gallows humor, and the punch line was at Krause's neck.

"No woods," Krause said. "I will say what I know."

"Well, well," Kaz said with a grin. "He does speak English. I thought as much."

"You want no woods?" I said, driving out of the village. "Answer our questions and tonight you'll be behind barbed wire being served American chow. Understand?"

"Chow?" Krause said.

"Food. Lots of it," I said. He nodded, as if agreeing to the terms of a business deal. "Start talking."

"No lies," Kaz said, his pistol still at Krause's back. "Or you will join your *Leutnant*."

"He was a pig," Krause said.

"Because he would have traded his life for yours?" I asked. "Would you have done different?"

"Officers should help soldiers. Not shoot them. Not give them to partisans."

"He was one of the officers shooting his men this morning?" I asked.

"*Ja*. He hates Russians. Good Russian, bad Russian, all the same to *Leutnant* Hauck," Krause said. "We were in the east together. Very bad."

"On the Eastern Front?" Kaz asked.

"*Ja*. Yes. Outside Minsk. Hauck was my *Leutnant*. I was made *Feldwebel* to lead Russian volunteers. Better for them to fight in France than against other Russians, the army says. So we bring them here."

"When?" I asked.

"Three months ago," Krause said. "France is much better. Russians like it here."

"The French do not like them much," Kaz said. "As you saw."

"Yes. Major Rast told our Ivans we are in France to hunt Communists. The Reds who wear the *foulard*," he said, coming up with the word in French. "Our Russians hate the Reds."

"Such as the boy who fed you soup?" Kaz asked. "Not exactly a ruthless commissar." As we drove past houses and through fields and farmland, a flight of aircraft flew low overhead. Krause ducked instinctively. They were Thunderbolts, looking to bomb and strafe his pals.

"*Bitte?*" Krause said as he looked up, following the flight of the fighter-bombers. Kaz gave him that last sentence again in German.

"*Ja.* He was kind. French Reds nothing like Soviets. No kindness in the east. Everybody kills. Partisans, Soviets, Germans, everyone. These Russians live close to death. You, a Pole, know this," Krause said to Kaz.

"I do know," Kaz said. "The French wear their red scarves proudly, but they are children when it comes to being Communists. They do not know what Stalin is like."

"I was Red when I was younger," Krause said. "In Kiel. Many who worked in the shipyard were Reds."

"What happened?" I asked.

"Brownshirts," he said. "Nazis came. Killed Reds. Too many Nazis. I quit the Party. Better to stay alive, *ja?*" We drove through a wooded lane, under cover of green foliage and dappled sunlight. It seemed to remind Krause that this could be a one-way ride. "I tell you things, okay? At POW camp."

"Where did you learn English?" Kaz asked, tapping Krause on the cheek with the barrel of his pistol, hinting that nothing was settled about his ultimate destination.

"In Kiel," he said. "Dockyard. Many ships from England, America, Russia. I learn a little of each language. The army sends me to Russia, I think, so I can talk with Russian volunteers."

"Volunteers? Are they really anti-Communist?" Kaz asked.

"Some. But mostly they know German camp means death. Prisoners starve, *ja?* And if they live, Stalin shoots them after war for giving up. So no choice if they want to eat. And live. Same with me. Officer tells me what to do. I must obey or die. You saw today."

"Does that include rape and murder? Burning homes and sending families to concentration camps?" Kaz asked. I wasn't sure if Krause understood all the words, but he got the drift.

"Russian boys have nothing. No country. No honor. No family to go home to. All they have is killing and to obey officers. Officers like Hauck. Is very bad, I know. But I do not join in. I fight, but I do not kill like them. Perhaps you do not believe me, but this is true."

"Tell us about Rast," I said, turning a corner and heading out through open fields again. I liked breathing in the fresh air a lot better than the stink of this guy's guilt.

Or I didn't like listening to him because his story made some logical, terrible sense. At what point would I disobey an order and risk a bullet for my troubles? Or let myself be marched off to a camp where I'd starve or be worked to death? We all like to think we're better than the enemy. But no one knows where that dividing line really is.

"When we get to camp, I tell you about Rast," Krause said. "I talk now, you shoot me in woods."

"Let's just get this over with," I said, pulling over slowly on the side of the road. "He doesn't know anything."

"*Nein, nein*, I do," Krause said, gripping the seat as if we were about to drag him away. Which was one possible outcome of the chat we were about to have. The sun baked down on us, nothing but a field of tall grass on either side of a lonely, dusty road. A fly buzzed Krause, and he swatted it away.

"Make me believe," I said. Sweat broke out on Krause's temple, and his face went pale. Perfect.

"Rast did not leave when we withdrew from Bricqueville," he said, his words tumbling out in frantic desperation.

"We know that already," Kaz said, thumbing the hammer back on his Webley.

"But his files. Do you know about the files?" Krause said, looking back and forth between us.

Kaz uncocked his revolver. "Of course," he said. "But tell us what you know. Perhaps there is something we have missed."

"Enough to save your life," I said, playing tough. "Maybe."

But Krause was wary. He'd stayed alive on the Kiel docks when the Nazi brownshirts came calling and survived the Eastern Front, so he didn't spook easily. He read our faces and then settled back in his seat.

"Let us go to POW camp. Have coffee and cigarettes, and I tell you about Rast and his files. Secret files. You know nothing, I can tell. *Ja?*"

Ja. We knew nothing, Krause had that right. I looked at Kaz, who grinned, enjoying the absurdity of the situation. Our hunt for clues had turned up nothing, even though we had the full weight and force of the US Army behind us. Now *Feldwebel* Krause, recently arrived from the Eastern Front, promised to reveal what secrets Rast had kept in his files.

All we had to do was give him coffee and cigarettes. It was a helluva war.

CHAPTER SEVENTEEN

WITHOUT A MAP, we were faced with a long return trip to Bricqueville. We knew the road back via Rubercy, but that looped us to the north, taking maybe an hour more than it had to. We found ourselves at an unmarked crossroads, one branch heading up to Rubercy, the other two in the general direction of Bricqueville and what we called home.

"Which way is POW camp?" Krause wanted to know.

"We can go through Rubercy, but that will take awhile," I said. I considered going that way to stop at the hospital and have another chat with Dr. Leroy, but decided to do that tomorrow without a prisoner in tow.

"We are not quite certain of the camp's location, I must admit," Kaz said. "All we saw on the way here was a party of prisoners digging graves, suggesting there must be a POW enclosure nearby."

"There's another option," I said. "We go back to *Pressoir* Janvier and have smokes and hot joe with Krause. Maybe a little calvados as well. Then we turn our *Feldwebel* over to Major Johnson."

"Who is Johnson?" Krause asked, sounding suspicious.

"The battalion G-2," I said. "Intelligence. He'll want to talk to you. Then he'll find you a camp."

"This is a promise?" Krause asked.

"Yes," I said. We hadn't met Johnson yet, but getting a prisoner to a POW cage was standard operating procedure for a G-2 officer.

"Then take this road," Krause said, pointing to the right. "It goes to Bricqueville."

"The other road?" Kaz asked, pointing to the left.

"It will take you to the German lines. Two, three kilometers and the machine guns will open up," Krause said. "I will show you the way to Bricqueville. I know it well."

"I will shoot you if it is a trick," Kaz said, rapping his pistol barrel hard enough against Krause's head to show he meant business.

"No trick. I am glad for my war to be over. I have seen enough, done enough. I am tired of people wanting to shoot me. I wish there was no war, but it came, I had to fight. You understand?"

"I understand plenty," I said, taking the right turn. "I understand you better deliver."

"*Bitte?*" Krause asked, turning to Kaz.

"Billy says you must tell the truth. And we must find it useful. *Wertvoll*," Kaz said. "Valuable."

"*Ja, wertvoll,*" Krause said. "It will be. This I promise, Billy. Rast was a strange man. A bad man, even for a Nazi."

"You're not a Nazi, then?" I asked, figuring there'd be damn few who claimed to be party members by the time we got to Berlin.

"*Nein!* I was a member of the KDP until Hitler ended it," Krause said, with enough indignation to make me think he really was telling the truth.

"He means the *Kommunistische Partei Deutschlands,*" Kaz added. "Strange that you ended up in the workers' paradise after all." Krause didn't catch all that, and Kaz had to translate. He laughed. A good, hearty laugh.

"*Ja!* Some days I think we are all fools, and the gods of war, they play with us. Go slow here, there are artillery spotters in the hills," Krause said, pointing to a ridge to our south. I did, easing up on the accelerator and coasting to a crawl so I wouldn't kick up dust with a hard brake.

"Thanks," I said.

"*Staub bedeutet Tod,*" Krause said.

"Dust means death," Kaz clarified.

Some things are the same no matter what side you're on.

"Will they send me to America? Or England?" Krause wanted to know, clearly enjoying the notion of being out of the shooting war.

"All I know is we're stuck here, so don't bring it up, okay? We may change our minds," I said. I'd read in *Stars and Stripes* about German and Italian prisoners being shipped back to the States, a lot of them sent out west to work on farms. A rest cure compared to the Russian Front.

"I am sorry, Billy," Krause said. He sounded like he enjoyed saying my name. Or maybe he was practicing sounding like an American. "My name is Anton."

He turned to Kaz, smiling. Kaz ignored him.

"Okay, Anton," I said. "How'd you like the Janvier place? Were you quartered there?"

"Quartered? You mean where I slept? *Ja*, I was. In one of the barns. The one where the calvados is made. *Das Kupfer*," he said, turning to Kaz for help.

"The copper still," Kaz said.

"*Ja*, we were ordered not to touch it. Calvados for officers only. Rast was very strict on this."

"I am surprised the copper was not taken away and sent to Germany," Kaz said, speaking up from the back seat as we rattled over the uneven road.

"In the East, we take everything. Here, the army wants calvados, so we leave alone. Rast punished any man who took even apples without paying. Very hard man, but kind to the French. Not the terrorists, but the people."

"They would not think of themselves as terrorists," I said, giving Anton a sideways glance.

"No, that is right. But it is what we call them. What the army calls them. Better than *Maquis*, which is *romantisch*. The *Milice* insist on it. To them, all who resist Vichy are traitors," Anton said.

"What do you think?" Kaz asked, with another tap of his pistol barrel.

"I think today I would rather be a *Maquis*, now that the Allies are here. Not *Milice* and not Russian. And I think there will be many who join the *Maquis*, now that the fighting is almost over."

"Do you know of Commandant Legrand and his men?" I asked as we came to another crossroads, this one out in the open at the top of a small rise.

"No secrets until I am POW," Anton said, frowning.

I didn't know I was asking about a secret. "Sorry," I said. "I thought it was well known that Legrand came late to the Resistance. I wasn't trying to trick you. Which way?"

"This way," Anton said, pointing out the next turn. "I will tell you all about Legrand. Later."

"With cigarettes and coffee," I said. Anton smiled.

Clouds blew in from the north. Dark clouds, heavy with water. A breeze turned into steady winds as we drove through a gutted village, its shattered church steeple and burned-out houses testament to the fighting that had raged here recently. Yesterday, last week, last month, it was hard to tell. The front lines rolled back and forth over these small villages so often it was amazing any two stones were still left standing.

"I am not sure where we are," Anton said. "This does not look familiar."

"Perhaps the village was intact when you last saw it," Kaz said, looking around as I stopped the jeep. There wasn't a soul in sight.

"I'll try the radio again," I said. I gave the call sign and got a faint response from Able Victor Two. It was Sullivan, from what I could make out through the interference. It was good to know we were close, probably at the far end of the radio's range. I described the route we'd taken and this village as best I could, then told him to alert Major Johnson that we were bringing in a prisoner. He said to stay put and that he'd be back in touch.

"Sullivan's checking," I said.

"This looks familiar," Anton said, getting out of the jeep and heading to what might have been a restaurant. He stepped gingerly as he navigated the rubble in his stocking feet.

"Here," Kaz said, getting out of the jeep with Anton's boots.

"*Danke,*" Anton said as he put them on. Kaz said nothing, resting his hand on the butt of his holstered pistol. It was hard to believe a few hours ago, Kaz was deciding whether to shoot Anton or his lieutenant. A drive in the country on a first-name basis and a bit of conversation tended to make an enemy more of a human being. Not that Kaz would ever admit it.

Anton kicked over building stones and timbers, uncovering a sign. It was charred, but intact enough to show this had once been the Restaurant Marcouf.

"This is Fierville," Anton said. "I passed through once. It was full of people."

We stood looking at the ruined church, the houses and shops, blasted beyond recognition. Who had done this? Our bombers? German artillery? American artillery? Or had everyone joined in the destruction to reduce Fierville to rubble?

Who was responsible? We could point to Anton or others who wore his uniform, decorated with a lot more braid and buttons. But this kind of total devastation went beyond finger-pointing, and Fierville was the wrong place to acknowledge anything but our roles as cogs in a machine that chewed up lives and left empty, ruined spaces behind.

"Able Victor One, over." Sullivan's scratchy voice on the radio crashed through the silence, like someone screaming during a funeral. I grabbed the receiver and acknowledged. I told him we were in Fierville, or what was left of it. He gave me directions back, telling us to be careful. German patrols had been reported in the area. I asked about Colonel Brewster's big push to take that hill. Sullivan said it hadn't gone well. Which was why there were Germans probing the woods around Bricqueville.

Raindrops began to fall from the darkening clouds moving in from the north. I told Kaz to keep Anton covered as I raised the canvas top. I didn't say anything about German troops in the area. No reason to give Anton any ideas, no matter how pleased he seemed to be about sitting out the rest of the war.

By the time we got underway, a steady drumbeat of rain was pelting the canvas and drenching the road. The good news was, we didn't have to worry about dust. But I did need to slow down to not run us off the road. Between Sullivan's directions and Anton's knowledge of the local roads, we gradually made our way to the outskirts of Bricqueville.

"It is not far," Anton said, as I slowed to make the turn. Vehicles emerged from the woods ahead, and we pulled off the road to make way for the two heavy trucks marked with red crosses. Casualties being taken to a field hospital, probably courtesy of Colonel Brewster's offensive. "Coffee and cigarettes, *ja*?"

"And calvados," Kaz said. "This is the perfect weather for it."

The trucks passed, splashing us with muddy water. I gunned the jeep, one tire spinning madly as it tried to gain traction in the wet soil at the edge of the road. I leaned out, looking back to see how deeply I was digging in.

A rifle shot cracked.

A warm spray of blood hit my neck. I jammed the gearshift into reverse, my foot heavy on the pedal. We flew backward as another round was fired, this one sounding muffled by the pouring rain and the pounding of my heart. I managed to get the jeep back on the road, my hand slippery with blood as I shifted into first and raced ahead, hoping speed and poor visibility would throw the shooter off.

I rounded a bend, putting a line of trees and a good distance between us and the spot where we were ambushed. I slowed, turning to check on Kaz. His face was flecked with blood. He held Anton by the shoulders, his fingers gripping the *feldgrau* uniform tightly and his white knuckles covered in gore.

"His head exploded," Kaz said, his voice reduced to a shaky whisper. "Exploded."

Anton had taken a bullet square above his ear. The entry wound was a sizable hole. Where the slug had exited, well, there just wasn't much of his skull left on that side.

Poor Anton. No coffee, no cigarettes. No calvados, no secrets to tell. I felt bad for him, and oddly enough, good about myself. I was sorry a Kraut was dead. Maybe there was hope for my soul after all.

"Billy," Kaz said. "Was that bullet meant for you?"

"I don't know," I said. In truth, I hadn't had time to think about it. If I hadn't looked backward, I might have taken the hit to the head. Was it a sniper from one of the German patrols infiltrating the area? Or someone else, someone who didn't want this investigation to go any further?

I stopped the jeep.

"If that was meant for me, why?" I asked. "It's not like we're onto anything."

"We may have been, if Anton were able to tell his tale," Kaz said, loosening his grip. "What should we do with him?"

"Can you keep hold of him? Let's get him back and give him a decent burial," I said.

"Yes," Kaz said, holding onto the corpse of his enemy. "There has been little decency to be had this day, so let us finish with a decent burial, by all means."

There was a flinty edge in Kaz's voice, and I really had no idea who he was angry with. And I didn't want to know.

CHAPTER EIGHTEEN

"WHY YOU GOT a Kraut with his head blown off?" asked a GI in a rain poncho as we pulled in at *Pressoir* Janvier, not far from the barn where Anton had once slept. The soldier had a pained expression on his face, which had less to do with the rain than with the prospect of digging another grave, especially for a German. He stood next to half a dozen corpses, leaning on a shovel and squinting as raindrops dripped from his helmet. Beyond him, other GIs were lowering bodies into hastily dug graves and tossing in shovelfuls of oozing mud.

"We were bringing in a prisoner," I said. "Someone took a potshot at us about half a mile back. Do us a favor and take care of him, okay?"

"You're lucky they missed you, Captain. Tough as hell on the Kraut, though."

"His name was Anton Krause," Kaz said, stepping out from the rear of the jeep and grasping Anton under the shoulders. Rain sluiced down Anton's ruined brow, sending rivulets of pink foam to pool on the ground. "And I would like him to be given a decent burial. I am not certain he lived every moment of his life with decency, but he should not be forgotten by the side of the road at the end of it."

Kaz laid out Anton's body and stood by it, eyeing the skeptical GI. Maybe it was Kaz standing there coatless, oblivious to the soaking he was taking. Maybe it was the sound of rain splattering against the tent halves covering the bodies of the dead. Maybe it was how Kaz rested his hand on the butt of his revolver. Whatever the reason, the GI didn't hesitate another moment.

"Sure, Lieutenant, I'll take care of him. Off to the side of these boys, but I'll do him right." He bent down, and tugged at the chain holding Anton's zinc identity tag. He snapped half off and went through Anton's pockets, coming up with his *Soldbuch*, which he handed to Kaz. Unlike American dog tags, the Germans used a single perforated disk with duplicate information on each side. One side stayed with Anton for burial, the other went with the *Soldbuch*, the pay book every German soldier carried, giving his identification and a full record of his units and postings.

"Give those to Captain Johnson," the GI said. "He'll want the dope about this guy, and it'll be a record of his death. Might help his family someday."

"Thank you," Kaz said, his hand dropping from his holster. "That is quite kind of you."

"Ain't much."

"In this world, it is more than many get," Kaz said, turning and walking away, his boots sucking up mud and despair.

I left Kaz and drove the jeep to the annex at the rear of Madame Janvier's house. I passed the medic's tent, marked with a red cross. Wounded men, most of them upright but swathed in bandages, made their way under their own power to the nearby barn. A jeep sped toward the tent, a casualty on a stretcher strapped to the hood. Kaplan and another medic raced out and grabbed the stretcher, carrying the wounded man inside.

It didn't look like the attack had gone well.

I parked at the annex where Captain Johnson had his office, one door down from the communications room. Madame Janvier appeared in the radio room doorway, soaked to the bone and cleaning her hands with a bloody rag.

"Oh, Captain Boyle, are you hurt?" she asked, as I jumped from the jeep and ran to the doorway. I realized I had blood on me, running a faded red with the rain.

"No, a sniper took a shot at our jeep," I said. "They hit a prisoner we were bringing in."

"The baron is unhurt?"

"Yes, here he comes," I said, as Kaz appeared, looking even worse than I did.

"Mon Dieu," she said, taking in the reddish-pink hue of Kaz's jacket. "This is a horrible day."

"Looks like it," I said. "Is anyone hurt in here?"

"Minor wounds," she said. "Lieutenant Friedman, among others. I helped with the less serious cases." I recalled she'd worked in a military hospital during the last war.

"Doesn't feel minor to me," Friedman said, exiting his office and holding a hand to his bandaged head. Two other men were on the floor, one with a bandaged hand and the other holding a compress to his thigh, where his pants had been cut away. Madame Janvier returned to the man, telling him that the medics would see him as soon as they could, and to be brave. He gave her a smile, the best he could muster.

"Was it bad?" I asked Friedman.

"Started out okay, I guess," he said. "Then the Krauts counterattacked, and we got ourselves kicked back to the starting line. The only thing that kept them from overrunning us was a good shelling. Those Second Armored boys may be a little shy about fighting, but at least they helped with a healthy dose of artillery."

If he only knew.

"Glad you're okay, Friedman," I said. "I've got to see Johnson now. We got mixed up in a *Maquis* ambush and had a POW to bring him, but one of the Kraut infiltrators fired on us. Shot their own man by mistake."

"Yeah, rumors are flying about Germans in the woods. But no one's actually seen one, far as I can tell. Hey, was it Legrand's bunch? Be nice to know they were actually fighting the Germans instead of each other."

"No. *Groupe Rouge*. A bunch of Reds led by a fellow named Jacques. Tough bunch. They were after one of Major Rast's units of

Russian volunteers," I said. "They were hoping to take Rast, but he wasn't there."

"From what I hear, Rast is a slippery bastard," Friedman said. "I'd hate to be in his shoes if the *Maquis* ever do get a hold of him."

"Jacques was not successful?" Madame Janvier asked, rising from treating her patient.

"He was, except for the part about capturing Rast. What can you tell me about Jacques?" I asked.

"Not now, there is still much to be done. I will talk with you and the baron later," she said, clasping her worn and soaked sweater to her breast and making for the door.

"I've heard he's a strange man," I said, following her to the doorway.

"I would say a puzzling man," she said, her face uplifted to the darkened sky and the pelting rain. "He could be brutal, but I suspect he was not entirely pleased with what he had to do. Quite the contrary, at times. *Au revoir.*" With that, she dashed into the downpour and ran across to the medical tent.

I darted out and found Kaz in the G-2 office, where Major Johnson looked in far better shape than Friedman. The battalion's intelligence officer had the look of a lawyer about him, from the pipe clenched between his teeth to his wire-rimmed spectacles and clean fingernails. He had flecks of gray at the temples and dark pouches under his eyes. If he stood up, I wouldn't be surprised to see pin-striped pants.

He and Kaz were quite a contrast. My partner's steel-rimmed glasses were glazed with a pink haze, and his dirty uniform was dripping streams of water on the floor in front of Johnson's desk.

"You're Boyle, right?" Johnson said, hardly looking up as he leafed through Anton's *Soldbuch*.

"Good news travels fast," I said. "That of any use to you?"

"I would have liked it better if the German who had this in his pocket was still alive," Johnson said. "We've wanted to know more about this security unit. They're not front-line troops, so we don't often get a crack at them. And when the Resistance boys do, they don't bother taking prisoners."

"Tell me what you see in that book," Kaz said, taking off his wool cap and shaking the water out. He pulled up a chair and sank into it, looking at his feet, as if just now registering the mud, filth, blood, and sodden wool. I sat on a bench by the window, raindrops lashing the glass.

"This Sergeant Krause was transferred here from the Eastern Front three months ago," Johnson said, his finger tracing the lines of German and translating as he went. "Originally mustered into the *Wehrmacht* in 1939. Born in Kiel. Civilian profession, dockyard worker. Sent to Russia in 1943 from a replacement company in Germany and promoted to *Feldwebel*. There's a note about his language skills, which seems to account for the promotion. Looks like he served here with a *Feldgendarmerie* made up mainly of Russian volunteers."

"Nothing out of the ordinary? He didn't serve with the SS or in any of the camps?" Kaz asked.

"No. The German military police are separate from the SS, as you probably know. They can be bastards, but not like the SS or the Gestapo. Why do you ask?"

"Yeah, all that fits with what Anton told us," I said, looking to Kaz. "Why are we going through this?"

"Two reasons," Kaz said, standing and brushing down his arms, sending thick droplets of mud and dried blood to the floor. "I will explain later."

He walked out. Johnson looked to me, eyebrows raised.

"Sorry about that," I said. "Kaz is usually very polite."

"He's the baron Madame Janvier is always talking about, right?"

"That's him. It's been a rough day. We got caught up in an ambush. You know the *Groupe Rouge*?"

"Excellent fighters," Johnson said, fiddling with his pipe. "The *Milice* have a special hatred for them since they're Communists. And it works both ways. It's a bloodbath when they get into a brawl."

I didn't bother mentioning the truckload of *Milice* who drove into the shooting match today. When it came to summary executions in the field, the less put down on paper, the better.

"Better fighters than Legrand?" I asked.

"Legrand has some value," Johnson said, tossing Anton's *Soldbuch* aside. "He's good at reconnaissance. Not so good at a stand-up fight. He was nowhere to be seen today, for instance."

"Did you expect him? You're the liaison with the local Resistance, right?"

"I am. I saw Legrand yesterday and asked him to scout our right flank again and try to locate those Second Armored tanks. Never heard from him. Might've gotten overrun when the Krauts hit us back, for all I know," Johnson said.

"It was bad?" I asked.

"Brewster's madder than a hornet," Johnson said. As if that was the worst part of a day that ended with bodies being buried in water-filled graves. "He wanted to take that hill real bad. Instead, they hit us hard right when we started the attack."

"You were there?" I asked. He gave me a sharp look, as if it were an insult to ask. Which I wouldn't have, if his ODs had had a speck of mud on them.

"Yes. I collected two prisoners. Yours would have made a grand total of three if he'd made it back in one piece. Not much to show," he said. "And now I've got Brewster demanding new intel so he can plan another attack." He shook his head at the injustice. He'd have to work all night at his desk, perhaps. Pity.

"Any chance Legrand or one of his men tipped off the Krauts?" I asked.

"Not a chance in hell, Boyle," Johnson said, his face flushing red. Which told me he'd been worried about that himself. "I've been working with Legrand since we came to this sector. He's been reliable, long as you don't ask too much of him. He might have a healthy regard for his own longevity, but that doesn't make him a traitor. Not in my book, by God!"

"Okay, okay," I said. "Don't get all hot under the collar. It's just that the more I see of how the French are going after each other, the more I wonder about how easy it would be to switch sides. Or play the double agent game."

"That's just it, Boyle. They hate each other too much to switch sides. It's like the Hatfields and the McCoys out there. But I grant you, the double agent angle is possible. Anyone who was captured or detained during the Occupation is suspect. If they're still alive, they're not to be trusted."

"Does the name Leon Dubois mean anything to you?" I asked.

"No, should it?"

"He's a schoolteacher over in Saint-Jean," I said. "He was a member of the *Groupe Rouge*, but shot off his mouth about it to a girl. She sold him out, and Rast arrested him. Then after a few days, he let him go. Fits the profile you described."

"You know, that's not the first time I've heard of Rast releasing prisoners. From what I've seen, the Kraut military police are not in the business of forgiveness. Even if they thought a Frenchman was innocent, they'd send him to a work camp anyway," Johnson said.

"You question any of the people he let go?" I asked.

"No reason to. My job is to evaluate the enemy's intentions, not how they ran their security. Does this have anything to do with your murder investigation, or are you just wasting my time?"

"I'm following a lead. Since I can't see why anyone would target Major Jerome, I'm thinking he was simply in the wrong place at the wrong time. So I'm curious about anything out of the ordinary at *Pressoir* Janvier. That includes Legrand, Rast, Madame Janvier, and Yvonne Virot."

"Madame Janvier? What's off about her? She's a nice widow who's had a tough time of it and kept this place up and running," Johnson said, tapping out the ashes from his pipe bowl into an empty can. From his tone, I think I found the one man here who wasn't entranced by Yvonne. He had a soft spot for the good Madame. They weren't that far apart in age, after all, and I had to give him points for not falling for Sleeping Beauty.

"You must know about her involvement with the Nemo Line," I said. "The Resistance gave her the code name Corday."

"Sure I do. She told me all about it. That took courage, especially with the Germans headquartered here. But that doesn't mean she's a suspect," he said. "Makes no sense."

"I didn't say she was. But there could be some unfinished business that Jerome got caught up in, something related to the escape line. Maybe a betrayal that demanded revenge," I said.

"Well, I don't think she would have betrayed anyone. Legrand, that's another story. As far as Yvonne goes, I don't think she's capable of hurting anyone, expect maybe herself," Johnson said. He shuffled papers on his desk, a signal that he was tiring of this conversation and my supposed suspicions of Madame Janvier.

"Okay, I'll get out of your hair," I said, standing and feeling the damp chill in my bones. The rain had lessened, but the air was cold, a north wind blowing in off the Channel. "One other thing. Ever hear of Dr. Mathis Leroy?"

"Leroy? No, don't believe I have. Is he involved in this?"

"Wish I knew," I said. "Say, have you interrogated those two POWs yet? I'd like to have a chat with them before you send them off."

"Affirmative. I've got Sergeant Fair watching them over in the barn where he's bivouacked. MPs are supposed to collect them later tonight and take them up to the POW cage in Carentan. Don't know how much you'll get out of them. They're survivors from the 352nd Division. Got chewed up pretty bad after holding us up on Omaha Beach. Probably been too busy staying alive to get involved with Rast and the *Feldgendarmerie*. But have at 'em. You speak German?"

"No, but Kaz does," I said as I left, eager to find him. He'd been acting strangely, with good reason. I knew it took a lot to shake him. And he was really shook. Why had he asked Johnson to review the *Soldbuch* when he could have easily done it himself? Why leave so suddenly?

I walked to the kitchen doorway and pulled off my boots. I knocked off as much mud as I could before going inside. One thing my mother drummed into my head when I was a kid back in Southie was never to wear muddy shoes into the house.

The kitchen was warm and inviting. I set my boots down next to

Kaz's by the side of the stove, where heat reflected off the brick wall. I hung my field jacket between Kaz's soaked wool jacket and a sopping wet rain slicker that must have been Madame Janvier's. Water pooled on the stone floor beneath the garments, and I stood by the stove for a moment, enjoying the warmth.

Then I headed upstairs, looking for Kaz. Yvonne was in her chair by the window, staring at the streaks of rain. Only the weather changed; Yvonne remained the same.

No sign of Kaz or Big Mike in our room. Thinking Kaz might be washing up, I walked up to the bathroom at the end of the hall. I knocked on the door and entered. I had to push against a pile of dirty clothes in front of the door, so it took me a second to take in the scene of Kaz in the tub of steaming hot water, along with Arianne, who shrieked but did nothing to cover her nakedness. Kaz wore his usual grin and nothing else.

I shut the door and backed off down the hall as laughter echoed from the room.

While I was worried about Kaz, his pistol was nowhere close at hand, and what was would keep him pleasantly occupied while I checked on the two POWs. Tracing my steps back to the kitchen, I tugged on my boots and reached for my sodden field jacket.

"Captain, please take my oilskin. It will keep you dry," Madame Janvier said as she appeared from the hallway. "It was my husband's and should fit you well." She shook off the water droplets that had beaded up on it and handed it to me. I tried it on. It wasn't a bad fit, and would keep me a whole lot drier than my soaked field jacket.

"Thank you," I said. "I won't be long."

"Do not worry, I am finished with the work outdoors for today," she said, arranging my jacket over the back of a chair near the stove. "Now I must find that lazy girl Arianne and make dinner. The colonel asked for a special meal, but I think that was when he expected a victory. Still, I must prepare something. Have you seen Arianne?"

Oh yeah, I'd seen her. I mumbled something about seeing her soaking wet, which was true enough, and made my escape.

The rain had lightened up, but the wind was still blowing it sideways as I put my head down and jogged over to the barn, glad of the waterproof coat. It was the only thing so far that had gone my way. Sad, when a dead man's slicker is the high point of your day.

"Sergeant Fair," I said, ducking into the barn. "How are your guests?"

"Hey, Captain," Fair said, seated on a stool, his rifle across his lap, opposite a horse stall where two Germans sat on the floor. He drew on his cigarette as he leaned back against the wall. "They're nice and quiet, now that I fed 'em. Had some extra tins of ham and lima beans, since no one likes that stuff. They devoured it."

"Heard it didn't go well today," I said, pulling an empty crate closer and taking a seat. I eyed the two prisoners, taking in their haggard appearance. Sunken cheeks, bags under their eyes, grimy uniforms, and hands dark with dirt. These were men who had been on the line for a while. They reminded me of Fair before he cleaned himself up.

"No. Krauts pushed back hard," Fair said. "I gotta admit, I'm a little less steamed at you for mentioning my hearing to the colonel. Taking a squad of new replacements into that attack woulda got us all killed."

"That them?" I asked, motioning to a group of GIs in clean uniforms at the other end of the barn.

"Yeah. I told them to steer clear of the Krauts 'cause I didn't want these two to bust a gut when they saw the kids I gotta lead," Fair said. I wondered about that. Maybe he wanted to commune with two chewed-up soldiers without the distraction of raw recruits asking a thousand dumb questions.

"Either of them speak English?" I asked.

"Naw. I was there when Johnson interrogated them. He speaks the lingo pretty well, and they didn't spout a word of English," Fair said, spitting out a piece of stray tobacco.

"He get anything out of them?" I asked.

"You ask him?" Fair said, looking at me as the smoke curled up into his eyes.

"I'm asking *you*," I said. "On account of that trip we took yesterday."

"Oh," he said. Harding would want to know if the Krauts smelled a rat, and Johnson wouldn't know what questions needed asking. "Hey, Miller, get over here."

"Yeah, Sarge?" asked a skinny kid who trotted over, an eager grin on his face.

"Jesus Christ, Miller," Fair said, rolling his eyes. "Go back and get your rifle. These are enemy POWs, for cryin' out loud." I eyed the Germans, who seemed to enjoy watching a GI get chewed out even if they didn't understand why.

"You got any booze?" I asked.

"I've been working on a bottle of calvados, not much left," Fair said. "But I got a couple of bottles of wine. For them?"

"Yeah, sorry," I said. Miller returned, his M1 held at the waist and aimed at the Germans, who were understandably alarmed.

"Miller, just hold your weapon close like a good boy, and don't aim it nowhere you don't intend to shoot, okay?" Fair said, rising to fetch a bottle of red wine and uncorking it. I handed it to one of the Germans. He might be twenty, tops, no older than Miller, but a whole lot wearier and worn.

"You speak German?" I asked Miller. He said his family was from Germany, and that he grew up speaking it with his grandparents. Good enough to get by, he claimed.

"Ask them if they heard of Major Hans Rast, of the *Feldgendarmerie*," I asked. Miller looked confused. "Military police," I added, figuring that term didn't come up much around the dinner table back home.

They both said they never heard of him. I took the bottle back, both of them having had a good guzzle. "Tell them this is the last wine they'll have for a long time. All I want to know is about this one officer. It's nothing that will endanger their friends. He's just a *Kettenhund*."

Chain-Dog. That's what the common German soldier called their military police, from the metal badge they wore on a chain around their throat. Nobody liked a cop except when they needed one, but the German military police were especially tough, and I figured it wouldn't take much to convince these boys to pass on any gossip about Rast. Then I'd move on to the Ghost Army. I watched the two of them whisper, and then their eyes moved to Fair, who had a new pack of Luckies in his hand.

That sealed the deal.

"Yeah, they ran into Major Rast's men plenty of times," Miller said, listening to them chatter and translating as he followed along. "The Chain-Dogs rounded up men who had been separated from their units and checked identity papers all the time. Sometimes they kept their comrades in confinement, but never for long."

"Did they know Major Rast?" I asked.

"No. They both saw him a few times, but never had any contact. But they think Rast's own men didn't respect him very much," Miller said.

"Open the other bottle," I said to Fair. He handed it over, and I had Miller press for details.

"It was because of his nickname," Miller said. "Rast's men called him *Amerika*, the joke being that's where he wanted to go after the war."

"Why?" I asked.

"Because right after D-Day, he started letting prisoners go. French prisoners," Miller said. "Terrorists, they call them. Rast would interrogate them and then let them go, so the scuttlebutt was he wanted to go to America after the war."

"Do they have any names?" I demanded.

"No, no, all they can do is repeat what they heard the *Kettenhunde* say. They thought it was funny, but didn't want to ask for trouble by asking questions," Miller said. Smart. No reason for a common soldier of either side to get mixed up in military police intrigues.

"Okay," I said. "Ask them if they came up against any of our new tanks."

"New tanks?" Miller asked me.

"Never you mind," Fair said. "Ask the damn question." He did. There were no new tanks, but I thought the question might come across as less threatening that way. Soldierly chitchat.

"Nope," Miller said. "They heard tanks in the distance, but never saw any. They said our artillery was bad enough, so they were grateful the tanks never attacked."

"Good," I said. "Tell them their new name is *Amerika*. They'll see it before Rast ever will. Or me, for that matter."

The two Germans got a good laugh out of that.

"You heading out in the morning, Sarge?" I asked as Fair walked me to the door.

"Yeah, I'm supposed to get a corporal for the squad, some guy with experience to help me wet-nurse these kids. He's getting out of the field hospital and should be here in the morning."

"I'll buy you a cup of coffee before you go," I said. "Stop in Madame Janvier's kitchen. I'm sure she'll put the pot on for us."

"Yeah, all seems to be forgiven," Fair said. "She told me I could say goodbye to Yvonne in the morning. With her as a chaperone, but I don't mind."

I stepped outside, glad that Fair would have a chance to see Yvonne and hoping that he'd forget about her after that. Where he was going, daydreaming about some dame was a quick way to get yourself killed. The rain had stopped, and the sky was dark with heavy gray clouds coming in low and fast, the wind whistling in the trees. Night was coming, and I was cold, wet, and hungry.

Not to mention confused. Why had Rast suddenly gone lenient with Resistance members he'd picked up? If he really had been trying to curry favor with the Americans, why hadn't he simply surrendered? And what was in his files, and where were they hidden? It sounded like he hadn't pulled out with his men, so where had he gone with that mysterious paperwork? Dead and buried was a possibility, maybe by the organized *Maquis* or a freelancer with an old shotgun. If the Resistance had caught up with him, they'd be crowing about it. Legrand sure would, and Jacques was still searching for Rast, so it hadn't been either of those two.

How many other *Maquis* groups were there in the area? That was a question for Johnson. I shouldn't forget the men and women of the Nemo Line either. It was a smaller, more self-contained unit, and operated in greater secrecy. Easier for them to pull off an assassination and keep it quiet.

I put my head down and trudged on. Tomorrow, we'd talk with Leon Dubois and get a firsthand account of Rast's quick-release program. Maybe pay another visit to Dr. Leroy and press him on the fate of any flyers taken from the hospital. After that? Maybe see if there were any captured *Kettenhunde* in the POW cages around here. Before the chain dogs got an all-expenses-paid trip to the States.

But tonight? Dry clothes, warm food, and figure out what the hell had gotten into Kaz.

CHAPTER NINETEEN

"So WHAT'S THE deal, Kaz?" I asked, toweling off my head after a quick cold-water wash-down, someone having used up all the hot water. "What's eating you?"

"I realized something profound today, Billy," he said, checking himself in a small mirror as he knotted his tie.

"That you needed a bath?"

"No, although that has brightened my outlook, I must say." Kaz had a cheery disposition most days, but it was a thin veneer, a cordial politeness hiding a state of wounded despair, and it wasn't hard for me to see through his false bonhomie. Tonight, his words had a lilt to them.

Which worried me. It called to mind writing a police report on a suicide who'd stepped in front of a trolley out in Mattapan. His family said he'd been down in the dumps for a while, but that morning he was the happiest they'd seen him in months.

"Okay, I'll bite," I said, sitting on the bed and pulling on dry socks. "What was it you realized?"

"That hatred is incompatible with hope," he said, turning away from the mirror and facing me once he was satisfied with his knot. "When I thought my entire family had been murdered by the Nazis, I had nothing but hatred to sustain me. Killing Germans was satisfying, if only to forestall the inevitable onset of darkness and depression. It provided the illusion of vengeance, but ultimately it is all meaningless. In the grand scheme of things, at least."

"What brought this on?"

"Anton Krause," he said. "An apparently ordinary man, put into a terrible situation. Was he guilty of crimes against civilians? Perhaps. But did he take joy in it? I think not. That is one reason I wanted Major Johnson to look at his *Soldbuch*, to see if I had missed anything about his war record. I hadn't. It was the first time I saw the death of an enemy soldier as a regrettable event. I find that as I hope for life for Angelika, I cannot help but hope for life for others. Others like Anton, at least."

"Well, that's good," I said, uncertain where Kaz was headed with all this.

"It is. But it also told me something else." He reached for his jacket and pulled it on.

"What?"

"That Anton was telling the truth about the files Rast spirited away. If he'd been Gestapo or SS, I wouldn't have believed him. But I doubt a common soldier would bother to come up with such a lie. So the files may be important. They may be the only important thing in this entire investigation, not counting the souls of the dead."

"I think there's something to that," I said. "It gives us a motive for murder, although why Jerome was killed, I can't figure."

"Yes. It's a pity we never got to question Anton. Coffee and cigarettes would have provided vital information."

"It's no one's fault he's dead," I said. "Except for a German sniper with lousy aim."

"I know, and I am glad he missed you. But earlier today I would have put a bullet in Anton's head myself without a second thought. Then I got to know him. Not very well, but well enough. And his death disturbed me. Greatly. More so than I expected."

"So I guess you and Arianne hopped in hot water to recharge your faith in humanity," I said. "How'd that work?"

"Arianne and I concluded a flirtation that began shortly after I arrived," Kaz said, working to keep down a smile. "It was fortuitous and enjoyable, but it has nothing to do with my state of mind."

"What does, then?" I asked, finally warming up as I pulled on my wool high-neck sweater.

"My sister Angelika. Now that I know she is alive, I can think of little else. I have hope, finally, for a real life after the war. Perhaps she and I can start our own families, and Clan Kazimierz will once again prosper," Kaz said, lacing up his boots, which had been not only dried but spit-shined. "To hold such hope is impossible when my mind is clouded with hate. The two cannot exist together. As long as Angelika is alive, or until I know for certain she has perished, I must strive for a future in which I can live as a decent human being. Frankly, I had not sought out a future. After Daphne was killed, I mean."

"I always worried about the chances you took, Kaz. Now I'm worried you'll hesitate the next time you need to fire your weapon."

"I am a soldier, Billy," Kaz said, buttoning up his jacket. "I will do what I must, but temper my actions with what mercy I can. I wish Angelika to recognize me when I find her, both in body and in spirit."

"That works both ways, Kaz," I said. "She won't be the kid sister you knew before the war." *If she's still alive*, I managed not to say out loud.

"I know," he said with a sighing weariness as he reached for his web belt. He adjusted it around his waist, snapping the holster shut. "But finding that I am no longer alone in the world has made me think about what will come after the war, when the guns go silent. Killing and violence have offered a momentary release, but nothing more. I must be a better man and find a better way. I am prepared to kill if need be, as a soldier must. But I will not be an executioner."

"You're not alone, Kaz," I said, standing and placing my hand on his shoulder. "I'm your friend." I'd seen Kaz dispatch many Krauts. Some, like the arrogant officer this morning, or the SS officer a few weeks ago, I wouldn't lose sleep over.

"Yes, and you are a good friend, Billy. Which is why it pains me to leave you now," he said, grabbing his raincoat and cap. "Since you are also my superior officer."

"What? Where are you going?"

"To Bayeux," Kaz said, as matter-of-factly as if he were stepping out for a cup of coffee.

"Kaz, we're in the middle of an investigation. You can't leave," I said. "Don't put me in this position."

"Billy, do whatever you must. I will not take it personally. Big Mike will be back soon to assist you. As for this investigation, it is going nowhere. Sadly, someone killed Major Jerome. But I see no resolution and, even more importantly, no threat to any potential victim. If I did, I would wait. But this endeavor is an absurd waste of time."

"What's in Bayeux?" I asked, not really disagreeing with his assessment.

"The Polish 1st Armoured Division, newly arrived from England," he said. "Sixteen thousand free Poles. They were the real reason I volunteered to stay behind at First Army to interrogate POWs. I expected the division to arrive soon, and I wanted to question their intelligence officers about the Polish underground."

"About Angelika, you mean," I said.

"Yes. Many of the men in the division made their way to England early in the war. Still, there has been a small but steady stream of escapees making their way through Sweden, the Balkans, or Turkey. Some may have recent information about the underground."

"Why not go through the Polish Government-in-exile back in London?" I asked.

"Because we have had very little time in London, and I do not expect to see our rooms at the Dorchester anytime soon. So I will make do with the soldiers of the 1st Armoured. Besides, they are fighters, not politicians and officials. They will help if they can without worrying about diplomatic niceties."

"Makes sense," I said, sitting down on the bed, not knowing what to do. My friendship with Kaz was more important than rank or even this assignment. My biggest worry was the trouble he'd be in if he stayed away too long and Harding found out.

"I am truly sorry, Billy. I must do this. And I must do it now, or I will lose my mind with grief and worry."

"Sorry, Kaz, I can't hear you," I said, getting up and walking to the window to stare out into the darkness. "Listen, head out to speak with Dr. Leroy again in the morning. Then report back. But I don't know where I'll be, exactly." I leaned against the glass pane and felt the coolness on my cheek. I closed my eyes, the door shut, and I was alone.

I understood what Kaz was going through, as much as possible when it came to understanding a guy who'd lost most of his family along with his one true love in the war. My own kid brother had found his way into this charnel house, and all that had mattered to me was getting him out of it. So if Kaz went AWOL for a few days, I had no trouble covering for him.

A few minutes later, I heard footsteps in the hallway and hoped it was Kaz returning, but at the same time I was angry at the thought he'd given up his quest. As the steps drew closer and louder, the heavy footfalls announced Big Mike's entrance.

"Billy," he said, sitting down heavily and tossing his jacket on the table. "What's up?"

"Long story," I said. "Let's get some chow."

Big Mike needed no convincing. We headed out, passing by Yvonne's room. I glanced in, expecting to see her in her chair by the window. She was gone.

"Maybe Madame Janvier took her to the bathroom," Big Mike said. But I could hear the lady of the house laughing downstairs, probably trying to lift the spirits of Colonel Brewster and his staff. We checked the other rooms down the long hallway and came up empty. We headed down the steps, treading lightly so we wouldn't attract the notice of the brass in the kitchen. I went to the sitting room where Major Jerome had been found.

Yvonne was standing by the fireplace, a couple of feet from where Jerome had fallen.

She spoke.

I couldn't make out the words. They came out in a croaking, faint jumble, only a few of them comprehensible. "*L'allemand . . . Le pêcheur . . . Gustave.*"

The last word, the name Gustave, came out as a sob, and as she collapsed to the floor, I caught her by the arms, whispering her name, trying to get a response.

She was out cold. Big Mike relieved me of her, enveloping her in his massive arms. We brought her to her room, stepping gingerly on the staircase so as not to alert Madame Janvier. Even though Yvonne had spoken the first words I'd heard from her, I knew Madame would not be happy. She was so protective of Yvonne that her only thought would be to blame us for Yvonne's wandering away from her room.

Which was unusual, given that she seemed permanently attached to her chair. What had led her to leave?

We laid Yvonne on her bed, propping her up on her pillows. She was thin, and her skin seemed stretched across her bones. Her eyelids fluttered as I held her hand, waiting to see if she'd wake up. I could feel the scab on her palm and wondered how she had come by that slash. The broken glass? Or the missing knife that had killed Jerome?

"What was she sayin', Billy?" Big Mike whispered.

"Something about a German, a fisherman, and a guy named Gustave," I said.

"Doesn't make much sense," Big Mike said. "Let's let her sleep. She might spook if she wakes up sudden like and sees us."

It was good advice. The last thing we needed was a screaming Yvonne, an angry Madame, and a gaggle of overprotective officers asking questions. We left, and I wondered about Gustave. Not to mention the fisherman and the German. Or maybe a German fisherman? Nothing made sense, so I filled in Big Mike on Kaz's departure as we walked to the mess tent. That, at least, I could make heads and tails of.

"Jesus," he said. "He's risking a lot."

"Not really," I said, as we lined up for meat-and-potato hash. "A few days in the stockade for a quick AWOL trip at worst. Besides, I kind of gave him a cover story. He's off to question Dr. Leroy at the hospital again."

"Oh," Big Mike said, holding out his mess kit for an extra topping of hash. "I get it. You think you'll be the one in trouble. But it could be Kaz, out there alone. Some trigger-happy GI might think he's a Kraut."

"Well, there wasn't much I could do. He'll be fine," I said, as we settled in at one of the rough plank tables. It was late, and most of the men had already eaten. A few lanterns under the canvas gave off a soft yellow light, and the mess crew was clanking pots, cleaning up, and getting ready for the morning meal.

"Did you get to Sam this morning?" I asked.

"Hang on," Big Mike said, shoveling a few forkfuls of hash down his gullet before answering. "I did. Guy at the roadblock let me through after they got Sam on the radio. I told him Brewster was sending his battalion in, thinking he had armor on his flanks. Sam ordered artillery fire on known German positions and ordered the Ghost Army guys to pull back. Said that's all he could do. Then I left for Second Armored. How'd the attack go?"

"They got ground up. Kraut patrols followed them all the way here. One of them took a shot at us as we were bringing in a prisoner and got him by accident. It was close."

"I heard. You and Kaz okay?" he asked, readying another forkful of hash.

"Yeah. What about Jerome?" I said, eating my own hash with considerably less enthusiasm.

"I talked with the G-2 officer Harding told us about. He said Jerome was a radio engineer back in the States and knew everything there was to know about communications. He was a little older than most of the officers and kept pretty much to himself. Not a big drinker or card player."

I could see how that would limit his friendships with his brother officers. Booze and games of chance were big spare time activities. Bridge for the brass, dice for the dogfaces. "Any enemies? Arguments?"

"No. I talked to the men in his Signals section. They all respected him, said he knew his stuff. He didn't exactly inspire, but everyone said he was fair, and no one held a grudge about anything. In his off-duty time, Jerome worked on repairing radio gear."

"A quiet guy, wouldn't hurt a fly," I said.

"Basically," Big Mike said. "He didn't like driving at night and wasn't happy he couldn't have a driver take him here, on account of the secrecy.

So that's why he left early and showed up just after dark. He figured he'd sack out here and wait for everyone to show up."

"Did Harding's G-2 pal know why he was ordered here?"

"Nope. He said he knew enough not to ask questions. Figured it was some kind of deception scheme, but knew enough to keep it zipped, since the orders came direct from First Army. He told me he wasn't surprised to hear Sam was involved. Said he was always one for the cloak-and-dagger stuff," Big Mike said, grinning at the description. To us, Sam Harding was a strictly by-the-book hard-ass.

"So who takes over for Jerome?" I asked, chewing on a bit of gristle.

"I thought about that," Big Mike said. "Command of a Signals detachment isn't much of a motive, but you never know. All they have is a lieutenant who seemed damn nervous about taking command. Said he couldn't wait for a replacement with more experience to be transferred in. I confirmed that a major from Corps HQ was already on his way in. So we can scratch career advancement off the list of motives." Big Mike pointed at my mess tin with his fork. "You gonna finish that?"

"All yours," I said. "We should radio Sam and ask him for the dope on Resistance groups in this area. It'll save us a lot of shoe leather to know if any members are suspected of working with the Germans."

"Like somebody who Rast would have kept files on," Big Mike said, inhaling the last of the hash. I gave him the rundown on Madame Janvier and the *Réseau Nemo*, along with Jacques's outfit.

"So you got the Nemo Line, the *Groupe Rouge*, and then Legrand's gang. Probably a few other groups we don't know about. Did you question Madame Janvier about her work with Nemo?"

"Yeah, although I never really got down to brass tacks with her," I said. "There might have been another Resistance group she was with. I don't know if she got her code name from Nemo or a different bunch."

"What code name?" Big Mike asked.

"Corday," I said. "Name of some dame from the French Revolution who was called the Angel of Assassination. The original Janvier home is out in the woods, overgrown and out of sight. She used it to hide escapees from the Nemo Line. I have a feeling she did more than work with Nemo. She might have been at the center of it."

"Whoa. That don't sound like the nice apple lady we got here," he said. "Think maybe she was mixed up in something more than hiding out guys on the lam?"

"Yeah. We'll ask Sam for all that. He's back at First Army?"

"Said he was heading out after I talked to him," Big Mike said. "Let's send him a message tonight. We might hear back by morning. Might as well ask him if G2 has the skinny on Major Rast as well. Who knows?"

"Sure," I said, getting up and rinsing out my mess kit.

"So where's Kaz headed?" Big Mike said. "He tell you that much?"

"He said the Poles were forming up near Bayeux," I said. "That's all I know."

"You want I should go get him?"

"Hell no, Big Mike, leave it be. Let me worry about it."

"Worrying ain't gonna help Kaz if he gets in trouble out there. Or does something stupid. You know he ain't never too far away from stupid for a guy who's so damn smart."

Big Mike stalked off. He was right about Kaz. He'd talked about killing himself often enough. Usually joking about being reckless, but we both knew what that was all about. I had to trust that Kaz's desire to see his sister alive trumped any thoughts of ending it all. So I let it slide, knowing Big Mike had a point but not wanting to admit it.

Something else was nagging at me, something that we could ask Sam about. But it stayed hidden, back in the recesses of my tired brain. We went to the radio shack and found Friedman. I wrote out a message, asking for dope on all Resistance groups in the area as well as background on Rast and any mention of Madame Janvier, code-named Corday. He promised to get it out within the hour.

Back upstairs, I kicked off my boots, poured a glass of calvados, and lay back on my cot, trying to conjure up what was just beneath the surface of my mind.

Sleep came first.

CHAPTER TWENTY

THE NEXT MORNING, I stumbled downstairs, testing the air for the aroma of brewing coffee, but found the kitchen empty, a cold pot sitting on the stove. Yvonne's door had been shut, so I figured Madame Janvier was tending to her. Or maybe to her apple trees. The lady was a hard worker. I hadn't once yet seen her relax and put her feet up. Rain or shine, she was out and about in her orchards, trimming branches and overseeing the clearing of trees damaged by war, weather, or neglect.

Yesterday's rains had given way to a mild breeze, clear skies, and a warming sun, so my bet was that she was out early in the orchards, inspecting her ripening crop. I heard footsteps coming down from the third floor, which was the domain of Colonel Brewster and his officers. I didn't look forward to another round of questions about the investigation, so instead of waiting for Big Mike, I slipped out the back door and made for the comm shack to see if we'd heard from Sam.

"Hey, Billy, wait up!" It was Fair, jogging toward the house, M1 slung over his shoulder. "Still got time for a cup of joe before I head out?"

"Sure. I haven't seen Madame Janvier, though. She told you it was okay, right?"

"Yeah. But you think she'd mind me calling on Yvonne when she ain't around?" Fair said.

"Don't worry," I said. "She might be with Yvonne for all I know.

The door was closed when I came down. Come on, we'll check it out." I headed back to the kitchen with Fair in tow. He was about to lead a squad of fresh replacements up to the front line, so checking on Sam's message could wait a few minutes. If Madame Janvier was nowhere to be found, I'd play chaperone and give him a minute with Yvonne. Fair was a little nuts, at least where his silent girlfriend was concerned, but he still deserved a few minutes of deluded happiness.

"Did Yvonne ever speak to you?" I asked Fair as we walked together. It was a whim, but it occurred to me that maybe last night wasn't the first time she'd managed to get a few words out. And Fair managed to spend more time with her than most.

"Well, yeah, once," Fair said, stopping to face me. "She must have been all mixed up. She called me by another guy's name. Gustave, it sounded like."

"What else did she say?" I asked.

"A couple of other words in French, but nothin' I could understand. That was it. Just a whisper, really. Then she kept staring out the window like she always does."

"Did you tell anyone?" I asked, trying to look Fair in the eye as he stared down at the ground.

"No. I shoulda, I know, but I told her my name a thousand times, and I thought one day she'd look at me and say my name. Allan. That's all I wanted. But then she comes out with Gustave. Is that a Kraut name?"

"Gustaf," I said, stressing the last letter. "But Gustave is French. I heard her say it too."

"What else did she say?" Fair asked, his eyes finally meeting mine, beseeching me to tell him lies.

"*L'allemand. Le pêcheur,*" I said. "That sound right?"

"Yeah. But not my name, huh?"

"Not that I heard," I said. "Gustave might be her brother, you know."

"Yeah, could be," Fair said. "Hey, Billy, could you hold this for me? I don't want to go up there with a rifle. Might scare her."

"Sure," I said, taking his M1 and slinging it over my shoulder. "How's your squad?"

"Nervous in the service," he said with a grin, the well-worn phrase telling me all I needed to know. Replacements. The army tried calling them reinforcements for a while, but nobody bought it. They were replacing the dead and wounded, and everyone knew it. "I got one guy I gotta keep an eye on. He's ready to hightail it outta here, and he ain't even heard a shot fired yet. Found him in his trench this morning with his rifle pointed at his foot."

"A self-inflicted wound is a court-martial offense," I said.

"That's what I told the poor bastard. The powder burns always gives 'em away, and then they got a hole in their leg and six months in the stockade. Plus, a lot of medics won't go out of their way to help a guy like that, especially if the lead's flying."

"Well, good luck," I said, movement by the house catching my eye. "There's Madame Janvier."

The kitchen door was open, and our host stood in the doorway, waving at Fair, a white handkerchief fluttering in her hand.

"Sergeant, come in," she said, sounding nearly cheerful, maybe at the thought of not having to put up with Fair anymore. Still, she didn't have to invite him in, so I gave her points for kindness.

"Thank you," Fair said, looking up at her. *"Merci."*

A rifle shot shattered the air.

A *thud* shuddered Fair's chest.

He wavered, stumbled, fell face-first to the ground.

"Sniper!" I yelled and grabbed Fair by his collar, dragging him behind the trunk of a poplar tree hardly wide enough for decent cover. I turned him over.

He was dead. The bullet had taken him square in the chest, doing the terrible damage that kills a man before he even falls.

Sniper, sniper, sniper, the screams and yells echoed as I saw Madame Janvier still standing in the doorway, hand raised to her mouth.

"Take cover!" I shouted, just as Big Mike grabbed her from behind and pulled her inside.

GIs began to fire at the tree line across the road, the smarter ones diving for slit trenches first. Others poured out of buildings, weapons at the ready, taking what cover they could. I lay prone behind Fair's body, resting his M1 on his ruined chest. It wasn't a plan, it was just how I'd tumbled to the ground. I looked through the iron sights, scanning the brush at the edge of the field and the trees beyond, looking for any movement.

More gunfire erupted, but it was all ours. I could hear the discharge of M1s, the slow and steady automatic fire of a BAR, and bursts from several Thompsons.

I don't think anyone knew what they were shooting at. The biggest danger right now was being shot by one of our own.

"Billy!" Big Mike yelled from the doorway.

"I'm okay," I said. No need to report on Fair. The red on his chest and his still limpness said it all.

"You need me?" Kaplan shouted as he ran a zigzag pattern from the barn to the side of the house. I told him to stay put. Most of the time, medics on both sides were safe from snipers. Most of the time.

"What the hell's going on?" Colonel Brewster demanded, bursting from the kitchen door, pushing Big Mike aside and brandishing his Colt automatic pistol. Johnson and another officer followed him, looking less certain about venturing out into the open. "Cease fire!"

"Get inside, Colonel! You'll draw fire," I yelled.

Brewster looked my way and saw Fair. He froze. Which made him a perfect target. Older guy, clean uniform, pistol for a weapon. Officer.

Big Mike burst out of the house, shouldered Johnson aside, and laid his paws on Brewster's arm, leading him firmly inside. Johnson and the other officer followed, reluctant to be sniper bait.

The shooting quieted but didn't stop. I did my best to calculate where Fair had been standing, and which way he faced. There was a clear line of fire across the field that ran along the road to the house. But it was some distance.

I pressed my cheek to the rifle and sighted in again, searching the area where the shot would have come from. It was useless. Too far away to be sure of a hit, or even a near miss. Over five hundred yards. Six or seven hundred, maybe. But the sniper had taken Fair down with one shot.

Which told me two things.

One, we had a real sniper on our hands. Not just a Kraut taking potshots with his rifle, but a sniper with a telescopic sight, capable of making a deadly hit from a third of a mile away.

Two, he was gone. Snipers never take two shots from the same spot. That gives their position away. Already, the heavy weapons platoon was busy setting up two mortars, which could shell the tree line easily. Snipers don't like shrapnel.

Calls to cease fire came from all directions. A couple of shots from excited GIs popped, followed by a deathly silence.

Then one shot, and a scream.

"Medic!"

Kaplan ran out from undercover, sprinting to the far side of the *pressoir*, where helmets started to bob up from foxholes.

"Get patrols out," Brewster snapped, stepping outside and issuing orders to his officers. "Sweep those woods. And make it fast." He walked over as I stood up, shaking his head as he viewed Fair's body.

"He was ready to head out with his squad, Colonel. Madame Janvier was going to let him say goodbye to Yvonne," I said.

"Fair was a good man. He took things hard, and I think he doted on that girl as a way to leave it all behind for a while. Damn," Brewster said, looking around and scanning the fields and woods. Men were already fanning out, rifles at the ready. Two jeeps crammed with GIs took off down the road. "That was one helluva shot."

"Definitely a trained sniper," I said. "One shot, some seven hundred yards out. Then he repositioned himself. Probably long gone by now."

"Or waiting," Brewster said. "Those German snipers are good at concealment. They can lay in wait all day and hardly move a muscle. Why did he have to pick Fair, anyway?" He glanced at his sergeant again, as if he couldn't believe Fair's luck had finally run out.

"Fair asked me to hold his rifle while he visited Yvonne. He didn't want to frighten her. The sniper must've thought he was an officer," I said. "It could have just as easily been me."

"A damn good shot," Brewster said, eyeing the tree line again, and kindly not commenting on the twist of fate that had put a slug in Fair's chest instead of mine. "Do me a favor, Boyle. Get some stretcher bearers to move Fair out of here, okay?"

"Sure, Colonel," I said, motioning for Big Mike to come with me. "You should get back inside, just in case."

"Yes, yes," he said, and stood there, eyes squinted as he scanned the fields. A perfect target.

We found Kaplan, kneeling in a slit trench and sprinkling sulfa powder on a nasty leg wound. He'd cut away the GI's trouser leg and removed his boot, revealing a bloody mess. A good chunk of the guy's calf was blown off, and he was writhing on the ground as a buddy tried to hold him down.

"Com'n, Joey, you'll be okay," his pal said. "Doc, give him some morphine, willya?"

"That looks self-inflicted," Kaplan said. "I'm saving the morphine for guys who deserve it."

"No, no," Joey said through gritted teeth. "I got out of my hole when they said to cease fire. The bastard got me in the leg. Gimme a shot, please."

"Look at the angle," Kaplan said, glancing at Big Mike and me standing above them. "He shot himself. Besides, you saw how Fair was hit. That sniper wouldn't aim for a leg."

"Sergeant Fair?" Joey's buddy said. "He's hit?"

"Dead," I said. "You in his squad?"

"Yeah. Who's gonna lead us now?" Joey was unconcerned. He was going home. I wondered if this was the guy Fair said was giving him problems. I leaned in to pick over the pieces of wool Kaplan had cut away from around the wound.

"No powder burns," I said. "Most guys who pull this stunt don't know about leaving powder burns. That's what gives them away. The smart ones get a pistol or a carbine, at least. An M1 slug does a lot of damage."

"Jeez, doc, a shot, I'm begging you," Joey moaned. Kaplan shook his head as he packed gauze pads around Joey's shattered calf and wrapped them with bandages.

"Jesus Christ, okay," Kaplan said when he was done. He slammed a morphine syrette into Joey's thigh, and I watched as the drug took effect. Joey relaxed as Kaplan pinned the empty syrette to his collar, so the doctors at Joey's next stop would know how much he'd had.

"What do you guys want, anyway?" Kaplan asked, climbing out of the hole. Two stretcher bearers carried Joey off to a waiting jeep, his pal trailing behind.

"Brewster wanted someone to take Fair away. He's sort of standing guard over him, I think," Big Mike said.

"They were close," Kaplan said. "Brewster liked him. Especially since Fair was a sergeant, like Brewster was in the last war. He watched out for him, you know?"

"Still is," I said. "And putting himself in the bull's-eye while he does it."

Kaplan jogged off, hollering to a GI at the medical tent to grab a stretcher. I looked at the ground around the slit trench where Joey said he'd been hit. No blood there. But there was plenty in the trench, and he could have tumbled right in when the bullet took him.

But this sniper didn't seem the type to hang around and take a second shot. Especially one that was nearly a miss.

I got into the trench, kneeling to examine the earth. It was hard-packed, except at the edges of the hole, where Joey hadn't trampled it down. I took my knife and scraped at the dirt, playing a hunch.

It didn't take long. My knife caught on a piece of burlap, covered with a thin layer of soil. I pulled it loose, shaking out the dirt, and held it up for Big Mike to see. It was a small sack, about the right size for a sandbag. It had been folded twice, and showed a bullet hole four times over. One section was peppered with powder burns.

"Joey was smart enough to use this to hide the gunpowder residue," I said. "He even managed to bury it after blowing half his calf off."

"He's still a damn bum," Big Mike said. "You give that to Brewster, and they'll cuff him to his hospital bed and then throw him in the stockade where he belongs."

"Yeah," I said, hoisting myself out of the trench and taking a deep breath. No one liked shirkers, especially at the front. One less guy doing his job could get other guys killed. Where Fair had been taking these raw replacements, the only thing they could count on was each other. Now Joey would have his bandages changed while lying on clean white sheets and probably head home on a hospital ship, leaving his buddies to fend for themselves.

We headed back to the house, watching as Kaplan directed the stretcher bearers carrying Fair to the graveyard by the road. Where Anton had his own little plot.

I held the burlap in my hand, sticky with blood, the rough fibers coarse against my skin. I could make life even more miserable for Joey with this clear evidence of a self-inflicted wound. But how would that help anyone? Joey had already botched things, giving himself a grievous wound. Maybe his hand was shaking. Maybe he was just a punk kid, too dumb to understand the damage an M1 slug fired at that angle could do. He'd go through life with an ugly knot of scar tissue over a hole in his calf. He'd tell lies about it, but he'd always know.

The army might still court-martial him without this evidence. Or not. All I knew was that I was tired of people dying and suffering the agonies of war. Even if the only person I could help avoid the smallest bit of pain was a bum like Joey, I had to do it. It wasn't right, I knew, but I couldn't help myself as I let the burlap cloth fall to the ground as we crossed the roadway.

It was wrong, and it felt good. And goodness was in short supply.

"Did they get him? *L'allemand?* The German?" Madame Janvier asked as we entered the kitchen. She stood by the sink, drying her hands on a towel, rubbing it nervously on her palms. The aroma of freshly brewed coffee filled the room.

"Sit down, Madame," I said, guiding her to a chair. I'd done what passed for a good deed, and now it was time to put goodness aside. Madame Janvier was shook up, scared, and distracted. Which meant this was the right time to press her on what life had been like with Major Rast in charge. She hadn't wanted to talk much about it, but right now she was vulnerable, and that was something I could use.

"No, they didn't find him," Big Mike said. "Not that I heard, anyway. There's lots of guys out looking, so you can rest easy. He won't be back anytime soon."

"Bien," she said, nodding mechanically. "Poor Sergeant Fair. He was a troubled man. *La guerre.*"

"Yes, too much of the war," I said. "But he was cheerful this morning. It was nice of you to allow him to see Yvonne."

"Alors, I felt I had to, you understand? He was always sneaking around, and I thought it best to let him say his goodbyes while I could watch him. Still, I am glad it helped to soothe his mind. It is all so sad."

"Has Yvonne ever spoken to you?" I asked.

"Never. Not a word. Why do you ask? Has she spoken to you? Or to Sergeant Fair?"

"No," I said, keeping mum about the few words she had uttered. "I thought you said Fair frightened her. Why do you think she would have chosen him to speak to?"

"Oh, who knows?" Madame Janvier said, giving a slight shrug of the shoulders while tilting her head to one side. "I thought of the sergeant only because of all the times he tried to see her. If she spoke, it could have been to him as well as anyone else. But tell me, why was Sergeant Fair being sent away? I thought he was helping you with your work about the murder of Major Jerome."

"Colonel Brewster needed an experienced sergeant," I said. "For the replacements."

"Ah, I see. But he did help, did he not? He spoke with fondness of working with you," she said, wringing her hands as if she still held the dishtowel. Excited voices sounded from outside, guys still high-strung after the shooting. She looked out the window, her gaze resting on the spot where Fair had died.

"I'm glad to hear that. Yes, he did help us to understand what happened here, even though he was reluctant to admit to his visits with Yvonne," I said, hoping he hadn't talked too much and spilled the beans about the Ghost Army. "It seems like we both gave him some comfort." That was an interrogation technique my dad taught me. Find some common ground and then exploit it.

"It would have been better if I had not," she said. "After all, had he not come to say farewell to Yvonne this morning, he would still be alive. That is how kindness kills, Captain Boyle. One never knows the consequences of even the simplest act."

"Here," Big Mike said, pouring a cup of coffee for Madame Janvier and filling the silence that followed with the clink of spoons against china as we all fiddled with our cups. It helped to make believe it was a normal morning at someone's kitchen table, if only for a moment.

"Do you know Leon Dubois?" I asked after a few sips. "He's a schoolteacher over in Saint-Jean."

"One of the *Groupe Rouge*, yes? I know who he is, but I am not well acquainted with him. I buy apples from his mother. She has a small orchard and sells to *pressoirs* in the area."

"Are there many women in the apple business?" I asked.

"For women of a certain age, those who lost their men in the last war, it is the only way to keep the land in the family. We must do what our husbands did and care for the trees and make calvados. The only alternative would be to sell to a stranger and live off the money, as long as it lasts. I could never do such a thing. To pass by my fields and orchards and know they were owned by someone else would be horrible."

"It must be hard work," I said.

"Yes, and Madame Dubois is older than I am," she said, looking at her own calloused hands. "But she works hard, and those men who were left after the Germans took away the able-bodied are glad for the work at harvest time. But why do you ask about Leon?"

"Did you know he was arrested by Rast? Apparently, he bragged about his exploits to a woman, and she betrayed him," I said.

"I heard he was let go," she said. "It does not surprise me he talked too much to gain a woman's favor. Leon is somewhat awkward and not very good-looking. He talks a lot about himself and his politics. He makes the mistake of thinking other people are terribly interested. Perhaps that comes from standing in front of children, obligated to listen to their lessons."

"Seems like you do know him," I said, smiling at her description.

"I only talk of his weaknesses," she said. "Leon was brave enough to fight, which many were not. I heard he did not return to the *Groupe*

Rouge after he was let go. Perhaps Jacques did not trust him. A wise precaution."

"We met up with Jacques and his men yesterday," I said.

"Yes, I know. One hears things. Especially from comrades in the Nemo Line."

"Dr. Leroy?" I asked, getting up to pour us more coffee. I smiled as I filled her cup, keeping up the pretense that this was nothing more than a kitchen table confab.

"Among others. But he is why I sent you to the hospital. He knows Yvonne's story better than anyone."

"We'll get back to Yvonne. Do you have any idea why Leon was released?" I asked.

"No." She shrugged. "Perhaps he convinced Major Rast that it was nothing more than a lover's quarrel."

"What was Rast like? You lived under the same roof for months. What's your opinion of the man?" I asked.

"I hardly can say, Captain. First, I was made to give up my bedroom. I had to share Arianne's room, which was cramped and unpleasant. We stayed clear of the *Boche* whenever possible. Even Arianne, who flirts with anyone wearing trousers, ignored them."

"But you must have had some interactions with them. Did they make you cook?" Big Mike said.

"No. They wouldn't trust a decent Frenchwoman not to poison them. You must understand, there is a certain code of conduct. We have to answer their questions and obey their commands, but the proper way to act is to ignore them whenever possible. It is a small thing, but a way to maintain some dignity. No smiles, no friendly greetings, nothing to give them the idea they are welcome. Soon they became used to it and left us to run the farm and make the calvados, which they then bought from us at ridiculous prices. It was barely worth picking the apples. But they left us some to sell locally, which helped, if only to keep the tradition alive."

"You must have heard of Rast releasing other prisoners," I said.

"Yes, certainly. He had a change of heart, it seems, soon after the invasion. He began to ignore orders to crush the Resistance. He performed the basic duties of German military police, but little else. It puzzled his men."

"How did you find this out, if you had nothing to do with the Germans?" Big Mike asked, polishing off his coffee and looking around the kitchen, probably hoping for a sighting of grub. The room was warm and inviting, with sunlight filtering through the curtains. The wooden counters were shiny clean, the tile floor sparkling. Had Rast sat in this very chair, admiring the peacefulness of a French country kitchen?

"We did not socialize, but we always listened. I speak German well enough, although I never let on. Whatever I heard, I passed on to others in the Nemo Line. With so many *Boche* here, it was impossible to shelter anyone. So I focused on providing what intelligence I could."

"Rast never succeeded in finding any of the Nemo people?" I asked.

"No. We are a tight-knit group. Unlike the Resistance fighters. Even though Jacques and Legrand are very different, the one thing they have in common is a tendency to talk too much. Legrand because he is vain, and Jacques because he wishes everyone to know it is the Communists who fight the hardest."

"Is that true?" Big Mike asked.

"In our area, yes. It is different elsewhere, I am sure. But this is all about after the war, and who will have power. I only wish the war to leave us and move on to Germany. And soon."

"Does the name Gustave mean anything to you?" I asked.

"No. Other than it was the name of my *grand-père*. Is it important?"

"Not if it doesn't mean anything else. Tell me, why did Rast change? Do you have any idea?" I said.

"He did make some comments critical of Hitler and the Nazis," she said. "Once to one of his officers, which I overheard. Then later, to me. He said someone should stop Hitler before Germany was destroyed. He seemed very upset."

"Really?" I said. "Anything else?"

"Well, yes. I think he regretted saying it. It was a sudden outburst, and he seemed to think better of it. He asked me not to repeat it, and said if I ever told anyone, it would mean torture and death for him.

He said it so fervently that I fully believed he was involved in some plotting against the Nazis. I never did tell anyone. Until now. It made quite an impression on me."

"You think he was telling the truth," Big Mike said.

"Absolutely. So much so that I feared for myself and the others here if he was caught. The Nazis would seek revenge on anyone associated with a plot against Hitler."

"If they weren't successful," I said.

"Of course. But after years of war and occupation, I hold out little hope for a miracle," Madame Janvier said.

The lady was a realist.

CHAPTER TWENTY-ONE

I JOINED BIG Mike in the mess tent. I'd sent him there, figuring it was dangerous to keep the big Detroit cop from solid food for too long, and gone alone to check with Friedman to see if we'd gotten anything back from Harding.

"Nothing from Sam," I said, joining him with a scrambled-egg sandwich balanced on my mess kit. The eggs were powdered, but at least the bread was fresh.

"He must be busy with something," Big Mike said. "It's not like we asked for a lot of dope."

"Hey, how'd you get bacon?" I said, seeing the mound he had in his mess kit. "They said they didn't have any."

"It pays to make friends with the cooks and bakers," Big Mike said. "They keep back a little for themselves and their pals."

Cooks and bakers.

I froze, my sandwich halfway to my mouth.

"Cooks and bakers," I said, hoping that by saying it out loud, it would make sense. The phrase had jolted something in my mind, something that sparked at the mention of cooks. And bakers.

"Yeah," Big Mike said. "What about 'em?"

"They're professions. A lot of the SOE spy networks are named after professions," I said. The British-run Special Operations Executive organized clandestine circuits to collect information on the enemy and maintain radio communications with London. A lot of them were named after professions. "Author, Farmer, Minister, that sort of thing."

"Okay," Big Mike said, his forehead furrowed quizzically.

"Fisherman," I said, blowing steam from my coffee. "Yvonne might have been referring to her circuit."

"Yeah, it could be. And maybe Gustave was a member," he said. "Or maybe Gustave is a fisherman. That's a pretty thin thread, Billy. And who's the German?"

"Maybe Rast," I said. "Since he brought her here from the hospital. Or the Kraut from the train, or whoever interrogated her after she was arrested."

"It's possible," Big Mike said, warming to the notion. "Maybe we should ask for help from SOE."

He winked as he said it. It wasn't a half-bad idea. For several reasons.

Right around the time Kaz lost the love of his life—Daphne Seaton—I met her sister, Diana. Diana Seaton was unlike any woman I'd ever known. Not only because she was British upper crust and had a father with a *Sir* in front of his name, which were damn few and far between in South Boston, but because she knew what she wanted and wasn't afraid to go after it. She volunteered for the SOE after her experiences as an auxiliary with the British Expeditionary Force in 1940. She'd gone to France to work on a headquarters switchboard, but found herself retreating with the rest of the troops as the Germans closed in on Dunkirk.

She'd made it onto a destroyer, only to have it sunk in the crossing. Diana watched helplessly as wounded men laid out on stretchers slipped from the listing deck and drowned in the cold Channel waters. She went overboard in her life jacket and managed to be picked up by one of the small civilian craft which braved the voyage. Some women, and men for that matter, would have stayed on dry land in England after that. Not Diana. Fluent in French, the SOE trained her for dangerous duty. Not long ago she'd been working with her own circuit, Noble, as a wireless operator. Probably one of the most dangerous jobs in occupied Europe.

We were pretty much opposites. She wasn't Irish or Catholic. I didn't volunteer for anything, and she put herself in the darkest danger imaginable. She rode horses on her family estate, while I rode the trolley back in Boston. Regardless, we'd fallen for each other.

Hard.

As far as I knew, she was still in England. We'd managed one night together before I was sent to Normandy. Between assignments, she'd headed north to Seaton Manor to see her father as I left for France.

Diana would be perfect. She knew SOE operations, spoke French, and as a woman would be able to question Yvonne gently. And maybe we could have a glass or two of calvados together, in between people shooting at me. Fun all around.

Big Mike and I talked it over some more and decided it really did make sense. I wanted to be sure before I asked Harding for a favor that he might see as purely personal. We rinsed out our mess kits and made for the comm room.

It was abuzz.

Johnson and Friedman huddled over a radio as a teletype machine chattered in a corner. GIs dashed in and out, their nervous energy charging the air with excitement.

"What gives?" I asked.

"They tried to kill Hitler," Johnson said. "Yesterday, at his field headquarters in East Prussia."

"Who?" I asked.

"A small clique of renegade officers, according to Adolf himself," Johnson said. "We just got the translation of his radio address. Some colonel named von Stauffenberg planted a bomb, but Hitler escaped with minor injuries. They tried for a coup in Berlin, but it failed. Too bad, huh?"

"We could've been home for Thanksgiving," Friedman said. "Those Nazi bastards are pretty good at killing, but they sure screwed up this execution."

"A plot by German officers to kill Hitler?" I said, glancing at Big Mike. "Who would've thought it possible?" Short of Madame Janvier, that is.

"You sure he's really alive, sir?" Big Mike asked.

"Positive, sad to say," Johnson said, rushing to the teletype as a new dispatch clattered in.

"There must be a lot of German officers on the run right now," I said. If Madame Janvier was right about Rast being involved, and he hadn't just been blowing smoke, then I wondered if he'd head for the American lines. If he hadn't already been put up against a wall and shot.

"No idea how many were involved," Johnson said, ripping off the sheet and scanning it as he spoke. "But we did get a report about German army officers arresting Gestapo men in Paris, then letting them go after the coup fell apart. Hard to tell what's really going on, or who's on which side."

"Yeah," I said. I couldn't have agreed more. "Any chance we can get a message out to First Army?"

"Maybe in an hour or so after things calm down," Friedman said, taking a message from one of his radio operators. "We're up to our eyeballs here."

"What gives, Billy?" Big Mike asked once we were outside. "Shouldn't we tell someone about Rast being mixed up in this thing?"

"Not yet," I said. "First, we don't know if it's true. He might have been saying that purely for the Madame's benefit. Second, I don't want word getting around. It might spook him."

"Spook him? You think he's hiding out in the barn? What are you talking about?"

"Look, if Rast is involved and still alive and kicking, his best bet will be to give himself up. The last we heard, his unit was heading to Paris. So if he was part of that failed roundup of Gestapo officers, he's going to want to get somewhere safe before the boys in black leather coats begin questioning him."

"Okay, that makes sense," Big Mike said as we stopped in the road to watch a pair of silver Mustang fighters swoop high above us. "I hear they start with a few fingernails just to show they mean business. But what makes you think he's headed back this way?"

"Gut feeling," I said. "Maybe he was trying to make friends by releasing people. Maybe he's got the goods on some collaborators in those files we heard about. I don't know. But how many choices does he have?"

"*If* he's a part of the plot, and *if* he was found out, and *if* he's not in Berlin by now," Big Mike said. "Then you might have something. But what's it to us? I can't see how this ties into the murder of Major Jerome."

"Hey, it's the one loose string I have to pull," I said. It was like my dad always said. When you're getting nowhere fast on a case, look for the one thing that stands out, like a stitch unraveling on a sweater, and start pulling. Sometimes that thread leads somewhere. Other times, you basically just ruin a sweater. "Rast had secrets. Files I'd like to see. I can't help thinking he's connected to Jerome's murder, one way or the other."

"Well, maybe, but I don't know how he pulled that one off in the middle of a battalion HQ," Big Mike said. "But I gotta admit, we have damn little else to go on. So what's next?"

"You stay here and get a message to Sam as soon as you can. Give him the lowdown on Yvonne and Fisherman and ask if he can get Diana assigned to this investigation. Find out if anything in Rast's background points to him being part of this bomb plot against Hitler."

"What are you going to do?" Big Mike asked.

"Pay a visit to Leon Dubois and find out how he got the get-out-of-jail-free card," I said. "If you don't hear back from Harding soon, go up to First Army and track him down. And bring back Kaz." I had a feeling things were about to heat up, and I needed him here.

"How am I supposed to find him?" Big Mike asked as we entered the kitchen by the back door.

"If I need to tell a guy named Miecznikowski how to find sixteen thousand Poles riding Sherman tanks in Normandy, then you don't deserve those stripes. They're somewhere outside of Bayeux, that's all I know."

"Okay, Billy, but you don't have to take it out on me," Big Mike said, frowning. "I'm not the one who let Kaz go off on this wild goose chase of his."

"Jesus, what do I have to do to get some respect from my non-com?"

I said, trying for a smile to show I was cracking a joke. But I wasn't. I was steamed at Big Mike, but more at myself for letting things get out of control.

"Act like a captain once in a while," Big Mike whispered, leaning down with his hand on my shoulder. "I know you like to stick it to the army, but every now and then giving orders and having them followed works pretty well."

"But we're talking about Kaz," I said, whispering right back between clenched teeth. "He's about to go off his rocker."

"He's *Lieutenant* Kazimierz and you're *Captain* Boyle," Big Mike said, punching a meaty finger at my chest in a way that said the chain of command didn't extend to him. "And Kaz is a whole lot safer with us to watch over him. You think he's going to feel better hearing stories of what it's like in Poland under the Nazis? Or that the latest news is his kid sister was sent to a concentration camp? That could push him off the deep end. *Sir.*"

"That's enough, Sergeant," I said.

"Not hardly," Big Mike said and stomped out of the room, nearly running into Madame Janvier, who'd come in carrying a bowl of string beans from her garden.

"Oh, your sergeant looks angry," she said, setting the bowl in the sink. We both glanced up as Big Mike's boots thundered up the stairs.

"It will pass," I said. "Have you heard the news?"

"About Hitler? Yes, such bad luck. Perhaps Major Rast was involved after all," she said, rinsing the beans.

"He must be pretty worried right now if he was," I said. "Tell me, were you here the day the Germans left?"

"Of course. Where else would I be? It was quite frightening, I tell you. We could hear the artillery coming closer, and the fighter planes overhead dropping their bombs. It made us nervous."

"It looks like the fighting came very close to you," I said.

"Yes, but that was after the *Feldgendarmerie* men pulled out. Most of the actual combat took place in the orchards, and new trees can be planted, the damaged ones saved. I was worried about my workers. I told them to hide in the woods until the Germans left. They are all

older men, but I thought the *Boche* might take them for slave labor.
Or that the *Milice* might kill them just for sport. I kept Arianne close
by my side, for reasons which are obvious."

"Did the *Milice* give you any problems?"

"No, they left quickly, frightened after the first aircraft flew over.
The Germans were too busy burning papers and loading their belong-
ings to bother us."

"They burned their files?"

"*Oui*, they had a big bonfire out back. Petrol is precious to them,
but they used a great deal. I imagine they had secrets which many
collaborators were only too pleased to see go up in smoke. Will you
join us for luncheon, Captain?" She snapped the ends off and tossed
the green beans into a pot.

"No, thank you. But tell me, did you see Major Rast that day?"

"*Oui*, I did. He was among the last to leave. He sought me out to
thank me for my hospitality. Not that I had any choice in the matter,
but still, it was a better end than I expected."

"Was there anything left of what they burned?" I asked.

"Nothing but blackened paper and ash," she said. "When the first
Americans arrived, some officers went through it all. I do not think
they found anything."

"Did Rast take anything with him?"

"Not personally, no. I saw his men load bags into a truck. It looked
like clothing, but I was not close enough to inspect it. I was desperately
waiting for their departure, you understand. It was our moment of
liberation." Wiping her hands on a towel, she smiled at the memory.

I asked if she'd show me where Rast had his office, and she led me
upstairs to the third floor. We passed Colonel Brewster's room, where
he and a couple of aides were rolling out a map. At the far end of the
hall, she opened a door, gestured for me to go in, and left without a
word.

The room was wide, with narrow windows on each side. A small
fireplace was choked with ashes, blackened curls of paper strewn
around the edges. Two wooden beams hung low, forcing me to duck
as I walked across the space. A single table and two chairs were shoved

under one window, an old feather bed covered with a threadbare duvet by the other. The floor was bare wood, worn shiny.

I don't know what I expected, but it wasn't this spartan room. It had the musty smell of an old attic, and cobwebs gathered dust on the windowsills. I took the poker by the fireplace and raked it through the ashes. Nothing but sodden soot.

What did I expect to find here? Some hint as to what kind of man Rast was. If this room gave any indication, he was at least a very neat hermit. Or maybe Madame Janvier had given the place a thorough cleaning to get the odor of the Occupation out.

I turned on my heel, frustrated at my inability to make some sense of this investigation. I stopped at our room, hoping to see Big Mike, but he was gone. I grabbed a jacket, my Thompson, and a stack of K-Ration cartons he'd squirreled away. I passed Yvonne's room and caught sight of her at her usual post, staring out the window. What did she see out there? The daily movements of a *pressoir*, or visions of a Gestapo jail cell?

"Madame Janvier," I said, catching her as she stepped outside wearing a leather jacket and holding trimming shears. "Can you tell me the quickest way to Saint-Jean?"

"It is not far," she said. "At the end of the drive, turn right and take the road east. Then follow the signs to La Croix. When you get there, go right in the center of the village. That road will take you to Saint-Jean. You are going to see Leon Dubois? He and his mother live in a farmhouse at the edge of the village. If you ask anyone, they can direct you. Leon is a schoolteacher, you know? Perhaps you should wait and find him at home this afternoon."

"I don't have much else to do, unfortunately," I said, as we walked outside. "Perhaps I can catch him at lunch. Is it possible to telephone him? You do business with his mother, right?"

"Yes, but they do not have a telephone. Mine has not worked in some time. I think it will be a while before they repair all the broken lines. You are not making much progress, it seems?"

"We are following leads," I said, giving the usual response.

"The baron is doing so elsewhere?"

"Other business called him away," I said. "Right now, it seems like Major Jerome was simply in the wrong place at the wrong time. Why it was wrong, well, that's the hard part."

"Do you really think Leon Dubois can help you?"

"Perhaps. He knew Major Rast under different circumstances than anyone else I've talked to. I'm hoping he may have some insight into why Rast began letting people go."

"And that will help you how?" Madame Janvier said, stopping by the gate to her orchard. "It seems only to speak to the major's change of heart, not a reason to kill. Quite the opposite, in fact."

"Yes," I said, watching her unlatch the gate. "That's a mystery. But maybe someone wasn't released, and they, or someone close to them, wanted to take their revenge."

"And mistook poor Major Jerome for Major Rast? Oh, good luck, Captain Boyle. I do not envy you your job," she said, ambling off, pruning shears in hand.

I didn't envy me my job either.

CHAPTER TWENTY-TWO

As MADAME JANVIER disappeared in the rows of apple trees heavy with ripening fruit, I drove away with something niggling at the back of my mind. Something was off. What was it?

The bedroom. Madame Janvier had said she'd been forced to give up her bedroom and bunk with Arianne. But given up for who? I'd assumed Rast, as the senior officer, but she'd just showed me his room. It certainly didn't look like the kind of bedroom befitting the lady of the house. Besides, she hadn't moved back in there.

Yvonne. It had to be Yvonne who took her room. But why? And why not reclaim it?

Which led me to wonder again what she planned to do with Yvonne, and why she hadn't yet done it. Yvonne Virot was a silent constant in this investigation. Always there, giving away nothing. Except when she found Jerome, and when we found her back in the room where he died.

Twice out of her room. Three words spoken. *Fisherman, Gustave, German.*

Whatever her eyes had seen was locked up tight in her mind, or what was left of it. If she'd been tortured and abused, she might never come out of her shell. I toyed with the idea of taking her back to the hospital myself. After all, what claim did Madame Janvier, or anyone else for that matter, have on her?

Best to wait and see if Diana could be sent over. If she spent time with Yvonne, we might learn something. Maybe I could have Dr. Leroy visit her. Or get an army shrink to assess her. *Not a bad idea*, I thought as I slowed the jeep and looked up at the sound of low-flying aircraft. A pair of Thunderbolt fighter-bombers screeched across the sky, heading south, hunting for Germans on the move. Or called in by a forward observer to take out a tank or a pillbox.

More Thunderbolts followed, their Pratt & Whitney engines ear-shatteringly loud as treetops swirled above me, the sound of their snarling engines fading within seconds. I pulled over as another flight approached, and ducked instinctively even though they were too far away to do more than shower me with leaves sucked from the over-hanging branches. Their shining aluminum skins sparkled in the sunlight, their beauty and grace in flight masking a deadly intent. Some Kraut bastards dug in somewhere to the south were about to suffer a storm of .50 caliber rounds, rockets, and bombs unleashed on their positions.

I waited, and in less than a minute I heard the first thuds of far-off explosions. I turned the wheel to get back on the road and froze as a fast-moving shadow caught my eye.

Had I really seen it? I scanned the road ahead, reaching for my Thompson as I did so.

There. The figure of a man flitting through the brush at the side of the road. The outline of a rifle. I swung the Thompson around as I got out of the jeep, settling my feet on the dusty road as quietly as possible. I caught a glimpse of movement headed away from me. The slow, deliberate moves told me I hadn't been spotted.

Crouching low, I darted across the road and ran to where the figure had entered the woods. I knelt, making myself as small as possible in case this was the sniper on his return engagement. Who else would be skulking around this far behind the lines?

I didn't have an answer to that, but I didn't want to take a chance and start spraying the trees with .45 slugs. So I slipped between two trees, staying low, trying not to make a racket. The guy ahead of me sure wasn't.

The good news was, he didn't have a lot of room to hide. About a hundred yards of neat lines of apple trees left little room for cover. The workers kept the rows between the trees scythed and weeded. On the other side of the orchard was a cultivated field of vegetables. The same field the sniper had fired across to take out Fair.

In the other direction, the road dipped and crossed a stream marked by a jumble of rocks and a sharp drop-off. Then the land rose and flattened out into another field of apple trees. So I knew my quarry was confined to a narrow strip of wooded cover, unless he made for the orchards or the field. If he did, I had him. If he didn't, well, then he might have me.

I worked my way along a slight fold in the terrain. Rocks jutted out from the ground, perhaps from when they cleared the land generations ago. I heard water running off to my side, the sound covering my footsteps as I crossed fallen limbs and stepped on rotting leaves.

A twig snapped.

Maybe five, ten yards ahead. I froze. Explosions echoed faintly in the distance. More Thunderbolts, or maybe an artillery strike. I took a deep breath, waited for the next salvo to hit, and took three quick steps to the cover of a thick tree trunk. The chattering of machine guns rattled dully in the distance.

My cheek pressed against the rough bark of an oak as quiet draped itself about the greenery, the ragged sound of my own breathing louder than the distant booms and mechanical rhythm of gunfire. Slowly, I moved my head until one eye peeked around the tree. No movement, no sound. I twisted my body, wincing at the multitude of noises it seemed to create. Leather creaked, the edge of my helmet scraped bark, the butt of my Thompson thudded against my hip. Even the deep breath I took echoed in my chest as I scanned the woods ahead, half expecting a rifle shot. Sweat dripped down the small of my back, a feeling in the pit of my stomach telling me I was being watched.

A rustle of leaves.

Maybe ten yards out, dead ahead. I went low and duck-walked to the next tree, my eyes fixed on where I thought the noise had come from. Hard to say in the forest, with leaves and scrub brush deadening sound. A bird fluttered up from the ground, flapping away and making a sudden racket before it settled into the low branches of a pine tree.

Had it been the bird, pecking at dead leaves and hunting for insects? Or a man, stumbling upon the bird and flushing it out?

If it was the guy I was following, he'd probably sit tight for a few minutes, waiting to see if anyone had noticed the frantic flight of that bird. Carefully, walking heel-to-toe to keep my steps muffled, I advanced to the next tree and took what cover I could, bringing up my Thompson. I eased around the tree, finger on the trigger, making no sudden movements or sharp noises. My sleeve brushed against the smooth bark, the brief grating thunderous amidst the quiet.

A bead of sweat dripped from my forehead. I was exposed, half of me presenting the perfect target, if anyone was there. Maybe it was a GI on patrol, which would be a good idea after the sniper attack. But a single dogface? Not so likely. Whoever it was, they were lying low, or so far ahead of me that I was worrying for nothing.

But worry in a war zone kept you alive, so I moved low and silent, ducking beneath a low-hanging branch and kneeling to scout out the scene ahead. Small trees, vines, scraggly bushes, and a tumble-down, dry stone wall that once marked a forgotten boundary.

Water. I heard the gurgling rush of water over stone.

It was impossible to see more than a few yards in any direction, but I could tell the water was off to my right. The orchards and fields were to my left, so it made sense that my guy—whether he was a GI, a sniper, or a local kid out to steal apples—was straight ahead.

If it was a sniper, I had one advantage. He'd be facing out over the open fields, looking for a target. Close in with all this brush, I'd be hard to spot until it was too late. I hoped. I veered right to get on his blind side. Meanwhile, I prayed it was a kid filching apples.

I stepped over the stone wall slowly, swinging my leg high and wide so as not to catch it on a rock and send it tumbling. A few yards up, I spotted a pile of stacked logs, green with moss and rotting into the ground. They'd been cut and laid there years ago, then forgotten. A woodcutter gone to war, perhaps.

I crouched low and made my way to the woodpile. It was good

cover. I went around one side, looking for a spot to hunker down and survey the ground ahead.

Wood tumbled down around me, logs rolling off the pile in a flurry of wet rot and dirty moss. The Thompson was knocked loose from my grip as my helmet went flying. I scrambled to get away from the logs, skittering backward on my butt.

"*Fils de pute!*"

It was Legrand calling me a son of a bitch, standing on the other side of the woodpile, a booted heel on the remaining logs and his rifle pointed at my chest.

I froze.

"What are you doing here?" he said, walking around the fallen logs and snagging my weapon.

"Following someone," I said. "You, I guess."

"Stand up," he demanded, which I liked, since this was a good place for an execution, and it was always easier to shoot a guy already laid out on the ground. "Tell me why you are here."

"I was driving to Saint-Jean, and I saw a man run into the woods. So I stopped and followed. I was worried the sniper was back. He isn't, is he?" I took a chance and glanced at his rifle. Standard issue German Kar 98k, no sniper scope.

"No, I am not your sniper," Legrand said, offended. "But I thought he may return and came to kill him."

"Then you can stop pointing that gun at me," I said, dusting myself off. Legrand was on the defensive, and if he hadn't shot me already, I didn't think he would.

"Yes," he said, lowering the rifle and picking up my Thompson. "I heard you but could not see. I hoped it was *le salaud Boche*, and I might have him." He shrugged at his misfortune and handed over my submachine gun, an apologetic grin slapped on under his thick mustache.

This was not the braggart I'd seen before. He was alone, without his usual gang of brutal pals, and stalking a sniper who possessed deadly aim. That took guts, and I hadn't pegged him as the type.

"Where are your men?" I asked.

"Hunting Germans as well. But this I do by myself. Too many men make too much noise," he said. "Come, help me with these logs. Otherwise he will know someone has been here."

We stacked the logs as quietly as possible. I watched Legrand, and his eyes flitted about, searching the woods for signs of movement.

"Why are you doing this?" I asked when we were done.

"Sergeant Fair was a good man," he said. "It was not right, what happened. It should have been you, I hear. I mean, an officer. That is what a sniper does, yes? Kill officers?"

"Usually," I said. "A good sergeant is a valuable man as well. But I agree. I think Fair was killed because I held his rifle."

"Foolish man," Legrand said. "Visiting that woman. She is trouble."

"Again, I can't disagree," I said, wanting to get back to why Legrand was skulking around in the woods. "But you're telling me you are out here alone to avenge Fair's death?"

"You doubt my word?" He jutted his chin out at me. This was the Legrand I knew.

"Yes, I do. I doubt you'd come out here and risk your life because a Kraut sniper put a notch in his rifle, whoever took the bullet. I doubt you'd risk your neck without a dozen of your men around you if there wasn't something in it for you. What's your angle?" Now I was the one thrusting my chin forward. With Legrand standing a few inches taller than me, it didn't have quite the same effect.

"Angle?" Legrand said. "I do not understand." A furrow ran across his brow as he tilted his head.

"Your purpose, your main reason for being here," I said. Legrand nodded, grasping my meaning. Interesting that he didn't take offense. I'd basically insulted his honor, and he wasn't doing much more than storing away a new vocabulary word. Instead of shaking his fist and threatening bodily harm, he sat down beside me on the mossy logs and sighed.

"Perhaps there is another reason," he said. "I often come to *Pressoir Janvier*, as you know. I do not like the *Boche* shooting at people there, you understand?"

"I think I do," I said, weary at the thought of another lovestruck guy pining after the silent beauty in the garret. "You're worried about Yvonne."

"What? No, not that poor wretch of a girl. What do you take me for? It is Madame Janvier I worry about. She is a fine woman, is she not?"

"Yeah, she's a brave one too," I said, resisting the urge to add "well-off." I knew Legrand had killed a man to buy his farmland cheap, but I didn't want to say anything to spoil this little heart-to-heart we were enjoying. "Being part of the Nemo Line, I mean."

"*Certainement,*" he said, nodding eagerly. "That is why I worry. Have you thought that the sniper could have been sent to assassinate her?"

"No. She's in and out all the time. A little bit of patience, and he would have had her in his sights. I think he took one shot, mistaking Fair for an officer, then got out fast."

"Well, perhaps that time. But who is to say I am not right? Who has done the most harm to the *Boche*? It is Madame Janvier. More than Colonel Brewster and his man Johnson."

"Major Johnson? You work closely with him, don't you?"

"Bah! He never listens to my warnings. And he wants my men to go into battle as if we were trained soldiers. We know how to prowl the night and set charges on rail lines, but we are not *infanterie*. A stupid man, he would throw away our lives."

"I wasn't that impressed with him either," I said. I watched Legrand's eyes as they darted back and forth, as if trying to find a version of the truth to settle down on.

"I told him there were no tanks close by, but he did not listen," Legrand said. "He only tells Colonel Brewster what he wants to hear. You should tell the colonel he is not well served by that man."

"I'll think about it," I said. Legrand would like that. Get Johnson in trouble, maybe transferred out, and there went his competition for Madame Janvier. With his upper-class manners, Johnson might be a good match for a land-owning Frenchwoman. If that was Legrand's game.

I had a feeling there was something deeper at work here, and this story was a good cover for it. I decided to let up on the interrogation for now so I wouldn't spook him with my suspicion. "Do you know where the sniper fired from?"

"I do, yes," Legrand said, stammering a bit as he realized we'd left an uncomfortable topic behind. "Here, I will show you."

We walked on, veering close to the border with the open field. The trees thinned out, and this narrow strip of land looked like it had been cleared and then gone to seed not too long ago. Saplings you could wrap your hand around dotted the ground where thick grasses grew.

"Here," Legrand said, holding up his arm to keep me from advancing. "Do you see?"

I did. The grass was matted down in places. The ground here was maybe a foot higher than the surrounding area, with enough elevation to provide a good view across the field. In front of the grasses, branches from a leafy shrub had been snapped back. I lay down and saw the view as the sniper had. A narrow cone of vision, leading straight to the rear of the house. Kitchen door on one side, the garden in the middle, and the entrance to the annex with the door to the comm room wide open.

Officer country.

"Perfect spot," I said to Legrand as I slithered backward and stood.

"It is a long shot," he said. "I could not hit anything at such a distance."

"I know," I said. His rifle didn't look well maintained. Traces of rust showed the beginning of corrosion on the barrel. It might do the job at close range, but it wasn't a sharpshooter's tool. I hadn't really been worried about Legrand being the sniper. What concerned me was that he still worried I might believe he was.

And that there was more to his story than defending the honor of Madame Janvier and protecting her from an assassin's bullet. I didn't buy the notion of the Germans putting a hit out on her. Her job was done. The Krauts had more to gain by knocking off a colonel or a battalion staff officer, and no one I'd talked to thought Legrand was the type to put himself in harm's way.

"Did you find anything else?" I asked.

"No. The old Janvier mill is close, but it is deserted. I checked it earlier," he said.

"Earlier? You've been out here before?"

"*Oui*, I arrived early this morning. I walked in and out twice, hoping to find the sniper. But you are the first person I saw," Legrand said.

"Show me the mill. This is where Madame Janvier hid people?"

"It is. Come. But no more talking," he said in a whisper, a finger to his lips. He set off, hunched over and rifle at the ready. Maybe the sniper was holed up out here, but if he was, Legrand would never spot him. German snipers were masters at camouflage. He probably wouldn't waste a shot on a partisan anyway. A captain? Probably.

I trailed behind Legrand, glancing back and checking our flanks. His faded brown jacket melted into the shadows amidst green leafy branches, turning him into a ghostly figure who vanished and reappeared like an armed and dangerous woodland wraith. Finally, he halted, kneeling at the edge of a stand of small pines.

He pointed. The original Janvier homestead was old, indeed. Really old. Walls of stone still stood, but parts of the roof were caved in, and the windows were dark, gaping, vine-choked holes. Shrubs and tall grasses sprouted everywhere, even in the open doorway, where a rotting wooden door hung lazily on one hinge.

"How long has it been like this?" I asked. It didn't look like much of a hideout, not even solid enough to keep the rain out.

"I do not know," Legrand said, keeping his voice low. "The Janvier family started here, but that was centuries ago, when this was a mill. Then they turned to apples and left this place to rot in the damp."

"A long time back?"

"When they cut off the king's head, I think." That qualified.

"I don't see any way inside," I said. "A man would leave a trace going through the weeds and vines."

"You are right. I thought to wait inside myself, but saw it would be impossible to do so without leaving a mark. Come. On the sides it is even worse."

Legrand was right. The side close to the river was an impenetrable tangle of weedy plants and stunted saplings. The wooden wheel that once powered the mill was rotted and disintegrating, covered in thick moss and ready to tumble into the stream from where it was set into the crumbling brick wall along the water.

It was the same on the other side, where a round stone trough marked where they had first pressed apples. Back when the queen told the starving Parisians to eat cake if they had no bread, this was a thriving center of business, grinding grain and making cider. But there was no trace of any activity now. The place was so overgrown it was impossible to even touch the building without a machete to hack your way through.

"The sniper couldn't have hidden here," I said.

"No. I believe he came for one shot, at least on that day, and left, knowing the Americans would send out patrols. Not that they found anything."

"Are you going to stay here?"

"*Oui*, I will make my own patrol and watch for his return. I may have some luck, who knows?" With that, Legrand gave me a lazy salute, brushing his hand against his black beret before vanishing into the trees.

I didn't trust him one damn bit. I didn't know what he was up to out here, but a guy who shaved the heads of young girls for sport didn't strike me as the sniper-stalking type. Maybe he was about to flip his wig over Madame Janvier, or at least her property, but I didn't buy his heroics for one second.

Not that I had a clue what he was really up to. Better to let him think I bought his story, especially since he could have me in his crosshairs. I scooted off, giving the old deserted mill one last look-see before I trotted off into the pines. Later, I'd ask Madame Janvier about how they hid escapees there. Or maybe the mill was the wrong place, and there was some tumble-down house along this waterway. But it didn't matter; this had been a wild goose chase.

Back at the jeep, I took a healthy swig from my canteen and listened for the sounds of combat in the distance. The faint, echoing *rat-tat-tat* of machine guns and the dull explosive *crumps* told me the fighting hadn't died down. I drove off, thinking about all the graves that would be dug tonight because of those distant echoes of violence.

CHAPTER TWENTY-THREE

I'D BEEN DRIVING for less than a minute when I spotted a Frenchman trudging along the road, a heavy sack slung over his shoulder. I slowed to offer him a ride as more aircraft roared overhead. It dawned on me that this road was a straight shot to La Croix, and that the air show I was being treated to was because they were following the road to their target.

The Frenchman ducked instinctively as I did, bending at the knees as if the propellers might snag his cap. He turned after they'd passed and grinned, clearly aware of how silly it was. I smiled back, nodding to show I understood.

"*Un tour?*" I asked, gesturing to the passenger seat.

"*Oui,*" he said, letting the sack fall to the ground. He looked tired. His face, partially hidden by his cloth cap, was covered in stubble and smudges of dirt. He looked about the same age as Legrand, and I wondered if he might be one of Legrand's men, out scouting for the sniper. But he had no weapon, which my cop's eye took in as I checked him out head to toe. He glanced down the road as the rumble of vehicles signaled a convoy headed our way.

"Come on," I said, patting the passenger seat.

"*Merci,*" he said and jumped in, picking up his bag and clutching it to his chest. We both craned our necks to take in the advancing jeeps and trucks, moving at a steady pace, but not too fast. Dust means death.

"Where to?" I asked, and then tried a little French. "*Où aller?*"

"*Chez moi,*" he said, waving his hand vaguely in the direction of the road ahead.

The approaching vehicles were almost to us, so I swung the steering wheel hard and gave it some gas, enough to jump out in front of the column. I didn't enjoy the notion of waiting until the tail end drifted by and eating exhaust for the next ten miles.

"Boyle! Slow down!"

It was Colonel Brewster, in the lead jeep just behind me. I waved and eased up on the gas, matching their pace. I took a quick look over my shoulder and spotted the scowl on his face. Maybe he didn't like me taking his lead spot. Or maybe he just didn't like me. Things hadn't gone well since I'd shown up. I'd seen it happen before in a murder investigation. Murder means something is rotten somewhere. Someone's angry, hurt, scared, or vicious, and violent death seems to be the only way to deal with the pain. The rot doesn't go away when the corpse gets carted off. It's still there, festering, turning all it touches foul.

Like Fair. He'd been at the edges of this thing, drawn in by the allure of Yvonne. Fair had survived a lot of lead flying his way up front, and then he took a sniper's slug in Madame Janvier's garden.

What if that hadn't been a German sniper?

What if the rot had gotten to Fair? What if he'd come closer than we knew, and the killer had taken him out and laid the blame on a Kraut sharpshooter?

Was that the same person who took a shot at me and hit Anton? Or had the presence of a real sniper given our killer the idea to take out Fair?

Maybe, but I couldn't see what that accomplished. We'd gotten everything we could out of Fair. He was headed back into combat and could have been killed or captured soon enough.

"*Ici,*" my passenger said, tapping me on the arm. I'd nearly forgotten about him as I worked my new theory. He pointed to the right where a dirt track crossed the main road. He wanted to be let off here, but I couldn't stop, especially with Colonel Brewster breathing down my neck. The road had narrowed, leaving no room for the column to pass.

I slowed and signaled for him to jump out. He got the message, giving me a big grin and a *merci* as he vaulted out and stumbled for a few steps before regaining his balance, the bag gripped in one hand. I gave him a quick wave and drove on, trying to get my thoughts back on track.

Had Fair simply been unlucky, or would he have been killed even if he hadn't handed off his rifle to me? Would I have been the target, a sure hit this time? Whoever the shooter was, he was good at it. The shot at our jeep had been in the driving rain, and he'd hit where he'd aimed, right where my head would have been if I hadn't turned to check that spinning tire.

Was it the same shooter both times? Impossible to know. The Germans used snipers a lot, more than we did. They were better at it, not just shooting, but camouflage, cover, and stealth. So there could have been more than one guy with a telescopic sight operating near a battalion headquarters, which was a good target. A decent amount of brass hanging around, but close enough to the front lines for a sniper to make his escape and work his way back home.

The road split, and I took the turn marked for La Croix. The column behind me took the other fork, and I pulled over, craning my neck to watch the parade. A dozen trucks followed Brewster's jeep, GIs crammed in the back, laughing and jostling one another like it was a Sunday drive.

I spotted a couple of Joey's pals. Unlike the rest, they wore solemn faces as if they were on their way to a funeral. Without an experienced non-com like Fair to lead them, it was a good bet they were. Towed artillery pieces followed the truckloads of infantry. Something was brewing. It wasn't a full-scale attack with the whole battalion, but Brewster was throwing a reinforced company against the Krauts not too far from here, by the sound of artillery up ahead.

I drove on, the road narrowing as I entered another stretch of hedgerows. They loomed darkly over the dirt road, ditches on either side thick with mud. Shattered and blackened branches marked where the hedgerows had been breached. Gaping holes gave a glimpse of wrecked vehicles in the squared-off fields. A blackened Sherman tank sat on its side in a ditch, a track spun off like a child's loose shoelace, the area charred by the fires that had scorched it.

Artillery fire sounded up ahead, but it was outgoing, in the right direction. I came upon a field, the hedgerows along the road completely cleared. Four howitzers blasted away, crewmen pressing palms to their ears with each thunderous volley. I drove off quickly, not worrying about dust. If the Krauts didn't spot this fire, they were already hunkered down. Or dead.

La Croix wasn't much of a town. It appeared suddenly, as if placed in the middle of a maze of hedgerows and then forgotten. A few houses gave way to a village square, with a water fountain at the center and the usual monument to the dead of the last war. A couple of shops were open, but most buildings were shuttered or damaged too badly to be occupied. Beyond the fountain, two roads veered off around a church dominating the square. The steeple lay in ruins, blackened brickwork strewn across the stone steps. It would have been a good perch for artillery observers or a sniper. Until mortars or a tank round blew it all to hell. Jeeps were parked by a café marked as COMPANY B HQ. A couple of medics lounged by the fountain, sporting red cross armbands on both arms.

"Hey, fellas," I said, braking to a halt. I wasn't wearing insignia, so they responded with supreme indifference. "I'm headed to Saint-Jean. Is that the way?" I pointed to the right, which was the turn Madame Janvier had told me to take, if I recalled correctly.

"Naw," one the medics drawled. "That road will get you an all-expenses-paid trip to a POW camp."

"Or shot," another said. "So don't head that way, partner. We got ourselves a quiet day here. Like to keep it that way."

"You sure?" I asked.

"Damn sure. Hauled casualties out that road yesterday. You want Saint-Jean, you go left here. No Krauts, just another dump like this one about three miles out," he said, waving his hand in the direction of the other road.

"Must have gotten my wires crossed," I said. "What's with the extra armband? Don't you wear one on the left arm?"

"Yeah, but some doctor in England came up with the idea to study wounded medics. Turned out there's way more wounds on a medic's right side."

"Where the Krauts can't see the armband," I said.

"That's the idea. So we're doubling up. Most of the time, the Jerries let us do our job, and we do the same for their medics."

"Except for the fucking SS," the other medic said. "They kill for the fun of it. That's who's waiting down that other road. The 17th SS Division. They massacred a bunch of wounded paratroopers from the 82nd Airborne a few days after D-Day. Not to mention the French villagers who had helped them."

"Thanks for the warning, then," I said and drove off, making sure I took the left turn.

Maybe Madame Janvier had been confused, or thinking about the return route. Or I'd misheard her. Either way, I was glad to have run into those medics. It saved me the embarrassment of being turned around at a front-line position. With the SS down the road, there were bound to be GIs dug in to keep watch. Worse case, my jeep would have drawn fire, and someone, most likely me, would've gotten hurt. At a minimum, I'd have had to put up with the grim stares and disapproval dogfaces reserved for staff officers who got lost near the front. Damned embarrassing.

In a couple of miles, I came to the outskirts of Saint-Jean. Then I realized, after the buildings thinned out, that the outskirts had *been* the village. The narrow road ran straight through it, with no turns or crossroad in sight. Which was a good thing for the people of Saint-Jean. It had kept their small village intact. No one had fought over this place. It had a small church with a stubby, gray-slated tower, not tall enough to serve as an observation post. The road itself ran parallel to the front, so it had been of little importance to advancing or retreating forces. A few small lanes meandered off the road, nothing but dirt tracks.

The café was open. Flowers bloomed in window boxes. A bakery sported a hand-lettered sign. PAS DE PAIN. No bread, but the windows were unbroken. Not bad for Normandy.

Two old men sat at a table outside the café. I asked if they knew Leon Dubois and where he was. I guess I didn't mangle the French language too badly because they both began to speak, faster than I could understand. I got them to slow down, and one of them pointed to the lane I'd just passed.

"*La maison de Dubois?*" I asked, and their heads bobbed. I backed up and took the hard-packed dirt road between buildings so close I could have knocked on each window. I kept going until the village gave way to fields, one with rows of greening crops and the other dotted with cows lazily munching grass. It all seemed unreal. Peaceful.

I spotted the house down a weed-choked drive. Apple trees spread out behind it, orderly columns behind a stone wall topped with rusting barbed wire. The house was long but narrow, stucco crumbling off the sides and revealing old stonework beneath. Vines ran up the sides, bright green against the reddish stone. A small garden finished off the picture of a quaint Norman setting.

I spotted an older woman in the garden, her hand to her back as she stood up from weeding. Madame Dubois, who I hoped spoke some English. I drove in and parked at the front door.

She was stout in a big-boned sort of way, but the skin hung loose from her jaw. Plenty of well-fed folks had thinned down the hard way during the Occupation. A shock of gray hair fluttered loose from a headscarf, rising and falling with a gusting breeze.

She didn't speak any English. She spoke a whole lot of French, wagging her finger in my face the entire time. I couldn't pick up a single word and backed up a step as I held up my hands in mock surrender.

"Leon?" I said, pointing at the house once she slowed down a bit.

We were saved from this linguistic impasse by the sound of bicycle tires crunching on stones. Leon, home from school, I prayed.

"Leon Dubois?" I asked as he drew near, halting and carefully leaning his bicycle against the house. Bikes were valuable these days, the only form of transportation for a lot of people.

"I am he," he said, in careful, deliberate English. His mother stood by, her face hard and grim, arms akimbo as she stared me up and down.

"I have some questions for you," I said. "*Je m'appelle Capitaine* Billy Boyle."

"No," Leon said, as if there couldn't possibly be a question he could answer. He shifted on his feet as if he were ready to run away. Leon was on the small side, thin, with shallow cheeks and a mop of thick black hair above a face which didn't seem large enough for it. Where his mother was formidable, he was shifty. Or maybe I was judging him too quickly. Could be because he was a teacher. School had never been my favorite place.

"Yes," I said, folding my arms and watching his reaction.

"Of course, of course," he said, almost dancing a jig on those jittery feet. "I did not mean I would not answer. But what do you wish to know?"

His mother interrupted with a question, throwing a quick glance in my direction. She seemed upset with Leon.

"Please, come inside," he said. "*Ma mère* insists." She was already at the door, waving us on impatiently. Leon gestured for me to go first, but I put my hand on his shoulder and gently pushed him forward. I didn't want to chance him grabbing his bike and taking off, even if the chances of his disobeying the daunting Madame Dubois were pretty slim.

We sat at the kitchen table, windows open to the breeze and a fine view of the orchard. The room was small, with an ancient stove and a hand pump for water on the wooden counter. Everything looked scrubbed to within an inch of its life. Madame Dubois poured wine from a jug into three mismatched glasses and nodded. That seemed to be the signal for me to speak.

"Are you done with classes for the day?" I asked, wanting Leon to sweat a bit before we got to the point.

"Yes. We have school only in the morning," he said. "Please tell me why you have come?"

"Your English is good," I said, watching as Leon's mother took a long gulp and set her glass down hard. Leon jumped, and she rattled off a question to him.

"Thank you," he said. "*Maman* wants to know if you have come to pay her for the trees."

"Trees? What trees?"

"Apples. In her orchard. You bombed them, and eight are gone. Burned. Do you have the money, she wants to know," Leon said, glancing at his mother and holding his glass with both hands.

"I didn't come about the trees," I said. "Please tell her I'm sorry about her apple trees."

"Then why are you here?" Leon said, a nervous tremor vibrating in his throat.

"Tell her," I said, nodding in the direction of his mother, who'd already finished her wine. He did. Then he looked everywhere except straight at me. His *maman* poured herself another glass and shot Leon a disapproving look.

They both knew why I was here.

"I want to ask you about Major Hans Rast, of the *Feldgendarmerie*," I said, leaning forward with my arms on the table. Leon sat back, either at the mention of Rast's name, or to distance himself from my glare.

"He arrested me," Leon said. "I am part of the *Groupe Rouge*, you know."

"Do you teach English at school?" I asked.

"Yes, but not during the Occupation. It was not allowed," he said, shaking his head and trying to follow the conversation. "Why?"

"Because you should have used the past tense. You *were* a member of the *Groupe Rouge*. Jacques said he kicked you out."

"Kicked?" Leon's forehead wrinkled in puzzlement. "Oh, I understand. No, I am still a member. We are comrades, you understand? It was to be safe. For everyone."

"A precaution," I said, seeing that he was searching for the right word.

"Yes! A precaution. I am still a member," he said, puffing out his thin chest. "I went on many raids and blew up the *Boche*. Trucks and trains. But now that is over."

"Where's the girl?" I asked. "The girl who betrayed you."

"Carine? She has fled. To the south, perhaps. I do not know." At the mention of the name, Madame Dubois snorted and poured herself more wine. She drew the stub of a cigarette from her apron pocket and lit it with a wooden match. I waited for her to comment, but the derision in the small noise she'd made said it all. She knew that Carine had gone south, all right. As in dead south. Jacques had said as much with a finger drawn across his throat.

"So Rast had you arrested based on her statement?" I said.

"Yes. I thought she could be trusted, but I was wrong. They came for me at school and took me out in front of the children," Leon said. "It was horrible."

I bet it was. And I felt bad about it, but I needed to push Leon harder. The way he was telling it, he was the hero of his own story. If I was going to get to the bottom of why Rast had released him and the other prisoners, I had to change that narrative. Leon had been brave enough to fight with the *Groupe Rouge*, but there was something in his anxious glances that told me he had a secret. A secret I needed to know.

"Was Rast there?" I said.

"No. It was his men along with the *Milice* who took me. But tell me, Captain Boyle, how can I help you?" Leon took a drink to mask his unease. He knew how he could help me, but didn't want to admit it.

"How long did they keep you in jail?"

"Three days. It was at the prison in Castillon, a terrible place. The *Milice* were in charge, and they are even worse than the *Boche*," Leon said, shuddering as he spoke the words. He took another drink, his movements more natural this time. He needed the wine.

"Did they torture you?"

"No. They hit and kicked me, but it was not torture. I told them nothing. When they said Carine had denounced me, I said she was only doing so because I would not ask her to marry me. They thought that was funny."

"But you never should have bragged to her," I said, tapping my finger on the table like a teacher pointing out an arithmetic error. "You endangered everyone in your group."

"Yes, yes, I know. But I did not know she was in the pay of the Nazis. She hid it well."

"How do you know she was a paid informer?" I asked.

"Major Rast told me," Leon said, his eyes darting back and forth. "He said she was well paid, and he trusted her, so I should admit the truth. But I did not. I kept to my story. It is best to stick with what you first tell the police. Jacques taught us that."

"In case you were caught out after curfew, for instance," I said.

"*Oui.* Some things can be explained away, if one is sincere. I told Rast Carine had wanted to marry, but I did not. I told him perhaps she wanted a husband before anyone found out she was a collaborator. I pretended I was angry with her."

"You weren't?"

"Well, yes, but I had to make-believe I was only angry as her lover, not as a partisan," Leon said. "There is a difference, don't you see? Rast believed me, and the next day I was released."

"Just like that," I said.

"*Oui.* There were others, I heard. Perhaps he was worried about the invasion and wished people to think him sympathetic."

"He didn't torture you at all? No threats, no promise to kill your mother and burn down your house, nothing like that?"

"No, no, I swear to you," Leon said, laying both hands on the table and leaning forward. "He just let me go."

"He didn't want anything from you?"

"Nothing. If he had tortured me and wanted information, I could have betrayed the *Groupe Rouge.* I could have given Rast names of the men I fought with, told him where their families live. But no harm has come to them, has it? So you see, I could not have betrayed anyone."

He sat back, a sigh escaping his lips. I lifted my glass and watched him as I drank the wine. He looked satisfied. He'd delivered his lines with a certainty that said to me he'd rehearsed them for just this moment. Something was off, but I couldn't put my finger on it.

I looked at Madame Dubois. She'd been taking this all in, not understanding the English, but hearing Rast's name enough to know what we were talking about. She should have been proud of her son. A Resistance fighter who refused to name his comrades and who smooth-talked his way out of jail.

The look on her face wasn't one of pride.

It was disappointment, tinged with disdain.

"What was the deal you made with Rast?" I said.

"There was no deal, no agreement, nothing," Leon said. "Remember, he released others. Ask them."

"I will," I said, standing. "You were the first one on my list. I'll find out. And when I do, you'll wish you'd told me the truth."

"You stay at *Pressoir* Janvier, yes? Ask Madame Janvier to tell you the names of those who were released. She knows," Leon said, sounding certain of himself.

"How did you know that?" I asked.

"Oh, I hear things. All of us in the Resistance have ways of knowing. Madame Janvier herself was very active," he said.

"Pffff," his mother said, waving her hand and shaking her head.

"Is that your *maman's* opinion of Madame Janvier? Doesn't she do business with her?" I asked, eyes on the old lady. She spoke to Leon, giving him a piece of her mind to pass on to me.

"She says yes, she sells her apple crop to *Pressoir* Janvier. As she did for years, and her *papa* before her. Her father and *Monsieur* Janvier were friends, and she was sad when Janvier died."

"Leon, that's a nice story, but I think there was something else she wanted you to say."

"Well, yes. *Maman* thinks Madame Janvier was not so sad, and perhaps even relieved when her husband died. She being a younger woman, with her own ideas about how to run the business. *Maman* thinks she should have mourned longer and with proper dignity," he said.

"What does that mean?" He shrugged and asked his mother.

"Ah, heavy mourning, the old people call it. A widow should wear nothing but black for one year and go out very little," he said. "Madame Janvier wore black to put her husband into the ground, and then things went back to normal. She even entertained men who came to visit. Quite improper, my mother thinks." He raised his eyebrows and canted his head in slight apology, and I felt a little sorry for him.

I tried not to let my pity show, or my relief at leaving this house. I told Madame Dubois *au revoir* and she gave me a half-hearted smile in return. I let myself out.

"Captain Boyle," Leon said from the doorway as I got into the jeep. He glanced back into the house and said something reassuring to his mother, then walked over. "You must trust me that I betrayed no one. Not a single person was arrested or hurt, not one."

"Okay," I said, not ready to buy his line but wanting to see where he was going with it.

"Is it possible Major Rast is dead?"

"Sure, but no one's found a body. Hard to say for sure. You'd be glad if he is, right?"

"Very glad. Again, I have betrayed no one."

"But he has a hold over you," I said. "Why are you so afraid? The Germans are gone."

"Not so far away, Captain. We still hear the fighting. I can tell you nothing more. Except that there was another man from Saint-Jean who was in prison with me, Eugène Brassens, who was not released. He escaped only when a policeman left his cell door unlocked. He lives just up the road, in the small house of brick with blue shutters. Go to see Eugène, and perhaps you will understand."

"Understand what, Leon?"

"The cost of being stubborn," he said, and walked back into the house, his head hung low.

CHAPTER TWENTY-FOUR

THE HOUSE WITH blue shutters was easy to find. It was within sight of the center of town, flanked by a larger two-story building of red stone on one side, a tin sign with the word AVOCAT marking it as a lawyer's office. Opposite a barn stood empty, smelling of wet, rotting hay. I pulled in by the barn and made my way to the front door, not knowing what to expect. Or what to ask, given how poorly my few words of French prepared me for this second interview in Saint-Jean.

I knocked and wondered if Eugène Brassens was associated with the law office or the barn. The house was small but well kept, the shutters freshly painted.

A woman answered the door, opening it barely enough to reveal her face.

"*Oui?*" Her eyes were as blue as the shutters, and my first thought was that Eugène chose the color for that reason. She was about my age, with wispy light brown hair, wearing a dirty apron and a fearful look. Her worried eyes were set above puffy gray bags. Not much sleep or joy in her life, and I didn't need to be a detective to figure that out.

"Eugène Brassens?" I asked, pointing inside. "*Puis-je entrer?*"

She nodded and let me in. I followed her down a narrow hallway to the kitchen. She gestured to a man sitting at the wooden table, his back to us as he faced the rear window. Without a word, she stood by the stove and stirred a pot of what smelled like vegetable soup.

"Monsieur Brassens?" I said, as I moved around the table to take a seat by his side. No response.

Then I saw his hands.

Clasped in his lap, they were swathed in bandages. His fingertips were oozing red. The blood had seeped into a towel that was laid across his lap. He didn't move.

His face was a welter of healing cuts. Scar tissue knotted itself across his brow and along his jaw. His head hung heavily to one side, a thin line of drool finding a home on his worn sweater. He'd been beaten hard and stitched up with only enough care to keep him alive for the torture of pulling out his fingernails.

"*La résistance?*" I asked, glancing at his wife.

"*Oui,*" she said, stirring the pot slowly, her eyes on her unmoving husband, perhaps hoping for a sign of movement, a signal of the man he had once been.

"The *Groupe Rouge?*"

She shook her head. "De Gaulle," she said, with little enthusiasm. The political divide between the Communists and General Charles de Gaulle meant nothing in this sad and quiet kitchen.

I spoke to Eugène for a while. I told him who I was, and that I wanted to know about what happened to him. It was all in English, and I didn't expect him to understand me. I just hoped for a response, a sign that he was still of this world.

He wasn't. He was gazing out that window just as Yvonne Virot stared out of hers. The only difference was he wore his scars on the outside, and his wounds bled red.

I stood and said goodbye to Eugène, on the off chance he was aware of me at all. His wife had slipped out of the kitchen, and I took a look in the soup pot as I left. Pretty thin stuff. I made my way back to the jeep and grabbed the K-Rations squirreled away in a rucksack in the back seat, along with two cartons of Lucky Strikes kept for bargaining and loosening tongues. I left them on the kitchen table. A fair trade for coming to understand the cost of remaining stubborn.

I drove through Saint-Jean, and the quiet village looked different on the way out. I had thought it unscathed by war, but I'd only seen the buildings standing intact and untouched. The people inside were a different story. Madame Dubois and her barely concealed disdain for her own son. Leon, who held a secret that shamed him. Eugène Brassens, who had withstood torture and now sat with useless hands while his wife simmered the thin soup of what was left of their life together.

Driving along the narrow lane heading out of the village, I thought about Leon Dubois. For all his nervousness, I believed him that he hadn't betrayed anyone. I'd been a cop long enough to develop a sense about when a suspect was lying. Leon had been as direct and as forceful as he was capable of. No hemming or hawing, no twists and turns in his story. But the careful wording hinted at a hidden truth.

You must trust me that I betrayed no one. Not a single person was arrested or hurt, not one.

No betrayal, no one hurt. And yet he clearly was holding something back. Leon had done something so terrible that he wanted me to see the evidence of what refusal would have looked like. Eugène, with his stubbornness and torn hands. Eugène had not given Rast whatever it was he wanted, and he'd come home a broken man.

I steered the jeep through the ruins of La Croix as artillery fire rumbled from the battery on the far side of town. The medics were gone from the fountain in the main square. The company HQ was busy, GIs darting in and out, drivers gunning their engines and zipping ahead of me.

The whistling of an artillery shell put a stop to all that. Men dove for cover and I hit the brakes, holding onto my helmet as an explosion erupted behind a building at the corner. Debris fell like rain all around, but no one appeared to be hurt. The two-story structure was already damaged, and the impact sent bricks and timbers sliding into the road, raising a cloud of dust as the whole side wavered and threatened to collapse.

Guys stood up and looked at one another, happy to be alive, distrustful of such good fortune. Only one shell? Was it one of ours from corps artillery somewhere in the rear, a short round that mercifully took no lives? Or a ranging shot from the Krauts, with the promise of more to follow?

Whichever it was, I didn't want to hang around. Another short could kill me as well as a barrage of Krupp steel. I sped away, brushing off bits of brick and mortar from my shoulders. I passed the artillery emplacement, the big 105mm guns blasting away as trucks rolled in with more ammunition. Something big was brewing. All this firing was more than the usual morning hate, as my dad and Uncle Dan called the daily German barrages back in their day. They'd gone to war with their oldest brother Frank, who didn't make it home from what they'd called the World War, probably never imagining people would like it so much they'd start numbering them.

Driving between the looming hedgerows, I couldn't stop thinking about Eugène. It wasn't his condition that stayed with me, although that was bad enough. It was the fact that he was still alive. Rast's men, or the *Milice,* could have aired out his brains with one pistol shot, once they were sure he was of no use to them. Or sent him to a concentration camp if they didn't want a corpse on their hands. Those were the usual rewards for any *maquis* unlucky enough to be caught.

But Eugène Brassens was alive, if you counted a vacant stare and torn fingers missing ten fingernails as much of a life. So the question was, why?

As an example? It was the only thing that made sense. To show the price of stubbornness, to demonstrate the power of Major Hans Rast. How that served Rast's interest was beyond me, but I was sure it did, as sure as I was that the murder of Major Jerome served his interest as well.

Right now, I was hoping Colonel Harding had come through with some intelligence on Rast, something that might give us a lead on what he was up to. My only other plan was to find the closest POW camp and look for Rast's men. German military police probably weren't any more popular with the common Kraut *Landser* than American MPs were with dogfaces. It wouldn't be hard to find a POW to point them out.

One other thing, I reminded myself. We still needed to check back in with Dr. Leroy. Jacques had suspected him of betraying the presence of escapees at the hospital. If that were true, we'd have to view everything he told us about Yvonne with a certain amount of suspicion.

We.

That was my other problem. Big Mike was plenty sore at me for letting Kaz go on his wild goose chase and not acting the part of a proper officer. Well, he was right about Kaz, anyway. I shouldn't have turned a blind eye to his jaunt for his own sake. If Kaz was going to get bad news about his kid sister, he should be with friends, not strangers. And given that all news out of Nazi-occupied Poland was bad to worse, odds were not in his favor.

As for being a proper officer, Big Mike should know better. We were both cops, more blue than khaki, and I wasn't going to start following regulations now. Not that I knew many to begin with.

So I had problems with one guy AWOL and the other pissed off at me. Basically, there was no *we* until I straightened out those problems. I put aside thinking about my two malcontents as I drove along the wooded lane where I'd spotted Legrand this morning, watching the shadows for anyone—German sniper or French partisan—snooping around with a rifle. The woods were quiet, unlike the skies, which had erupted in a snarl of engines as another flight of fighter-bombers headed for the front lines.

A big push was on—all the signs pointed to it. I hoped it turned out better than Brewster's last attack. From all the air power and heavy artillery being thrown at the enemy, it seemed a helluva lot bigger than a battalion-size offensive. It looked to be something Colonel Harding and First Army might be involved in. I began to worry about all my witnesses being chewed up in the upcoming struggle through the hedgerows, and then I remembered I didn't really have witnesses. Except for Yvonne, and she wasn't talking.

I pulled into *Pressoir* Janvier. Everyone was gone. Tents, trucks, and the constant chaos of a battalion HQ, all vanished. The place looked deserted, but what I was really seeing was how it looked when there wasn't a war on. Except for the foxholes and trenches dug in along the fields.

It was quiet. Peaceful.

I pulled around the back and saw a couple of jeeps and a truck in front of the comm room. Big Mike came out of the kitchen and gave me a casual wave, as if this morning's tiff hadn't happened.

"Where'd everyone go?" I asked, keeping my voice neutral. I wasn't ready to kiss and make up, not by a long shot.

"Colonel Brewster took the headquarters company up on the line," Big Mike said. "The rest of the battalion staff are ready to go. Looks like this is going to be too far to the rear for an HQ pretty damn soon."

"Lots of activity down the road," I said. "Something's brewing. Who's still here?"

"Major Johnson. He's inside saying his goodbyes to Madame Janvier. I left when he gave me a look that said 'scram.' I think he's makin' a play to come back for a visit. And Lieutenant Friedman is still around. He had some last-minute radio signals to send out."

"Any news from Harding?"

"Yeah, he said he'd send what we needed, so I didn't have to go up to First Army. A motorcycle courier brought a bundle of files about an hour ago. Madame Janvier made some coffee, and I was about to go through it. Didn't know when you'd get back," Big Mike said. "Sir." He stood with his hands held behind his back. His tone was proper, which for Big Mike meant he was still steamed. Fine by me.

Behind him, Johnson paused in the doorway of the kitchen, looking spiffy in his pressed ODs. He shook Madame Janvier's hand, holding on for those few extra seconds that claimed a hopeful ownership of the person at the other end. She smiled and waved as he donned his tin pot and vaulted into the passenger seat of the waiting jeep, putting on a good show for the lady of the house.

"Where to, Major?" I asked.

"Le Mesnil-Durand," Johnson said. "That'll be our forward HQ. It's on a ridge just west of Saint-Lô, overlooking the Vire River. The Germans are retreating out of Saint-Lô, and we've got to hold the river line to keep them bottled up. I got a feeling this whole front is about to bust wide open!"

He tapped his driver on the shoulder, and they drove off, followed by another jeep with a mounted .30 caliber machine gun. Officers liked traveling with a high-powered escort. Especially ones in clean uniforms spouting off about the front busting wide open, which meant bodies in dirty ODs burst open in the process.

"He's making a play for the Madame," Friedman said, tossing a duffel bag into the back of his jeep.

"Yeah, we noticed," I said. "He making any progress?"

"Hard to say. Madame Janvier is a smart lady. She knows how to play nice and end up with a good supply of food. Nothing wrong with that either, in my book. She's playing the best hand she has. Got to be hard for a woman, running a place like this during the Occupation and now with all this shooting going on."

"She'd be a good catch for a guy like Johnson," Big Mike said. "Imagine coming back to this after the war?"

"Nah, most guys who daydream about marrying a French girl want to bring her back to the States. Johnson's a real straight arrow. Don't see him learning French and picking apples for the rest of his life. Anyway, we gotta go. You solve the case yet, Billy?" Friedman asked.

"No. Not yet," I said. "I may catch up with you at Le Mesnil-Durand. Keep your head down."

"Best advice I had all day," Friedman said, and then they were gone.

"Quiet all of a sudden," Big Mike said, looking around.

"Yeah, the place seems empty."

"About this morning, I was out of line. I shoulda kept my mouth shut. This is a small outfit, and you're the boss, so run it any way you want. I'm just a non-com." He made it sound like he was doing me a favor.

"Yeah, that's what I thought," I said. I hadn't meant it to come out like that, but something was distracting me—the thought of life here after the war. Now that the battalion HQ had pulled out, the place looked more like a peaceful French farm than a military base. It would be a nice place to settle down. And Madame Janvier, if Madame Dubois were to be believed, might like a man like Johnson by her side. Besides, I didn't need Big Mike's permission to do what I thought best.

"Jeez, Billy, I'm trying to apologize here," Big Mike said, clearly offended.

"Then apologize. And forget about it. You don't have to remind me you're a sergeant."

"If that's the way you want it, Captain, fine. It's forgotten about," Big Mike said. Not that I believed him when he resorted to calling me by my rank.

"Have you heard from Kaz?" I asked.

"Nothing. Should I head up to Bayeux and look for him?" Big Mike said. "He could have gotten in trouble, driving around without a pass. He could get mistook for a Kraut real easy. Some of these guys at roadblocks are pretty nervous about German spies."

"Maybe in the morning. I'm sure Kaz can talk himself out of any jam," I said.

"What if that Polish division got sent up to the line already? You know Kaz. He'd follow a tank assault if it meant finding out about his sister," Big Mike said. He had a point, not that I'd admit it. Or had thought about it, for that matter.

"I don't think the army moves that fast. Kaz said they'd just arrived from England, so don't worry about it. Right now, let's see what Harding sent us on Rast and the Resistance groups around here," I said.

"Coffee's on the stove," Big Mike said, hitching his thumb in the direction of the kitchen, his tone neutral. "Friedman's right. Madame Janvier knows how to work the system. She could open up a coffee and tobacco shop right now. All the officers were falling over each other to thank her for her cooking and company."

"Johnson most of all?"

"Oh yeah. I think he really fell for her," Big Mike said. "He's kind of pompous, but I saw them together in there. He's like a puppy dog. I'm not sure he would mind being lord of the manor after the war."

"That reminds me," I said, stopping before we entered the house. "I talked with Leon Dubois today. His mother, who does business with Madame Janvier, isn't a fan of hers. She thought Madame Janvier wasn't exactly broken up when her husband died. Leon's mother is a grim lady, and her family was friends with the Janviers from way back, so she may be biased. But she thought the widow Janvier should have mourned longer and not had men come visiting right after her husband died."

"Sounds like village gossip," Big Mike said. "Or is there something I'm missing?"

"I don't know," I said, keeping my voice low and taking a few steps back, leaning against my jeep. "I feel like there's some missing piece to this puzzle, but I don't know what the hell it is."

"Yeah," Big Mike said, taking up a post next to me, his arms crossed against his chest. He seemed more comfortable discussing the case, and so was I. "We were focused on the Second Armored and the Ghost Army guys, and now that seems to have gone by the boards. Colonel Brewster walked right by me and didn't even ask if we'd made any progress. You get anything useful out of Leon?"

"Maybe," I said. "He swore he didn't betray anyone to get released from prison, and I believed him. He was nervous as hell, though, and wouldn't say why. But he did send me to visit a guy up the road from him. He'd been badly tortured. Beaten something awful, all his fingernails pulled out."

"What'd this guy have to say?"

"Nothing. Which was why Leon sent me there. To see what happened when a prisoner didn't cooperate with Rast," I said.

"I'm surprised the bastards didn't shoot the poor fellow," Big Mike said.

"I think that was the point. To send him home as an example."

"Of what?"

"If we knew that, we might know why Major Jerome was killed," I said. "Leon is frightened, but I can't figure out why. No one was arrested after he was cut loose, and he's got a solid reputation as a fighting member of the *Groupe Rouge*. He should be home free."

"You said this other guy was just up the road? Maybe he's an example to Leon of what might happen to him."

"If the Germans come back? It's not impossible, I guess. We might be stuck in this damned hedgerow country, but I don't see the Krauts rolling through us. They're trying to hold ground, not take it."

"And what did Leon do for Rast to earn his release?" Big Mike said, kicking a stone with his boot. "Nothing makes sense."

"It all makes sense to whoever killed Jerome, remember that," I said. That was the advice my dad had given me on my first murder investigation. Lucy Arsenault had been reported missing by her husband. I suspected the husband of doing away with her, since it was usually the husband in a case like that. But there was no evidence of trouble between them, or him stepping out on her and wanting to get free. It was late winter, and the Arsenaults owned a small three-story apartment building. In a corner of the courtyard out back there was a spot where residents dumped their ashes. One day, I saw a guy empty a pail full, and on a hunch I had the ash pile dug out. There was Lucy, right where she'd been for a month, with a dent the size of a half-dollar decorating her skull.

Her husband Alphonse was a wreck. He seemed genuine, no overplaying the dramatics or vowing vengeance to anyone who'd listen. I was stumped. Dad told me the night we found the body to remember it all was perfectly logical to the killer. So I listened to the old man, him being an experienced homicide detective, and went back to the apartment house and interviewed everyone again. And the neighbors on both sides.

Then I saw it. A neighbor lady name of Sophie Mullen. A good-looking woman with rosy cheeks and stout legs. She brought a pie over to Alphonse one day when I stopped in to see how he was doing. She gave a little start when she saw me, but that wasn't what gave her away.

It was the pie.

I checked up on her. Her husband had worked in a garage and died in a car accident a year before. It turned out he was a gambler who had welshed on his debts to a bookie. A bookie with connections, who liked to set examples. The brakes had been tampered with, and his death was ruled suspicious. Which meant little to Sophie, who was left with nothing but an empty bank account and a crummy one-room apartment where she was behind on the rent.

I went back and asked Alphonse if her pies were any good. He said they were terrific. She'd been baking them since the funeral.

Sophie confessed as soon as we brought her down to the station. Like Dad had said, it all made perfect sense to her. She was alone and abandoned, nearly destitute, her bum of a husband having left her nothing but a Plymouth with a smashed front end and bloodstains on the front seat. Lucy had everything she didn't, and Sophie seized the opportunity to take her place. Perfectly logical, if you were the kind of person who didn't mind whacking a neighbor on the head with a ball-peen hammer and burying her in the dead of night under an ash pile.

"Billy?" Big Mike said, nudging my arm.

"Yeah? Sorry, I was recalling an old case. Sophie Mullen. I haven't thought about her in a long time."

"She the victim?" Big Mike asked as he shoved himself off from the side of the jeep, looking at anything but me.

"Killer," I said. "She wanted what she couldn't have, and she murdered another woman to get it. Didn't work out well for anyone. But it all made sense to her at the time. That's what we need to find here. The time and the place when killing Major Jerome was the logical thing to do."

"Well, until we do, let's go over the dope Sam sent down for us. Reports on Resistance groups and background on Rast."

"Okay," I said, following him to the kitchen. "And coffee."

The sound of grinding gears caught our attention as a jeep and an open truck came down the drive. The truck was full of young men, civilians by their dress. But the driver of the jeep was unmistakable.

Kaz. With a big grin on his face. His passenger was dressed in a British army uniform, with the same *Poland* red shoulder patch.

"Billy! Big Mike!" He leapt out of the jeep as the truck pulled in alongside him. The civilians were all chattering in what sounded like Polish. "Meet Lieutenant Feliks Kanski."

We shook hands with Kaz's passenger as he introduced us. Big Mike cut loose with a volley of Polish, and in short order I had no idea what anyone was talking about.

"Kaz, who are these people? The civilians," I said. It was evident that Kanski was with the First Polish Armoured Division by his shoulder flash, black beret, and British uniform.

"Poles, or at least many of Polish extraction," Kaz said.

"We are on a recruiting drive," Kanski explained, his English clipped and precise, as if he'd learned it at a British boarding school. "There are many Poles in this part of France, some of them escaped from forced labor camps, others whom the Germans pressed into service with the *Wehrmacht*. Most of them deserted or surrendered as soon as possible."

"Word spread that a free Polish unit was in the area, and these fellows volunteered," Kaz said. "There is an obvious difficulty with obtaining Polish replacements, so every recruit is valuable. The men were gathered at Bonneval, not far from here, so I offered to guide Feliks there."

"That's great," Big Mike said. "But did you find what you were after?"

"Yes," Kaz said, clapping Kanski on the shoulder. "Feliks escaped both the Nazis and the Soviets, fought with the underground Home Army, and was forced to go into hiding when the Gestapo put a price on his head. Last year he crossed the Baltic Sea to Sweden and made his way to England."

"You knew Angelika?" I asked, eyeing Kanski. He looked too youthful to have done all that, but war demanded much from the young.

"I *know* Angelika," Kanski said. "She is a courier with the Home Army, and I worked with the intelligence division in Poland."

"Feliks worked with the Polish Government-in-Exile in London," Kaz said, his eyes wide with excitement. Behind him, the new Polish recruits chattered excitedly, their enthusiasm evident by their broad grins and arms across one another's shoulders. "He's been in contact with her unit and confirmed she is still alive. As of two months ago, at least."

"Kaz, if she's kept herself alive this long, the last two months shouldn't be a problem," I said, hoping my logic held true in Nazi-occupied Poland.

"Angelika is very smart," Feliks said. "She has an uncanny ability to move about without attracting attention. I myself did not have that talent and was forced to flee. But now I am part of this mighty division. We will have our revenge."

"Good luck, Feliks," Kaz said as they embraced.

"And to you, my friend," Feliks said. "Contact me if you need me. I will help any way I can. It is an honor to meet Angelika's brother at long last. She spoke of you often."

Feliks got into the truck, and they drove off, the new recruits smiling and laughing. Kaz looked away, a hand brought up to his face, hiding his eyes.

"Damn dust," Big Mike said, throwing a giant arm around Kaz's shoulders. We watched the truck disappear down the drive, and I tried to imagine what Kaz must be feeling. Incredible joy at learning his sister was alive. Terrible fear at her doing such dangerous work. Pride at what she, the Home Army, and this armored division were doing to fight back, here in Normandy and under German occupation. Kaz's life had been rough, as rough as his nation's own odyssey in this war, but these Poles were still alive, still in the fight. As was Kaz. It hadn't always been so straightforward with him.

And it was only going to get bloodier. For the Polish armored division about to go into combat. For the Home Army, as the Soviets drew closer to the Polish border and their country once again became a battleground. There was still a lot of war to be fought.

CHAPTER TWENTY-FIVE

"BARON! WELCOME BACK!" Madame Janvier greeted Kaz with a double-cheek kiss and an embrace as energetic as Feliks's had been. Kaz was popular coming and going. "It is good to see you again. Will you be staying now that Colonel Brewster has taken his battalion into battle?"

"If you don't mind," I said. "This is as good a place as any, but I imagine you might want to be free of the military after all this time."

"Not at all, you are our liberators. I insist you stay! And it is only the three of you, so no trouble at all. Now I will leave you to your work. But soon I will cook for you. *Lapin à la Moutarde.* I have already prepared the sauce." With the cooking smells wafting through the kitchen, we didn't argue about dinner. Making ourselves comfortable at the kitchen table and armed with hot coffee, we gathered the intelligence files to read.

"You pick up any other information on your jaunt?" I asked Kaz.

"No. Feliks is one of the few to make it out of Poland in the last year or so. He is assigned to the intelligence section of the division, so he still has contacts with the Government-in-Exile. He's promised to watch for any mention of Angelika. The Home Army provides a lot of useful intelligence about German units, so there is a constant flow of communication via radio."

"I'm glad you got good news, *bliski kumpel*," Big Mike said, his hand resting on Kaz's arm as he used an affectionate Polish term. We were both happy, as much for Kaz as for Angelika. Relieved, really, at not having to contend with the kind of deep depression Kaz had been subject to not that long ago. Some of the tension between Big Mike and me seemed to dissipate, but I saw Kaz studying us both, and I wondered if he'd picked up on it.

Before we dug into the files, I filled Kaz in on my visit to the Dubois and Brassens households, keeping Leon's mother's comments about Madame Janvier to a few hushed whispers. It felt important enough to mention, but there was no need to upset our host with what her gossipy acquaintance thought of her.

"So there is something Leon wishes us to understand from your visit to Eugène Brassens, a man who could not speak," Kaz said, setting down his cup and laying his hands on the table. "That sums up this case quite well."

"Excuse me, gentlemen," Madame Janvier said, donning an apron as she bustled through the kitchen. "I need this for *les lapins*." She grabbed a long kitchen knife and left by the back door, leaving it open to a pleasant breeze.

"That's rabbit, right?" I said.

"Yes. Prepared the traditional way with mustard, it is a delicious dish," Kaz said.

"I feel bad for the rabbits now," Big Mike said. "But I think I won't take it so bad by dinnertime."

"That's the way of the world," I said. "One day you're being fed carrots and greens, the next day you're in the cook pot." Which also summed up where we were. I'd been fed bits and pieces of information, just enough to keep me nibbling away at the truth. Someone was stirring the pot and having a good laugh as they waited for me to fall into it.

"What do we do next?" Kaz asked, walking to the stove to pour more coffee.

"Review these files," I said. "Learn what we can about Rast's background. Go over the Resistance groups in the area and see if any of them had a beef with anyone here. Pray for a clue to jump out at us."

"Has anything else happened since I left, other than your visit to Dubois?" Kaz asked as he took each of our cups and gave us refills. Big

Mike coughed and shifted in his chair, busying himself with the file folder in front of him. Neither one of us wanted to admit the rift that had opened up between us, so I went with business as usual.

"Yeah. A German sniper got close. He picked off Fair. He's dead," I said, and gave Kaz the lowdown on my guess that Fair had been mistaken for an officer.

"Interesting," Kaz said, taking a slow sip of the hot joe. "Two people have been shot at by a sniper. Both are involved in the investigation. And both were right next to you."

"Yeah, but the shooter might have targeted Billy," Big Mike said. "Maybe his aim was off."

"Well, either fate determined it was Sergeant Fair's day to die, or it was more important to silence him specifically than Billy. Which makes more sense?" Kaz said.

"We were just talking about not making sense of all this," I said. "Only the killer knows."

"Perhaps we should ask ourselves if Sergeant Fair knew something he hadn't told us," Kaz said.

"But that only works if the sniper came back to kill Fair," Big Mike said. "Odds are he thought he was picking off an officer, not a sergeant."

"We're going to run ourselves in circles unless we get something new out of these files," I said, opening one of the folders, holding down the papers as the wind gusted briefly through the open door.

"Hey, we didn't tell him about Diana," Big Mike said with a grin. "We asked if she could be assigned here to look after Yvonne. Billy thought she might get something out of her."

"It was Big Mike's idea, at first anyway," I said, feeling a little embarrassed as Kaz grinned and nodded his approval. "By the way, I also ran into Legrand on my way out this morning." I took a sip of strong coffee and felt thankful for the jolt of caffeine.

"Where?" Big Mike said. "What was that clown up to?"

"I saw him on foot with a rifle as I drove out this morning. I followed him, and he claimed he was hunting the sniper. Said he was worried the Krauts may have sent him to assassinate Madame Janvier

because of her Resistance work, and that he'd be back for another try."
I told them how he'd shown me the spot where the sniper had lain to
take his shot, and the tumble-down ruins of the old Janvier homestead.

"Do you think Legrand is sweet on her too?" Big Mike said. He
told Kaz about Johnson's farewell play for our hostess.

"He doesn't seem the type to get weak in the knees over a dame,"
I said.

"Yeah. Besides, Madame Janvier was standing by the kitchen door
when Fair was hit. It would have been easy to pick her off. Easier, really,
with her framed in that doorway," Big Mike said. "Legrand's gotta be
up to something out there, but I doubt he's hunting a Kraut sniper.
He's definitely the type to get weak in the knees when the odds aren't
stacked in his favor."

"As you say, whatever Legrand is doing, it makes sense to him," Kaz
said. "I think we should presume it is connected to this case, as was
the sniper attack on Billy and Sergeant Fair. To treat them as random
shootings is to invite complacency. And perhaps another bullet."

"But there's a war on, Kaz," Big Mike said. "A sniper this close to
the front just ain't that unusual."

"Exactly," Kaz said, leaning back in his chair. "It would be the perfect crime. Or was, in the case of the sergeant. And Anton, who took
the bullet meant for Billy."

I thought about that. Kaz hadn't been gone long, but gaining some
distance from the problem may have allowed him to see things more
clearly. I'd been too close to the action to consider the shootings to be
anything but combat related. Especially since a slug had nearly parted
my brow.

"Like I said, the sniper's aim could have been off. Doesn't take much
at that distance," Big Mike said. "Windage, air pressure, you name it."

"Okay, let's assume we have a sniper targeting me, or anyone else
involved in this investigation. If that's true, we're a lot more vulnerable
without a headquarters company and staff surrounding us day and
night," I said.

"Maybe it was one of them," Big Mike said. "A guy could have snuck
away, taken the shot, then blended into the search."

"Except I haven't seen anyone with a Springfield," I said. "Much less one with a telescopic sight. It would have stood out." The old bolt-action M1903 Springfield was the army's standard issue sniper's rifle.

"Nevertheless, it would be a good question to ask Colonel Brewster," Kaz said. "Does he have any marksmen operating as snipers?"

"That's a long shot," I said. Kaz shook his head at my unintentional pun. "Sorry. Let's get to work on these files." But it wasn't a bad idea, and I filed it away to follow up on later. We could radio Friedman and ask him. Brewster wouldn't take kindly to the suggestion Fair had been shot by one of his own.

Kaz took the report on the *Groupe Rouge*. Big Mike went through the Nemo Line file while I read one on the local FFI organization. That was de Gaulle's French Forces of the Interior, and the pro–de Gaulle unit in this area was called the *Maquis Tigre*. Many of their fighters were already being organized into the Free French army, with others serving as scouts with the American forces. Eugène Brassens didn't merit a mention, but there was a note about the excellent security for which *Maquis Tigre* was noted. No double agents or betrayals. It was a tightly knit group, made up of men and women from the area who already knew each other. Several members had been assassinated by the *Milice*, and a dozen or so were listed as killed in action. Thirteen downed airmen had been passed on to the Nemo Line through their efforts.

"Not surprisingly, the *Groupe Rouge* defies all attempts at control," Kaz said, leafing through the far thicker file on Jacques and company. "They reject orders from London if they do not agree with them. Note is made of the tendency of some members to talk too freely of their actions, and of their demands for more weapons. The SOE was reluctant to air-drop arms at first, but given the fighting record of Jacques and his men with weapons they captured from the Germans, SOE gave in. Now more weapons and equipment have been delivered directly to them. They operate across the lines and are known to target the *Milice* with a special fury. They have been quite effective in passing Allied aircrew on to the Nemo Line, with twenty-one to their credit."

"Fits with what we saw," I said, and reported on what I'd found in the FFI file.

"The Nemo Line report is pretty thin," Big Mike said. "But that's a good thing. Excellent security, small, compartmentalized cells. The *Groupe Rouge*, the *Maquis Tigre*, and several other Resistance outfits had established contacts, but only with one person. They were very careful, and brought out over fifty fliers. Nemo is listed as currently inactive due to the advance of Allied forces. There's a list of code names, including Corday, but no real names or locations."

"How did they get the fliers out?" I said.

"Three Lysander landing spots, south of here. Outside the coastal restricted area that the Krauts set up. And with more open ground," Big Mike said, flipping through the pages. "Plus a secluded beach on the west coast of the Cotentin Peninsula for submarine pickups in an emergency."

"Did the Germans know about the Nemo Line?" I asked.

"Yes. Intelligence reports showed an increase in German antipartisan activity aimed at eliminating the Nemo Line and locating their landing sites," Big Mike said, running his finger along a page of typewritten lines. "Looks like a couple of escaped POWs being moved closer to their Nemo contact were betrayed along the way, and the theory is, that's how the Krauts got wind of it."

"Who was bringing the POWs to Nemo?" I asked.

"The *Pêcheur Réseau*," Big Mike said, sounding out the French words carefully.

"Fisherman," Kaz said. "The Fisherman Network. Sounds like an SOE group."

"The Fisherman, Gustave, and the German," I said. Kaz looked perplexed.

"Yvonne spoke those words to Sergeant Fair," I said. "He told us about it. They're the only words anyone's heard from her."

"Hang on," Big Mike said, grabbing a file and flipping through it. It was marked *Pêcheur*, but I hadn't picked up on it. "Gustave is one of the code names. He was the wireless operator. Maurice is the organizer, and Madeleine was the courier."

"Was?" Kaz said.

"The network was blown four months ago. No communication. And reports came from other SOE networks that several Allied airmen had been swept up, along with half a dozen members of Fisherman. Conclusion was that they'd all been taken prisoner or killed."

"And it was after Sergeant Fair told you of this that he was shot," Kaz said.

"Yeah," I said, my eyes drawn to the ceiling as I thought of Yvonne above us, staring out her window. Thinking of Gustave. Or the German. Maybe later I'd have Kaz speak to her in French, and see if she recognized any of those names.

"I think it was you who taught me that there are no coincidences, Billy, only undiscovered connections," Kaz said, reaching for the last file. Like the others, it was marked with red tape, the word *CONFI-DENTIAL* in large capital letters across it.

"Major Hans Rast, originally of Cologne, Germany," Kaz read, skimming the slim file. "Before the war he worked for an export firm, which took him to England, Sweden, and France regularly. It seems the firm was owned by his father-in-law, who has family in Sweden. He's adept at several languages, which must have helped with business. There are some newspaper clippings from British and Swedish newspapers about his firm. Nothing unusual. Oh."

"What is it?" I asked.

"His wife and her parents were killed in a bombing raid in 1942. The obituaries were noted in a Swedish newspaper. Sad, but not unusual these days. Rast was posted to the Russian Front and wounded in 1943 during an antipartisan operation. After being discharged from hospital, he was chosen to head up a special training camp in Poland. For snipers."

There are no coincidences. That one came from my dad, who always tried to teach me to search out those undiscovered connections. And this one was a beauty.

"He's a sniper himself?" Big Mike asked.

"All it says is that he was a member of a shooting club before the war and won various amateur competitions. From the brief description, it may have been an administrative posting, not as an instructor."

"So he knew how to shoot already and probably picked up some pointers from experienced instructors," I said. "Then he came here?"

"Yes. Earlier this year," Kaz said. "There is reference to his wounds being fully healed. The sniper school may have been a temporary post while he recovered. His assignment was to eliminate the route for getting escaped POWs, downed airmen, and Resistance leaders out of northern France."

"Where do they get all this inside dope on the guy?" Big Mike said.

"Some of it is prewar information," Kaz said, coming to the last page in the file. "The rest is likely pieced together from radio intercepts and reports from Resistance networks. As we know, the Polish underground passes on much information to London about German forces. As for his assignment here, a new antipartisan effort in Normandy by the *Feldgendarmerie* would be of keen interest to our SOE chaps."

"Anything about him being involved in the plot against Hitler?" I asked. "He told Madame Janvier he was part of an anti-Nazi group."

"No," Kaz said, skimming the pages. "But that would be something Rast would keep well hidden."

"That him?" I said, seeing the picture clipped to the last page.

"Yes," Kaz said. "Cologne, 1941, when he was newly commissioned as *Leutnant*. Again, the source is a Stockholm newspaper. Some of them are quite pro-German and play up any Swedish connection."

He slid it across the table. It was a studio photograph, the kind you had taken on a special occasion, perhaps to give to your wife. The original was probably buried in the rubble that once was Cologne. The photograph, I mean, but she could be there too, beneath tons of timber and stone that had been bombed again and again.

The uniform was spotless, the way they are before the blood and mud ruins them. He wore the police eagle patch on his left sleeve, the symbol of the German MPs. His hair was wavy jet-black, his eyes gleamed with pride, and it looked like he was struggling to keep back a smile. It was the face of a young man on the winning side with a beautiful bride waiting at home. The future was his. The only problem was, the future was here and his world was shattered. His city ruined, his wife dead, and all he had was a sniper's rifle and a helluva deadly aim.

I looked closer at the photograph. Held it up, looked at it from the side. I covered his hair with my hand, where a cap would obscure his head. I tried to see him with a few days' stubble and dirty clothes. I didn't have to try too hard because I had. Earlier today.

"Rast is here," I said. "And Legrand is hunting him."

CHAPTER TWENTY-SIX

"THAT'S HIM," I said, tapping my finger on the photograph. "That's the guy I saw on the road right after I left Legrand in the woods." I explained how I'd given him a lift, but he didn't hang around when the other vehicles rolled up.

"Who was hunting who?" Big Mike said. "Was Rast after you? Or Legrand? Maybe Legrand had a point about Madame Janvier being a target."

"Did this supposed Frenchman have a weapon?" Kaz asked.

"Not that I saw. He carried a bag but nothing big enough for a rifle, although he could have had one stashed nearby."

"Is the old Janvier home close to where the sniper had been?" Kaz asked.

"Yes," I said. "Damn close. But the place was a mill and backs up to the river. There were weeds and brush growing all around it. There wasn't a sign anyone had gone through the undergrowth to get in."

"Did you check the water side?" Big Mike asked.

"No, I didn't even give it a thought," I said. "If you don't mind getting your feet wet, there's probably a way in."

"And a place to hide a rifle," Kaz said. "We should investigate."

"Absolutely," I said, glancing out the window. It was getting dark, and heavy clouds were rolling in. "First thing in the morning. I don't want to be stumbling around in the pitch-black if anyone's lying in wait. It could be Rast, but I wouldn't put it past Legrand to stash a sniper's rifle out there. The Kar 98 he was carrying was poorly maintained. Now I'm wondering if that was for show."

"We still have no idea why either of them would target anyone here," Big Mike said, as a low rumble sounded in the distance. "Artillery?"

"No, it is thunder," Madame Janvier said, entering the kitchen with four skinned rabbits. She flopped them on the wooden cutting board, her hands speckled in blood. She washed at the pump and carefully cleaned her knife. "The storm is coming."

We gathered up our papers and headed upstairs, leaving her to cut up rabbit carcasses, the knife edge snapping sharply on the cutting board as she sliced through muscle and bone. With her busy in the kitchen, I figured this would be a good time to check on Yvonne. I handed off the files to Big Mike and signaled for Kaz to follow me.

I gave the door a light knock and entered, expecting to find Yvonne in her usual chair. But it was empty. She was in bed, the sheets strewn about and her hand clenching a nightshirt to her breast. Her eyes were closed, and a sheen of sweat glistened on her forehead. Her breathing came in uneven heaves as she turned on her side, oblivious to our presence.

We backed out of the room.

"I do not think I have seen her move on her own before," Kaz said.

"Right. Looks like she's sick," I said. I was half tempted to wake her to find out, but what common sense I had told me that would be a bad idea.

Back in the room, Big Mike had already sprawled out on the bed and shut his eyes.

"Tire yourself out doing nothing all day?" I said, taking a seat and picking up the file on Rast again, trying to sound nonchalant but not too friendly. I had to work with the guy, but it seemed like our days of palling around were over.

"Staying away from the brass when a unit is pulling out is hard work," he said. "I didn't want Brewster or Johnson ordering me to pack their suitcase."

"Let me guess," Kaz said. "You hid out in the mess tent."

"I tried, but those guys were busier than anyone. I had to clear out when Johnson came by to snag some rations for Madame Janvier. She's going to be rolling in coffee and sugar."

"No wonder they were making nice," I said, idly flipping through the pages of the file, looking for something that wasn't there. I was certain Rast was at the center of all this, but it was becoming increasingly obvious the reason wasn't going to be in an intelligence file.

"Do we search the old house in the morning?" Kaz asked as he poured himself a calvados and raised an eyebrow in my direction. I nodded, and in a moment the three of us were clinking glasses. The calvados cut through the road dust but didn't penetrate the confusion swirling in my head.

"And I want to find out if there's a POW cage near here where Rast's men would have been taken. Someplace closer than Carentan. We might learn something looking at this from the Kraut side of the street." I told Big Mike to get on the radio and contact Lieutenant Friedman. As the communications officer, he should know who to get in touch with.

Johnson, as the intelligence officer, would have been the logical choice, but there was something about the man I didn't like, and I saw no reason to let him know our business. Maybe I was feeling protective of Madame Janvier. Or maybe I just didn't care for Johnson's smug attitude.

"Now?" Big Mike said, smacking his lips after another slug.

"Yes, Sergeant, now. You'll want to do it before it rains, anyway," I said.

"Okay, you're the boss," he said. "I'll put the top up while I'm out there." I figured Friedman was within range of the radio in our jeep. If not, we'd have to drive closer to the front. Or Big Mike would. I might as well take his advice and start acting more like an officer.

"There is some difficulty between you two?" Kaz asked after Big Mike left the room.

"Why do you say that?" I asked.

"Because I wondered about it. Now, however, I am sure, since you avoided answering the question," Kaz said, sipping his brandy. "You have taught me a few things about detection, Billy."

"Okay. He's sore that I didn't order you to stay here. He was worried you might get into trouble. And I'm ticked off that he's trying to tell me how to do my job."

"Were you worried?"

"I wasn't, not until he pointed out that if you had to trail the Poles into battle to make contact, you'd go right ahead. That sounded too much like you for comfort," I said.

"Big Mike is quite protective," Kaz said. "Of us both. I admit, I have been reckless at times. But now that I know Angelika has survived, I have no desire to take foolish chances with my life. I hope to survive this war as well."

"Then be careful."

"As careful as circumstances call for," Kaz said. "I am sorry I caused this rift."

"You didn't. I was the one who let you go. And if Big Mike wants me to act more like a regular officer, then I'm happy to oblige," I said.

"No, you are not," Kaz said, picking up one of the folders and leafing through it.

He was right. I was never going to be a regular spit-and-polish officer. I only knew how to do things one way, which was the way that felt right in my heart. And I knew Kaz had to search out anyone who might have had news of his sister.

I shook my head in frustration and returned to the file, flipping through the pages that outlined Rast's career. I wondered about his wife, and what kind of life they'd had before the war. Before she died in an Allied bombing raid.

Could that have anything to do with this? Some sort of revenge plot? Did Rast sneak back to *Pressoir* Janvier and knife Major Jerome? Did he take a shot at me and then Fair? There were plenty of ways to kill Americans in Normandy these days. Plenty of Germans were doing it all up and down the line. So why would he take so many chances to kill men who had no special connection to his wife's death?

He wouldn't. Like everything else in this case, it made no sense.

I turned a page and noticed a smudge along the margins. Brownish-yellow, with a tiny dark speck at the edge. I sniffed it. I wet my finger and rubbed it, then tasted.

Dijon mustard. Madame Janvier had snuck a look at Rast's file while we were outside, leaving a telltale trace of evidence from the sauce she'd prepared for tonight's rabbit.

Why? Curiosity? Maybe. She'd been forced to live under the same roof as the man for months, so a little peek was understandable.

Or was there a reason why she wanted to know what we knew about him? Did she want her own revenge for the crimes Rast committed while quartered with her? Had he killed someone close to her? That might be worth following up on. After a good meal, of course. My brain was in low gear, but my stomach was growling. No reason to interrogate the cook before the meal was served.

On the way down to dinner, I saw Madame Janvier exiting Yvonne's room with a covered enamel pail. I asked how she was, not letting on I'd looked in on her earlier.

"She may have influenza," Madame Janvier said. "It is best if you do not enter. Unless you wish to be sick to the stomach yourself." She wrinkled her nose and glanced at the pail. I caught a whiff, and it almost made me lose my appetite.

It returned as I entered the kitchen. Rain was pelting down outside, making the warmth and aroma coming from the stove even more enticing. I felt a pang of guilt over the GIs out on the line eating K-Rations in their muddy foxholes, but I knew any of them would think a guy crazy to pass up a home-cooked meal. So I joined Kaz at the table, where a jug of cider was at the ready.

"*Un moment,*" Madame Janvier said, busying herself at the sink. Big Mike burst in, rain slicker dripping. He hung it on a peg by the door, puddles forming on the stone floor.

What did that remind me of? I watched the drops of water splash as they fell, and knew it reminded me of something. Something that mattered. What, I had no idea.

"Billy," Kaz said, in the way people did when you hadn't been listening. He nodded toward Big Mike.

"You ignoring me, Captain?" Big Mike said.

"No, I'm not," I said. Normally I'd explain myself, but I was getting fed up with his attitude. "Have a seat and report."

"I got through to Lieutenant Friedman," he said. Kaz handed him a glass of cider and gave me an eye roll. I wasn't popular with anyone tonight. "There's a POW cage up in Canchy, a little north of us."

"It is not far," Madame Janvier said as she pulled a roasting pan from the oven. "A half hour to drive, perhaps."

"He know if they have any of Rast's men?" I said.

"He got on the horn to them. Turns out they got MPs in spades. About a half dozen Kraut chain dogs and our very own lieutenants Sewell and Moretti."

"So that's where they were transferred to," I said, then explained to Kaz about their sudden reassignment after we arrived to investigate Jerome's murder. It had to have been part of the security scare surrounding the Ghost Army. Someone at First Army probably figured it was better to get them out of the way so they wouldn't put Jerome's murder and the phony Second Armored guys together. But I'd have to fill Kaz in on that later, when Madame Janvier was out of earshot. Right now she was transferring the rabbit to a platter, and I didn't want her to go anywhere.

"Yeah, and Friedman spoke direct with Sewell. He wants to get back with the battalion, so Friedman's working on it. In the meantime, Sewell expects us tomorrow. He's got the Kraut MPs all lined up. They use them to help maintain control of the POWs."

"The other prisoners must love that," I said. "Still bossed around by a bunch of *Kettenhunde*." The aromas wafted from the pan as Madame Janvier poured in red wine, the leavings in the pan crackling in an explosion of steam.

"Nobody likes a cop until they need one," Big Mike said, swallowing half his drink in one gulp.

"Maybe we'll get lucky and one of them will be a real cop from civilian life," I said. "Might be easier to get information on *Amerika* Rast."

"America?" Madame Janvier said, setting out platters of food. Crispy pieces of rabbit served with a mustard sauce along with bowls heaped with green beans and carrots. It was kind of hard to concentrate on her question, but I did my best while she served each of us, doling out an extra portion along with a smile for Big Mike.

"*Amerika* was the nickname we heard Rast's men gave him," I said. "This came from a POW who told us his own troops wondered why he went easy on the French Resistance after the invasion. They figured he wanted to go to America after the war and was setting the stage."

"The stage?" Madame Janvier said as she sat down. "Oh yes, I understand. You think he wanted the Americans to favor him."

"I think it likely his men were joking," I said. "The common soldier often likes to criticize his officers, if only to pass the time." Another eye roll from Kaz. Big Mike was so focused on the rabbit I didn't think he picked up on the barb.

"Yes, I am sure my workers often say things about me I would prefer not to hear," she said. "Even if only in jest."

"Does anyone use the old mill anymore?" I asked, taking a drink of the sharp cider.

"Not since the Americans arrived. We used it for a temporary hideout, but only for a night at most. It was too dangerous with the Germans so close."

"I saw Legrand near there this morning," I said, spearing green beans. "He claimed he was waiting for the sniper to return."

"That man is a fool," Madame Janvier said, serving herself. "And a coward. If he was alone, he was up to no good."

"It didn't look like there was any way to get into the house, it's so overgrown with weeds and brush," I said.

"*Oui*, that is how I like it. The *Boche* never bothered to get inside from the river either," she said, turning to smile at me. "You did not want to get your feet wet, Captain?"

"Didn't even think about it," I said. "There's a way in?"

"Next to the water wheel is a small door. There is a flat stone beneath the water to step on. The water will be quite high after this rain, but you can look tomorrow," she said.

"The sniper may have used it for a hideout," Big Mike said, managing to distract himself from the food disappearing from his plate.

"Perhaps. I have not checked it for some time, so who can say? *Bon appétit.*" She poured herself a glass of cider and dug in.

"Will Arianne be joining us?" Kaz said. I held back asking if he needed a bath.

"No, I gave her the evening off to be with her family."

Too bad for Kaz. We focused on eating. The rabbit was tender and delicious. We complimented the chef, drank cider, ate, and otherwise forgot about the war for a while. Big Mike and I even managed a few exchanges that were nearly normal. But beneath the small talk was the knowledge that men were fighting, suffering, and dying not far away. Behind the lines, French men and women were risking their lives, helping to liberate their nation, as we nibbled meat from the bone.

We toasted Madame Janvier and her work with the Nemo Line. She played at being embarrassed, but I could tell she was proud. When the food was gone, she brought out the calvados.

"Here's to the Liberation," I said, raising my glass.

"And to the peace," Madame Janvier said as she touched my glass. "The war goes on, I know. But I must say, it is wonderful to have the *Boche* gone from our land. I pray the end comes soon for all."

"If those German officers had been a bit handier with their bomb, it might have been over already," Big Mike said.

"Ah, yes," Madame Janvier said. "They were brave to try, in any case."

"Did Major Rast mention anything about what kind of anti-Nazi group he was involved in?" I said, twirling the glass of amber liquid.

"No, no," she said, with a dismissive wave. "It was an unguarded comment, nothing specific. As I said, I think he wished he had not said it."

"Was he trying to impress you?" I said.

"Major Rast was not the type of man to worry about impressing people," Madame Janvier said. "But he may have felt some guilt about what he had been ordered to do. Perhaps he wanted someone to know in case the worst happened."

"The Gestapo?" Kaz said.

"The Gestapo, the Resistance, your fighter-bombers, a transfer back to the Russian Front, take your pick," she said. "Life and death, they both hold surprises for us, do they not?"

"The things Rast was forced to do," I asked, not bothering to answer the unanswerable, "did they happen to anyone in the Nemo Line? Or friends of yours?"

"No. We lost a number of young men from the village when the slave labor roundups began, but that was not a duty of the major's. Two members of the Nemo Line were arrested, but that was the Gestapo, not the German military police."

"What happened to them?" Kaz asked.

"Dead, or in a concentration camp. They were part of a group of three, and the third person was never picked up, so we know they didn't talk. Which means they endured tortures beyond imagining."

"I saw a man today, Eugène Brassens, in Saint-Jean. He'd been tortured by Rast and then released. Apparently as a warning of what to expect," I said, looking at my own hands as I remembered his ruined fingers.

"Terrible," she said, finishing her calvados. "Was it Rast himself who did it? He seemed too refined for such bloody work."

"He either did it or ordered it done," I said. "Neither is the sign of a refined man."

"Yes. But it is the sign of a guilty conscience," she said. "Thank goodness it bothered him. He saved many others from the same fate by halting his antipartisan efforts."

That was one way of looking at it, but I doubt Eugène Brassens would have been impressed.

CHAPTER TWENTY-SEVEN

MORNING FOUND US in the woods, tracing the route I'd taken to the old Janvier place. The ground was wet, and leaves dripped moisture from last night's rain. I didn't think there was much chance the sniper would return now that Brewster and his men had pulled out. Even so, we advanced quietly, weapons at the ready.

We got to the woodpile where I'd encountered Legrand, and I motioned for Kaz and Big Mike to go low. I listened. Nothing but the swiftly running current of the swollen river, splats of heavy raindrops from the trees, and the chattering of birds. I raised my head slowly above the moss-covered logs, scanning the woods and the old mill.

The grass had been trampled. Vines and weed-choked brush had been pulled away from around the entrance. It looked like someone didn't want to get their feet wet. I motioned for Kaz and Big Mike to take each side as I ran low for the door. The undergrowth beneath my boots crunched with each step, and I kept my Thompson trained on the doorway. I darted inside and flattened myself against a wall, waiting for my eyes to adjust to the dim light.

Part of the floor had rotted away and collapsed into the basement, which was covered in black water. Below, I could see the waterwheel through the missing planks, and the door Madame Janvier had described on the wall. A ladder led from it up to the main level. Floor-boards creaked and groaned as I moved around, and I became more concerned with falling through decayed timber than stumbling into a sniper.

The place was covered in dirt and debris. Leaves and crumbled plaster crinkled under my feet. This floor was one open room, and the only place to go was up a flight of stairs. I caught sight of Big Mike through an open window and signaled that I was headed up. Given all the noise I was making, I could have hollered it out loud, but why chance it? I took the first step, moving aside a branch that had fallen through the hole in the roof. The stair felt firm. Same with the next one. I brushed aside dirt and who the hell knew what else and checked the wood. New. Not brand-new, but not centuries or even decades old. The stairs had been repaired, which meant the hiding place was behind the door at the top of the landing.

I didn't bother turning the knob. I kicked the door open with my foot and took a step in, Thompson at the ready.

Nobody home. But it wasn't a bad hideout. The room held a low bed, a table and chair, a worn carpet, and a chest of drawers. An intact window gave an unobstructed view outside. Not a bad place to spend the night while on the run.

I did holler this time, telling Big Mike and Kaz it was all clear. Then I began the search. First thing was to take in the obvious. The place was clean. The slightest layer of dust covered the surfaces, the bed was made, and the chair pushed neatly under the table.

"Anything upstairs?" Kaz called out from the bottom of the stairs.

"Yeah, a room with a view. I'll search up here, you check out downstairs. Tell Big Mike to stay out, the floor is pretty rickety."

I tossed the bed. Nothing underneath or hidden in the blankets. I turned over the table and chair, found nothing tucked away there. The chest was empty except for yellowed newspaper used to line the drawers. I went over each wall, looking for a hiding place. The thick wood planks, some of them soft with age, did not give up any secrets. But near the door, a section looked newer. I pried the wood apart with my knife, and two pieces fell away from the wall neatly, revealing a long, narrow hiding space along the floor.

An empty hidey-hole, just the right size for a rifle. I stuck my head in, checking for anything left behind. I caught a whiff of something and traced it to one corner of the hole. I pawed at the spot and came up with a patch of fabric. I sniffed it. Gun oil.

"The sniper was here," I said, giving Kaz the fabric. He gave it a smell and nodded.

"Nothing down here but junk," he said. "Did you find anything else?"

"Clean as a whistle," I said as we headed out the door. I showed Big Mike the gun-cleaning swab.

"We may have missed him by minutes," he said, pointing to the freshly snapped stems and leaves in the trampled undergrowth.

"Lucky for him," I said before we returned to the *pressoir*. Or lucky for us, as the scent of gun oil in my nostrils reminded me.

A jeep with First Army markings was parked in front of the house. Inside, voices were raised. Madame Janvier didn't sound any too happy.

"That's Sam's jeep," Big Mike said. Then I heard the other female voice.

Diana. Colonel Harding had come through, but she wasn't exactly getting a warm welcome.

"No, I will not have it!" Madame Janvier said, waving her finger at Harding as they stood toe to toe in the sitting room, right where Jerome's body had been found. "It is an insult."

"Madame," Kaz said, moving close to her and speaking in French, trying to calm her down. It took me a moment to register the fact that the good lady was all dolled up. She wore pumps and a nice dress, far from her usual work outfit. Then it dawned on me. It was Sunday, and she was headed to church. With her hair fixed and red lipstick on, she presented an entirely different image. A pleasing one, trim figure and all. If Major Johnson had caught a glimpse of her one Sabbath day, that might have made him a churchgoing man if he wasn't already.

Harding looked at me and shrugged. It wasn't the first time one of my ideas had backfired on him. Not that I much cared as I sidestepped him and sat on the couch next to Diana.

She was dressed in her First Aid Nursing Yeomanry uniform. That was the outfit the Special Operation Executive used for their female agents. Diana's, of course, was especially tailored for her. She was a lady, which generally means you had some old country estate in your family along with some title given for services rendered to the Crown. Which she did have, plus a whole lot more. Her wool serge uniform set off her auburn hair, and her leather belt gleamed, as did her eyes. Or maybe that was a spark of anger. She didn't seem all that glad to see me and kept her arms folded tightly across her chest. I didn't expect a cuddle with all this hullaballoo going on, but a smile would have been nice.

"What am I doing here, Billy?" she said, flicking a stray strand of hair away from her face. "And why is that terrible woman going on so?"

"Who do you call *terrible*?" Madame Janvier demanded, turning away from Kaz and advancing on Diana. "Get out of my house!"

"Madame Janvier," I said, standing to intercept her. "I apologize. I asked Miss Seaton here because I thought she could help you look after Yvonne. I did not mean it as an insult."

"This is too much," she said. "I offer you my hospitality, and you bring in more people and accuse me of not caring properly for Yvonne. You must all leave. *Allez maintenant!*"

"I am not staying, Madame," Harding said, struggling to get a word in.

"None of you are! I have had enough with soldiers and the war. Please leave my house quickly!"

This wasn't going the way I planned at all.

Madame Janvier was steamed. Diana sat there glowering at me, while Kaz and Harding stood helplessly by. Big Mike was leaning in the doorway, wisely staying out of the line of fire. Then I saw him step backward, his eyes widening.

Yvonne stepped into the room, wearing a stained nightdress. Her eyes were red and puffy, mucus ran from her nose, and sweat shone on her skin. She wavered, as if about to fall over, then steadied herself with a hand on the wall. She searched the room, leaning forward and squinting, as if she were peering through thick fog.

"Juliet?" Her voice came out as a harsh croak. Then her eyes rolled up and she fell in a slump to the floor.

"Madeleine!" Diana said, vaulting up from the couch and kneeling next to Yvonne—or Madeleine. Then it hit me. Juliet had been Diana's code name on her last SOE mission. And Madeleine had been the wireless operator in the Fisherman network. So of course they knew each other by their code names.

"Mon Dieu," Madame Janvier said, backing up with her hand clasped over her mouth.

"Help me," Diana said. We got Yvonne—Madeleine—to her feet and guided her upstairs, Madame Janvier trailing behind us.

"Perhaps you are mistaken, Madame," Diana said, with as much kindness as she could muster. "And you could use some help to care for this brave woman."

"You know her?" Madame Janvier said as we laid Yvonne on the bed. She moaned as we did, but her eyes remained closed, her hands clutching at the duvet, fingers digging into the soft whiteness.

"Yes. And I know of you and the Nemo Line," Diana said. "But do you mean to say you have no idea who this young girl is?"

"No. We call her Yvonne, but it is just a name. She has not spoken," Madame Janvier said, wringing her hands.

"Billy, please leave while we take care of Yvonne," Diana said. "Let's use that name, shall we? Best not to let on otherwise."

I left, thankful they seemed to have called a truce. And wondering about the Fisherman network.

"The young lady does not look well at all," Harding said.

"Last night Madame Janvier said she had the flu," I explained. Then I told Harding about Yvonne, and the story of her wandering away from the bombed train and being helped by Doctor Leroy, then taken here by Rast. I went over what she had said about the Fisherman, Gustave, and the German. It made sense that she was the wireless operator, Madeleine, and that she'd escaped Gestapo custody after the attack on the train.

What that meant for our investigation, I had no idea.

"Outside, Boyle," Harding said, giving a nod to the stairs. He didn't want to be overheard.

"Yes, Colonel?" I asked, once we were out by his jeep. I looked around, amazed that only a few short days ago I had pulled in at this very spot, with Major Jerome's body still warm on the sitting room carpet.

"Listen, Boyle. First Army G-2 is convinced there is no security threat to the Ghost Army. They've pulled out and are headed to another part of the front," Harding said.

"So? Major Jerome is still dead. Someone tried to kill me, and Sergeant Fair, the driver you originally assigned us, was shot by a sniper. All probably linked to this case," I said. "Sir."

"Maybe," Harding said. "But there are snipers all along the front. You're not the first guy to almost take a slug, and the sergeant sure as hell isn't the first to buy the farm. You've done a good job here clearing the air about any security issues, which is why you were sent here. Time to stand down."

"Colonel," I asked, trying my best not to explode, "doesn't it make sense for us to continue the investigation, if only for a while? Otherwise someone might tumble to the fact that we were only here as part of a cover-up."

"You may have a point," Harding said, rubbing his chin as he thought. "We still need to report back about this SOE operative you've discovered here. I can give you a few more days, but that's it."

"That's all we need," I said, with more certainty than I felt.

"So who killed Major Jerome?" Harding asked. A very reasonable question.

"Someone linked to Major Rast," I said. "I think Jerome simply was in the wrong place at the wrong time. He witnessed something he shouldn't have and paid with his life."

"You think Rast's sniper experience fits into this?" Harding said.

"I'd bet my life on it," I said, and filled Harding in on what we'd found in the old mill.

"Doesn't prove much," he said. "That could have been left by a regular German sniper holed up in a convenient shelter. Or by an Allied airman or one of the Resistance cleaning their weapon."

"Hidden behind a wall? I don't think so, Colonel. I think Rast came back here and tried to kill me. Then he went for Fair and made his shot. Maybe it was meant for me and missed, but I doubt it."

"What could Fair have known that put Rast in jeopardy?"

"I'm not sure, but it may be linked to Yvonne. He was always mooning over her. Madame Janvier banned him from the house since he was underfoot every chance he got. He may have picked up some dope and not even known how important it was."

"Okay. Have Miss Seaton stay with her, and let's keep her true identity a secret for now. I'll contact the French section at SOE and let them know she's alive. Once she's better, we'll get her back to England."

"She looks pretty sick. Maybe we should get her to a doctor in town," I said. Madame Janvier called it the flu, but it looked like a pretty bad case.

"Tomorrow, if she's not better," Harding said. "Today, focus on getting what information you can from her. Now, I'll take those files I sent you. They of any help?"

"Except for identifying Rast as a sniper, not much. Although the Fisherman file explained why Yvonne had mentioned that word, along with Gustave. But we would have learned that anyway when Diana saw her."

"Find out what you can," Harding said. "SOE suspected the network was betrayed. She may be able to tell us by whom."

"Which might be a motive for murder," I said.

"Hers, yes," Harding said. "But she's alive, so there goes your theory. Keep me posted."

"You going back to First Army HQ?" I asked.

"No. I'll be at VII Corps headquarters, not far west from here," he said. "Radio me there with any news."

"Something happening?" I asked.

"Something big," he said. "Really big. All I can say is that the Ghost Army was part of it, and their deception was important. So good work on keeping the news tamped down."

Files in hand, Harding took off for whatever was cooking over at VII Corps. It occurred to me that Sergeant Fair knew the secret of the Ghost Army. But why that would earn him a bullet to the chest, I had no idea.

"How is she?" I asked, poking my head into Yvonne's room. Diana sat next to the bed, wiping Yvonne's brow with a wet cloth.

"Quiet, at least for the moment," Diana said. "She's very uncomfortable, and the perspiration won't stop. Madame Janvier is making a broth for her."

"Sorry about her response to you. I had no idea."

"I suppose you don't get the code name Corday by being cheery," Diana said. "She's actually quite famous in the SOE. In a secretive sort of way."

"And Yvonne?" I whispered her name as she twisted a sheet in her hand. Her eyelids fluttered, but she did not wake.

"I met her in training. We rehearsed our identities together, practiced our French, that sort of thing. A pleasant girl, and brave, but I don't really know much about her. I wonder what horrors she went through. Madame Janvier said she was brought here by a German officer?"

"He took her out of the hospital," I said. "But no one understands why. He apparently had no romantic attachment to her, although she's had that effect on a number of men." I told Diana the story of the train wreck, and Doctor Leroy's rescue.

"So she had been captured," Diana said. "Poor girl. It's odd that you say she attracted men. I don't think that happened in England. She was a bit shy, actually."

"The Sleeping Beauty effect, then," I said. "She's an unattainable princess."

"That fairy tale is quite horrible. I remember reading it when I was a child, and it gave me nightmares," Diana said, wetting the cloth and rubbing Yvonne's arms.

"What scared you?" I asked, taking a seat in Yvonne's chair by the window.

"Everything," she said and told the story.

Once upon a time, a king and queen have a baby. They invite seven fairies to be godmothers. One of them feels slighted by the royal couple, so instead of a gift, she gives the baby princess a curse. If the child ever pricks her finger on the spindle of a spinning wheel, she will die. Another fairy steps in to stop the curse, but all she can do is alter it. Now a pricked finger will put the princess into a deep sleep from which she can only be awakened by a kiss from a king's son.

Even though her father orders all the spinning wheels in the kingdom destroyed, one is left in his castle. The princess, now a young woman, discovers it and, unaware of the curse, touches the spindle. Blood flows, and she falls asleep. The fairy who tried to stop the curse returns, and puts everyone in the castle to sleep so the princess will not be alone once she wakes. She also summons forth a forest of vines and brambles to grow over the castle to hide and protect those within.

A hundred years pass. One day, a prince happens by, climbs the vines, and enters the castle. He kisses the sleeping beauty. She wakes, and then so does everyone else in the castle. The pair are married in secret, since the prince's mother is descended from a line of ogres and is unfriendly to humans. The young couple has two children, and when the ogre mother learns of this, she demands that the children and their mother be cooked and served to her at dinner.

The mother is tricked into falling into her own cook pot, which allows everyone to live happily ever after.

"That's strange," I said.

"Indeed," Diana said, as Madame Janvier entered with a bowl of soup.

"No, I mean that we have a vine-encrusted castle here. Except it's an old mill house."

"Vines and everything else that grows in the forest," Madame Janvier said to Diana. "It was an excellent hiding place, accessible only from the river." She'd changed her tune and sounded almost friendly. Maybe talking shop with Diana had calmed her down.

They pulled Yvonne upright and began feeding her spoonfuls of clear broth. Yvonne shook her head, fighting it. Then she took one sip, followed by another. I edged out of the room, not wanting to disturb this small victory.

The fairy tale bothered me. Not because it was gruesome. Most fairy tales in their original form are. It was the vine-choked house, the protected family, the secret marriage, the ogre mother ready to consume her own grandchildren. The happy-ever-after ending.

I couldn't put my finger on it. Any more than I could put my finger on why I felt uneasy when I walked into the kitchen and stared at the jackets hanging on pegs by the door.

CHAPTER TWENTY-EIGHT

IN THE AFTERNOON, we split up. Kaz and I headed up to Canchy, hoping to get something useful from Rast's chain dogs. It was a long shot, but it didn't take three of us to work the POW angle. I needed Kaz to translate. So I sent Big Mike to the Sarlat Hospital for a chat with Dr. Leroy about the Allied airmen who'd been picked up by the Gestapo on their way to the Nemo Line. Jacques hadn't trusted Dr. Leroy after that, and I wanted to find out why Dr. Leroy hadn't mentioned it. I tried to make a joke about sending him to the funny farm, but it fell flat. Guess it wasn't officerly enough for him.

"We found evidence of the sniper using the old mill house," I said to Madame Janvier as we prepared to leave. "Or at least someone cleaning a weapon there. It could have been one of your people."

"Maybe. Or it may have been that buffoon Legrand. You saw him sneaking about yesterday, *n'est-ce pas?* He is not to be trusted."

"Perhaps," I said, detecting a note of concern, or maybe even fear, in her voice. "I just thought you ought to know. Has Legrand bothered you?"

"Every time I see him," she said. "He is not a good Frenchman. Some people say he collaborated with the Germans."

"Is there any proof?"

"Ha! Those who said something all ended up dead or with the *coiffure* '44. Women know what will happen next if they speak out. The men are already dead. You witnessed this yourself, Captain."

"Yes, I did. Perhaps if we capture Rast, we can find out the truth," I said.

"About who killed your Major Jerome?"

"That, and much else. If Legrand is a collaborator, and why Rast targeted Sergeant Fair."

"I thought you said it was because you held his rifle, and the sniper thought the sergeant an officer?"

"Yes, but now I think it was deliberate. As was the attempt on my life."

She shrugged. It was the all-purpose Gallic shrug, her arms outstretched and lips in a thin pout. *What can one do? Such is life.*

There was nothing to say to that. Maybe I'd expected something more, a touch of understanding or even solace. But this woman codenamed Corday had endured too much hardship to be so easily moved. I asked if we were still welcome to stay, and she did manage an apology of sorts for her behavior. Certainly we could stay.

Big Mike had already departed when Kaz and I pulled out. I'd taken a few chocolate bars and a pack of smokes from the supplies he had stashed in his jeep. I'd left everything from mine in the Brassenses' kitchen, and I wanted a few goodies to entice the Kraut POWs. Big Mike had been quiet, which was unlike him. I didn't know how to get out of the jam we were in, and I didn't think he had a clue either. So we'd wished each other luck and gone our separate ways.

"I'm not sure what to say to Big Mike," I told Kaz as I shifted gears and took the first turn. "Maybe I should order him to forget all about it." That jest fell flat too, and I felt Kaz eyeing me as we hit the main road.

"Big Mike looks up to you, you know," he finally said as we drove out of the hedgerows and into the low-lying marshes that made this part of Normandy hell for advancing troops. Burned-out tanks and charred trucks littered the roadside, shoved into narrow ditches or swampy water to make room for the advance.

"Funny, I got the feeling he was looking down on me," I said, steering around a knocked-out Tiger tank. "And I mean both altitude and attitude."

"He respects you, Billy. Whether he is right or wrong about how you responded to my departure is not the point. What is important is that it crossed some line for him. Now he has to look at you as a flawed person and flawed in a way that matters deeply to him."

"Hey, I've got plenty of flaws, Kaz. I know that."

"Yes. But many of those flaws are what make you good at what you do. This flaw is different. Big Mike feels let down by your inaction, and it is personal for him."

"I don't get it," I said. "Why?"

"You should ask him," Kaz said. "Remember, he became angry with you when you let me leave without permission. Perhaps he felt you weren't doing all you should to protect a friend, which is obviously something he values."

"You talked to him," I said, shooting Kaz a glance as we came out into open country. Kaz waved a hand as if to say maybe, maybe not. Then he remained silent until we came to the POW cage, which was fine with me. Quiet made life simpler.

The barbed-wire enclosure ran along the edge of the road and held hundreds of German prisoners. Hostile eyes stared at us from inside as we slowed to show our papers at the gate. The POWs were ragged and dirty, some of them sporting bandages, and many wearing the shocked and dazed look of soldiers fresh from battle. There were the usual German army *feldgrau* uniforms, a sprinkling of *Luftwaffe* infantry in blue, and plenty of the camouflage tunics favored by the Waffen SS. The SS men scowled and sneered as they stared at us. They stood together, a tight-knit group that seemed to ooze disdain for their fellow prisoners. A few POWs smiled and laughed, probably happy to be out of the shooting war and enjoying the prospect of summer in England, or maybe even America.

Lieutenant Sewell waved as we were let through the gate, directing us to pull up in front of a large tent. Sewell snapped off a salute, and I introduced Kaz.

"Didn't think I'd see you again after they yanked me out of Bricqueville," he said. "Sorry I couldn't stick around to help, but the orders were to leave immediately. Damn strange. It wasn't like they needed more MPs here."

"You know how the army is," I said, remembering Sewell didn't know about the Ghost Army as we followed him into the tent. Two sides were rolled up to let in the breeze. There were a desk, a few chairs, and a table with a coffee urn. "You have some Krauts for us to talk to?"

"Yeah," Sewell said as he handed us a couple of chipped enamel cups filled with hot joe. "Three of our chain dogs were from Rast's outfit. Hey, you got any clout with Colonel Brewster? I'd like to get back with my unit."

"I might if we solve this murder," I said. "Looks like a big push is coming up. They've moved up to the line. You sure you want to go back?"

"Hell, yeah, I do. This place is the worst. I got nothing to do all day. Besides, all my buddies are with the outfit. Doesn't feel right to be stuck out here babysitting Krauts."

"No promises, but I'll try. Now tell me about Rast's men. Three, you said?"

"Yeah. But one refused to talk, on account of the Geneva Convention doesn't require him to answer questions about his unit. He's kind of a stickler for that stuff. Another Fritz just transferred in to Rast's unit from southern France. Never even met the guy."

"I hope number three has a bit more to offer," Kaz said, taking a seat and crossing his legs. He tasted the coffee and set the cup down, his lips puckered in a grimace of distaste.

"He does," Sewell said. "In spades. He hates Rast."

"Bingo," I said. I took a gulp of joe. It was blisteringly awful, but I didn't care. A German who had it in for Rast was just what I needed.

Sewell brought in *Unterfeldwebel* Walter Dassler, a non-commissioned officer. He wore the *Feldgendarmerie* metal gorget on a chain around his neck. He was a tall guy, with a long neck and a sharp, sloping nose. His dark eyes assessed us, pausing briefly as he took in Kaz's uniform and shoulder patch. His eyes went wide, but he recovered quickly. Any German would have good reason to worry about a Pole coming for them in a POW camp.

"Yes?" Dassler said, looking to Sewell as his protector.

"You speak English?" I said.

"Little bit," Dassler said, smiling as he held two fingers close together. "I learned at school. Then the army taught me more. We were to question American and British prisoners. Now I am here. Funny, is it not?"

"*Eine Tasse Kaffee?*" Kaz asked, nodding in the direction of the coffee urn. Dassler looked surprised at the kind offer and poured himself a cup. He took the seat offered by Sewell, who also gave him a cigarette. Dassler lit up and sat back, enjoying the moment. Hot coffee and a smoke. Not much, but a break from the dull routine of prison camp.

"Major Hans Rast," I said, setting down my own cup and leaning forward.

"Is he here?" Dassler said. I told him no. "Too bad. I would kill him if he was."

"Why?" Kaz asked, all smiles.

"He left me to be captured. The day we left the *pressoir*. He is a *Schwein*. I do not like any officers, but Rast I hate."

"You were with him that day?" I asked. Dassler took a long drag on his cigarette as he studied us. I could see the wheels turning. He'd been quick to reply when he heard Rast's name, given that he loathed the guy. But he'd caught on to the fact that we wanted something from him. Needed something. Which put him in a position to bargain, which was a powerful commodity when you were stuck behind barbed wire.

"Why? What do you want?"

"Information," I said. "About Rast."

Dassler shrugged. He took a sip of coffee and nodded in appreciation. POWs must get some awful swill here if he liked this stuff.

"I want to go to America," he said. "Like Rast."

"*Amerika* Rast, you called him," I said.

"Yes. We called him that when he stopped fighting partisans. It was to laugh. What is the English word? *Ein Witz*."

"A joke," Kaz said.

"Yes, a joke. On Rast, because he became soft."

"Why do you think he did?" I said.

"No answers. I want to go to America. I have been here too long," Dassler said, pinching off the glowing ember of his smoke and putting the butt in his pocket. He folded his arms across his chest and waited. He had the time, and we didn't. A breeze luffed the sides of the tent, scattering papers across the table.

"We just process POWs here," Sewell said, gathering them together. "Most of 'em are shipped out within a week. Our German MPs aren't too happy staying here, but we need them to help keep order and communicate with the prisoners."

"Why would they help you?" Kaz asked.

"Better rations, decent quarters," Sewell said. "It isn't really that bad."

"Then why do you want to leave, *Leutnant?*" Dassler said, grinning as he finished his coffee.

"Shut up, Walter, and answer the man's questions," Sewell said, obviously irritated that his prisoner had struck a sore point.

"Who could organize a way out for our friend here?" I said.

"Not me," Sewell said. "But I could make a recommendation to the CO."

"So can I, *Unterfeldwebel.*" I tapped my shoulder patch. "I work for General Eisenhower. I can get you out."

"*Geben Sie mir Ihr Wort?*" Dassler said, his eyes on Kaz.

"Yes, you have our word," Kaz said. "If what you tell us is useful."

"I do not know what you want with Major Rast, but I think you will find this *interessant.*"

It *was* interesting. The story Dassler told—with some translation help from Kaz—was that the day the unit pulled out from *Pressoir Janvier*, Dassler had been assigned to drive Rast in his staff car. Everyone was in a hurry, with the American artillery coming closer, and fighter aircraft searching for targets. They were the lead vehicle. After driving for thirty minutes, Rast ordered Dassler to pull over. The rest of the column passed them by on their way to Saint-Lô, where they were to regroup with another military police unit and make for Paris. Rast told him to take a side road, then along a deserted stretch ordered him out of the vehicle. Rast got into the driver's seat without a word and drove off.

"I was surprised he did not shoot me," Dassler said. "I was as good as dead out there. If the partisans find one of the *Feldgendarmerie* . . ." He drew his finger across his throat. The rolled-up tent flaps gave a good view of nearby ground, and he relaxed when he seemed sure there weren't any fellow Fritzes nearby.

"How were you captured?" I asked.

"I started to walk to Saint-Lô," he said. "Then I saw a roadblock. The SS, one of the panzer units. I had no papers, no reason to be out alone, away from my unit. They would hang me dead."

"*Ironisch,*" Kaz said.

"Yes, I thought so too, I must admit. The situation was often reversed. I turned around and went north. I ran into a patrol of *Amis* and surrendered. Rast almost got me killed, and for what? I wish I knew."

Dassler gestured to Sewell for another cigarette. I gave Sewell a nod, and he turned over the rest of his pack. Smokes were like gold in a POW cage, and Dassler deserved a reward for talking. We'd see if his reward amounted to anything more than a crumpled pack of Chesterfields.

"I'm not sure I buy it," I said. "Why wouldn't he simply have driven himself?"

"He never drove himself. Always with a driver," Dassler said with the self-assured tone of a guy telling the truth. "Also, people might question why he went alone and never came back. But with the two of us, it would seem like we had bad luck and were killed by partisans."

"It would help to know where he was going," I said. "That might tell us why he did it."

"I have an idea where he was going," Dassler said. "But first, you write out an order, yes? For me to go to America."

"A request to the commanding officer, Walter," Sewell said, standing and patting him on the shoulder. "I'll type it up now."

While Sewell stepped out, I gave Dassler the chocolate bars I'd brought along, just to reinforce our goodwill. He sniffed the Hershey bars deeply, smiled, and stashed them in his pocket. In a few minutes, Sewell returned with a typewritten sheet. He showed it to Dassler, then gave it to me. I signed it and held it in front of Dassler.

"Where?"

"Quibou, a small town to the west of Saint-Lô. He went there often, on a special antipartisan mission."

"What kind of mission?" I was beginning to think Dassler deserved a first-class ticket to the States.

"He speaks fluent French, you know. He had created a false identity as a Frenchman from Alsace. One who had fled the area when it was taken over by the Reich. As many did. That would also explain any accent. He had an apartment there. He often brought back information about the local Resistance groups."

"Why Quibou? Isn't that far from your area of operations?"

"Yes. It had to be somewhere he would not be recognized. And there was a local train that ran to Quibou, so he could easily make his way. He always carried his *Feldgendarmerie* identity papers hidden, in case he was stopped by any of our men."

"You are telling us that Major Rast had a secret identity?" Kaz asked, leaning forward. "Papers, a residence, all that?"

"*Ja, ja,*" Walter said. "Papers in the name of Phillipe Bonnet. The major is very clever. But not that clever. He should have shot me on the side of the road. Then you would never know all this. So, not so clever, *ja?*"

"I don't know, Walter," I said, thinking through the implications. "Pretty damn clever, I'd say. Tell me, did he have a rifle with a telescopic sight?"

"Oh *ja*, he did. He won medals in shooting before the war."

"Was it in the staff car?"

"Of course. I packed it myself. He would not have been without it."

"And his files," Kaz asked. "Did you pack them as well?"

"No, he had a man, *ein Schreiber*, for that."

"This clerk put the files in Rast's vehicle?" Kaz asked.

"*Nein.* There were boxes of files. They went in a truck. Except for his special files, of course," Dassler said.

"Special?" Kaz and I repeated at the same time.

"*Ja*, his files from the Quibou mission. He also kept some reports on the terrorists we captured."

"How do you know this?" Kaz asked.

"Major Rast typed up the Quibou reports himself. Everyone knew this, that it was a secret operation. He also wrote secret reports on terrorists, the ones he let go and earned him the name *Amerika*."

"Was one of them Leon Dubois? A schoolteacher from Saint-Jean?"

"*Ja!* That fool who told a woman about fighting with the Reds. He didn't even get her in bed for all that trouble. I was there when we arrested him. Rast let him go after two nights in the cells."

"Why? He didn't believe the woman?" I said.

"You tell me why. Dubois confessed before we laid a hand on him. He was, ah, *erschrocken, ja?*"

"Frightened," Kaz supplied. "He was scared."

"Rast made certain Dubois would know what to expect. He put him in a cell with a fellow who wouldn't talk. It would scare me too."

"Did Dubois betray his group?" I asked.

"I do not know. The report went into Rast's secret files, and the next morning Dubois went free. It happened often after the invasion."

"Do you recall other names?" Kaz said.

"There was only one other where I was present," Dassler said. "A one-eyed man, apprehended after curfew. I forget his name. Rast took over immediately."

"Legrand?" I said.

"*Ja*, Legrand. Same thing, two nights in the cells, then he was let go. No report filed with headquarters. Is this what you wanted?"

"It's not what I expected, Walter, but it will do," I said. "Now tell me about Yvonne."

"*Ach*, no one understood that," Dassler said. "Rast found her in that hospital during a security check. There was a rumor they might be hiding terrorists or escaped soldiers. But all Rast came up with was this girl who never spoke. Very pretty. We thought he wanted to have some fun with her, you know? But he kept her locked up, with orders no one was to go near her. He made Madame Janvier look after her, which she did not like."

Dassler's eyes were riveted on the paper that promised him a free ride to *Amerika*. We were in dangerous territory now. So far, he sounded like he was telling the truth. But as soon as he began to worry it wasn't good enough, he'd start embellishing, spinning wild tales to pump up his own importance. So I handed him the document.

"Danke," he said, his shoulders relaxing as he held the paper delicately, not wanting to wrinkle even a corner.

"Yvonne is still there," I said, watching for a reaction.

"Ja? I thought the Janvier woman would have sent her back to the hospital. She complained about having to feed her, even though Rast gave her extra rations. I think she did not like having the younger girl around."

"How do you know that?" I said.

"I saw her watching Rast. I think she liked him even though he is German. Which is bad for a Frenchwoman these days. She had no husband, and there are not so many Frenchmen for company anymore."

Because they're in POW camps in Germany or drafted into slave labor, I wanted to say, but I wasn't here to debate the point. "No, I mean, how did you actually know? Did she tell you she didn't like having to care for Yvonne?"

"Ja. She speaks German very well. She often said she wished to be free of Yvonne."

And yet just this morning, she said she wanted to care for Yvonne all by herself.

Dassler had nothing else to give us. Sewell said he'd process the request for transfer to a POW camp in America. Then he made me promise to get him back with his battalion. I did, but my mind was on Yvonne, Legrand, and those secret files.

CHAPTER TWENTY-NINE

"YOU HAVE HAD more dealings with this Legrand than I have," Kaz said as we motored south from the POW camp. "What do you think it means?"

"I'm not sure," I said. "If there had been a sudden increase in arrests, I'd say Legrand talked and betrayed his colleagues. Men in his own group, or others like the *Groupe Rouge* or the *Maquis Tigre*. Or the Nemo Line, for that matter. But there's nothing, as far as we can tell. Everything quieted down after the invasion, about the same time Rast was letting these people go."

"*Amerika*," Kaz said. "I wonder if there is something to that."

"But what's he up to? He could have traded information for a trip to the States, just like Dassler."

"Perhaps he does not wish to trade barbed wire in France for barbed wire in America," Kaz said. "Although I cannot pretend to understand what he gained by letting Dubois and Legrand go, along with the others."

"Me either," I admitted as I braked to a halt. At a road junction ahead of us, a column of trucks turned onto our road, moving fast. We were too far north to worry about dust, except for choking on it if we followed too closely. "It's the same with Yvonne. What purpose did she serve, and why hasn't Madame Janvier moved her back to the hospital?"

"Our hostess may simply have a fiery temper," Kaz said. "She may have truly been upset at Diana's sudden appearance. And she may have complained about Yvonne in order to extract more rations or favors from Rast. I am more interested in what Rast wanted with Yvonne, if not to indulge his carnal instincts."

"Well, I've tried to get information out of Dubois, but he's too scared to talk, that was plain to see. Yvonne can't talk, at least not yet. So that leaves Legrand."

"Then we must have a chat with Monsieur Legrand," Kaz said as I shifted into first and followed the column at a safe distance. "Where can we find him?"

"In Bricqueville," I said. "He should be easy to spot. Last time I saw him there, people were cheering him on as he shot two supposed collaborators and shaved the heads of young girls."

"Charming fellow," Kaz said. "I cannot wait to question him."

It was slow going on the return trip. More convoys of trucks bearing troops and supplies were all headed south, clogging the roads, churning up mud, and getting snarled in traffic jams at every intersection.

"Colonel Harding told us something big was in the works," I said, gesturing at a line of tanks parked under the cover of trees. Real tanks, this time. "This must be it."

"Look," Kaz said. At a four-way intersection, the bulk of the traffic took a turn to the right. The road marker pointed to Saint-Lô. "We just took Saint-Lô. A large-scale offensive push must be next."

It was a good guess. The city of Saint-Lô stood at the junction of seven main roads. It was a fair bet that we'd use those roads to strike south, deeper into German-held territory.

"That's where Colonel Brewster and the rest of 30th Division are now," I said. "At Le Mesnil-Durand. It anchors the right flank on the far side of the city." Flights of fighter-bombers zoomed overhead, heading for the enemy lines.

We left the convoy traffic behind as we went straight, following the markers to Bricqueville. The town square, where men had been butchered and women humiliated in the name of the Liberation, was quiet. Rubble was still strewn across the road in places, as if no one was sure whose job it was to clean up after this latest round of battle.

I parked in front of a café and let Kaz ask the questions. What he got in return was a lot of hand-waving and what seemed like an argument between the barman and two old gents at an outside table.

"What was that all about?" I asked as Kaz returned.

"One of the older fellows called Legrand a blowhard. The barman said he was a true patriot. All they agreed upon was that Legrand had two more of the *collaboration horizontale* women with him and drove through town with several vehicles filled with his men. The barman thought one of the women was Madame Janvier, but he is not certain."

"That can't be right. Which way did they go?"

"Towards Saint-Lô," Kaz said. "Less than thirty minutes ago."

"Damn," I said, jamming the jeep into reverse and backing out. "I would have preferred a nice, quiet conversation, not another mob scene."

"Why is he going to Saint-Lô?" Kaz said, hanging onto his cap with one hand and the seat with his other. "He has a built-in audience here."

"Saint-Lô was just liberated. Maybe he likes the atmosphere. No rules, nobody in charge. Gives him a chance to be the boss."

"And to settle scores," Kaz said as I floored the accelerator, hoping Legrand would be slowed by the steady stream of vehicles headed in the same direction he was.

"With Rast, you mean?" Kaz nodded. It was possible. Quibou was on the other side of Saint-Lô, but why make a spectacle of it? Protection, maybe. Legrand had his own private bodyguard this way. "Say he was after Rast. How would he get him to come forward?"

"Wait," Kaz said, laying a hand on my arm. "He has two women with him. If one of them is Madame Janvier, could the other be Yvonne?"

"Damn!" I said, smacking my hand against the steering wheel. "That makes sense. Rast has some sort of connection to Yvonne. That might draw him out."

"Which means he certainly is going to Quibou," Kaz said. "We should be able to find him there. It is much better than having to search Saint-Lô."

"Yes," I said. "But who is the other woman?"

"It may be a real collaborator. Or at least a young girl who slept with a Fritz."

"Or it could be Madame Janvier. Or Diana."

"My God, he wouldn't take a woman in a British uniform, would he?"

I didn't answer, just drove faster. I'd seen a small suitcase in the hallway, and I'd guessed that was Diana's. If she had civilian clothes, she might have changed into them to care for Yvonne. Or perhaps Legrand had her along to serve as a nursemaid. If so, then what happened to Madame Janvier?

Too many questions. For all I knew, Diana was still spooning broth into Yvonne and listening to Madame Janvier complain.

I passed four trucks crammed with GIs, narrowly missing a tank destroyer coming at me. Kaz, never the calmest passenger, managed not to complain.

The country road descended from the heights and gave us a view of the city of Saint-Lô. Or what once was a city with that name. The sight was so stunning I pulled over and gazed at the scene below. All I could see were mounds of rubble as high as a man, with the occasional skeleton of a building or church steeple still standing, half buried in debris. Jeeps, trucks, staff cars, and ambulances snaked through narrow cleared passages that might have once been streets, alleys, or parks.

The devastation was total. Great blocks of concrete and granite lay tumbled upon one another, covering God only knew how many civilian and enemy dead. The living scrambled over the scorched debris, searching for remnants of their lives. Close by, two kids covered in chalky dust and grime sat atop a shattered building, their shoeless feet dangling over the edge. GIs stood gawking at the destruction, as if unable to take in that this had once been a city, teeming with people and purpose.

We drove farther into the city, the only sound that of grinding gears and the treacherous echo of stone on stone as shaky structures continued their collapse all around us. Deeper in, it felt as if we were descending into a pit, a giant hole in the earth that had belched up ancient ruins to replace a modern city.

"How could anyone live through this?" I said, my voice strangled into a whisper.

"Cellars," Kaz said. "They go into cellars. Some come out."

I hoped most of the population had fled before Saint-Lô became a battleground, absorbing artillery shells and bombs until the rubble bounced. Tires crunched on gravel as we moved slowly forward, trailing an ambulance, the shrieks and groans of the wounded inside growing louder as the cleared roadway became more torturous and uneven.

Near what seemed to be the city center, the road opened up. An MP at an intersection let the ambulance through and then halted us as two more trucks emblazoned with the red cross rumbled by, turning north and away from the fighting. He wore an MP armband and a helmet with a faint gray stripe. In the rear areas, they wore all-white helmets, earning them the nickname "snowdrops," which I couldn't imagine went over well.

"Be a few minutes, Mac," the MP said, waving a column of half-tracks in the opposite direction. The GIs aboard swiveled their heads, watching and listening to the casualties pass them by.

Welcome to the battlefield.

"You see any FFI vehicles pass through here?" I asked.

"The Fee-Fees? Yeah, a truck and a coupla cars, about five minutes ago. They went left, toward the cathedral. Or what's left of it. We sure liberated the hell out of this place, didn't we?"

"Worse than anything I've seen," I said. "Hey, is that the way to Quibou?" I point to the shattered spire of the cathedral a few blocks away.

"It is, but that's Kraut real estate," he said.

"You sure about that?"

"Sure enough that I wouldn't take a joyride out that way, Captain. There's Kraut paratroopers and *beaucoup* tanks over that next ridge. Quibou's about three miles thataway," he said, pointing past the cathedral. "First one's easy. The next two are killers."

"Thanks," I said as he waved us through.

"That takes care of our Quibou theory," Kaz said. "I wonder what Legrand is up to."

"I'm not so sure it doesn't still hold," I said, craning my neck to see up ahead past a truck towing an antitank gun. "Remember, Rast is used to moving between the lines. He's got false French papers and his German ID. Covers all the bases."

"You think Legrand is meeting Rast?"

"I think we're about to find out," I said, spotting a truck with *FFI* painted on a side panel. I pulled into an alley and parked the jeep between two piles of bricks. I grabbed my Thompson and hopped out, Kaz right behind me with his Webley drawn.

We made our way around the block, so we could approach the cathedral from the next side street and get a good view of what Legrand was up to. We climbed over tumbled-down chunks of granite and concrete, and wriggled through shell holes in the wall of a building opposite the open ground in front of the church. Perhaps this had been a park or a promenade in more peaceful times, but today it was a field of sharp-edged stones.

"Here," Kaz whispered, tapping my arm and leading the way to the second floor of the building, climbing up planks of wood someone had obviously set up as a makeshift ramp. I followed him through a hole in the wall, hitting a brick with my elbow as I slithered through, dislodging it. I winced as a small avalanche followed, covering my head as I was showered with dust. But the wall held, and we moved on to the first window and the view it afforded of the square.

We weren't the first ones there.

A man lay sprawled on his back, flies already busy around the red hole in his forehead. He wore an FFI armband and a wide-eyed look of shock. A British Lee-Enfield rifle sat at his feet.

I pulled Kaz away from the window, and we flattened ourselves against the wall.

"One of Legrand's men," I said, recognizing him. "His rifle is clean and well oiled. He might be what passes for a sniper in this outfit."

"Legrand sent him here to ambush Rast," Kaz said. "Who was one step ahead of this unfortunate fellow."

I chanced a glance out the window. I figured it was safe enough since Rast had already eliminated the threat from this position. There was a crowd gathered by the church, a gaggle of men and women shouting and shoving their way to the front. The cathedral once had two towers, but one was totally destroyed, and the other had its top sheared off halfway up. The roof of the nave had collapsed, with stones and timbers spilled out into the street, as if the devil himself had spewed it out from the depths.

A cheer rose from the group, some of them wearing the FFI arm-band, others simply drawn to the event by the noise and drama. I could see a line of FFI men armed with rifles, leading four women toward the group. None of them was Madame Janvier, so perhaps the barman had been mistaken. One was very young and frightened, tears running down her cheeks. Another was older, mid-forties, maybe, and walked with a regal bearing, as best as she could manage on heels going through rubble. The other two were in their late twenties and looked resigned to their fate. Working girls, I'd bet. They were no strangers to being used and abused by men.

I still couldn't see who else they had in front of the crowd, but I could hear Legrand's voice, mocking and scornful, as he whipped up the onlookers. Far as I could figure it, he'd brought Yvonne to this settling of scores in newly liberated Saint-Lô, and somehow sent word to Rast in Quibou. My guess was, he'd offered an exchange: Yvonne for whatever Rast had on him. Evidence of betrayals, or whatever else he'd done those two nights in Rast's custody.

But where was Yvonne? I strained to see who was up front, but there were too many people blocking my view.

"Let's go," I said. Kaz picked up the rifle and followed. We found a stairwell and took it to the ground level, which had a convenient hole in the wall big enough to walk through. We ran across the street, past the crowd with their backs to us. We scrambled up a heap of rubble and found ourselves in what once had been a sitting room, except now it was half a sitting room, exposed at the end facing the cathedral.

Below us, the FFI men marched the four women to the front, shoving them into a group of three others. But Yvonne wasn't one of them.

I saw Diana and Madame Janvier, both with hands tied behind

their backs and mouths gagged. Diana struggled, trying to loosen the rope binding her hands. As the new arrivals huddled together, pushed and prodded by their captors' rifles, Diana fell backward, rolling on her side and grimacing beneath the gag.

"We must stop this," Kaz said, kneeling and aiming his rifle. At this close range, he could pick off any of them in a heartbeat. Legrand continued to harangue the group, working them into a frenzy, walking in and out of the crowd, patting people on the back, and arguing with the few who seemed to object to the proceedings. If Rast was lining up a shot, he might hit anyone.

"I'm going down there," I said.

"I will announce you," Kaz said, and aimed his rifle at the top of the tower. The shot rang out, echoing against the stone as the ricochet zinged between the ruins.

That got everyone's attention. Rifles swung in the air, seeking targets. I noticed Legrand melting farther into the crowd. I stepped forward, Thompson held at the ready.

"Halt!" I shouted. "By order of General Eisenhower, I order you to disband!"

Kaz hollered out the same in French, rising to one knee so they could see the rifle aimed at them. I stepped down the pile of loose brick and stone, praying I wouldn't stumble and ruin my entrance.

"It's not going to work, Legrand," I said, wading into the crowd and working my way forward. Holding a submachine gun with my finger on the trigger had a way of parting the crowd quite nicely.

"You have no place here. This is French soil," Legrand said, puffing his chest out but standing behind one of his tallest men. "And this is French justice."

"There's a lot of guys who would be glad to leave the rest of the fighting to you, Legrand. And as for justice, there's damn little here. Now come up and tell these people to disperse. Show's over."

"Never!" Legrand said, and ordered two of his men to guard the women.

They shot me nervous glances, but climbed the small pile of stones to where the captives were on display, putting themselves between me and them. They probably thought I wouldn't spray the whole group with .45 slugs. They were right.

I gave Diana a quick look. She winked. I saw her move her arm slightly, and I knew she'd freed herself. I stepped up on the rocks and swung the butt of my Thompson against the head of the man nearest me. Diana rose swiftly, bringing up the brick in her hand against the temple of a second rifleman, who fell in a heap on top of the first.

The group began to murmur, the momentum of Legrand's frantic speech gone. A few men and one woman still yelled and shook their fists at the captive women huddled together, but most whispered among themselves, unsure of what to do or who the hell I was.

"Billy, give me a pistol and I'll shoot this man myself," Diana said, after tearing off her gag and freeing Madame Janvier. "He kidnapped us at gunpoint."

"Do not listen to them," Legrand shouted at me. "We are here to take justice and to trap a German agent. You are helping him!" Then he told the same thing to the crowd, which only seemed to frighten them. Public head shaving and humiliation were one thing, but a German agent, that sounded dangerous.

"Break it up, Legrand," I said. "You're coming with us. We'll get you out of here safely."

"I do not need you. My men are all around." He waved an arm in a grand gesture, taking in the buildings and the church tower.

"Like the man with this rifle?" Kaz said, standing so Legrand could see the Lee-Enfield. "He is dead. Killed by a sniper before you arrived, I would guess."

"Louis!" Legrand called out. "Vincent! Pierre!"

The names went unanswered.

"Rast got them, Legrand. Come with us. It's your only chance," I said. FFI men, those who had been in on the plot, began edging away, eyes darting about as they prepared to run to the nearest cover. Their sudden fear communicated itself to the rest of the crowd, and slowly people at the edges began to clear off. Then more, including Legrand's own men.

"No!" he yelled the moment those closest to him melted away. He spun on his heel, ready to run into the cathedral, but before his foot hit the ground, a rifle shot sounded, echoing harshly off stone. He fell face first, blood and dust spraying off his back.

"There!" Diana shouted, picking up a rifle from the poor guy she'd clobbered. Counting on us to see where she was shooting, she knelt and fired. I saw a hit take a piece of brickwork off a building behind us on the main road. She worked the bolt and fired again, this shot sending a puff of concrete dust flying near a window. "Go!" she said and fired again.

I ran, jumping over Legrand's corpse, legging it for the structure Diana was firing at. I could see she was working the windows, keeping Rast guessing in case he planned another shot. It gave us good cover, but from what I knew of the man, he was a smart sniper. A one-shot sniper. I was aiming to spot him as he exited the building. Once he got clear, he'd be impossible to find in this city of ruins and rubble.

I scrambled over piles of debris, keeping close to the edge of the building, looking for a way in and staying out of Rast's crosshairs, if he was still up there.

"What's going on?" The MP from the intersection was coming at a run, right down the middle of the street, other GIs not far behind.

"Sniper!" I shouted. "Take cover!"

It was good advice, and the MP took it, diving behind a burned-out truck. I doubted Rast was still looking to take a shot, but I didn't want to waste time answering a lot of questions from a well-meaning snowdrop.

The top floors of this building had been blown off, and the rubble rose to the top of the ground-floor windows. I found one with enough space to squeeze through and waited for Kaz to catch up.

"Cover me," I said, handing him my Thompson. I tossed my helmet through the opening, in case Rast was waiting and might be suckered into firing off a round.

Nothing but the clatter of a steel helmet against stone.

I slithered through, sliding down the mound of brick and mortar that had flowed in through the shattered window. It made a helluva racket. At the tail end of the noisy avalanche, I thought I heard a board snap above me, somewhere on the second floor.

Kaz handed me the Thompson and his rifle, then slid into the room. My finger went to my lips to tell him to be quiet, which was rewarded with an eye roll. Yeah, a bit late for that. I pointed up, and Kaz got the message. I grabbed my helmet, and we made for the door, stepping over debris barely visible in the darkened room.

In the hallway, the light improved, mostly due to the fact the roof was in the basement. Wide boards had been laid across the collapsed hallway above, and I spotted a broken one at the far end of the hall. I waved Kaz forward, and we scuttled over the timbers and roof tiles littering the ground, trying to keep an eye out for Rast and not break a leg at the same time.

A pistol shot echoed off the walls, the zing of a bullet overhead making us duck. He wasn't bothering with an aimed rifle shot, just trying to slow us down.

So I went fast, weapon at the ready, hoping to catch him off guard as he worked his way through the fallen timbers. Kaz stayed on my heels, falling once with a grunt, then catching up as I came to a back door blasted almost off its hinges. I pushed it aside carefully with the barrel of my Thompson, ready to fire at any sign of movement.

I had a clear view of the rear of the next building. Its roof was little more than charred timbers, and the back wall had a gaping hole where a shell must have hit. The rest of it was intact, but the hole led to a perfect view of the cathedral. If Rast was targeting anyone else, he might take a shot from there. And Diana could be in his sights.

"Cover," I said to Kaz as he knelt beside me. He leveled his rifle at the space between the building and a steep granite outcropping behind it. I raced to the hole, leaping over a section of collapsed wall and flattening myself before I slipped through the opening, watching for movement. I couldn't take more than two steps. The upper floor had fallen, and I was faced with a jumble of desks, chairs, masonry, and thick wooden beams scorched from the fires.

I backed out and signaled Kaz to move up. Beyond the building the granite outcropping rose even higher, above the field of rubble by the church. Several medieval turrets were still standing, miraculously in one piece. Green grasses grew thick on the sloping ledge, like long abandoned and forgotten parkland.

"The ramparts," Kaz whispered. "The old section of Saint-Lô has walls built up along the river for protection. The Germans were digging tunnels from this side. Look there." He pointed to what looked like a cave opening, with a large warning sign.

DANGER. The same in English and French.

"Rast may have used them to approach the cathedral," I said.

"And to get away," Kaz said, pointing to another opening farther down. "We should follow."

I saw him wince. He was using his rifle to hold himself up. His trouser leg was ripped and soaked in blood.

"Jesus, Kaz, are you okay?"

"I cut myself when I fell," he said. "Clumsy of me."

"Listen," I said. "I need you up here. If you can walk, take that path above the ramparts. Watch each of the tunnel entrances for Rast. Can you do that?"

"Absolutely," he said. "I much prefer the open air in any case. Go, and I will take a pleasant stroll with my new rifle."

"Okay," I said, grasping his shoulder for a moment. "Watch yourself."

"You too, Billy. Wait, look there." He pointed to the rear end of the cathedral, not a hundred yards away. It was Diana, trotting toward us with her rifle at the ready.

"Don't let her follow me," I said. "Tell her you need help." I got up and waved her on, pointing at Kaz. Then I ran to the tunnel entrance and darkness.

Light filtered in for the first ten feet or so, and then it was nothing but pitch-black. I kept my shoulder to the wall and edged forward, feeling with my feet for any obstruction, or worse yet, a sudden drop-off. My shin hit something, and I felt the top of a table, then what turned out to be a cot. Farther on, another cot with a crate next to it. I heard something drop to the floor and discovered a candle set in a tin can, with a small box of matches inside. I took a chance and lit one, then the candle. I figured with no light, I couldn't move fast enough to catch Rast. And he'd never think his pursuer would be dumb enough to light himself up.

As the match flared, I saw why the Germans had tunneled under the rampart walls. It was a makeshift hospital. Overturned tables and cabinets had been emptied, leaving nothing but empty cots and rust-colored bandages on the floor. I slung my Thompson and drew my revolver, trusting I could handle the .38 Police Special one-handed better than my tommy gun.

The flickering light was enough to guide me through the tunnel without my tripping over the remnants of the underground field hospital. I held the candle as low as I could, hoping to keep my eyes accustomed to the dark as I strained to see just a few yards ahead. I stopped, listening for footsteps or any sound that would betray Rast's presence.

Nothing. Which meant he wasn't even here, or else he was quietly lying in wait. A few yards ahead, the tunnel branched out in two directions. I darted forward, squatting as I got to the split. The left might take me to an exit on the far side of the ramparts, down by the Vire River. That would lead to Quibou. The right would lead out to open ground, where Kaz and Diana were waiting.

I went left.

The tunnel narrowed, and I had to duck a few times to keep from hitting my head. My helmet clunked against the rock above me, so I took it off. The Thompson was knocking against my side, so I laid it against the wall next to the helmet. Quiet was my friend in this tunnel, and if I needed more firepower than six .38 caliber slugs in this narrow chamber, I'd be in a world of trouble. An underworld of trouble.

The passage widened again, the yellow glow from my candle reflecting off crates stacked floor to ceiling, marked *Granaten, Explosiv, Munition.*

Grenades. Explosives. Ammunition. Maybe it wasn't a good idea to spray automatic weapons fire around in here. I eased past the crates on either side of the wall, going sideways where they were packed close. A single crate was open, revealing neat rows of German potato masher grenades. One was missing. Rast might have grabbed it, but it'd be suicide for him to toss it my way with all the explosives stacked up in here.

In front of me, the two-foot-wide space was blocked by a couple of crates set in the path, one after the other. I froze.

I'd been channeled into this contained space. If I wanted to move forward, I'd have to step up on the first crate. That would put my skull square up above the ammo crates. A clear shot, with no risk of setting anything off.

It was a cunning sniper's trap.

I went low, reaching up and placing the can on the highest crate. I tipped it over, the open end facing ahead. It rolled, the flame guttering as it sent its meager light trembling against the shadows.

The shot was incredibly loud, echoing over and over again in the enclosed space, the stone walls and ceiling bouncing the sound around until it faded to a harsh ringing in my ears. The can was gone, sent spinning by the round that was meant for me.

The light was out. Darkness enveloped me. Total jet-black inkiness, except where the flash of the rifle shot imprinted itself on my eyes. I lay on the ground, willing my breathing to calm so I could listen for approaching footsteps, Rast coming to check my corpse and apply the coup de grâce.

I did hear footsteps, but not headed my way. Maybe Rast thought I was dead. Or maybe he just wanted to get away, counting on me to hunker down in the dark.

I wanted to stay hunkered down. The complete darkness was suffocating and disorienting, and I was already unsure of which way was forward. I found the boxes blocking the path and slithered over them, keeping to my hands and knees, crawling until I felt the cool packed earth of the tunnel wall, loose stone and gravel cascading at my touch. I stood, keeping one hand on the wall and the other extended, revolver at the ready.

This part of the tunnel was empty and much smaller. I could reach out and touch the other wall, the passageway barely wide enough for two people to pass side by side. As the ground began to slope downward, damp, putrid odors wafted in my direction, a sign that I was nearing an exit, with fresh air blowing in from the river.

The farther I ventured ahead, the less fresh the air smelled. It was rancid, and I held back coughing as the odor rose into my nostrils. I let go of the wall and held my arm against my nose, trying to keep the stink at bay. Without anchoring myself on the wall, it felt like I was walking into a deep, dark hole filled with the stench of decay. I stumbled over something, tried to stay upright as I took the next step, and tripped as my boot hit a surprising softness.

I fell, my free hand landing on a face, the unmistakable outline of teeth and nose hard on my palm. I rolled away, another body beneath me, the vile, sickly odor of death at the back of my throat. I scrambled away, gasping, wishing for one clean breath of air. I found the wall and backed up against it, chest heaving, wondering what kind of charnel house I'd wandered into. And if Rast had led me here for a final bullet.

I still had matches, and as much as I wanted to see my way out, I knew I couldn't risk it. A single spark would be a bull's-eye. I went flat and crawled on my belly, pulling myself over a pair of legs. I could feel a thin layer of earth covering the limbs, and for the first time was thankful for the total darkness. The cursory burial hadn't done much to stanch the fetid fragrance of death, but at least I didn't have to look at the rotting corpses I was dragging myself over.

After a few minutes at a slow crawl, the smell seemed to fade. I felt the breeze wash over me and blinked my eyes as the faintest shimmer of light played against the wall. I rose and ran, making for the outside, hoping Rast wasn't waiting around the next bend. The tunnel grew brighter and I squinted as my eyes adjusted to the light.

A *clunk* echoed against the walls.

A grenade bounced in my direction.

I spun around, ran three steps, and dove for the ground, hands covering my head.

The explosion felt like it went off inside my head. The concussive waves rattled my brain and banged on my eardrums, as if my head was being slammed against the ground over and over. Debris showered me, and I tensed, waiting for another explosion or a cave-in, telling myself I had to get up, had to defend myself in case Rast came at me.

I rolled over and pushed up, breathing in dust and smoke as I felt around for my revolver. I found it and stood up, my head spinning and a thrumming noise in my ears. Hacking and coughing, I stumbled, then righted myself and found the exit, a narrow cleft in a rocky field sloping down to the river. I squeezed through in time to see a figure running on the path along the riverbank, a rifle slung over his shoulder. He moved with an uneven gait, favoring one leg with a loping limp that might have resulted from his fall in the bombed-out building.

He went blurry. I raised my pistol, which seemed to waver as I worked to put him in my sights. I felt dizzy, and the ground fell out from under me.

I saw sky and heard shots.

Maybe not in that order.

CHAPTER THIRTY

I DIDN'T KNOW why people were dragging me by my arms. They were yelling, and there were grenades falling everywhere. I forced my eyes open, and went from dazed to alert in no time flat.

Those weren't grenades. It was artillery fire. Mortars from the look of the explosions blossoming by the riverside, each one a few yards closer.

"Billy! Get up!" It was Kaz, pulling on one arm while our MP pal grasped the other, the two of them hauling me up the steep, grassy hillside. I tried to work my legs, and they surprised me by cooperating, getting me upright and then running pretty damn fast. My brain felt sluggish and blurry, but my feet knew enough to get the hell out, pronto.

We made it up and over the embankment, collapsing behind one of the stone turrets that stood watch on the heights. Diana was there, concern wrinkling her brow.

"Did you see him?" I asked.

"No," Kaz said as Diana examined me, her hands in my hair. They came away sticky with blood. The MP doused my head with his canteen, and Diana daubed at a cut I was just beginning to feel at the back of my head.

"We heard the explosion and ran up here," she said. "Then saw you on the ground as the Germans started shelling. They're right across the river."

"Rast got away," I said, waving my arm vaguely in the direction he'd run. "We should go after him."

"He's too far away by now," Kaz said. "He could have doubled back into the city or vanished into the trees along the river. He might know a safe crossing place farther to the west."

"He's a slippery bastard," I managed. "How's your leg?"

"We should get both of you to an aid station," Diana said. "Baron, you may need stitches."

"Baron? And an English dame toting a rifle out here? What kind of outfit is this anyhow?" asked the MP.

"Trust me, you don't want a transfer," I said. "What's the status of the FFI crowd?"

"We scattered 'em," he said. "A few of them threw stones at those women. I got a medic down there doling out bandages and sympathy. Maybe he could look at that leg."

We descended the ramparts, Kaz limping as he used his rifle as a crutch. My ears were still ringing from the grenade, and the MP was casting quizzical glances my way, still trying to figure out who the hell we were. Diana looked more like a soldier than any of us.

On the cathedral steps, a medic was winding a bandage around the head of one of the young girls. The older woman next to her held her hand, patting it reassuringly. She managed to keep her aristocratic bearing even as she held a compress to her cheek, stanching the flow of blood that had stained her blouse. Madame Janvier rummaged in the medic's kit and came up with sulfa powder and a new compress, cleaning the woman's wound and wrapping a length of gauze around her head to hold it in place. She murmured her thanks and arranged her hair around the binding, making it look almost fashionable.

Coiffure '44.

The girl wept, whether from the pain of the blow or her situation now that the Germans had retreated, I couldn't say. By the heavy makeup and the cut of her dress, I pegged her for a prostitute. All that meant was, she worked for some criminal who told her to sleep with whoever had the dough to pay, and in occupied France, that meant

Krauts. Her pimp was probably safe somewhere, sitting on a fortune in francs, while his working girls were left to the mob.

The rich lady, who knew? Maybe she fell in love with a German officer. Maybe she ran a shop and made a good living selling finery to the cash-rich Fritzes who wanted to send real French doodads back to their girlfriends. It didn't really matter. Unless these women had fought for the Germans or the Vichy militia, they didn't deserve the degradation served up by men eager to display their bravery with razors and clippers.

"Are you all right, Madame Janvier?" I asked as the medic turned his attention to Kaz, cutting away the fabric of trouser leg.

"Yes, now that the fright is over. It was terrible, Captain Boyle. Legrand had gone insane. Madness! Oh, Baron, you will need the stitching. But it is not too bad."

The medic nodded his agreement, sprinkled sulfa, and tied a tight bandage around the gash. He told us there was a new field hospital set up in Pont-Hébert, near VII Corps headquarters, and that we could expect fast service.

"Must be a big offensive coming up," he said, giving my noggin a quick look. "They got *beaucoup* medics and empty beds. No waiting, at least today. And you're lucky, Captain. You might have a slight concussion, but it's just a scratch."

"Thanks, but if I was really lucky, the other guy would be the one bleeding into his collar."

The medic wrapped a bandage around my head and told me to keep it on for a couple of hours, and I'd be okay. I told the MP about the munitions in the tunnel and the hastily buried bodies.

"We haven't had time to check all those tunnels yet," he said. "We've found other bodies. The city jail had a dozen corpses in the cells. Krauts musta shot 'em before they pulled out. The others could have been slave labor. We found a few of them still alive, believe it or not. They were practically skeletons."

Then he and the medic loaded the two women into a jeep, promising to see them safely home. Assuming they had a home still standing. The lady wrapped her arm around the young girl, who leaned into her shoulder and wept as the jeep lurched away over the rubble.

"I need a minute," I said, raising my hand as Kaz got up, wincing as he put weight on his leg. "Tell me what happened back at *Pressoir Janvier*. Exactly."

"That maniac stormed in with several of his men," Diana said. "He called Madame Janvier a traitor and said she'd betrayed members of the Resistance. I asked what proof he had, and under whose authority he acted, but that only angered him more."

"Then he took me and Miss Seaton too," Madame Janvier said. "He knew he could not get away with this in Bricqueville, so he brought me here to be part of this charade."

"But why?" Kaz asked, sitting on a pile of broken granite. "He apparently made contact with Major Rast and expected to ambush him here. Why would Rast play into his hands?"

"First, Baron, you must understand Legrand was unbalanced. *Maboul*. I think when my husband died, he thought he would call on me after a time. I told him no, and perhaps not in the nicest way."

"He did act strangely," Diana said. "I feared for our lives as soon as he set foot in the house."

"But there's something else," I said. "The second thing."

"Yes," Madame Janvier sighed. "A few months ago, I had a moment of weakness, I am ashamed to say." She looked away, out over the destruction of the city, unwilling to meet our eyes.

"With Major Rast," Kaz said.

She nodded her head abruptly, once, keeping her face turned away. She was ashamed and smart enough to know this was dangerous information.

"Legrand knew, and thought Rast would come to your rescue," I said.

"Legrand did find out, yes. I don't know how. Perhaps one of my workers, or even a German talking in town. But he did know. Why he thought the major would risk his life to rescue me, well, that is ridiculous."

"But Rast did come," I said, fingering the bandage on my forehead.

"He came to kill," Madame Janvier said. "Not to save me. I don't wish to put my shame on display, but I will tell you it was a sudden thing. A thing that happened once. It is hard for a woman to run a business, especially when the old wagging tongues say I am a witch for not mourning in black. Who can do such a thing when there is work to do, I ask? Should I have mourned properly and let all my husband's work fall apart? No! I was weeping one night, and Rast came across me. He was kind in that moment. He is the enemy, but it must be said, he is a cultured man, as far as any German can be. And fair to look at. So I forgot all the things I should have done and, for once in my life, did what I wished. For that, Legrand would have shaved my head. For some insane reason, he thought to use that to trick Rast."

"It wasn't insane," I said. "I think there's a good chance Rast has an incriminating file on Legrand for betrayals real or imagined. Legrand may have been hoping to get his hands on those, or simply do away with Rast."

"It does not surprise me that Legrand was a collaborator," she said. "Tell me, did Rast do this to you?" She gestured at Kaz's and my wounds.

"Yes," I said. "But he got away."

"Ah, well, the war has a way of finding those who deserve justice," she said.

"We should go," Diana said. "We need to get back to Yvonne."

"Of course," Kaz said, rising unsteadily. "Perhaps you should drive."

"I'm fine," I said, and got up. Then promptly sat back down. "Okay, Diana drives."

We made it to the jeep in one piece, just in time to hear our call sign on the radio.

"It's Big Mike," Kaz said, answering the call. "He found Yvonne alone, and he's looking for us."

"Tell him we're headed to the field hospital and to meet us there," I said.

"Oh, I can take care of Yvonne," Madame Janvier said. "She will be fine, I am sure."

"It won't take long, Billy," Kaz said. "We should take Madame Janvier back and decide about Yvonne. Then to the field hospital."

"I can wait if you can," I said. He agreed.

"Then hang on," Diana said, starting the jeep. "It looks like we may need an ambulance before this day is done."

We made good time back to *Pressoir* Janvier. It looked like most of the heavy stuff was already up front. There were plenty of vehicles marked with red crosses, trucks weighed down with ammo, and staff cars full of officers, all headed to the front. Final preparations, complete with sightseeing brass. Whatever was in the works, it was going to be big.

"What's going on?" Big Mike demanded as we pulled up at the front door. He took in our bandages and ran to the jeep to help Kaz out. "Are you guys okay? What happened?"

"Where's Yvonne?" Diana said, vaulting from the jeep and making for the door.

"Upstairs. I cleaned her up best I could, but she don't look so good. Someone tell me what's going on, willya?"

I filled in Big Mike on what had happened, leaving out Madame Janvier's confession.

"How bad you hurt?" Big Mike asked.

"This is nothing," I said. "But Kaz needs to get that gash sewn up. We wanted to check on Yvonne first, then head over to the VII Corps field hospital. We'll take her if Diana thinks she needs it."

"She does, believe me. We coming back here?" Big Mike asked.

"I don't think we need to," I said. "We're going to Quibou soon as we can to find Rast. You mind grabbing our duffels, Sarge?"

"Sure," Big Mike said. "Glad you two knuckleheads didn't get yourself killed."

"As are we," Kaz said, once Big Mike was inside. "It seems he is back in good humor."

"Wait until we tell him Quibou is behind enemy lines," I said.

CHAPTER THIRTY-ONE

"WE HAVE TO get her to hospital," Diana said, holding Yvonne upright, one hand tucked around her waist and the other grasping her hand over her shoulder. Yvonne made fumbling attempts to walk, the blanket Diana had wrapped around her trailing at her feet. Her head lolled, and her eyes barely stayed open as I helped her into the jeep.

"She doesn't look good," I said.

"It is the influenza," Madame Janvier said. "I pray she will be well. Please let me know, will you?" Her hand went to her mouth as if to stifle a sob. It was the first real display of emotion I'd seen from her as far as Yvonne was concerned. I promised we'd get a message to her as soon as we had news.

Big Mike tossed all our bags into the two jeeps, and we set off for the field hospital at Pont-Hébert. Kaz went with Diana and Yvonne, holding Yvonne steady in the rear seat as Diana drove. Big Mike got behind the wheel, and I checked the map for the quickest route.

"Head south," I said. "Take the road to Airel. Looks like it should take a half hour or so."

"Okay," Big Mike said, glancing back to be sure Diana was following. She was practically on our bumper. He hit the accelerator, and she stayed close. "I was worried about you. All of you."

"It must have been a shock to find everyone but Yvonne gone," I said.

"Yeah, and it looked like the place had been ransacked," he said. "Lousy job, pretty slapdash, but Legrand must have been after those files. But why the hell did he take Madame Janvier and Diana?"

"Keep it under your hat, but she and Rast evidently had a roll in the hay. One time, a moment of weakness, according to her. Legrand found out somehow and thought Rast would come to her rescue. I think he grabbed Diana so he wouldn't leave a loose end behind."

"I guess that makes sense," Big Mike said, rubbing his chin with one hand. "And I will keep that on the QT. If that's all that happened, she doesn't deserve the kind of punishment these people hand out. People make mistakes, you know?"

"Yeah," I said. "I made one, Big Mike. I shouldn't have let Kaz disobey orders to take off like that. He could've gotten in trouble. You were right."

"I know I was right, Billy. Because I once did the same thing you did. But it didn't end up all swell, like Kaz showing up with good news. It ended real bad. That's why it got to me, I think. I didn't want anything to happen to Kaz, but I didn't want you to have to live with it either." He kept both hands hard on the wheel, knuckles white with tension.

"Here's the turn," I said, pointing to the road sign ahead. "What happened?"

"It was back in Detroit. I'd been on the force a couple of years, and they assigned me a rookie. Kid by the name of Freddy Bielak. Freddy had an uncle who was a union organizer. Worked at the Hudson plant in Detroit. You ever hear of the Black Legion?"

"Sounds like the SS," I said, hanging on as Big Mike took the turn with an anxious look over his shoulder to be sure Diana was keeping up.

"Close. Buncha wackos who thought the Ku Klux Klan was too soft. They went after Negroes, Catholics, Jews, and union guys. A fair number of Detroit cops and politicians were on their side. They wore black robes with a skull and crossbones. Really violent bunch. They murdered mayors in Michigan towns if they hired colored folks for city jobs."

"I can't believe I never heard of them," I said.

"They kept a lot of stuff out of the newspapers. They finally got broke up pretty good before the war."

"So what happened to Freddy?" I said, touching the tender spot on my bandage where the blood had dried.

"His uncle's union was demanding higher wages. Henry Ford and his automaker pals didn't like hearing that. Freddy said his uncle was getting death threats and had been warned not to speak at a labor rally out in Monroe. He asked me to go with him. I knew what the Black Legion was capable of, and I told him not to go. I said even if there was two of us, there'd be twenty of them, and his uncle should sit this one out. I even made sure he was assigned the second shift that night, so he couldn't go. But he called in sick. I shoulda known. I shoulda stopped him."

"What happened?"

"Freddy and his uncle were found in a car riddled with bullets, about ten miles from Monroe. I was his partner, so I notified his parents. They didn't say anything out loud, but I knew. I knew they wondered why I didn't go with him."

"It wasn't your fault," I said as Big Mike slowed to pass a farmer leading a cow along the road. He was a skinny old guy who tipped his wool cap and grinned, revealing maybe half a dozen teeth beneath a heavy gray mustache. That he and his cow had survived the Occupation was a tribute to rural living.

"You know, you can pretty much convince yourself of anything if you try hard enough," Big Mike said after giving the guy a friendly salute. "But I ain't never talked myself into believing it wasn't my fault. I didn't want you to end up the same way. And I didn't particularly like being reminded of Freddy, to tell the truth. It put me in a real bad mood. So I know I was pretty rough on you."

"I'm sorry about Freddy," I said. "The kid had guts."

"Yeah, he was a lot like Kaz. Except for the scar, the fancy talk, and a boatload of dough. Basically a skinny Polack kid who tried to do the right thing."

We drove on in silence, letting the story of Freddy Bielak and the

Black Legion fade into the past, where it belonged. Not forgotten, but no longer a nightmare sowing doubt and guilt over each misstep, each mistake that led to a hail of gunfire on that lonely country road.

"What'd you get from Dr. Leroy?" I said, after we passed through a village and descended into the sunken roads of the *bocage* country. Shell holes and blasted, blackened hedges marked the course of the hard fighting over the past weeks.

"He knew about the two fliers who were taken by the Gestapo. But he said they never made it to the hospital, and the Gestapo never questioned him about it. But one interesting thing was that the fliers were in the care of the Fisherman network."

"Yvonne's group," I said, giving a quick glance back. Kaz had his arm around her, holding her steady as Diana drove on.

"Exactly. Which may explain what happened to her. Someone betrayed the network, and the two fliers were picked up while in their hands," Big Mike said.

"I think we've been looking at Yvonne all wrong," I said. "So many guys were entranced by her, we assumed Rast was too. That he took her out of that hospital because he was smitten with her otherworldly charms."

"But what if he was collecting members of the Resistance?" Big Mike asked, wagging his finger. "Like Legrand and Dubois. Some kind of insurance policy."

"Could be," I said. "Stands to reason the Gestapo would circulate her picture if she escaped custody. Rast may have recognized her and snatched her for some purpose we don't yet understand."

"Makes sense," Big Mike said, slowing for a curve. As the road straightened, we had a clear run between rows of stately plane trees, the paved surface marred with tread marks but in good shape. He floored it. "But I can't figure his angle. What's in it for him?"

"And how did Major Jerome fit in?"

"Maybe Rast hid those files in Madame Janvier's house," Big Mike said, snapping his fingers and quickly putting his hand back on the wheel as we bumped over road damage from Sherman tanks and German Tigers before them. "He sneaks back in after we occupy the place, in the middle of the night, of course. Jerome is there and spots him, lights out for the major."

"Remember the three glasses of calvados," I said as I grabbed onto my seat. "One laced with morphine."

"Yeah, that doesn't add up."

"Unless Madame Janvier knew he was coming and wanted to knock him for a loop. Maybe he forced himself on her, and she dressed it up for us."

"You know, I could see that if it wasn't for the third glass," Big Mike said. "A night cap with a Nazi who raped you isn't the kind of thing you invite a pal along for."

"We're here," I said, pointing to a sign directing us to the 51st Field Hospital. We pulled into a field chewed up by more tank treads and truck tires and parked by a large tent, one of many marked by large red crosses on white backgrounds.

Four nurses were seated outside on wood crates, having a smoke, dressed in oversized fatigues. The medic had been right—there were a lot of tents and not many patients.

"We have a French civilian who's very sick," I said. "And a British officer who needs his leg looked at."

"Come on, girls," one of them said. "Let's lend our allies a hand. What about you, soldier?"

"It's only his head," Big Mike said. "He don't use it much."

This got a laugh, and a couple of the nurses began to flirt with Big Mike while the others looked Yvonne over.

"We think she has the flu," I said. "But she's also been mute and nonresponsive for quite some time. The Gestapo had her." The look in the nurse's eyes told me that was all she needed to hear.

"She's in bad shape. Stretcher," she said, calling out for help and tossing off a quick salute. "Lieutenant Myrtle Kent. These are my nurses. Who are you?"

"This is Diana Seaton," I said, after I'd introduced myself. "She works with this young lady, who we call Yvonne. It's not her real name."

"Hush-hush, is it? Okay, let's get her loaded up," Myrtle said as two nurses hustled out bearing a stretcher. Yvonne moaned, her skin pale and sweaty.

"I must stay with her," Diana said. "It's quite important."

"All right, but leave your rifle in the jeep," she said. "We have an empty tent in the next row, we'll put you there. These are the staff tents, not for patients. That way you can stay off the books."

"You're wonderful," Diana said. "And please take care of the baron as well."

Of course *baron* got their attention. What with a spy and a nobleman to look after, I hardly rated a second look.

"It's just a cut," Kaz said, grinning as more nurses materialized and rushed to his side.

"I'll be with Yvonne," Diana said. "Can you find Colonel Harding and ask him if he's gotten in touch with SOE? Once she's stable, we need to get her back to England."

"Will do. I'll come back as soon as I talk to him. Be careful."

"Why do you say that? We're perfectly safe here."

"Because I'm missing something. An important part of this puzzle. I know it, and it makes me worried," I said.

"You be careful," Diana said, and gave me a kiss, then ran after the nurses carrying Yvonne. Myrtle had noticed the kiss and winked as she led Kaz, limping, to a medical tent. I told Kaz we'd be back for him, and he told us to take our time.

We found Colonel Harding at VII Corps HQ, about a half mile down the road, situated in a stout stone farmhouse surrounded by camouflage netting, tents, and vehicles parked between rows of apple trees. A motorcycle courier roared off as we parked, and GIs buzzed around the place, carrying papers, files, and an urgency you could read in their earnest faces.

"What's going on?" Harding demanded once we reported in and he took note of my bandage. He was in a small room at the back of the farmhouse, a table full of files, maps, and an overflowing ashtray. We sat across from him as typewriters and teletypes clacked away outside the door, keeping beat to the hum of frantic human activity. Boots on stair treads and shouted orders echoed against stone walls.

On the front lines, GIs huddled in foxholes, quietly waiting, while here at HQ, clerks, typists, couriers, and high-level brass created a cacophony of rising noise.

"Legrand kidnapped Diana and Madame Janvier," I said. "We got them back, but Legrand's dead. Rast took him out with a sniper shot."

"Why the hell did he do that? Is Miss Seaton all right? What about Yvonne?" Harding asked, as full of questions as we were.

"Diana's fine," I said. "She and Madame Janvier were unhurt. Best I can figure, Rast has some sort of dossier on Resistance members. Maybe it's for blackmail, I can't really say. All I'm sure of is that people are scared of what's in it." I gave Harding the rundown on what happened in Saint-Lô and how we almost caught Rast.

"We brought Yvonne to the field hospital," Big Mike added. "She's pretty sick. Diana's with her. Kaz is getting his leg sewn up; he got hurt chasing Rast."

"Bad?" Harding said, concern etched in his face.

"He'll be fine," I said. "Nasty gash, but nothing half a dozen fawning nurses can't take care of. Diana asked if you've heard back from the SOE yet."

"No, but I've got a stack of radio messages to go through. I'll let them know she's here."

"Looks like she was betrayed along with the rest of the Fisherman network," Big Mike said. "I talked with Dr. Leroy at the Sarlat Hospital. He told me the network was blown around the same time the Gestapo picked up two downed airmen making their way to the Nemo Line at the hospital. They never made it."

"Okay, SOE is definitely going to want to debrief her, if she ever snaps out of it," Harding said. "So do you think Major Jerome's murder had something to do with Rast's dossier?"

"Yes. It's possible he went back to the house to retrieve his files and encountered Jerome there. We know the major arrived ahead of schedule, when no one expected him. Can't say for sure, but one thing we do know from a POW interrogation is that Rast operated undercover out of a town not far from here. Quibou."

"Undercover? As a Frenchman?" Harding asked, leaning back and lighting another Lucky.

"Phillipe Bonnet from Alsace, to cover up any accent. His file said he spoke fluent French," I said. "He may have infiltrated the Resistance and gathered information for his dossier. I'm sure that's where he ran off to and where we'll find his secret files. I think he injured himself in the same building Kaz did, so I'm hoping he's holed up in his safe house right now."

"The only problem being a lot of Germans between you and him," Harding said, blowing blue smoke toward the ceiling.

"Hey, Sam, can we get some food?" Big Mike asked. Big Mike was always ready to eat, but this time I was with him. It had been a long time since I'd eaten, and the mention of chow made me hungry. Harding knew Big Mike well and smirked as he called out to a GI to bring us bacon sandwiches and coffee.

"I'd like to find out what Rast's game is myself," Harding said as we waited. "He might be putting together a stay-behind operation. Or even spies to infiltrate the French army. General de Gaulle is asking members of the *Maquis* to join up. There's still lots of opportunities for collaborators to help the Germans."

"Hard to see why," Big Mike said. "It's not like the Krauts are coming back."

"Money," Harding said. "And politics. The French have their own brand of fascists. Some of them are diehards and know they'd be killed or prosecuted if they're caught. Rast might be offering them new identity papers in exchange for spying or sabotage."

"Could be," I said. "But he had something on Legrand. Something so dangerous that Legrand gambled with his life to get at Rast."

"And lost," Big Mike said. "He wasn't the brightest guy around. Maybe he did collaborate and was desperate to stop Rast from spilling the beans."

"We've heard a lot of bad things about Legrand," I said. "Collaboration wasn't one of them. Sorry, Colonel, we're just going around in circles right now. What we need is Rast and his dossier."

The bacon sandwiches and coffee made an entrance, and we

stopped to dig in. Big Mike's vanished before I finished half of mine.

"You may be able to get to Quibou soon," Harding said after he polished off his sandwich. "I'm sure you've noticed the preparations for a major offensive."

"A new field hospital with plenty of empty beds and a lot of staff cars ferrying brass close to the front," I said. "Pretty obvious there's a big show in the works."

"Operation Cobra," Harding said, moving papers on his table and unrolling a map. "It kicks off tomorrow morning. It might blow this whole front wide open."

Harding briefed us on the plan. In the morning, troops along a stretch of the front by the road from Saint-Lô to Périers were going to pull back twelve hundred yards. Beginning at 0930, Allied air power was then going to pound a box about three and a half miles long and one and a quarter mile deep with saturation bombing. Six hundred fighter-bombers would attack a strip of land closest to our troops, on the theory their low-level attacks would be more accurate than the high-level bombers. Eighteen hundred heavy bombers would follow, working over the rest of the box with their payloads. Nearly four hundred medium bombers would finish the job from the air. That was a lot of high explosive for a relatively small area, not counting the shelling from over a thousand artillery pieces. The infantry would go in first, at 1100, and clear out any defenders left standing.

"Then the tanks," Harding summed up. "Probably the next morning. And that includes the Second Armored Division. That's why the work of the Ghost Army was so important. We couldn't let the Germans know we pulled them out of the line for this offensive. I think we're really going to catch them by surprise."

"Where's Quibou in all this?" I asked, studying the map, which was filled with arrows and all slicing through that rectangular box.

"Right here, on the south edge of the box," Harding said. "I might be able to arrange a ride with Second Armored in two days. If all goes well, they should be in Quibou that afternoon. You can comb the place for Rast."

"Okay," I said, tracing my finger along the route the armored column would take. I noticed a familiar division number on the left flank. "Is the 30th Division in on this?"

"Yes," Harding said. "Colonel Brewster's battalion will be in the spearhead. They're on the left flank and will cover the Vire River approaches to the east after the breakthrough."

"I'll have to look Brewster up after we nail Rast," I said. "He's been hounding me for results."

"He's got a lot on his mind right now, but I'm sure he'll be glad to hear it. Now go get some rest. I'll check with SOE and let you know what I find out. If you don't hear from me, check back here tomorrow night. I'll let you know then about going in with Second Armored."

I gave him Lieutenant Myrtle Kent's name and told him they were treating Yvonne off the record. Big Mike grabbed the last bacon sandwich for the road, and we left Harding to his maps.

"We ain't waiting for Second Armored, are we?" Big Mike said as we got in the jeep.

"Rast will be long gone," I said. "With that much firepower headed his way, he's bound to run. Our only chance is to grab him while the situation's confused and wait for the cavalry to arrive."

"You make it sound easy," Big Mike said.

"You don't have to go," I said. "This is strictly a volunteer mission."

"Damn," he said, driving back to the hospital. "I wish I'd never told you about Freddy."

CHAPTER THIRTY-TWO

I TOLD KAZ. I didn't tell Diana.

He was in no shape to hike through a battlefield, and he knew it. Diana was preoccupied with helping care for Yvonne. Evidently, she was a little better and beginning to manage a few words, even though nothing made much sense. Diana wanted to stay close in case Yvonne came around and she could get any information from her about Fisherman. A doctor was due to examine her, but I couldn't wait.

I told Diana I had to see Colonel Brewster and that I'd be back. She nodded and smiled, more focused on feeding Yvonne a clear broth than on what I was saying.

She believed me. I hoped I wasn't lying to her. Or myself.

Kaz told me to be careful and to keep my head down. It was what I told guys whenever they were headed into the fight. It always felt like I was giving them good advice. Now I knew how useless and empty it sounded. But I promised I would.

Big Mike and I drove to Le Mesnil-Durand, where Johnson had told us the battalion HQ would be. I told Brewster what the plan was, and he said it was my funeral, but I was free to come along. He told me he wanted the man who'd killed Sergeant Fair, but he couldn't spare us anyone to help. I told him that was fine, and we were counting on moving fast and skirting any Germans who were still in one piece after the bombardment. He had us outfitted with weapons, gear, and extra ammo, and gave us a foxhole on the withdrawal line. Men were starting to pull back as night fell. In the morning, the rear guard would come in an hour before the bombing.

Flares and flashes of artillery fire lit the night sky. We didn't talk much. Didn't sleep much either.

AS SOON AS the sun rose, cooks brought up coffee and chow from the company kitchens, about half a mile back. Trucks backed up to the foxholes as close as they dared. Guys lined up for coffee and oatmeal, still steaming as it was served into mess kits. It was better than a cold breakfast K-Ration. For some, it would be their last meal.

We watched the rear guard filter in as we finished the last of the coffee. They cast anxious looks over their shoulders, knowing there was nothing but air between their backs and Krauts in their forward positions.

"Kinda hard to imagine what it's gonna be like," Big Mike said, craning his neck and searching the sky. A lot of guys did the same, counting down the minutes until the massive bombing run.

"I was bombed in North Africa, but that was a small raid compared to what's coming. It was bad enough," I said, almost feeling pity for the enemy. Almost.

There was a lot of nervous chatter all around us as GIs waited, hoping for the best, praying it wouldn't come to the worst. I know I was. We were far enough from the Krauts that men gathered together, smoking and talking, wandering around behind the hill where we were dug in, too keyed up to sit still, but with nowhere to go. Nervous in the service once again.

A faint hum turned into a distant drone and grew more insistent, louder and more piercing as the seconds passed. Officers shouted orders for their men to get back into position. Non-coms rounded them up, pushing them toward foxholes while staring up at the sky.

It was the fighter-bombers, swooping in low in groups of four, attacking the German line closest to us. Red smoke flares were set off right behind us, signaling our position to the pilots. One low-flying

P-47 waggled his wings, setting off a cheer that rippled up and down the line.

Tank destroyers moved into position down the line, their treads grinding up the ground and engines at a low idle. It was good to know we'd have some armored support going in, even though the big armored formations would follow tomorrow, exploiting the gap that bombs, shells, and infantrymen would open up today.

"Hey, Billy!" I turned to see Lieutenant Sewell, grinning broadly as he trudged forward.

"Looks like you got your transfer," I said, involuntarily ducking as a flight of four P-47s swooped in low over us.

"Yep. Colonel Brewster told me I'd find you here. I wanted to say thanks. It feels good to be back with my unit," Sewell said.

"Thank me when it's over," I said. "What do they have you doing?"

"Traffic control, mostly. We need to keep the men moving and supplies close behind. Not to mention getting the ambulances through. They're about a half mile back," Sewell said, jerking his thumb to the rear. GIs liked knowing medics in their unit were close by. But they didn't need to see how many trucks and ambulances with big red crosses were waiting. Too demoralizing. "I gotta go. Thanks again, and good luck."

"Keep your head down," I said. Force of habit.

"I hope he knows what he's in for," Big Mike said as bombs crashed into the landscape before us. Machine guns chattered and fighter-bombers strafed the positions they'd just hit.

"I hope *we* do," I said. "He'll be safe enough, sorting out road traffic."

Another wave of fighter-bombers hit the Germans, then soared away, leaving behind blossoming clouds of bright orange flame. Napalm, the stuff they used in flamethrowers. The fire raged, incinerating forest and flesh.

Then quiet, nothing but low murmurs from the men and the faint roar of whirlwinds whipped up by the raging fires. A rumble in the sky got everyone looking for the source. The sound was everywhere, the droning loud and insistent, filling the air with a thunder of engines.

The heavy bombers, very high up, coming closer and closer. Hundreds of them, the formations so high and far away the individual bombers blended into the cloud cover.

"There!" Big Mike shouted, as the lead bombers released their bombloads. The other aircraft followed suit, and we could trace the clusters of bombs as they fell from that great height, hurtling to the ground, erupting in great geysers of smoke and fire.

A line of explosions shook the ground under our feet. The salvo of bombs crept our way, finally stopping short. Another bombload erupted, even closer, and it looked like the earth was exploding from within, spewing out destruction and death.

Closer. They came closer, each bomber releasing their payload nearer our lines. The air was filled with clouds of choking dust, and I rubbed my eyes to see clearly, looking straight up and seeing tiny black dots grow larger and larger as a stick of bombs came right at us. Big Mike shoved me down into the foxhole as the earth shattered and shook around us, a rain of dirt and debris showering us until I feared we might be buried alive.

More explosions threw us back and forth in the foxhole, slamming our bodies against the earthen walls hard enough to dislodge dirt and gravel, burying us even deeper. I began to cough, hacking out the dust filling my mouth and nostrils.

The bomb hits faded, the ground shaking less as the explosive devastation moved away from our position. Big Mike pulled me up, flinging me out of the foxhole as the sides caved in. He shook off the dirt coating his body, which had protected mine. We exchanged glances and a quick nod. We were okay, not that we could say it out loud. The steady throbbing of engines, the constant explosions, and the ringing in my ears made it hard to speak or hear.

Until the screams.

Standing, I saw the carnage. Several bombs had hit our positions. Smoking craters dotted the ground, bodies with blackened flesh and flowing red blood flung out of them like scorched rag dolls. A leg lay a few yards from us, the boot laced up tight by a GI who minutes ago thought it would propel him into battle. Instead, battle had come to him.

Bits of flesh and burning GI wool uniforms lay scattered on the ground. A sergeant with one arm shredded by shrapnel walked straight down the road, dripping blood and calling for his squad. Men with torn bodies and shattered limbs writhed on the ground as others tried to fight through the fog of shock and help them.

We went forward as the ambulances raced toward us, slamming on brakes and disgorging medics with packs and stretchers. Dozens of wounded were cared for and carried off. About twenty dead were laid out in rows, waiting for Graves Registration. They, like the medics, were close by, hidden from view.

One of the twenty was Sewell. He had not a mark on him, nothing but the unmistakable limpness of death, as if the body understood it would soon be interred and had begun to melt into the earth.

"He was with his buddies," Big Mike said, surveying the scene. "That's something."

I didn't reply. I was too busy fighting off the guilt I felt for helping Sewell get back to the battalion. But it was his wish, his choice. I kept telling myself that as we waited, watching the medium bombers work over the box, glad that they were flying lower and could actually see what they were blowing to hell.

Finally, it was time. Colonel Brewster came forward, delivering the news. The battalion had taken casualities, but the attack was still on. Non-coms got their men ready. The last bombs were dropped, the sound of aircraft engines fading in the midday sky. Artillery kicked in, adding their shells to the violence, a creeping barrage creating a concussive curtain of steel before us.

Ahead was nothing but dust, a giant wall of it, churned up by constant bombardment, fires, and swirling wind. The men moved out, dazed and bewildered by their own bombs, still shocked at so many casualties before the enemy had fired a shot.

But they advanced. They stumbled into the dust cloud, running low, covered in dirt, dusty uniforms bound tight by webbing, belts, canvas ammo pouches, field packs, knives, canteens, and more ammo hung from belts, the cloth, leather, and metal softly clinking and bouncing, creating a faintly musical sound as they ran.

It was like walking through fog. A gritty fog, laced with acrid smoke and arch fear. Big Mike and I followed a line of men as they made their way through a hedgerow that had been blasted away in places. GIs filtered into the next field, littered with bomb craters overlapping one another, with black, smoking earth thrown in all directions. Artillery continued to fire over our heads, and we walked on with increasing optimism. No Krauts yet.

Then I spotted one. Flat on his back, legs twisted at impossible angles, dead.

Another one appeared, walking out of the brush holding his rifle, a wide-eyed look of shock and bewilderment on his face, his uniform casting off wisps of smoke. I don't think he even registered our presence. A GI put a round in his chest, and the Kraut crumpled.

Shouts and screams came at us, and everyone went flat. No machine gun fire came our way. We crept along a stone wall and found a burning truck with Germans spilled out around it, the dead, wounded, and shocked nearly impossible to tell apart.

One of them, dully taking notice of the Americans advancing on him, raised his rifle.

They were all cut down.

We spread out and followed the road, coming upon a Panzer IV tank upended and on the edge of a huge bomb crater. Smoke curled up from the hatches, the vile smell of burning flesh burrowing into our nostrils. More Germans dead in the road, looking much like our dead, except for a slight difference in the uniform color, the shades of gray and brown not so far apart after dirt, fire, and blood had their way.

"Maybe it worked," Big Mike said as we knelt in a shell hole, watching the men of Brewster's battalion fan out and make their way across the cratered ground. "Looks like they're all dead or crazy."

"Let's hope," I said, scrambling up out of the hole and following the line of GIs. I knew I'd almost lost my head when those errant bombs hit us. The enemy soldiers in front of us had endured much more. But I knew there was one big difference. "If they were dug in good, a lot of them are probably getting into position now. They may be shook up and half deaf, but that doesn't mean they won't fight."

In the middle of the field, three Germans lay dead. The ground they lay upon was untouched, as were their bodies. All around them, huge craters hissed smoke from blackened earth. Concussion had hit them from all directions, killing them instantly and leaving them almost as they were, crouched and holding their weapons, huddled together in their last moments.

A farmhouse with one wall blown out came into view as the dust settled and the air cleared. We stepped around a cow split in two, losing sight for a moment of the squad in front of us. A stone barn was completely destroyed, its roof gone and nothing left but a pile of shattered granite. A blackened corpse smoldered beside it, one arm pointing to the heavens.

A stone slid to the ground, the harsh scraping sound followed by another.

A hand appeared. It was chalk white from the granite dust and bright red from rivulets of blood. Big Mike and I ran over and dug out the rocks covering the hand. We pulled, and the guy screamed. We got more stone off him, revealing a Kraut coal-scuttle helmet.

We got him out. His leg was broken, and he had a shell-shocked stare that didn't seem to register who we were. He jabbered in German, probably delirious and in shock. Big Mike gave him some water, but there wasn't much else we could do. We left him beside the barn, hoping a medic would find him. He wasn't going anywhere, but we were.

Machine gun fire rattled off to our left. A few shots echoed from ahead, and we took cover behind a fallen tree. Big Mike nudged me, and I looked back to see another squad coming up from behind. They passed the German we'd pulled from the rubble, and one of the GIs casually pointed his M1 at him, fired, and walked on, not missing a beat.

Maybe it was quicker that way.

Firing increased to our front. The whistle of mortar rounds sent us running, the shells exploding in the road. The rapid firing of a German machine gun kicked up, bullets slashing the air with a frenetic *thrum* as they passed close by. The Bonesaw, GIs called it, the

Kraut MG42 that could fire twelve hundred rounds a minute. That was a lot of lead.

"This way," Big Mike said, pointing to where the field sloped off into what looked like a streambed. I nodded, and we ran for it, giving the growing fire fight a wide berth. It felt strange to be skirting the battle, but we weren't here to assault machine gun nests. We were here to find a killer. Not a hard thing to do in this France of July 1944, but I had a score to settle with a particular killer.

We left the streambed after making good time for about ten minutes and took a break within a bombed-out hedgerow, where we could keep a good lookout. Rifle shots crackled around us, but the heaviest fire was to our sides and rear.

"We may have snuck through the first line of resistance," Big Mike said, looking down the lane. A single truck burned at the side of the road, likely abandoned. No bodies in sight.

"Yeah. I figure what's left of the defenders are going to naturally group together, like the machine gun and mortars back there. If we can get around them, we should be okay until the reinforcements start showing up," I said.

"How far to Quibou?" he asked as a flight of four P-47s raced overhead, fragmentation bombs under their wings. I sent up a prayer for them to find whatever armor the Krauts were sending our way.

"If I'm right, Les Fontaines should be dead ahead. Then it's about a half mile."

"Straight ahead," Big Mike corrected me.

We went straight, working our way through torn hedgerows with the occasional sprint along the road. It was slow going, but we found a crossroads with a road sign for Les Fontaines—on the ground in several pieces, but it meant we were on the right track. We went around the small village, not much more than a collection of blown-out houses and what might have once been a church. The rubble looked like a good defensive position, and we found a spot on a small rise to observe.

"Over there," Big Mike said. A staff car drove in from the direction of Quibou, followed by a truck towing an antitank gun. If we were lucky, they were moving forward from Quibou and setting up shop here.

"Infantry," I said, spotting field-gray uniforms filtering out of the woods and making for the ruins. "They're staying well away from the road. *Staub bedeutet Tod.*" The truck and towed gun were kicking up a fair amount of dust.

"What?"

"*Dust means death*, in German," I said. As if on cue, the snarling engines of two P-47s in a dive proved the adage. The Krauts hit the dirt, and we took off, taking advantage of the bombing to avoid being spotted.

An hour later, we crossed the railroad tracks on the outskirts of Quibou. A slate-roofed train station stood intact next to a row of shops with windows blown out. A church had lost its roof, and bombs had churned up the graveyard, as if we didn't already have enough rotting corpses lying around.

A priest stood outside the church, his black robes billowing in the wind. He looked lost, and I wondered what he thought about God at this moment, his dead parishioners unearthed before him and his sanctuary open to the elements. We watched from the cover of a low stone wall and saw no one else. No dust, no vehicles, no shouts in German.

I stood up and waved, stepping over the stone wall. The priest's mouth gaped open, and he covered it quickly, eyes wide with surprise. I put my finger to my lips as we got closer.

"American," I said. *"Américain."*

"Oui, oui," he said, smiling excitedly and shaking our hands. He was a thin guy, short, with gray, wispy hair. He had to look up to greet Big Mike. He began to fire away in French, but I held up my hand and showed him the picture of Rast I'd taken from Harding's file.

"Phillipe Bonnet?" I said. "Quibou?" I pointed to the village center, visible from the height of the churchyard. The road from the station and the church crossed a stream to where a cluster of houses gathered itself against the outside world. Burned-out vehicles dotted the road, and smoke rose lazily from a house that had been hit, but otherwise Quibou wasn't the total ruin other towns had been.

"Phillipe? *La Résistance*," he said, but I couldn't understand if he was asking or telling me. I finally understood we could find Phillipe at 32 Rue des Moulins, in a second-floor room above a cheese shop, in the center of town.

"Merci," I said, and turned to scout out a safe route into the village. As quiet as it looked, I wasn't about to saunter up the main road.

"Non, non!" The priest said, grabbing my arm. *"Boche.* Panzer."

"Combien?" He held up four fingers. Four panzers.

I tried to get more details, but I didn't have enough French to cut through his excitement and understand most of what he was going on about. But four Kraut tanks was all I needed to know. I thanked him and got the old fellow to go back inside.

Big Mike and I knelt by the cemetery wall and stared at the town, a short stroll away.

"Four tanks, plus support," Big Mike said. "Could be a platoon over there."

"Then why aren't they in forward positions? I'm thinking they're just four tanks that pulled out once the bombing started. They might be using the village as cover. And look at the bright side."

"What, there ain't fourteen Tigers in there?"

"No. I'm betting Rast is hiding from the Germans as well as us. With them in town, he doesn't dare go outside. That means we can grab him at his apartment."

"Oh. So the good news is that we get to do what Rast ain't dumb enough to do himself. Walk through a small village and avoid four big Kraut tanks," Big Mike said.

"That's one way of looking at it," I said. "How about we do it after dark? Better?"

"No. Those guys in Les Fontaines might get pushed back. Then we'd have more trouble."

"Okay, have it your way. We'll go now," I said.

"I gotta eat," Big Mike said, sitting against the wall and pulling out K-Rations. It seemed the sensible thing to do, given that there was no reason to die hungry.

CHAPTER THIRTY-THREE

I WENT FIRST. Big Mike was a good guy to have at your side in a fight, but when it came to sneaking up on a position, he was too damn big to make a stealthy approach. I told him to stay twenty yards back and stop whenever I did.

I crawled along the base of the raised roadway, slithering through the muck as I came to where a squat stone bridge arched the slow-moving water in the streambed. I hugged the foundation, glancing in every direction. I could hear voices raised in the village, echoing off the buildings, impossible to pinpoint. German or French? I strained to hear, but it was all garbled shouts. Windows were shuttered, wisps of smoke still curling up from the fire we'd spotted earlier. I hoped any civilians still left in Quibou were hiding in their cellars. For their own safety and ours as well. The last thing we needed was for the locals to start cheering, thinking we were the vanguard of liberation.

I crouched low and ran across the stream, barely a foot deep. From beneath the arch, I scanned the road leading into the village. No one guarding the perimeter. Maybe my theory of a disorganized retreat was holding water. If the Germans were defending Quibou, I should've spotted them by now.

The ground rose up from the stream to the edge of the village, so I gave up on crawling. If anyone was watching, they'd have a fine view of my prone approach. Instead I duck-walked, making for what looked like an alley on the backside of a building facing the road. I went flat against the cool stone, my Thompson aimed down the shadowy passage. Nothing moved.

I took a couple of steps to a door set into the windowless wall. I pressed down on the latch, the ancient hinges creaking as the door swung open. It was an old garage, empty except for a rusting Peugeot waiting out the war up on blocks and a workbench piled with tools. I waved Big Mike forward, and we both slipped inside as voices were raised from the road.

German voices.

We each went to one side of the single window facing the road. Opposite us was a low brick building attached to a tumble-down house with a stone foundation. Four Germans came out, looking furtively up and down the street. Their uniforms were mud stained, the stunned looks on their ashen faces showing they had fled the Operation Cobra maelstrom. A shouted command and the *tromp* of boots came at them, an officer with his pistol drawn in the lead.

"Stragglers," Big Mike said. "Maybe looking to surrender."

"They should have stayed put," I said, watching the officer march them away. Three of them. Where was the fourth? Big Mike nudged me, cocking his head to the right. There he was, backed up in the recessed doorway of the brick building. He bided his time, then crossed the street.

A latch turned on a small access door set into one of the double barn doors. Big Mike darted over and grabbed the hand that pushed on the door, yanking him inside and thrusting his tommy gun under the Kraut's chin.

I pulled the door shut, fingers to my lips as I stared at the wide-eyed German. I kept nodding and tapping my finger to my lips until he got the message. He shook his head in agreement, sweat dotting his forehead.

"*Kamerad,*" he whispered. "*Kamerad.*"

"We're all comrades," I whispered, as I took the rifle hanging from his shoulder. I patted him down, taking the knife from his belt. He carried no other gear.

"What do we do?" Big Mike said, lowering his Thompson but

keeping a tight grip on our visitor. He was a *Gefreiter*, a corporal, according to the vee-shaped stripe on his sleeve. He looked to be no more than eighteen. Which didn't mean he wasn't a hardened killer. But he wasn't SS and looked damn scared. Of us, maybe, but certainly of any officer who found him shirking his duty.

"Tie him up," I said. I rummaged through the junk on the tool bench and came up with electrical wire, enough to tie his hands and feet, and a rag to gag him with. With gestures and a few words of German, I got him to understand he was our prisoner and we'd be back for him. He didn't argue, even when we opened the rear door of the Peugeot and tossed him in.

"I don't think he's going anywhere," Big Mike said. "What about us?"

"Let's go find a cheese shop." I didn't worry about our Kraut corporal. He didn't want to draw attention to himself any more than we did.

We went out the back, darting from door to door, watching and listening. At the end of the alley, we came to the Rue Saint-Pierre, the street name painted on the stucco siding of a shop at the corner.

"Looks like this might be close to the town center," Big Mike said. Down the street was a bank and a café, but no *fromagerie*. The bank sat on a corner, but I couldn't read the name of the side street. I listened, swiveling my head in every direction, cupping my hands around my ears. Nothing. Maybe that Kraut officer was done sweeping the town for deserters. Maybe they'd all pulled out.

Maybe I'd live forever.

I darted down the street, ducking into a doorway just before the bank, Big Mike at my back. Now I could see the faded street sign at the corner. RUE DES MOULINS.

"We're close," I whispered.

A door slammed. Heavy steps on pavement, then the *scritch* of a match and the smell of Kraut tobacco, which always smelled awful. More steps, the footfalls coming closer as we backed up into the doorway as far as we could. Big Mike tried the latch, but it was locked.

A figure in a camouflage smock emerged from the Rue des Moulins, his back to us. He stopped and looked up and down the street, turning far enough for me to catch a glimpse of his SS collar tab. I held my breath, willing him to not turn around.

He didn't. He walked across the street, rifle in hand, maybe searching for more stragglers, or maybe checking out his own escape route. I waited until he was out of sight, handed my helmet to Big Mike, and went to the corner. With my face up against the edge of the wall, I moved slowly, bringing one eye to bear on the road. Without the helmet, I didn't risk a clunking sound of steel against stone.

The first thing I saw was the barrel of a tank's gun, aimed straight at me.

Or so it seemed. I'd found the four tanks. And the cheese shop. Unfortunately, the *fromagerie* was directly across the street from the tanks. Down the road, I could see the smoldering and collapsed building that had been the source of the smoke we'd spotted earlier.

"Good news and bad news," I said to Big Mike, back at the doorway. "Four Kraut tanks, Panzer IVs. They're backed into buildings on this side of the road. Good cover from the air, along with the smoke from that fire."

"I sure as hell hope that's the bad news," he said, looking warily up and down the street.

"Yeah. Good news is, the cheese shop is still standing. Across the street from the tanks." Which was bad news too, but I tried to dress it up for Big Mike.

"Christ," Big Mike cursed, as the roar of low-flying aircraft sounded over the horizon. He looked up, searching for the source. I figured so was everyone else, so I tapped him on the arm and ran across the street, hoping the tank facing us wouldn't open up with their machine guns.

We dove for cover in the cellar stairs leading under the main entrance to the café. I looked up in time to see two P-38 Lightnings zoom over, rockets slung under their wings. Headed for Les Fontaines, no doubt. Which meant a retreat in our direction could come at any moment.

More shouts came from the street ahead, and we ducked down, hiding behind barrels of trash set by the cellar door. It was the Kraut SS officer along with several men, including the cigarette guy. They were dragging a regular *Wehrmacht* soldier, no rifle, helmet, or belt. He was talking a mile a minute, but they weren't listening. The men threw him to the ground and stepped back, and the officer put a bullet in his head.

The men laughed, then clomped up the steps above us and smashed open the locked door to the café. By the shouts and sounds, they were fueling up with alcohol for the next round of executions.

"We gotta go," Big Mike said. "One of them comes down those stairs, he'll spot us for sure." He was right. As quiet as we could, we climbed the steps on our hands and knees, crawling under the window. Blood and brains drenched the paving stones a few feet away.

There wasn't a convenient alleyway, but we found a small stationery shop with the door wide open. We slipped inside, shuffling through paper strewn across the floor, and went out the back, where a narrow lane dead-ended at the rear of the café. The cheese shop was four doors down.

"Let's hope those SS bastards are seeing double," Big Mike said in a low voice. "At least they'll think there's four of us."

"I'm not worried about them," I said. "They're not looking for us. But Rast, he's got to be nervous. With his pals running around drunk and shooting deserters, I don't think they'd buy his undercover routine. He's got to be hunkered down and watching."

"I want to get my hands on him just to find out what the hell he's doing," Big Mike said. "I can't figure it out."

"So let's bust in on him. We'll interrogate him while we wait for the good guys."

"Solid plan, Billy. Except the good guys might drop a few five-hundred-pound bombs on our doorstep. Especially if they spot those tanks."

"Our first problem is Rast hearing us coming. He may have a bolt hole ready. He's smart that way," I said. As I finished, the rumble of tank engines starting up turned into a steady, deep, throaty roar from the other side of the buildings.

"They ain't moving," Big Mike said, leaning close and whispering loudly. "A lot of Kraut tanks need to run their engines when they've been sitting still. They have to charge the batteries to run their radios and rotate the turrets."

"For how long?" I asked. He wasn't sure. Which meant we had to go now to take advantage of the cover the engine noise gave us.

We sprinted for the back door of the cheese shop, making it in seconds. I spun around and trained my Thompson on the café, in case any of the drinkers had taken note. Nothing. I tried the door. Locked.

Big Mike unlocked it with his foot, and we went in. A door to the left was half open, revealing the nearly empty shelves of the cheese shop.

Then an SS trooper filled the doorway, a smile on his face and a round of cheese in his hand, grinning as if he thought we were his comrades come to join in the looting. I swung the butt of my Thompson at his head, catching his helmet and sending him to the floor. An MP-40 submachine gun was slung across his chest, and even after he took that blow, his hands were clawing at it, trying to bring it to bear. One burst, and it would be lights out.

I stomped on his hands, trying to kick away the weapon. His mouth was open, but with the engines right outside, I couldn't tell if he was screaming or in shock.

He got one hand around the grip, bloody knuckles closing in on the trigger.

Big Mike dove for the floor, shoving the Kraut's jaw up to close his mouth while driving a blade into his chest. There was some thrashing and gurgling, but not for long.

We looked at each other, glancing at the open front door, not certain if he had a pal with him. We had to hide the body.

But where?

Big Mike pointed upstairs. Logical. Crazy, but he hoisted the body over his shoulders. I stashed the submachine gun behind the counter and led the way upstairs. The engine noise was almost deafening. At the first landing, a window gave us a view of the street. More SS in their distinctive camouflage smocks stood around the tanks, looking up at the sky. Nervous in the service, Kraut style.

Up the stairs, on the landing, a single door waited for us. It was undoubtedly locked, so I used my skeleton key, who wore size-twelve boots and carried a dead Kraut like a sack of potatoes.

CHAPTER THIRTY-FOUR

RAST STOOD AT the window, peering through the curtains. He jumped, his mouth gaping. But not so surprised that he didn't flatten himself against the wall next to the window, making sure he wouldn't be spotted from the street below.

I went in first, my Thompson pointed straight at his chest. Big Mike followed, kicking what was left of the door shut and dumping the dead SS man. There wasn't much to the room. One wide, tall window. A bed, a dresser, a small table and chair. An enamel sink was on the wall behind me. Next to it were a few pegs where shirts and a jacket were hung. That was it for creature comforts.

I had to hand it to Rast. He went right into his Gallic routine, jabbering on and gesturing like a deeply wronged Frenchman. Seeing me, and Big Mike carting a corpse, didn't even jolt him out of character.

"Can it, Major," I said, advancing with the Thompson raised. "Sit down."

The engines stopped. The silence was thick, marred only by Big Mike's heavy breathing. Rast seemed to draw in on himself, standing straighter, his arms dropping to his sides.

"Be very quiet," he said in a calm voice. He perched on the edge of the bed.

"They're shooting deserters out there, Major," I said. "Or should I call you Phillipe? Phillipe Bonnet?"

That shook him.

"Yes, I know. Which is why you must not act rashly," he said, recovering nicely. "Why are you here? What do you want with me?" He managed to keep his voice steady, no mean feat with SS outside and two corpse-bearing Americans in his room.

"We want you and the files," I said.

"And we want to know what your plan was," Big Mike said. "What's this all about, Rast?"

Big Mike could be a frightening kind of guy when he was upset. Particularly when there was fresh blood on his hands from the Kraut he'd just knifed. Rast reacted, fear passing over his face, followed by something else. Relief? Had Big Mike tipped him off that we were missing a big piece of this puzzle?

"You should have killed Walter Dassler instead of leaving him by the side of the road," I said.

"Walter is a prisoner, then? Well, good for him," Rast said, smiling as if he'd heard good news about an old friend. "Killing a fellow soldier would be murder, Captain Boyle. This is war, but that is still a capital crime in any army."

"How do you know my name?"

"It is expected that a *Feldgendarmerie* officer will utilize his intelligence contacts to identify the enemy, particularly those associated with command headquarters. As you are, Captain. May I smoke?"

I thought about saying no, since I didn't like his smug attitude. But the more relaxed he was, the more he'd talk. I could already tell he liked the sound of his own voice, and I wanted to give him every chance to spill his own beans. A crumpled pack of Gauloises lay on the table. I shook one out and tossed it to him. He slowly put his hand in a jacket pocket, pulling out a box of matches, as we trained our weapons on him.

"Ah, good," Rast said, exhaling and tossing the match into an ashtray on the floor. "Now, what are your plans for me?"

"We could slit his throat, Billy," Big Mike said, lowering his Thompson slightly. Bad cop.

"No, I'm sure the major can explain his actions," I said. "No need for knife work unless he doesn't come up with the files." Reasonably good cop.

"What files do you mean?" Rast said, tapping ash from his smoke and glancing idly out the window as if he were waiting for a friend.

"The files on Leon Dubois, Claude Legrand, Eugène Brassens, and anyone else you planned on blackmailing," I said.

"What would I want with those people?" Rast asked. "Besides, Legrand is dead."

"You killed him, along with Sergeant Fair and Major Jerome," Big Mike said. "Like you tried to kill Billy."

"This is war, my friends. Killing each other is the entire point of this foolish endeavor. I do not know who Sergeant Fair is. And if I did put an end to Legrand, it is not a crime to shoot a terrorist. If you knew the man, you would hardly mourn his loss."

"You're in civilian clothes," Big Mike said. "You could be shot as a spy."

"Yes, indeed. If I were captured behind enemy lines. But this town is still occupied France, and I may dress as I wish without fear of a death sentence. An official sentence, of course. Do you plan to murder me?"

Rast was one cool customer. For a guy hiding out in a cramped dump like this, and hiding from his own army, he acted like he was holding aces.

"Did you kill Major Jerome in Madame Janvier's sitting room a few nights ago?" I asked.

"Yes," Rast said. Nothing else. "Although I did not know his name. But a major at that location, yes."

"What were you doing there?" I asked as I motioned for him to back up. I opened the drawers, searching for a weapon. There was nothing but worn work clothes and toiletries, just what you'd expect of a guy living in a one-room joint above a cheese shop. His cover was good.

"Routine reconnaissance," he said, frowning as I pawed through his duds. "I saw vehicles leaving and decided to take a closer look. Your security was quite lax, by the way. The fellow surprised me, and he had to be silenced. It was not my original intent, but *c'est la guerre.*"

"You hid in the old Janvier mill house," I said.

"I did. Adequate for my purposes, but quite uncomfortable."

"You're a trained sniper," I said. "A good one."

"As you know," he said, smiling at the compliment.

"So you're not just a military policeman directing traffic and hanging deserters," I said. "You take on dangerous missions. You're well trained with the rifle and other weapons."

"The role of the *Feldgendarmerie* is more operational than your military police, so yes, you are correct. But what happens next? Do we sit here all night and talk about my career?"

"Get up," I said. "Hands against the wall. Big Mike, frisk him."

Rast crushed out his cigarette and narrowed his eyes as he gave me the once-over. He was trying to figure out what I knew, and which of my questions were a threat to whatever he was holding back. I wished I knew myself.

Big Mike patted him down and came up with a knife tucked into his boot. A small kitchen knife, nothing military about it. Not very sharp either, except for the tip. A thrusting weapon.

"Your recon mission to *Pressoir* Janvier," I said. "You went in your Phillipe Bonnet disguise, right?"

"Of course. It was a risk if I were caught, but going in uniform was an even greater risk. Even your lazy sentries would have noticed a German officer prowling about," Rast said.

"Handy knife," I said. "Doesn't look like anything special."

"That is the point, Captain."

"I understand," I said. "But tell me, if you'd already deserted, why conduct this mission at all? What was the point? You'd already abandoned Dassler and gone underground, hiding from your own people."

"I did not say I was a deserter. I was acting as a soldier on a mission and acting under the rules of war," he said as voices were raised on the street below. "Perhaps you should be more concerned with those fanatics. Quite unpleasant fellows, I assure you. Second SS Panzer Division." Rast leaned against the wall, smiling as if he had the upper hand. He gave a knowing glance at the corpse of the SS trooper we'd carried in. Our death sentence if we were discovered.

"They're hustling men into formation," Big Mike said, glancing outside. "Stragglers and their own guys. Something's up."

"Rast, we're going to find those files. We found your hiding place in the old mill house, where you stored your rifle. I'll rip this room apart board by board. The entire building if I have to."

"That will be very noisy," he said. "You should wait until the SS depart. They've been shooting civilians and deserters all day. They have no desire to take prisoners, especially not ones who have killed a *Kamerad* of theirs."

I hefted the knife in my hand. Wood handle, short blade. But there wasn't much distance between the skin over your ribs and a beating heart.

"Why did Legrand think he could trap you by bringing Madame Janvier to that mob in Saint-Lô?" I asked.

"He evidently thought I had an attachment to her," Rast said. "It was easy to see through his plan. I simply arrived at dawn and waited."

"How did he contact you?" Big Mike asked, checking the French window again from a few feet back.

"I do not know how he found out, but there was a message for me at the café. The telephone lines are still intact, and I have an arrangement with the owner. For a few francs, he takes messages. Legrand said he would exchange both Madame Janvier and Yvonne for the file I had accumulated on his activities. But he only showed up with the Madame and another woman I had never seen."

"You and Madame Janvier were not close?" I asked.

"No. Evidently Legrand thought so. The man was unbalanced, as I am sure you noticed yourself."

"Why Yvonne?" I asked, turning as one of the Krauts shouted, "Manfred, Manfred," over and over again beneath our window. Manfred didn't answer, probably because he was the corpse on Rast's bed.

Rast took a half step toward me, stopping as I turned back to face him, knife at the ready. He spread his hands apologetically.

"I didn't mean to startle you, Captain Boyle. As for Yvonne, if you have spent any time around her, you will have seen the effect she has upon men. Legrand thought that was my interest in her. But, I assure you, it was not. Here, I will tell you something. She had been arrested by the Gestapo. She was part of an English spy network. Her interrogation was especially brutal. She escaped during transport to another Gestapo office for further questioning. She was given shelter in a local hospital, and I discovered her there. The Gestapo had circulated a warrant for her arrest with a picture. I recognized her immediately."

"And out of the goodness of your own heart, you hid her in your own headquarters," I said.

"Perhaps there was some goodness involved, yes. But also guilt, and a desire to survive the war and the aftermath. I wanted to do something decent for a change. She would not have survived another interrogation, that is certain. I thought the English might want her back."

"And put in a good word for you," I said. "But what happened?"

"We had to leave very quickly. Madame Janvier was caring for her, so I left it at that. Legrand, and probably some of my men, thought I had designs on her. But that was not the case. The poor girl is in terrible condition and never spoke once. Perhaps she is permanently damaged."

"She's recovering," I said, tapping the knife against my palm. "She spoke to me."

"No," Rast said, surprise showing in his widened eyes and the slightest gasp of breath. "What did she say?"

"She spoke about a Frenchman named Gustave and a German," I said. "And the Fisherman network."

"I don't believe it," he said, a stunned look passing over his face. He believed it, all right. He was just having trouble with the truth of it. "She spoke of Gustave and Fisherman to you?"

"Yes. And a German, but she wasn't quite able to name him yet. The other woman with Madame Janvier? The British sent her to care for Yvonne. She's an expert in these things," I said, improvising as I went. "She expects Yvonne to make a full recovery."

"Where is Yvonne now?" Rast asked, his eyes darting back and forth between Big Mike and me, and then out the window to the SS below.

"In a field hospital outside of Saint-Lô," I said. "Receiving the finest medical care. You did well to save her, Major."

"Yes, yes," he said, holding his head in his hands. "That was my intent. To do some good in the midst of this terrible war."

"Yvonne will be able to speak about what happened to her," I said. "That will bring justice, don't you think?"

"Justice," Rast said, his voice low and mournful. He shook his head as the tanks started their engines. Big Mike kept him covered as I checked the window. One tank lurched into the road, bricks sliding off its back. Soldiers climbed aboard.

"They're pulling out. We'll leave after they do," I said. "When we have the files."

"Under the bed, there is a loose floorboard," he said. "Legrand's file is there, along with the rifle."

"Only Legrand's?" I asked.

"There are others. Including one on Madame Janvier. I suspected her of Resistance activities, but I could never prove anything," he said, standing and brushing down his stained corduroys, as if he were wearing his dress uniform. "As for Legrand, he and I each had information which could damage the other. I thought you were getting close, and that is why I tried to kill you, Captain Boyle. Twice. I did hit the wrong man each time, luckily for you. The night I encountered Major Jerome, I was looking for Legrand. To kill him. I was forced to kill the major instead. I did not expect to encounter him, and he was about to raise the alarm. So, I killed him with that knife. Yvonne will tell you much the same, if she has regained her senses. She witnessed it."

"Why tell us all this now?" I asked.

"It is what you came for, *nicht wahr*? The truth? The truth is, I wanted Legrand to vouch for me after the war, to clear me of any wrongdoing. That is why I released him, Dubois, and the others."

"But not Eugène Brassens," I said.

"He was troublesome," Rast said. "Most unfortunate. And it was not all up to me. My men were watching, as was the Vichy *Milice*. There was nothing I could do for the man. Legrand demanded too much, and we had a falling-out."

"He was an informer?" I asked.

"He is dead. What does it matter? I should have known I could not escape my past. The things I saw, the things I did in Russia, they were beyond imagining. All I wanted was for the war to end and to be left alone. An impossibility, I know that now. It seems the past catches up to us all."

In two long steps, Rast was at the window, surprising us both with his sure, quick movement. He flung it open and glanced back with a wistful smile as we stood frozen in place.

"*Vive la France!*" Rast yelled, shaking his fist at the SS below. "*Vive de Gaulle, vive les Allies!*"

Machine gun fire spat through the window, a burst hitting Rast square in the chest, sending him sprawling back against the wall. His blood sprayed scarlet as he slid down to the floor, dead, his hand still clenched in a fist. Big Mike and I looked at each other, waiting for a flurry of boots on the stairs.

Instead, engines roared, treads clanked, and men laughed and jeered as the tanks and infantry moved slowly down the street, away from the tide of battle, leaving death and a terrible silence in their wake.

I stared at Rast's ruined body as blood dripped from the garments he'd hung on the pegs. It was then I knew for certain what I'd begun to suspect. The blood puddling on the floor brought me back to a sight I'd seen before. It puzzled me then, enough to wedge itself in my mind and stay there, just below the level of conscious thought, like a sliver in your finger, noticeable only when you brush against it.

Now that memory answered everything. And it was the last damn thing I expected to find at the end of this case.

CHAPTER THIRTY-FIVE

"WHY THE HELL did he do that?" Big Mike asked as the last of the Krauts marched off, following the panzers.

"I'll explain later," I said. "Right now, let's get those files."

We pried up the floorboards. The rifle was there, just as Rast had said, next to a stack of files marked *Geheime Reichssache*, Kraut for "top secret." Each one was stamped with the *Feldgendarmerie* insignia and tied off with thick red string. I put the files in a small rucksack, and then began to search Rast.

It was a sticky, unpleasant job. He had his phony papers in an inside jacket pocket. I found an opening in the lining at the back. Reaching inside, I pulled out his *Wehrmacht Soldbuch*. Inside was a neatly folded letter on official *Feldgendarmerie* stationery. It was written in German and French, probably in case he got picked up by the *Milice* while masquerading as Bonnet. I couldn't read most of it, but I got the gist. It was his get-out-of-jail-free card.

"Grab the rifle," I said to Big Mike as I hoisted the rucksack and stepped over the two corpses. He shouldered it and checked the window one more time.

"It's clear," he said. A single aircraft flew low, then around and high in a graceful arc.

"We have to get out of here," I said. "If he spotted anyone moving, they'll be back in no time."

Out in the street, I could hear the distant, fading sound of tanks as

the small German column retreated. Other than that, silence. We made
our way back to the church, sure that any German soldier still in hiding
would be waiting to surrender, not to take potshots at us.

I hoped.

The sun was low in the sky as we vaulted the wall around the churchyard cemetery and watched for any sign of movement in the town.
Quibou was quiet, but the rattle of small-arms fire echoed from the
direction of Les Fontaines.

"We oughta wait here," Big Mike said. "If we head into a firefight,
no telling who'll be shooting at us."

"You're right," I said. "Look over there." A half dozen or so Germans
hustled down the road toward Quibou. Probably the first of many to
melt away from the fight.

"The church," Big Mike said. "Good cover and a clear view of the
road."

I gave him a nod, and we waited until the Krauts on the road were
out of sight. We approached the large oak doors and listened for a few
seconds before I pressed on the old iron latch. The door opened slowly,
revealing frightened faces huddled behind the priest's robes.

Half a dozen kids gathered around him as he spoke to them in
calming tones. Men and women rose from the pews, some of them
sporting bandages, all of them with hesitant smiles.

I managed to get across that there were only two of us, but the *Boche*
were retreating, and we needed to wait. Quietly. Big Mike reached into
his gear and came up with candy bars, making him an instant hit. The
priest pulled on my sleeve, then led me to a pew near the altar.

A German soldier was laid out there, a bandage on his shoulder,
another wrapped around his leg. He was scared. Scared at the sight of
me, scared of dying, scared of being alone with all these French people,
just plain scared. The field dressing was grimy and thick with blood.

He was a kid, but then a lot of them were kids. Kids good at killing.
But I put that thought aside and got out my medical kit. I pulled back
the gauze bandage. He winced, and I didn't blame him. He'd taken a
nasty hit in the shoulder. A few inches lower, and it would've killed
him outright. As it was, this wound might kill him slowly.

I tried to remove his tunic, but he yelled in pain, attracting more attention than was healthy for a wounded German, even in a church. A couple of older gents, wearing scowls beneath their graying whiskers, walked by, muttering to each other.

I took out my knife, and the German cried out again. I lifted his unbuttoned tunic and cut away at it. I kept the blade sharp, and it easily sliced through the wool. I folded the flap back and washed out the wound with my canteen. It was bad. Bone splinters protruded from a gaping hole, maybe from a .50 caliber machine gun round. I rinsed out bits of cloth and sprinkled sulfa powder over the oozing hole. If he didn't get medical care soon, he wasn't going to make it.

"Bad?" Big Mike asked as I packed the wound. I nodded, the kid's frightened eyes on me. I took out a morphine syrette and gave him the shot. He relaxed immediately, eyelids sliding shut. I pinned the syrette to his tunic to keep track of the doses. I was glad he wasn't in pain, but mainly I was glad I didn't have to look him in the eye.

I slumped back in the pew. For the first time today I realized how tired I was. Big Mike rummaged through my pack and took my K-Rations. He gave them, along with his own more substantial supply, to the priest.

"These people are hungry," he said, sitting in the pew behind me. He sounded like he needed to convince himself giving away all his food was a good idea.

"Blessed are those who hunger and thirst for righteousness, for they shall be satisfied," I said, reciting a passage from Matthew I remembered from Sundays back in Boston.

"Don't go all holy roller on me, Billy," Big Mike said. "It was K-Rations and Hershey bars, not righteousness."

"Depends on your point of view," I said, glancing at a kid of about six or seven licking the last of the chocolate from his fingers, probably the first he'd ever tasted. But Big Mike knew what he was talking about. This wasn't salvation or righteousness. This was damnation.

"You gonna explain to me what the hell happened back there?" Big

Mike said. "That was the last thing I expected. I mean, he knew those SS would fire on him, didn't he?"

"He knew," I said. "It was the only choice he had after I told him about Yvonne."

"But why?"

"I need to think about it some more," I said. "I think I have all the pieces, I just need to get them in the right order."

"Okay. You think, I'll stand watch."

I didn't really need to think. I needed to sleep. My eyes felt like they were full of sand, and my legs were stiff. I watched my Kraut patient for a while and then slumped over, giving in to the darkness which kept the dead and dying at bay, at least for a while.

During the night, gunfire erupted in the distance. Artillery struck not too far from us. Children cried, the priest prayed, and the German died.

At dawn, we departed. I wanted to get closer to our men and tell them the church was full of civilians, so they wouldn't call down suppressive fire on it. We took up position in the railroad station, its stout walls a good defense against any Germans beating a retreat from Les Fontaines. I glanced at the ticket counter where Rast must have paid for his fare many times. I almost felt sorry for him.

Big Mike had given up asking me about Rast. We were too busy right now keeping a lookout for Krauts making a run for it anyway.

"Hear that?" Big Mike said. Tank treads. The clanking drew closer, and I thought I saw flashes of olive drab filtering in along the sides of the road. A Sherman tank turned the corner and halted, its turret traversing as if looking for a target.

"Let's get out of here," I said. Suddenly the thick walls didn't seem so thick. We darted out the back and came face-to-face with a GI about to pull the pin on a grenade.

"You ain't Krauts," he said, sounding almost miffed.

"Sorry, buddy," Big Mike said. "Hey, what's your outfit?" He nudged me and pointed to the guy's shoulder patch.

"Second Armored, pal," he said. "Hell on Wheels, that's us."

We passed on the dope about the civilians in the church as his squad moved out. We leaned against the wall of the station for a while, watching the real Second Armored Division roll by. The Ghost Army had done its job, and now this division and others were busting through the Germans, chasing them to who the hell knew where. Paris, I hoped, for a start.

CHAPTER THIRTY-SIX

WE HITCHED A ride back to the field hospital and found Kaz lounging on a chair outside the nurses' tent, one foot resting on a crate as he read *Stars and Stripes*.

"How's the leg?" Big Mike asked.

"I am in terrible pain but bearing up well. Should I assume you had success?" He nodded at the rifle with its telescopic sight.

"We found Rast," I said.

"There's more to this story," Big Mike said, then explained what had happened in Rast's room. "Billy wanted to wait until we got back here to explain it to everyone."

"Do you know why Rast did it?" Kaz asked. I could see him trying to puzzle it out as he furrowed his brow.

"I think so," I said, then caught sight of Diana.

"Billy, are you all right?" Diana ran up, gave me a hug, checked me for bullet holes, and then stepped back. "How could you do such a stupid thing? Sam was beside himself. You too, Big Mike."

"They found Rast," Kaz said. "He is dead."

"Good. But it was still a dumb stunt. You could've been killed." Diana said, taking the other chair as Big Mike and I lowered ourselves onto empty crates. I didn't even try to argue the point. "But I've got news about Yvonne. They've been drugging her."

"Morphine, right?"

"The doctor thinks so," she said. "He was suspicious of her

symptoms and checked her veins. She'd been injected all over her body, in different locations to hide the marks. She didn't have the flu, she was going through withdrawal. How did you know?"

"That's part of a long story. How is she now?" I asked.

"She was improved enough that they flew her to England this morning. Improved physically, at least. She told me about her capture. She betrayed them, Billy. She betrayed her own network, including her lover, Gustave."

"She'd been tortured," I said. Less of a statement than a question.

"A different sort of sadism. They made her watch others being horribly tortured. She gave in after twenty-four hours and told them everything. Then they raped her. She doesn't remember anything after that. Nothing about the train or the hospital. Just the German, as she called him."

"Rast," Big Mike said.

"Yes. Her mind is shattered. She remembers bits and pieces, but she really doesn't understand what's happened to her since her escape." Diana looked past us, out to the rows of tents with their big red crosses. Then at me, a sad look that told me her own experience back in North Africa was never far from her mind. And never would be. But she hadn't been shattered, hadn't been brutalized as Yvonne had been.

Thank God.

"But she knows of her betrayal," Kaz said, his voice a trifle loud, enough to pull Diana back from those memories.

"Too well," Diana said with a sigh, returning her gaze to Kaz with the smallest of smiles. "She may never recover emotionally. SOE has a place in the country for agents who have suffered like this. Hopefully, she will get decent care there."

"Did she know about the drugs?" I asked.

"She was confused. She thought that was at the hospital. But she insisted it was the German who injected her."

"What about Major Jerome?" Big Mike asked. "She was covered in his blood."

"She told me the German was there," Diana said, waving to Myrtle Kent, who walked by on the way to her tent, her face worn and tired, her eyes barely focused. She'd probably been on duty since the first of the casualties from Operation Cobra came in, and it showed.

"That fits with Rast's confession," Big Mike said.

"What else did she tell you?" I asked.

"That she tried to help, and that's how she ended up drenched in blood. As was Madame Janvier," Diana said. "She remembers being awakened by voices from downstairs, voices in German. The doctor thinks her previous dose of morphine may have worn off, and the shock of hearing German got her out of bed, perhaps to flee. Instead, she came upon the body of Major Jerome. She remembered Madame Janvier helping her."

"That wasn't Madame Janvier helping her. That was Madame Janvier murdering Major Jerome."

That was greeted with a chorus of questions, drowned out by the growl of Thunderbolts overhead, a full squadron returning from its sweep, low enough for the snarl of their engines to echo against the buildings.

Then we adjourned to the mess tent, Big Mike insisting he needed food to listen to this. It would take a pretty strong stomach, I had to admit. Kaz had a cane and managed to make it look fashionable as he hobbled along. We got our coffee and found bench seats at one corner of the tent, where Big Mike told me to hurry up and spill.

"Everything happened because Hans Rast and Regine Janvier fell in love," I said. I took a sip of hot coffee and felt it filter through my veins, waking up body and soul.

"That's crazy," Big Mike said.

"No, not when you look at it from their perspective. I've said all along this crime makes sense to someone. It made perfect sense to them."

"How?" Diana asked.

"I don't know when it happened. We do know that they were caught once, and Legrand got word of it. My bet is they were extra careful after that. An affair between them might mean a death sentence for Madame Janvier," I said.

"And Major Rast might not survive the war," Kaz said, tapping his finger on his chin as he worked it through. "Nor would he be welcome in France if he did, having hunted the *Maquis*."

"Right. So they came up with the idea of blackmailing members of the Resistance into helping them," I said, handing the rucksack with the secret files to Kaz. "It's all here."

"But what is it?" Diana asked. "What could he blackmail them with?"

"I believe these are official documents stating they were informers for the *Feldgendarmerie*," I said. "To be revealed if they didn't cooperate. If they did go along, I think he had another set of reports showing that they had resisted his interrogation and were released. Leon Dubois, for one. He was terrified that Rast would release his phony file. It would mean his life."

"In return, they had to speak up for him after the war," Diana said. "When he came back to marry Madame Janvier."

"Yes. I doubt she was planning to move to Germany."

"But what did Major Jerome have to do with all this? Why kill him?" Big Mike asked, grabbing another doughnut from the plate he'd brought for all of us.

"Wrong place, wrong time. Legrand wasn't manipulated as easily as Dubois and the others we'll probably find in those files. He had some extra leverage and was trying to use it. For money, land, whatever he could get," I said.

"The three glasses," Big Mike said, snapping his fingers. "One had morphine traces. That was meant for Legrand."

"Exactly. Rast told us he snuck back here that night. They likely had a meeting planned with Legrand, telling him they would meet his demands. The plan was to drug and do away with him. But Jerome wanders in unannounced. I figure he heard German being spoken and got suspicious. Remember, Madame Janvier speaks it as well as English," I said.

"Then they try to explain things," Big Mike said, working it out like any cop would. "They have a drink together, deciding it's more urgent to use the Mickey Finn on Jerome."

"But Yvonne walks in on them," Diana said. "And Jerome gets

suspicious, perhaps feeling the effects of the morphine. He tries to leave."

"And our dear, sweet Madame Janvier rips his throat out with her trimming shears," Kaz added, understanding dawning on his face.

"Right. It had to be her. It was a sloppy kill, a frantic attempt to stop him from getting away and telling everyone about the Kraut in the house," I said. "Rast would have knifed him clean, between the ribs."

"Like I did yesterday," Big Mike said.

"Yeah. That's what got me thinking," I said, and described how Rast's blood had dripped from his coat after he'd been shot. The puddling blood reminded me of the water on the floor of Madame Janvier's kitchen the day Rast had shot at me and killed Anton. When we got back, she was soaked through, wearing only a sweater, out in the rain to help with the wounded. But her slicker had already taken a soaking. I remember the water pooling beneath it as it hung on a hook near the stove. She'd been out somewhere else not long before that. It hadn't meant much at the time, but it stuck with me, burrowed in somewhere in my subconscious. "We'd radioed in for directions when we got lost in Fierville. She was in the radio room, patching up Friedman. She must have overheard us, grabbed her raincoat, and snuck out to tell Rast, who was hiding out at the old mill. He knew right where to ambush us."

"Then she came back, hung up the slicker, and returned to her nursing duties as if she never left," Kaz said. "This also puts the shooting of Sergeant Fair in a different light."

"That was my fault," I said. "I mentioned to her that Fair had been a big help with Yvonne, and that she had spoken to him. We also spoke about it in her kitchen, which she likely overheard. They couldn't take a chance on Yvonne opening up to him again."

"So she put him in the crosshairs to put an end to that," Big Mike said.

"She and Rast," I said. "Quite a team."

"But where did the morphine come from?" Diana asked. A gaggle of nurses with their mess kits piled high walked past us, and I waited until they settled down a table away. This wasn't a story that deserved to be bandied about.

"A medical truck was hit by artillery not too far away. The supplies, including several crates of morphine syrettes, were brought back to *Pressoir* Janvier," I said.

"Yeah, a medic from the battalion aid station told us they was all busted open. Madame Janvier musta used 'em once she saw Yvonne was starting to come out of her coma, or whatever it was," Big Mike said.

"Ah. And I assume Rast would claim that he saved Yvonne from the Gestapo at some point," Diana said.

"Yes, and perhaps Madame Janvier would also reveal that she knew, and together they worked to hide her. That, along with his self-proclaimed armistice with the *Maquis*, might buy him enough forgiveness that they could live here free and clear after the war," I said. "He also told us there's a file here on Madame Janvier, stating he tried to prove her Resistance connections but failed. A nice touch, especially when she speaks up after the war and forgives him."

"And remember, she also claimed he spoke of being involved in the German resistance to Hitler," Kaz said. "They may have encountered hard feelings, but perhaps some sympathy for his change of heart. They could have gotten away with it."

"All this killing, blackmail, and manipulation," Diana said, shaking her head slowly. "Done for love. It is hard to believe."

"Rast died taking the blame for Jerome's death," I said. "He knew that if Yvonne talked, Madame Janvier would take the rap. It was hearing about the Fisherman network that did it. That proved she'd talked. He exonerated Regine Janvier with his confession and his final, flamboyant gesture."

"The irony is, nothing can be proven," Diana said.

"Why?" I asked.

"Because Yvonne, or Madeleine, as I know her, could not be a witness," she said. "Because of her condition, which any lawyer could use to impeach her testimony. But more importantly, a French court would never be sympathetic to an Englishwoman who betrayed her French colleagues, not to mention her lover. A mob would be more likely to shave her head. Besides, SOE will hide her away so her secrets can never be told."

"Perhaps the army could bring charges against Madame Janvier?" Kaz suggested.

"No," Big Mike said. "Even though she killed an American officer, the civilian courts would have jurisdiction. General de Gaulle would throw a fit if we tried and sentenced a French citizen."

"There seems to be little we can do," Kaz said. "The French are still sorting themselves out, replacing Vichy magistrates and mayors. Even if we had real evidence, it would take ages to bring her to justice. Legrand could have testified, but he is dead. Leon Dubois and the others could do little but testify to Rast's blackmail."

"Well, all I can do is report to Colonel Harding," I said as I stood. "He'll have to decide what to do next." That was the nice thing about the chain of command. You could always boot a tough question upstairs.

"I'll walk over with you," Diana said. Side by side, our hands brushing, we made our way to the headquarters building.

"I have to go, Billy," she said, placing a hand on my arm. I stopped in my tracks.

"You just got here," I said. "We haven't had a moment together."

"Orders," she said, with a shrug and a downward look.

"Back to England?" I asked. Again, she shrugged, avoiding my eyes. It wasn't England.

"I have to leave now," she said. "I'm overdue already. It's so sad, Billy. Rast and Regine. I almost pity them."

"I know. I know what it's like to find the love of your life, and then worry about losing her."

"But we know we'll be together after the war, don't we? Promise me that," she said.

"I promise," I said. I embraced her, the feel of her close to me the most solemn promise we could exchange. She pressed her face against mine, her sweet skin warm against my dirty, unshaven face.

She stepped back, her fiercest gaze on me. Then she left, not another word spoken, only the glistening wetness of her tears on my cheek.

I promised. I hoped.

HARDING HELD OUT no hope. I briefed him on what happened and what we discovered, after listening to him bawl me out over our little hike to Quibou. I let it wash over me, thinking the whole time about where Diana might be headed. There still was a lot of France occupied by the Germans. Same with Italy, where she'd been on assignment with the SOE before. She spoke French and Italian fluently, and I thanked my lucky stars that she never took up German.

After Harding calmed down, he agreed that Madame Janvier was a problem for the French judiciary, and since our main witness was unavailable and legally unreliable, there was little chance the local courts would bring her to trial. He promised to forward my report with a recommendation for prosecution, but that was a formality. He gave me a couple of days to search out any new evidence, and then ordered me back to First Army HQ with Big Mike. Kaz was getting a week's leave to recuperate.

I thanked him and told him I understood.

Then I went to get Kaz.

CHAPTER THIRTY-SEVEN

THE NEXT MORNING, I told Big Mike to relax, and that I was driving Kaz to the air base at Saint-Lambert to catch a flight back to England. He didn't mind that one bit and ambled off to the mess tent for coffee and chow.

I tossed Kaz's duffel into the back of the jeep, along with Rast's sniper rifle. Using the cane for support, he eased himself into the passenger's seat.

"I finished reading through Rast's files last night," he said. "They were as you thought. Two sets for each person, one incriminating, the other stating how they had resisted interrogation."

"He could make those people heroes or traitors," I said. "That's the power of life and death in liberated France."

"I, for one, will be glad to leave the newly liberated France behind. It is not entirely to my liking. I look forward to my soft bed at the Dorchester," he said, exhaling as he fell back into the seat. "And room service." Kaz kept a suite at London's Dorchester hotel. It was the last place he'd seen his family before the war, and I had the feeling he'd never leave the place. Too many good memories. With all the bad memories we were accumulating, good ones were worth safekeeping. Besides, Kaz was rolling in the green stuff, so he could afford it.

We didn't speak on the way to Bricqueville. We were beyond words. Kaz, of all people, understood the need for justice. Most of his family had been unjustly murdered, and he was in this war to set that right. He knew some crimes could not be left unavenged.

It was a hot drive, the sun beating down on us from a cloudless sky. I parked the jeep in front of Madame Janvier's house, just as I had that first morning when Major Jerome's body was cooling on her sitting room floor. Kaz remained in the jeep. I grabbed the rifle and went inside.

Regine Janvier was in the kitchen, setting a basket of apples on the table. I held the rifle chest high. Her eyes went to mine, then to the rifle. She dropped the basket, apples rolling off the table and hitting the floor as she backed up, grabbing the counter for support.

"He's dead," I said.

"What? Who is dead?" I had to hand it to her, she tried to work the bluff. But the color had drained from her face, and I could see her breath quicken.

"Hans Rast," I said.

"Why do you tell me this?" Her voice quivered.

"Dead, like Major Jerome," I said. I worked the bolt, ejecting a round. It pinged and bounced on the floor.

"Like Anton Krause." Another cartridge spun out as I pulled the bolt, the metallic grating harsh in the confined space. I did the same for Sergeant Fair, and a fourth for Yvonne, who was dead in spirit.

"No," she said. A denial. Not of her crimes, but of Rast's death.

"Yes. We tracked him to Quibou. Nice little town."

"Why are you here, Captain Boyle? And why enter my home with that *Boche* rifle?"

"To show you proof of his death, Madame Janvier. You know this weapon well enough, don't you? It's well cared for. The wood is polished, the mechanism well oiled. You probably know every nick in the stock, every scratch in the leather strap. A gun is like a person, don't you think? Once you get to know it, you realize no two are the same."

"I have seen it, of course," she said, raising her chin in a defiant gesture. "Many times. What of it?"

"I know," I said. "I know about you and Rast, your plans and schemes. About how it went wrong when Major Jerome showed up. How you killed him."

"I am a *patriote*," she said. "I am Corday. I do not kill allies of the French."

"You didn't plan to, I know that. But you had to, or else Jerome would have sounded the alarm about a German in the house. And you didn't plan to keep Yvonne drugged all this time, but you needed to be sure she didn't remember. And Sergeant Fair, well, since Yvonne unexpectedly spoke to him, he had to go. You couldn't help that. And poor Anton, he took the bullet aimed for me."

"You must leave! Go!" She shouted and stamped her foot. If her pruning shears were close at hand, I wouldn't have been surprised to see them flash in my direction.

"I will. I just wanted you to know that there's not enough evidence to bring you to trial. But you'll never have the life you planned with Rast. He's dead. In a small, sad room in Quibou."

I kicked a cartridge away and left the kitchen. Out front, I stashed the rifle in the jeep and gave Kaz the high sign. He gunned the engine and drove off down the drive, disappearing behind the trees in seconds.

I raced around the house, ducking low under windows until I came to Madame Janvier's office. The window was open, a light breeze blowing in the curtains. I heard Madame Janvier enter and lift the receiver. After a minute, she spoke.

"Bonjour, Regine Janvier à l'appareil. Puis-je parler à Phillipe Bonnet?"

That was all I needed to hear. She knew Rast's false identity. I figured she'd think, or hope, I was bluffing. She was calling on the line that a few days ago she claimed wasn't working. Right now, the café owner, probably readying the place for GI business, was writing out a message that would never be picked up.

I walked to the road. I couldn't say I felt good about what was going to happen next, but it was the only thing I could think of. It would have been worse to do nothing, to let the dead lay in solemn graves, unavenged.

We drove to Bricqueville. We stopped at the café where we'd heard guys arguing about Legrand a couple of days ago. The proprietor had been a big Legrand supporter. Today, it was a larger group, some of Legrand's gang as well, just what I'd hoped for.

We sat at a table outside, under the shade of an awning. I propped the rifle against the wall as Kaz ordered two beers. We'd immediately attracted attention, and not the welcoming kind. Legrand's men undoubtedly recognized us from the hair-trimming party in Saint-Lô. But things warmed up when the owner brought our drinks and I offered to buy a round for the half dozen men. It was only a couple of words and gestures, but I managed to get the point across.

Kaz chatted with them and found out they'd buried Legrand yesterday. I gathered he was a big hero now, a lot more popular dead than he had been alive. Finally, one of them pointed at the rifle and asked about it.

Kaz simply told them the truth. That it was Rast's rifle. He'd used it to kill Legrand as well as others at *Pressoir* Janvier. When he told them Rast was dead, they nodded their approval with angry, grim smiles. But, he was sad to say, we could not do a thing about Rast's accomplice.

Madame Janvier. The well-to-do landowner who had never properly mourned her husband, who we understood to be a good man born in this town. Yes, she'd slept with the German and hid him in the old mill house. They all remembered the ancient Janvier place on the river, and one said Legrand had gone hunting there for Rast on several occasions. Kaz told them I'd once joined Legrand, we brothers-in-arms, in a search of the mill house.

We bought another round as the righteous indignation grew. After an hour, we were all fast friends. After handshakes and double-cheek kisses, we drove off, leaving them in a huddle, arguing about what to do.

I left the rifle against the café wall.

By late afternoon I dropped Kaz off at the Saint-Lambert airfield. We shook hands, and I made him promise to rest and take care of himself.

"I will, Billy," he said, gripping his cane. "The first thing I shall do is take a long bath and wash away the stink of liberation."

I watched the C-47 lift off, carrying a load of officers and the walking wounded back to England. I wondered if Diana was on a similar plane, already in some distant land. Or close by. Part of me wished I was going with Kaz, but I knew I had to stay here. I was likely to be closer to Diana.

And I needed to witness what we'd set in motion.

I drove back to Bricqueville.

Back to *Pressoir* Janvier.

A thin wisp of smoke marked my destination.

AUTHOR'S NOTE

THE GHOST ARMY, designated in a deliberately opaque manner as the 23rd Headquarters Special Troops, was an actual unit of the US Army in Europe during the Second World War. Its unique mission was to impersonate other, larger units to deceive and confuse the enemy. These 1,100 men conducted a traveling road show during the campaign in Northwest Europe, utilizing sound trucks, phony radio transmissions, inflatable tanks, and a flair for camouflage in their twenty battlefield deceptions.

The story of the Ghost Army remained top secret for forty years after the war, perhaps to keep their secrets from the Russians, in case the Cold War turned hot. Even today, some of their operations are still classified. Security during the war was extraordinarily tight, not only to guard the overall deception campaign, but to protect the Ghost Army itself. The Germans could have made short work of these eleven hundred specialist troops if they had ever discovered the truth of the small force opposite them.

Ghost Army soldiers were encouraged to be creative and to use their talents to outwit the enemy. Many were recruited from art schools, Broadway, and other venues in which creativity was thought to flourish. Veterans of the Ghost Army included fashion designer Bill Blass, who makes a cameo appearance in these pages, along with the well-known artists Ellsworth Kelly, Art Kane, and Arthur Singer.

After the Allied D-Day landings on June 6, 1944, much of the fighting occurred in *bocage* country of Normandy, particularly in the American sector. Known as hedgerows by the GIs, *bocage* is a land of mixed woodland and pasture, with fields and winding country lanes sunken between narrow low ridges and banks mounted by thick brush that severely limits visibility. The Germans made good use of this ideal defensive terrain to halt the advance of the American troops and inflict heavy casualties. This close-quarters conflict was devastating not only to the soldiers on all sides, but to the French civilians caught between them.

The city of Saint-Lô was itself a casualty, with over 97 percent of the city destroyed. It was dubbed the "Capital of Ruins" in a radio broadcast authored by Samuel Beckett.

"We sure liberated the hell out of this place." As stated by an MP in this book, this phrase was reported as being uttered by an unknown GI as he surveyed the ruins of Saint-Lô for the first time.

The slogging match between the American and German forces came to a head with Operation Cobra, in late July 1944. Kicked off by a massive bombardment, which did produce American casualties, as depicted in this story, the offensive opened up the German lines and destroyed the fighting effectiveness of many enemy units. The stalemate was over, and American units were finally pouring into the French countryside, liberating wide areas and heading for Paris.

The Polish 1st Armoured Division played a significant role in that breakout, helping to trap a significant number of German *Wehrmacht* and SS divisions in the Battle of Falaise.

Following the Liberation of France and the establishment of de Gaulle's government, a "legal purge," or *épuration légale*, was carried out. A series of trials were held from 1944 to 1949, meting out justice to collaborators and officials of the Vichy regime. Nearly seven thousand people were sentenced to death, but in the end, only 791 sentences were carried out.

What is described in this book is quite different; the *épuration sauvage,* or the "wild purge," was carried out immediately following the collapse of the German occupation authority and before de Gaulle's provisional government was in place. Historians estimate these extra-judicial activities resulted in 10,500 deaths. Many of these were certainly fascists who had hunted and tortured their own countrymen and women. In some cases, old scores were settled, and no one can be sure that in the enthusiasm of Liberation, those scores had anything to do with the war.

The treatment of women during the wild purge is also disturbing. The standard practice was to shave the heads of women known to have had relations with Germans. Other abuse, including tar and feathers, was sometimes applied. Some of these women were prostitutes. Others were young women who made poor choices, and some were willing horizontal collaborators. But studying the pictures from the time, there is a sense of savagery in the air that made me wonder if the humiliation felt by men defeated in 1940, long repressed during the Occupation, found an outlet in the treatment of these women and the application of the *coiffure* '44.

For those with an interest in learning more about this, I heartily recommend *Les Parisiennes: How the Women of Paris Lived, Loved, and Died Under Nazi Occupation* by Anne Sebba. I found it moving and invaluable.

ACKNOWLEDGMENTS

IT IS AN ongoing pleasure to work with the talented folks at Soho Press, who are committed to making each book as good as it can be and working to get it in front of booksellers and readers. The publishing leadership, editors, marketing, and publicity people are all the best, and I'm proud to be associated with them.

I am incredibly lucky to have book covers illustrated by Dan Cosgrove, of Cosgrove Design. Each one is a gift.

I am also thankful to first readers Liza Mandel and Michael Gordon, who help tighten up these stories with their sharp eagle-eyed reading. My wife, Deborah Mandel, listens, comments, edits, and helps improve the narrative at every point in the creative process, from testing out story ideas to the placement of commas. There are so many shades of her in Billy and these characters.

Finally, this book, the thirteenth Billy Boyle novel, is only possible due to you, the reader. You know who you are; you've stuck with the series and helped make it a success. Thank you.